Brick by Brick

Brick by Brick

Martha Marie

The Third Irish Novel

PATJAC

About the Author

The second eldest of ten children (one of whom is now a very well known Irish comedian) Martha Marie was born and went to primary school in Dublin. She immigrated to London in the late 1950s after the clothing factory where she had worked since she was fourteen closed. She is now seventy-three, a widow of nearly two years, three grown sons, two teenage grandsons, eight living siblings and a few dozen nieces and nephews; studied with The Open University and gained a BA in 1984.

As a form teacher in a multicultural state school she was responsible for teaching the personal social and health course to her pupils. Many of the discussions she had with them involved talking about different cultures and families. During lessons she was constantly pressed to talk about growing up in Ireland, and what it was like to be one of twelve living in one house. It was through telling these stories about her own life and the life of her friends also from large families that she decided to write this trilogy.

Brick by Brick is the third novel in the trilogy, *The Irish Novels. Move Over* is the first and *Growing Up* the second.

PART ONE

Chapter One

Maura lifted her head up off the pillow when she heard the hall door close. The familiar pain in her arm warned her not to use her elbow to take the weight of her light body when she moved to sit up to see if her young son was still asleep.

Five minutes staring at the ceiling with her mind going over the last four weeks of her life, Maura still hadn't thought about what she would do now that she was home.

When she had decided to come from Canada she had imagined that the house would be the same as it had been eight years ago when there had been barely enough room for her and her husband to sleep. She wasn't expecting her older sisters Josie and Una to be here. They had already moved to England before she had gone to Canada to live with her sister Pauline but she wasn't prepared for an almost empty house.

During the ten years since she had left her family home in Dublin, Maura had never written to any of her brothers or sisters. And although none of them had written to her either she expected they thought about her constantly because they always sent her wedding invitations, and cards when their babies were born.

She rolled her small body over on her side and sidled out of the double bed. Although the curtains were drawn there was enough light in the room for her to see the dark hair of her young son. He was fast asleep in the single bed that was on the other side of the room near the front window. She walked quietly over to the door.

A light breeze blew into the hall when Maura was at the bottom of the stairs; the letterbox had flapped open, then shut again. She knew that the letters wouldn't be for her so she left them on the floor. The cold draught reminded her of why she had never liked the house. She was thirteen when the family had moved into the house and she was eighteen when she had left for Canada.

Ten minutes later she placed her cup of coffee on the windowsill of the small window on the landing at the top of the stairs and looked out on the large garden. She dragged on her cigarette and scorned at the unkempt garden. For a moment she imagined she felt scratching on her legs from when she had to hang out or taking in the washing.

But it wasn't hanging out or taking in washing she imagined she saw now. Her thoughts went back to when a marquee covered most of the garden and the family were having a party for her. She opened the window and threw out her cigarette end.

She didn't want to stay in the cold, silent house on her own so she decided she would walk into the village. After she had dressed her son and given him some cornflakes, she drank another cup of coffee and smoked two more cigarettes. Then holding her son by his hand, she walked down the road towards the Ballyglass village. She was halfway down the road when she met a girl she used to go to school with. She didn't want to talk to her so she lowered her head and kept her eyes on the ground.

'It's Maura Malone, isn't it?' the girl called out when she was close enough to see the pretty face of the blond–haired girl that used to live in number 43.

'Maura Grant,' Maura corrected.

'I haven't seen yeh fer years,' the girl said. 'Are yeh home fer a holiday?'

Maura giggled and looked down at her son.

'Yer sister Una was home a few weeks ago,' the girl continued, lowering her head to the little boy and asking, 'Is that yer youngest?'

'And the eldest,' Maura said and started to walk on.

'I have two meself,' the girl said, 'a boy and a girl. They are back at school now. I'm just on the way up te see me ma.'

'Then I won't keep you,' Maura said and started to walk on while she added, 'I'm in a hurry to get to the post office.'

'Yeh can take yer time,' the girl said, 'yeh have an hour because they have just closed fer lunch.'

'I have a few other things to do as well,' said Maura, walking away from the girl.

'Yer still a snobbish little bitch,' the girl mumbled to the back of Maura's jacket, 'just like yer mother.'

By the time that Maura was crossing the main Ballyglass road she was almost dragging her child. She was also tired. She had forgotten that it used to take her half an hour to walk into the village. She was sorry she hadn't taken a bus. She had sauntered around the small shops, then walked into the cinema. The large building that she used to queue outside on a Sunday afternoon was now a supermarket. She didn't want to buy anything but she walked along the aisles scowling at all the packets and tins of food that were stacked on the shelves. She felt she was back in Canada and for a few seconds she wondered if her husband was missing her yet.

'Strawberry or raspberry?' the girl behind the confectionary counter asked as she folded a light piece of white card into a small box.

'Strawberry,' Maura said, pointing to the cakes on the tray that were under the glass counter. She didn't want the cakes. She was buying them from habit because she always bought her mother-in-law cream cakes when she went to the supermarket. She thought about money when she handed over a five-pound note to the girl behind the counter. When she had changed her Canadian dollars for Irish pounds she was only given half of the Irish notes back when she had handed over her dollars. She had expected a difference in the exchange rates but the three hundred dollars she had saved from her tips felt paltry in her purse when she had walked out of the bank. She checked that she had her chequebook in her handbag before she picked up her box of cream cakes and walked away from the strong smell of cream, fruits, jams, and freshly baked bread.

Chapter Two

Maura was happy when her husband Carl had decided to move his small family into his parents' house. The house had three bedrooms and Carl's father was away for months at a time working on the oilrigs. Carl had started to work for a timber company and he was also going to be away during the week. They had been driving home from a movie when Carl told her they would be able to save money quicker to buy their own house with not having to pay rent and all the other bills if they moved in with his mother. She had nodded her head but she hadn't been listening. She had been thinking about how she wouldn't have to be nice to so many people so that they would mind Jerome when she was at work. And she wouldn't have to mind their children either when they went out in the evenings. She also would be able to do more evening shifts because Janet would be there to mind Jerome. The tips were always better in the evenings.

Less than a month after Maura had moved into her mother-in-law's house she was working five evening and two afternoon shifts every week. After six months Carl had saved enough money for a generous down payment on a new car.

Rain was threatening when she left the supermarket so she decided to take the short bus ride back to her family home.

'That's mine,' Maura said, holding her hand out to a young man for the small white box that had fallen down the stairs of the bus.

The young man smiled at the little boy behind the small blond lady who was holding out her hand for the box and said, 'All the children always want to go up teh top on teh bus even if yer only goin' a few stops.' He helped Maura to get off the bus, handed her the box, then walked away.

Maura nodded her head, blushed, giggled and looked after him. She wondered if, like the woman she had met on her way into the village, she had known him before she had left Ireland. He had blond, straight hair falling over his bright blue eyes. He turned back and waved to her. She remembered she was a married woman but she wondered if another man would want to marry her if she didn't go back to Canada.

Nearly all the women and girls she worked with in Canada were divorced. Some of them had married again, and some of them had children. She walked slowly because she didn't want to catch up with the young man. She was turning the corner into Plunkett Road when she recalled that her sister Pauline had been living on her own since her husband had left her over seven years ago. And she had two children.

Divorce for Maura would be married bliss. But it would have to be a Catholic separation like Pauline's.

Belief in, or religious feelings for any Christian doctrine had nothing to do with Maura's desire for a Catholic divorce. She assumed her sister's divorce was special because she was a Catholic. It had to be because she had generous payments from her husband. Pauline had her own house, her own car, and she didn't have to go out to work.

Panic and temper swept away the pain in Maura's shoulder when she raised her arm to open the hall door. The key wasn't in the lock. She was panting with impatience when she slid her hand into the letterbox. She had no memory of her family ever leaving a key on a string, but she remembered that some of the neighbours used to. The letterbox snapped shut when she pulled her hand out, and the hall door rattled when she kicked it.

'Cathy won't be back till after six,' a woman's voice called from the pavement. She continued to walk down the road when she shouted, 'And Mrs Malone is away.'

Children shouting on the far side of the road told Maura that they were probably coming home from school so she estimated it must be around four. She also realised that she would have to wait nearly two hours until Cathy came home from work to get into the house. She wasn't going to do that so she walked down the path ran her eyes over all the windows with the intention of getting one of the children to climb into the house and open the door from the inside. By the time she had seen that all the windows were shut, the woman from the house next door on the other side opened her kitchen window and called out, 'There's nobody in.'

The woman had never seen the small, blond haired woman before, and when the girl didn't answer the neighbour was reminded of Mrs Malone. The neighbour had only moved into her house a year earlier. She had learned from Cathy that there were ten children in the family and two of her sisters were living in England and two were living in Canada. Cathy had also told her that one of her sisters was coming home from Canada for a holiday. When the small woman wearing the blue padded jacked closed her eyes and tilted her chin up the neighbour was sure that the girl was Cathy's sister so she called out again, 'There's nobody in.'

Maura closed her eyes and turned her back on the neighbour's window.

'Are you Cathy's sister home from Canada?' the neighbour asked. She was now standing at her own hall door. Before Maura had raised her head from the pavement she said, 'Yeh don't look a bit like Cathy.'

'Could I get somebody to get over the wall at the back and try the back door?' Maura asked.

'Yer welcome to get over yerself,' the woman replied.

'Cathy'ed never talk te me again if I let anyone get over her wall, let alone inte her house.' She ignored Maura's scowl and continued, 'I think her friend Mrs Dolan across the road has a key. Yeh could try her if yeh like.'

'What number?' Maura asked closing her eyes and clenching her teeth. She was furious at the woman for saying Cathy's house.

'Thirty-one,' the woman replied, 'she may not be in, but yeh could try.' She closed the door and went back into her house. 'Yer yer mother's daughter,' she said from behind her curtains while she watched the small blond woman drag the young boy across the road. A snotty-nosed little cow.

'Can I have the key for number thirty-four?' Maura asked the woman with the pony tail who had opened the door to number thirty-one.'

Angie Dolan didn't say hello either although she recognised the girl that had stepped back as if she was afraid a dog might jump out at her. She pushed her glasses up on her nose and said, 'What fer?'

'I want to get into the house,' Maura said coldly, holding out her hand.

It was because the young boy holding Cathy's sister's hand looked so tired that Angie didn't ask the girl who she was. 'I won't give yeh the key,' she said, 'but I'll let yeh in.' She closed her door and went back into her house to get her coat and the keys to Cathy's house.

Maura turned walked down the path.

'Yeh hev changed yer clothes, and yeh look more than ten years older than teh last time I saw yeh but yer still a very rude young woman,' Angie whispered to the ground when crossing the road to open the door of her friend Cathy's house.

Some of the neighbours on Plunkett Road saw Angie Dolan as a nosey old cow. But none of them had ever known her to be a gossip. She was nearly forty when she had moved into her new house with her two young daughters fifteen years before she opened the door of number thirty-four for Maura Malone.

Angie had known her husband had tuberculosis before she married him but she had enjoyed ten years as his young wife until the disease had taken him. Before she could afford to buy a television she had spent many afternoons standing at her window watching the children playing out on the road. During those hours she had learned more about her neighbours' children than she did about their parents.

It was Saturday afternoon in 1959 when Angie had stood at her window and prayed that the rain wouldn't come for another hour. She had guessed that it would take the new tenants that long to carry their furniture and boxes off the lorry into number thirty-four. The rain didn't come and she had counted ten children before the empty lorry had pulled away.

'I'll take the key now,' Maura said, holding her hand out.

Angie pulled the key out of the keyhole, pushed the door in, then turned her back on the rude girl and walked back to her own house.

Chapter Three

Cathy came into the living room with her arms full of clothes. She was annoyed that Maura hadn't taken the washing in before the late afternoon rain shower. 'Will yeh sit up straight or yeh'll be left like that,' she snapped, her irritation with her sister ringing in her voice as she made her way to the far side of the room. She threw the clothes onto a chair while she added, 'I don't know how yeh can read in that light anyhow.' Her tone continued to reflect her growing impatience with constantly finding her sister slouched over the table reading her magazines, or doing a crossword during the two weeks since she was home.

'I suppose I should be getting Jerome in for his shower,' Maura drawled.

'We don't have a shower,' Cathy returned sharply.

Maura closed her eyes, sighed, then snapped her hand on the table as she stood, then walked over to look out of the front window to see if her son was about.

'What's yer hurry?' Cathy said. She looked over at her spoilt sister and added, 'It's only gone seven and yeh don't have teh leave here till half past eight. And anyhow yer brother is yer boss so yeh can arrive when yeh like.'

'It's getting dark,' Maura said, turning round from the window. She had been counting the hours all day so she knew how much time she had and she wasn't going to be late. But she didn't say that to Cathy. Her sister was too young to understand why it was important. The girl was only nineteen.

It wasn't getting dark. It was only the middle of September, and it was only seven o'clock in the evening. The clocks didn't go back for a few more weeks, but Cathy decided not to argue. She wanted to be friends with her sister. 'I see yeh have ironed yer blouses,' she said when she removed the lid off the large basket that stood in the corner by the back window. When she stuck her arm into it and moved the clothes about her temper rose again. While she was flattening the clothes back down so she would have enough room for the ones that she was folding she thought that Maura could have ironed a few pillowcases while she had the iron on.

'I ironed them this afternoon,' Maura said. 'I borrowed the hangers from the wardrobe in the back room.' She punched the top of her skinny hips lightly with her knuckles and stood watching Cathy shove the rest of her clothes into the ironing basket and said curtly, 'I suppose that was all right.'

Cathy forced the lid back on the basket as she thought what a little bully her sister was. Then when she saw Maura shove her chin forward as she dropped her head back to look down her nose at her she knew that her sister was daring her to ask what she wanted the hangers for. Every time Maura displayed one of her old hoity mannerisms Cathy found it difficult to like her.

At the same time Maura hadn't tried to endear herself to Cathy. The second stab of jealousy she had felt for any of her five sisters was when she saw Cathy standing at the hall door on the afternoon she had arrived home. Her youngest sister was as tall as her older sister Una and nearly as slim as her older sister Josie and they were both over five and a half feet. Cathy was only twelve when Maura had been home before.

'If yeh mean them wire things that came from teh dry cleaners there's a box of them in teh shed,' Cathy said. She placed one of her hands on her hip, then rested her other on the back of a chair, moved her shoulders towards her sister and snapped, 'Yer welcome te take them all back te Canada with yeh if yeh want them.'

Maura closed her eyes.

'Yeh have a black spot on yer mouth,' Cathy said. She took a small mirror off the table and held it out.

'It's not a spot,' Maura said, holding the mirror out so that she could examine the rest of her face. 'I have never had any spots,' she said, smoothing her eyebrows. She posed for a final check of her makeup, then lowered the mirror from her face.

'I'm very glad te hear it,' Cathy said, 'because we are not a spotty family.' She had no idea if any of her other older four sisters, or her four brothers had ever had spots. She was the youngest of ten children and by the time she knew what acne was her three eldest sisters had left home.

'I have never had any,' Maura assured her younger sister in a tone that was clearly saying that she didn't care about anyone else.

'Neither have I,' Cathy returned, walking over to the fire-place. She sat in an easy chair, lit a cigarette and knowing that any praise of Josie would annoy Maura, continued, 'Er Josie has skin like porcelain.'

'I'm not sure I would like to be that pale,' Maura retorted, recalling the first time she had been jealous of any of her older sisters and it had been when her husband had leered after Josie. She left the room abruptly as if she was running away from the memory of Carl staring at Josie's legs.

'Yeh must be thinkin' ev someone else,' Cathy called back, resting her head on the back of the chair. She was nearly fin-ished smoking her cigarette when Maura came back into the room, sat down at the table, picked up her biro and scribbled on the top of her magazine.

'That biro is leaking,' Maura snapped and threw the plastic tube into the fire.

The crack the biro made when it hit the back of the fire grate before it shot back out on to the floor reminded Cathy that Maura used to throw things when she was living at home. 'There was no need te throw it like that,' she said, leaning down and picking up the biro, 'it's a spiteful thing te do.'

'You use it,' Maura snapped, then started gathering her magazines and asked, 'What time will you get in at?'

'In where?' Cathy asked, combing her thick dark brown short curly hair with her fingers. She threw the end of her cigarette into the fireplace and asked, 'In here on in Tony's place?'

Maura tossed the magazines on top of the laundry basket, then hit her hips with her fists and shouted, 'Why do you keep calling it Tony's place all the time when the two of them own it?'

'Because,' Cathy spoke calmly and slowly like she was talking to a child and said, 'It started out as Tony's, and he still owns most of it.' She stood and asked, 'Why does it bother yeh?'

Maura cringed, hooshed her shoulders, then raised her hands up to her head to secure her hairpiece that had started to wobble.

Ten years, Cathy counted again. I didn't know her then I don't know her now. She tried to remember something nice about her sad-looking sister while she watched the girl push some hairpins back into the bundle of false hair that was half-secured on the crown of her head.

'I was only asking a simple question,' Maura said, cringing again and lowered her hands.

'Here,' Cathy said, 'give them teh me, and I'll fix it fer yeh.' She held her hand out for the hair clips that Maura was struggling to insert into her hair. When Maura cringed again and frowned, Cathy asked, 'Have yeh got a pain in yer neck or somethin'? Yeh look as though yeh can hardly raise yer arm.'

'Sometimes I get a crick in the neck, but it soon goes away,'

Maura lied. She cringed again and held one of her elbows as she handed her sister the hairpins.

'Sit down so that I can see what I'm doin'', Cathy said, pulling out a chair. 'I won't be able te do as good a job as Josie but I'll do me best.'

'I should think that Josie would be good,' Maura sneered and giggled, 'after all she has been a hairdresser for nearly thirty years.'

Annoyed at Maura for deriding Josie, Cathy said, 'That's amazin' because she doesn't look a day over twenty-five.'

'I didn't mean exactly thirty years,' Maura returned.

'Just teh same yer not far out,' Cathy said. When she placed her hands under Maura's chin to raise her head, her sister kept her shoulders folded forward like she had seen people do when they were cold. She removed the last of the hairpins. 'Josie was thirty-seven this year and she's been at teh hairdressin' since she was fourteen.'

Maura coughed. She didn't want to talk about her older sisters.

'There's plenty ev tablets in teh bedside cabinet in mammy's room if yeh want teh take somethin fer teh pain in yer shoulder,' Cathy said, removing the hairpiece and throwing it down on the table like it was a wet cloth.

'I know, the top drawer is like a drug store,' Maura said as she picked up the bundle of synthetic hair, rested it on her lap and smoothed it with her hands like it was a kitten and asked, 'What on earth are they all for?'

Here we go again, Cathy thought. More demands to know what is this for? And where did that come from? She combed her sister's wispy hair with her fingers and recalled that Maura was always asking questions, but she never listened to the answers.

'Where did she get them from?' Maura demanded.

'Why do yeh still wear that thing?' Cathy asked, nodding

her head to the hairpiece Maura was combing with her fingers. 'It went out ev fashion years ago.'

Maura sighed and closed her eyes.

'I'll have teh brush yer own hair out and tie it all back up again,' Cathy said. 'I'll get teh standin' mirror from teh bathroom so yeh can see what I am doin'.' In the bathroom Cathy examined her face for spots in the mirror she had taken off the windowsill and wondered why Maura had come home now. She must have known that their mammy would be away.

'Bring the lacquer as well,' Maura called out. 'I think my hair is a bit too soft and slippy. I washed it this morning.' She brought her head down to her hands and patted her hair and lied, 'I didn't have the time to set it.'

When Cathy came back into the room Maura had the hairpiece lying across the top of her, smoothing it with her hands. She was surprised at how frail and delicate her sister looked with her shoulders folded over and her thin wispy hair pressed to her head, and some of it sticking out around her face. She picked up the hairbrush and said, 'I pin up Angie's hair sometimes when she goes to teh bingo.'

Disgusted with Cathy for comparing her to one of the neighbours and to avoid any other reference to the woman that wouldn't give her the key to the house, Maura said, 'What time are your friends coming up at?'

'When they're ready,' Cathy returned. She was sorry now that she had said she would go into the Beggars Lodge with her friends to see how great her sister was at pulling a pint. 'I told yeh that we might come. We don't usually go out drinkin' durin' teh week.'

Maura closed her eyes.

'Anyway yer likely te have Maurice call in at about ten after his football,' Cathy said. 'He often calls in on a Thursday so at least yeh'll have one pint te pull.'

All the Malone children had always had their disagreements,

but the only dislike in the family had been between Maura and Maurice. Maura was the fifth baby and when her mammy was pregnant with her she had led her daddy to believe she would give the baby to her childless friends Pam and Joe O'Hara. Maurice was born ten months after Maura, and when three other children arrived in the family it was still always Maura that their daddy had spoilt.

'Cover yer eyes while I spray some lacquer on yer hair,' Cathy said, shaking a tin tube the size of a small milk bottle, 'teh sides are still stickin' out too much.'

'That lacquer is very sticky,' Maura moaned.

'Most ev them are,' Cathy said, 'they're nothin' but watered down varnish anyway.'

Maura sighed, closed her eyes again and asked, 'What are all the tablets for?'

Cathy removed the hairclips from her mouth and said, 'I wouldn't be able te tell yeh which ones are fer which. But there is one fer high blood pressure, one fer low blood pressure, one fer angina, one fer diabetes, one fer thick blood, one fer thin blood, there's about five fer agein' bones, some sleepin' tablets, wakin' up tablets, slowin' down, and keepin' yeh goin' tablets, and all sorts of vitamins.'

Furious with Cathy for being so flippant, Maura moved the mirror to try to get a glimpse of her sister's face and asked, 'Where did Mammy get them all from?'

'I think that will do,' Cathy said, smiling smugly into the mirror that Maura was moving about.

Maura moved her head, and the mirror around; she patted her hair all over, and examined her eyes and her teeth. She then held the mirror out for a full check. She smiled brightly when she said, 'Thanks.'

Cathy patted the sides of her sister's hair. 'I'll just give it a light spray teh keep teh side hairs in,' she said, 'some of them are very short.'

'Whose are they?' Maura asked again.

'What?' Cathy asked. She picked up the container of lacquer and started to read the label.

'The tablets?' Maura snapped. 'Who has diabetes, and heart problems?'

Cathy looked around the living room. It is much the same as it had been when her brothers had helped to decorate it after Joan had come home from England. The slide-out leaf table was up against the wall facing the fireplace that continued to be graced with an easy chair on both sides. The long, sturdy bookshelves in the recesses beside the fireplace were as full as ever they were, but they were now furnished with ornaments and stand-up picture frames. 'Nobody has diabetes,' she said, then picked up the mirror and walked out of the room.

Screams, and cries of laughing from the children playing out on the road floated in through the open window when Cathy walked into the kitchen. Her mind shot back ten years to when she used to play out late into the evenings. She closed her back teeth to prevent her memories going back further than two years.

The weekend of her sister Joan's wedding was a turning point in Cathy's relationships with her two eldest sisters. They were both old enough to be her mother, and it was the first time she had gotten to know them. She smiled at the dirty pot on the cooker. Josie bought the pots. Josie didn't like washing up, but she was a great cook. She is still a snob, but she is warm and kind. Even though Maura is only eight years older than her right now she wondered if she had ever known her at all. She couldn't recall playing out on the street with her.

'Who has a heart problem then?' Maura asked when Cathy came back into the living room. She handed her sister a cigarette.

This was the first time Maura had given Cathy a cigarette. She sat down at the table at a right angle to her sister with her back to the wall. She rested one of her elbows on the table and started to brush her own hair. She picked up the small mirror that Maura had left on the table and held it out so she could see what she was doing. She didn't want to fight anymore so she needed to think about what to say. 'That I know of,' she spoke slowly and quietly, 'nobody has anythin' teh matter with them.' She leaned over and lit her cigarette from Maura's lighter. She then put the brush down on the table and leaned back in her chair. She returned her elbow to the table, and pulled the ashtray over towards her.

Maura was sitting back a little from the table with her legs crossed; her body bent forwards, and her hands resting on her knees. Cathy thought she looked all squashed up and very tiny; like an old woman who was growing back into being a baby again.

For the past year Cathy's life had revolved around her girlfriends from the factory where she worked. She enjoyed a sort of star ranking among the girls because her brothers owned the Beggars Lodge and she was able to get them into the pub when their favourite groups were doing a gig there. She grew very fond of listening to all the stories and the gossip they told her. She spent more time with her girlfriends than she did with boys because she loved to sit and chatter.

'If mammy doesn't have diabetes then what is she doing with the tablets?' Maura continued, blowing out smoke from her cigarette.

Although Cathy was ready for a chat with Maura about anything, she wasn't going to tolerate an interrogation and she didn't want to fight with her either. She tried to recall some happy memories to talk about even though she was still annoyed about the way Maura had thrown the biro into the fire.

Seething with temper, Maura brushed the knees of her skirt with her hands, lowered her head and patted her hair, then rolled the end of her cigarette in the ashtray. She squinted up her eyes and demanded, 'Where did all those tablets come from?'

Cathy tapped the ash off her cigarette and said, 'They're not mine, and nobody else is livin' here.'

For the third time in an hour Maura wanted to punch the smiling face of her sister in her nose.

Cathy imagined she felt the punch her sister was glaring at her. 'She doesn't take them,' she said then sat back and added, 'not most of them anyhow.'

'Why does she have them then?'

'I don't know why she has them,' Cathy said, 'I only know she gets them from her friend.'

'I suppose you mean Ena?' Maura said. She had never like her mammy's tall friend. Every time she saw a bar of toffee she saw Ena Dwyer's big hands. When they were living in Arbour Hill the tall woman with the loud voice used to break a slab of toffee into small pieces and share them out between Maurice, Donal, Sean and herself. And she always gave her brothers the biggest pieces.

'No I don't,' Cathy snapped. She liked Ena. 'I mean Pam.' Cathy also liked Pam. But at the same time she was jealous of the two of them because her mammy had always given them so much of her time.

'Pam,' Maura whispered, raising her eyebrows. She could barely recall her mammy's pretty friend. But she remembered when was very young feeling a lovely soft fur coat when Pam used to hug her. 'Where does Pam get them from?' she asked, 'And what do you mean by she doesn't take most of them?'

'She gets them from teh nursin' home,' Cathy said softly, recalling when had she discovered half as many tablets and went running to Donal because she had been so frightened. She pressed her head back against the wall again looked at the mirror that was still hanging crooked over the fireplace and said,

'I think I know what's goin' through yer head. I was teh same meself when I found teh first lot.'

'What nursing home?' Maura panted, pulling at the top of her cigarette packet and withdrawing another little white tube from the packet, but she didn't offer Cathy one.

'The one she goes inte when she needs te dry out,' Cathy said. 'Every time Pam leaves teh place they give her a bag full of all sorts of tablets and she gives them all te Mammy. And anyway they are all only bits of sugar.'

'How do you know that?' Maura sneered.

'Because I phoned Ena and asked her,' Cathy said.

'I'd better get Jerome in and get ready,' Maura said turning her body to look at the clock but she stopped quickly when the pain in her shoulder shot into her neck.

'I'll bath Jerome, you go ahead,' Cathy said. She wanted her sister to be gone. She decided that if her friends came up she wasn't going to go to the Beggars Lodge. She turned back at the door and said, 'I might see yeh down in Tony's later. I'll just slip over and tell Angie to take her time because I won't be goin' out till after nine now as teh girls haven't shown up yet.'

'Are you sure?' Maura giggled. Although the pain in her neck had eased it was still there and it had hurt her badly the last time she had bathed her son.

'I'd love teh bath him,' Cathy said. She felt sorry for the quiet little boy. Maura didn't seem the least bit bothered about him. 'Go on,' she said, 'get ready and go, I'll bring him in when I've seen Angie.'

Chapter Four

Donal moved his eyes to the old clock over the bar after he had seen his sister walk into the pub.

'I won't be a minuet taking my jacket off,' Maura said, walking behind the bar through the opening in the counter.

'Take yer time,' Donal smiled, then lowered the counter top after his sister had walked through. 'Yer not late and we're not busy.'

Neither Tony nor Donal had wanted Maura to work in the pub but she had been so insistent they eventually agreed when Joan had reminded them that the people who came in during the week were mostly men playing darts, or pensioners after the bingo. They weren't busy evenings.

At twenty-seven, Donal was nearly two years younger that Maura. He stood five-feet-eight in his socks, weighed eleven stone. He had a round pleasant face and was always smiling. He wore his light-brown, thin, straight hair over his collar. He was the seventh child in the Malone family and from the time he could remember his life was so full of his family he had hardly gotten to know any of them save for the three that were born after him.

Watching Maura as she went about the bar and lounge on her third evening working in the pub, Donal wondered why she had come home at this time. She must have known that their mammy would be away. Maura hadn't said anything about going back to Canada, and there had been no talk about Josie or Una coming home. He thought that was odd too because Maura hadn't been home or seen her older sisters for over seven years.

On this, the last evening that Maura would be working in the Beggars Lodge, Donal collected the empty glasses as soon as he noticed them. He hoped it would prevent Maura from wandering around the lounge. He had decided she didn't know the difference between a pub and a restaurant. He also didn't know how to tell her.

The clock over the bar showed a quarter past ten when Donal put the last two empty glasses on the counter. He smiled at his sister while he said, 'I'll go over to teh corner and tell teh lads te get their last drinks in.'

Maura was returning her brother's smile when her eyes were drawn over to the door. She beamed with pleasure when she saw a man standing in the doorway looking around the room. She ignored her brother and started to walk down the bar.

Donal didn't know the man that his sister was so pleased to see but he was glad the man was on his own. On the rare occasion when even a small party of four people came into the pub this late they didn't leave until they had finished two drinks. He walked over to the corner watched one of the lads finish his throw at the darts board then called out, 'Twenty minutes.'

'Would yeh take a look,' a lad called Jim sneered as he looked over Donal's shoulder.

Donal turned round. All he could see were the backs of a couple of men sitting at the bar but he didn't know them. He picked up another empty glass then glanced enquiringly at Jim.

'The big bloke in the velvet jacket,' Jim said, jerking his head towards the bar. He then picked his darts up off a small table and walked away.

'Twenty minutes,' Donal called again.

'I'll get them,' Jim's pal Pat said, and walked over towards

Donal, gesturing with a twist of his head to go on out in front of him.

Pat waited at the bar until Donal had closed the counter opening. 'Four Guinness when yer ready,' he said and glanced down the bar.

'Do yeh know him?' Donal asked, nodding down the bar to the tall man Maura was laughing with.

Pat rubbed his chin and said, 'Not very well, but I believe he is a bit of a cheat with the darts.'

'He won't be goin' in there tonight,' Donal said, 'it's too late now.' He stole another glance down the bar after he had put a pint of stout on the counter. He was sure he had never seen the man before. 'Thanks fer tellin' me Pat,' he said then asked, 'Do yeh know his name by any chance?'

'Noel, Noel Larkin.'

When Maura saw her brother walking towards her, she slid off her stool. She winced, grabbed her arm and swayed so much that she nearly fell over.

'What's teh matter with yer arm?' Donal asked.

'It's nothing,' Maura giggled. She cringed again; 'I've got a creek in my neck that's all.'

Donal bowed his head to Noel then turned back to his sister and said, 'Get yer things and I'll take yeh home.'

'That's all right,' Maura replied quickly. She smiled brightly and shrunk her head into her neck and said, 'Noel will take me.' She giggled again: 'You do remember Noel? Don't you?'

'Really nice place you have here,' Noel said, removing his elbow from the bar. 'Your sister has been telling me how you have renovated the place.'

Donal took a small step back so that Noel could move away from the bar. 'Can't say I do,' he said.

'Nula's brother,' Maura said, giggling again.

Noel held his hand out to Donal.

'Are yeh walkin' or do yeh have a car?' Donal asked, noticing Noel was tall and skinny. He was surprised at how slender and soft the hand he held was.

'He has a Porsche,' Maura smiled proudly.

'A Peugeot,' Noel corrected, his mouth showing small white teeth when he smiled at Maura. He smoothed his dark straight hair back from his forehead, then brushed a sleeve on his jacket.

Donal decided that if people have long faces then they were bound to have long noses.

'I'll get my jacket,' Maura said. She held her left arm when she sauntered down the lounge before she turned into the storeroom behind the bar.

'Are yeh parked outside?' Donal asked, tilting his head towards the front of the building.

'No,' Noel replied, 'I'm around at the church.' He glanced out through the top of the long window that faced out onto the main road. He returned one elbow to the bar and leaned against it as he said, 'The Ballyglass Road is very busy.' He parted his jacket and put his other hand on his skinny hip.

Donal moved away and shoved a chair under a table. He couldn't think of anything he wanted to say to the tall skinny man.

'It's a different place,' Noel said, looking up at the ceiling, 'I hear you're packed out at the weekends.'

'It's an old place and we kept as much of the old wood as we could,' Donal replied proudly.

Noel continued to look around the large room.

Donal looked proudly at the old bar he had renovated. He had no memories of his sister's friend Nula, and he wondered why a bloke who looked older as Una's husband Jack would be taking his married sister home when she didn't need him to even if he was a friend's brother. 'It's a long way from Phibsboro,' he said.

Before Noel had replied, Maura came walking smartly back towards them with her jacket across her arm.

Donal didn't want his sister to go with her friend's brother. He was also worried about what Jim had told him about Noel when he moved close to her: 'I'll walk yeh round to teh church,' he said. He could hear a group of male voices outside in the street and he was afraid they belonged to Pat and his friends, and that they might be waiting for Noel.

'Donal, there's no need,' Maura giggled. She handed her jacket to Noel while she said, 'We both know the way.' She had to change the arm she was inserting into the sleeve of the jacket first because of the crick in her neck.

'I'm goin' fer fish and chips anyway,' Donal lied and tried to sound casual when he added, 'It's on me way.' He assumed that Maura wouldn't know about the lads in the bar. He pointed to a door with a printed sign that read private in black capital letters and said, 'We can go out this way.'

Out in the lane, Donal was relieved to find there wasn't anyone waiting for them. By the time he had eventually made the proper clicks in the three locks, Noel and Maura were about twenty yards down the lane. He kicked the door, hoping they would stop at the sound. He couldn't bring himself to call out, 'Wait fer me.' When he looked up Noel had stopped and he was looking around him as though he was admiring the view in the old lane.

'I must have another light put over teh door up there,' Donal said once he had joined Maura and her friend.

Maura slid her hand around Noel's elbow and asked, 'Why didn't we come out the usual way?'

'It's shorter to teh church,' Donal lied. When they reached the end of the lane he was relieved that none of the lads that had been playing darts were about, but he was disturbed at the way that Maura was snuggling into her friend's brother.

Chapter Five

Yer wastin' yer time doin' that, Sean.'

'Don't I know,' Sean Malone answered his grumpy old neighbour without getting up off his knees. He was a couple of stone too many for his five and a half feet height so he found it easier to kneel than to bend over.

'The kids have too much money,' the neighbour complained.

'I think yer r-right there,' Sean continued to pick the sweet, and crisp wrappings from under his rose bushes. He wasn't going to argue with the old man who always complained about something the children were doing. He stood before he said, 'Sure some of the stuff always gets blown about when the bins have been emptied.'

'Yer not workin' today?' the old man said by way of asking why, running his eyes over Sean's blue shirt and beige trousers.'

'I have a few things te do,' Sean returned. He wasn't going to tell the old man that he had worked late every evening during the week so that he could be home all day when his sister Maura came out. The grumpy old man would ask if his sister had also been born in Arbour Hill, and Sean didn't want to spend the next half hour listening to a lecture about how the people that lived in the city were better neighbours because their houses were closer together. He also hated to look at the warts on the man's nose.

'Ah sure there's always plenty ev paper work te do when yer

workin' fer yerself,' the old man said again by way of asking if that was why Sean was at home. He had nothing to do with his days but talk to all the neighbours that would talk to him so he knew that Sean was always busy. He had a cousin that lived a couple of streets away who was already waiting three months for Sean to build him a new porch on the front of his house.

'Yer right a-gain,' Sean agreed, turning his round pleasant face up to the sky as he said, 'it looks like teh rain is goin' te hold off fer a f-few hours.'

The old man watched the light ginger curly hair blow around Sean's forehead for a few seconds then went back into his house.

Five minutes after his neighbour had left, Sean closed the boot of his car. His attention was drawn to a double-decker bus that had stopped two houses up the on the far side of the road. He scanned the windows on the bus so he could return a wave to a neighbour or a friend. When the bus had moved on Sean glanced at the bus stop from habit but he wasn't expecting to find anybody he knew because the bus was almost empty. He watched a woman walk back and forth, studying the gates and doors of the houses. She was dragging a large bag and holding a small, dark-haired boy by the hand.

The bag and the small child encouraged Sean to believe the woman was a gypsy. He wasn't expecting his sister to come out on the bus but the woman reminded him of Maura because she had a lot of blond hair piled on the top of her head like the way he recalled Maura used to fix her hair.

Even though there were fewer gypsies or itinerants roaming the housing estates over that past few years, Sean walked down the path and closed the gates. He didn't want to make it easy for them to get into his garden and steal his roses. When the woman put the case down and waved to him he felt embarrassed because he had been watching her so he turned away and started walking back up towards his house.

'Sean,' Maura screamed when she saw her brother making his way back up his garden path. 'Sean,' she screamed a second time and waved wildly when he turned back and looked over at her again.

After a couple of seconds Sean waved, and called over to her to stay where she was. He had to wait until another bus had rumbled by before he crossed the road. 'Y-yeh didn't come out in t-teh bus on yer own?' he asked before he picked the bag up off the pavement. 'I thought D-Donal would bring yeh out. Yeh s-should have phoned and I would've come out fer yeh.'

'I wanted to give Jerome a ride on the bus,' Maura lied. She had changed her mind about asking Donal to bring her out five minutes before she had left the Beggars Lodge with Noel Larkin. 'Cathy told me what busses to get,' she said then pulled on her son's arm and said, 'say hi to uncle Sean.'

'Hi,' Jerome said raising his head from the road then re-turned to watching the bus again.

'He's like his daddy,' Sean chuckled. Although he hadn't seen his sister's husband all that much when he had come home with her eight years earlier he remembered that Carl was very handsome with dark hair, a broad forehead and square chin. He also remembered that none of the family had liked him and that they thought at forty he was too old for Maura.

'He is,' Maura said smiling down at her son.

'Nearly all er children are like er other half,' Sean continued. 'Una's two, Pauline's two, and Maurice's two, and Josie's Eileen and Rory.'

'We can cross the road now,' Maura said, stepping into the kerb, 'the traffic has eased.'

'Hi there,' Maura said when she saw her sister-in-law Flo standing at the gate with a young girl in her arms.

'Yer lookin' well, Maura,' Flo lied, opening the gate. Because her mother used to wear thick makeup to hide the bruises her father had given her Flo always saw deception of some sort when other women used so much make-up during the day. The flutter of a smile Maura returned was enough to tell Flo that her young sister-in-law was as cold as the last time she had seen her. She recalled the little bitch had hardly spoken a word to her the evening she had gone up to Plunkett Road to meet her eight years ago.

'So are you,' Maura giggled. She didn't take her memory back the eight years since they had met. There had been nothing remarkable about Flo to help her to remember the girl. She decided her sister-in-law was too fat to be wearing a short skirt let alone a ribbed jumper. She wasn't as tall as Sean and she must weigh over ten stone.

Flo hadn't gone over with Sean and her sons to Ballyglass the day after Maura had come home this time. She had used the excuse that Angela had been cranky with cutting her teeth. 'Say hi to your Auntie Flo,' Maura said to her son.

'Hi,' Jerome said, then turned his head out to the road.

'He likes te watch teh buses,' Sean laughed. He put the bag down and held his hands out to Flo for his daughter.

'Make sure teh gates are locked then,' Flo said, walking over to Maura and giving her a hug because she thought she should. She always hugged Josie and Una when they came home. She was also always delighted to see them.

Maura accepted the hug like it was her duty, then turned to watch her son.

'D-Don't worry, they all p-play out teh back,' Sean said when his sister turned her head towards the road. 'We n-never let them play out here.' He was suddenly afraid that Maura would change her mind and not leave Jerome with them for the night because of the traffic on the road.

'It's a lovely wide road,' Maura drawled.

'Y-you two go on in,' Sean said. 'I'll s-stay here with Jerome.' He held Angela out to Flo and added, 'I want teh f-finish clea-nin' teh car anyway. Yeh can c-call me when the lunch is ready.'

'Is it a girl?' Maura giggled. 'I thought you had two boys.'

'We have two boys,' Flo said, turning her daughter so that Maura could see her face. Angela was a year old on teh day yeh came home. Did yeh not get teh card I sent yeh when she was born?'

'We moved this time last year,' Maura said and giggled again. 'I thought she was a boy with the trousers.'

Flo hadn't been surprised when Maura didn't reply to the card she had sent to let her know that her brother had a daughter. She tossed her head to forget that she had been annoyed when the selfish girl hadn't sent a thank-you note for the present she had sent out to Canada for Jerome.

'Is the bathroom upstairs?' Maura asked, walking behind Flo through the porch into the hall.

'It is,' Flo replied, dropping Angela into her playpen. She sighed and thought here we go again. Bathroom; toilet, garbage; rubbish, post; mail what difference does it make anyhow. She prayed that Maura wouldn't go too far with her Canadian language because she knew that Sean was looking forward to having her in his home and he was determined to try and like her. 'In here,' she called from the kitchen where she was cutting tomatoes for the lunch when she heard Maura walking back down the stairs. She pushed the door from the hall into the kitchen open and added, 'Yeh found it all right.'

Maura ran her eyes around the small kitchen. 'No problem,' she said, 'there were only four doors.'

Bitch, Flo thought. She held her hands under the tap and decided that Maura was probably thinking how small and dingy the house was compared to Joan's house. She didn't know that Maura hadn't seen her sister Joan's house.

'You have plenty of light in here,' Maura said, running her eyes around the small kitchen.

'That'll be a problem when we build teh extension,' Flo said, 'but I'll have te put up with it. I'd prefer te build on than move. I like it here, and I don't want te move out any further from teh city.' She exercised her shoulders as she dried her hands on the towel and thought a promise to have patience with her husband's sister.

Maura didn't usually notice what rooms looked like. She had never had the opportunity to decorate a room because she had never lived in a house, or an apartment long enough to want to change it. She wondered about what changes she would make in her family home if she didn't go back to Canada.

Chapter Six

Flo glared at the plate of food before she scooped it into the pedal bin. She estimated Maura had eaten half of a tomato, a slice of cucumber, and half a slice of ham. No wonder she is so skinny she thought as she slid the plate into the hot water. She left the dishes to dry and went back into the living room. She picked a dish of cornflakes off the floor and called out, 'Come on in here and sit at teh table.'

'I don't want them,' Jerome said and continued standing at the front window that looked out onto the street.

'Yeh asked me fer them,' Flo said, kicking a red ball with her foot as she walked across the room to bring the boy back to the table. 'Yeh haven't eaten yer apple either,' she said, bending down to retrieve the red ball from under the window.'

'I don't want it anymore,' Jerome whined and continued to look out of the window. 'I don't want anything.'

'Oh yes yeh do,' Flo whispered to the floor frowning at the two small bits the boy had taken out of the apple and mumbled, 'Yeh want a good slap on yer ars.'

'I want to go over there,' Jerome pointed out the window at two children that were playing in a garden across the road.

Yer like yer mother, Flo thought; 'I want, I want, I don't want'. She pulled the curtain back and saw what the child was gazing at. Three children were playing in the garden of the house across the road.

'Cathy lets me play out,' Jerome said, smiling up at his new aunt.

Flo knew it was no use telling him why he couldn't play out on the street. The child was too young to understand the road was different to where he was staying with Cathy.

Expecting that his aunt understood what he wanted and used to getting his own way, Jerome walked over towards the door while he said, 'I don't want my coat.'

'Stay where yeh are,' Flo called out. When the child turned round it wasn't a small replica of his father she saw in his eyes. They were just like his mammy's; a mixture of defiance and sadness.

'I want to go,' the child pleaded.

'I know yeh do,' Maeve said softly, 'and yeh will when Kevin and Brian get in from school.' She noticed how thin and small the boy was as she said, 'Come into teh other room and eat yer cornflakes first. By the time yer finished Sean will take yeh round to teh school fer yer cousins and then yez can all play out in teh garden.'

Jerome let his hand drop from the handle of teh door and asked, 'How many cousins?'

'There'll be two cousins and two boys from next door,' Flo said and moved back from the window.

Jerome followed his aunt into the other side of the room. She sat him on a chair at the table and moved his dish of food over to him.

'Now eat it up quickly or Sean will go without you,' Maeve said, then went out the back door and joined Maura and Sean at the plastic table where they were drinking coffee.

Chapter Seven

Conversation with Maura consisted of television programmes and movies.

Sean looked at his watch then at Flo and said, 'J–Josie and Mike should be on their way now.'

Maura raised her face from her hands. She felt a light tingle under her ears at the thought of her eldest sister being in Plunkett Road for two weeks. She stretched her hand onto the table for her cigarettes and said, 'Cathy never said anything about Josie coming home.'

'Limerick,' Flo answered. 'They've been down there fer teh last two weeks. Josie said they'd try and get up te see yeh.'

Sean tried to fold his short arms across his wide chest.

He had just about managed to get his hands under his armpits when he said, 'J–josie d–doesn't have as much say in their holidays like she used to.' He tipped Maura on the arm and added, 'D–don't get me wrong, t–they'd have come up if they could. But it's not that easy te change teh f–ferry tickets. To be sure ev te t–times they wanted they had te b–book them at Easter.' His chair scraped the ground when he leaned over into the table and shouted, 'T–there's as many E–english cars on teh roads here in teh summer as er own.'

'Why did they go to Limerick?' Maura asked, shoving her chair back so she could cross her legs. She was relieved that Josie wouldn't be coming home for two weeks. When she was a child there were times when she felt that her eldest sister Josie was her mother. At the same time she was always jealous of Josie. There were also times when she felt her older sister Una was her mother, but she had never felt jealous of Una. Una was always fighting with their mother.

Maura had never fought with her mammy, or any of her sisters or brothers. She had never needed to because she had always gotten what she wanted. Although she often wished she were assertive like her second eldest sister, Maura was afraid of Una. Una could never tolerate laziness or lies. Maura walked away from Una more often than she did anyone else because she was terrified of the second question her sister would ask. And it never worked to agree with Una either because she always asked why you agreed.

'A f-funny family the Cullens,' Sean said, raising his head and squinting his eyes as though he was studying something down at the bottom of the garden. He still found it hard to believe that Mike's father was in jail for killing a man. And Mike had only told Josie about him two years ago.

'Can't be any worse than ours,' Maura said, laughing nervously. Her feelings with being at home this time were confused. She felt lonely because the house in Plunkett Road was so empty, and at the same time she didn't want to see her two eldest sisters. Being the fourth girl and the fifth child to be born in the family the house was always full of people. When her sixth sister, and ninth sibling Cathy was born, the new baby made little difference to her. At nine she was old enough to help with the other children but she never did. Joan and Liam played with Cathy and her daddy and three older sisters managed the housework and most of the cooking. She had never liked Josie because she saw her as her mammy's favourite.

There were the same number of beds to make after her older sisters had moved away, but there was more room in them, and the house was less crowded. Pauline was the last to leave, and it was only when Pauline was gone that she missed her older sisters. The sheets on the beds weren't changed every week, her clothes weren't ironed, and she had to peel potatoes, and do washing up.

Eight years ago, and a few days after she came home with her handsome husband, Maura hated Josie when she saw Carl leering after her. She joined her brother in laughing at Josie.

'Mike's grand though,' Sean said, laughing with Maura as he said, 'L-let's face it we all have er problems.' Just the same he was glad when he heard that Mammy was goin' away at t-teh same time as they were c-comin'.'

All Maura could remember about Josie's husband was that he was thin with straight hair, and he was a little taller than her sister. She had only met him once when he had come home for Pauline's wedding. Although she couldn't remember Mike doing what Josie wanted, she agreed with her brother because her sister was always telling everyone what they should do all the time. Right now she wondered about Josie knowing her mammy would be away now. She un-crossed her legs and leaned into the table towards her brother and asked, 'Did you say Josie knew that at Easter Mammy was going away in September?'

'We all d-did,' Sean said, moving his eyes from his sister's hands to the top of her head a few times. 'T-that's why we were all so s-surprised yeh came now. W-we thought yeh were comin' at teh beginnin' ev A-august.' He noticed two shades of blond in Maura's hair and the clips that were holding the hairpiece on her head when she lowered her face to the table again. Although she kept her head bent down over her hands, Sean saw creases across her forehead. He cast Flo a worried quick glance and continued, 'Una was exp-pectin' yeh te be here when she came a couple ev weeks ago.'

Hot tears stung Maura's eyes. She wasn't used to feeling tears because she only cried when she was throwing a tantrum and she was always able to control the amount of water that flowed. She raised her head sideways from her hands so she could avoid looking at her brother. Her face was flushed and her eyes were moist as they followed the birds across the rooftops of the houses that backed on to the end of Sean's garden. The tears that were burning her eyes had nothing to do with disappointment at not seeing her sisters.

Sean was now fed up with his sister looking away and closing her eyes. 'W–why de yeh ask?' he asked impatiently.

Maura ran the flat of her hand along the table as though she would find the words she needed under the surface. She kept her head down and looked over her forehead at Flo and said, 'I was to come in early August. I changed my ticket when mammy wrote and told me that she was going away then and she wouldn't get back until the second week in September. She also said she couldn't change it because she was going as a member of the staff.'

Sean frowned and asked, 'W–when did yeh learn she was goin away in teh end of August?'

Maura was now so near to crying real tears that she pretended to have a fit of coughing. The pain in her shoulder shot up into her neck and it took all her willpower not to cry out. 'The evening I came home,' she said, and coughed again.

The bitch, Flo thought. She remembered that Sean's mammy had done the very same thing three times before. Once when Una came, and twice when Josie came. However, Una and Josie had only come from England and between them they came home twice or three times a year.

'That's Mammy fer yeh,' Sean said. He tapped on the table with the flat of his hand as if to stress that what he was going to say had already been stated in a court of law and said, 'S–she's so caught up with that b–bloody job ev hers that n–nobody knows where she is h–half ev teh time.' He didn't know why, and he didn't care, but he was certain that his mammy either didn't want Maura to come home, or she didn't want to be at home when Maura was here.

'Job?' Maura bellowed. 'Mammy has a job?'

'She's t-tellin' all sorts e-ev s-stories,' Sean said. He stood so that he could do some breathing exercises. He could feel his stammer before he even spoke. He inhaled deeply and said, 'I couldn't believe me ears when C-cathy told me she was doin' night duty.'

'She goes on is if she's a nurse half ev teh time,' Flo interrupted, 'and she's nothin' but a gofer.'

'What's a gofer?' Maura demanded as though she was a policewoman talking to a group of teenagers. It was the only tone she knew how to adopt when she didn't want her real feelings to show.

'L-like an apprentice in teh old days,' Sean said. 'It's teh one who g-goes fer this, and goes fer that, and goes f-fer everythin'.' He sniffed, then looked straight at Maura and shouted, 'M-mammy and Ena go to teh b-bookies, most of the time fer Pam.'

'What was the night duty then?' Maura asked, closing her eyes at Flo so she would make it clear that she was asking her brother. After all, Flo wasn't really family. She recalled what Cathy had told her about Pam O'Mara being an alcoholic. 'Does Pam have any children?' she asked her brother.

The spasm of sympathy Flo had felt for Maura vanished when she saw coldness in the girl's face. She wondered what Maura would be like now if Sean's mother and father had given the girl to the O'Maras when she was a baby.

'She doesn't,' Sean said, sitting down again. 'Joe O'Mara has a family down in Limerick.'

Maura giggled and sneered. 'How can he have children that aren't Pam's?' she asked, implying her brother had said something stupid.

Sean tried to cross his arms again and said, 'Teh way every man can.'

'Just teh same Sean yeh know as well as I do that Pam is really is sick this time,' Flo said.

'Yeah, y-yeah I know, I know,' Sean said, turning his face up at the sky. 'It still annoys me t-teh see p-people like them gettin' others teh r-run after them j-just because they're loaded. It really d-does.'

'It's Cathy being on her own durin' teh night that worries me,' Flo said. 'When Pam can't sleep yer mammy and Ena stay up all night and play cards with her. That's teh night duty.'

A light buzzer sounded from the kitchen: 'That's me call fer te get teh boys,' Sean, 'anyway, t-they're both doing all right out of it. A six-week cruise on teh Mediterranean is a nice free holiday.'

'That'll waken Angela,' Flo said, when she heard the hall door bang after Sean had left to get his boys from school.

Maura closed her eyes and glanced at her watch.

They are all different; Flo reminded her thoughts. She was married to Sean before she had met any of his older sisters, and because she had been pregnant at the time she had expected they would have shunned her in some way. Ten minutes after she had met Josie she saw the girl was a snob and she was terrified of upsetting her mother. Una frightened her at first because she spoke her mind all the time. She had two children the first time she had met Pauline and Maura. She liked Pauline. Now she decided the girl that was trying to break the little glass object with her hard stare was more like her mother that any of Sean's other sisters.

The only sounds came from a breeze blowing through the few newly planted trees in the gardens and birds chirping. Flo's plastic chair sounded angry as it scraped the ground when she shoved it back from the table so she could move away from Maura.

Maura winced when she moved her arm to glance at her watch again.

'Sean'll run yeh back to Ballyglass when yeh want,' Flo said. When Maura continued to stare down the garden like she hadn't heard anything that had been said, she was tempted to lean across the table and slap the girl across her face.

But just the same Flo felt some pity for the rude girl. She recalled it hadn't been easy for herself to see, and then to admit that her own mother had been selfish. She had needed to believe that her mother had loved her so she had refused to accept that her mother hadn't known that her daddy had hit her, and her sister and brother so often. It was also some years after her daddy had left them that Flo forgave her mammy.

Noticing again the amount of make-up Maura had on her face Flo recalled how her mammy used to be more worried about the bruises on her own face than she did about the pain her children were suffering after her daddy had beaten them all. She didn't want to see the sullen face of Maura so she turned her head towards the bottom of the garden and asked, 'What club did Nula say she was takin' yeh te tenight?'

None of your business, Maura thought as she said, 'I have plenty of time.' It was tomorrow night she was going to a club with Nula, her husband and her brother Noel but she hadn't told Sean that when she had phoned and asked him to mind Jerome.

Cathy went out on Saturday evenings, and she couldn't bring herself to ask Angie Dolan to mind her son. She didn't want to stay at home on her own for the Friday evening, and she didn't want to go to the Beggars Lodge with Cathy and her friends either. She had met Cathy's friends the evening Noel had taken her home from the Beggars Lodge and when the stupid girls weren't asking her what it was like to live in Canada all they talked about was the factory where they worked.

Flo lit a cigarette and threw the packet into the table.

Maura crushed out her cigarette, shoved her chair back, stood and said, 'I'm not going straight back home. I want to go into town for a few things first.' She was moving towards the back door of the house when she added, 'The bus will do fine.'

Five minutes later Flo stood at her front gate and watched her sister-in-law walking quickly towards the bus stop. She didn't know why, and she didn't care why the girl was in such a hurry to leave. Although she felt hurt that Maura couldn't wait to say hello to the children she prayed that the bus would come and that Maura would be gone before Sean came home from the school.

Chapter Eight

Cleary's clock showed half past four when Maura strolled up O'Connell Street towards the Savoy cinema. She was too early to go to see a movie, but she wanted to know what film was showing. She remembered there was another cinema in a side street near the GPO where Pauline used to take her before she had started going out with Harry so she crossed the road to see what was on there.

Crossing the wide main Dublin Street with crowds of people all around Maura felt alone. She missed not having someone take hold of her hand while she moved with the throng of people. One of the reasons why she never liked going into town on her own was because she was terrified of crossing O'Connell Street. She never knew whether to wait for the traffic lights to change to green or to move with the people who took no notice of them at all.

With her memory aroused and her mind on some of the films she had seen with Pauline, Maura forgot to look for the other cinema after she had crossed the road. She pulled her jacket closed when she walked past the GPO. The tall grey pillars of the huge building always made her feel cold. Again because there were so many people rushing about her, and she wasn't in any hurry she turned into Henry Street. She decided she would walk around Arnott's for a while. It was a much nicer department store that Cleary's, and it was always warm.

Memories of roaming around the lovely store swam into

Maura's thoughts as soon as she walked in through the glass doors. There was no mistaking the scent of polish and perfumes that hung in the air. Cleary's used to have the same smell but it was never as delicate. She remembered that it was over twenty years since she had walked through the same door with her mammy. Her first thought was to walk back out again because she didn't want to remember when she was there before.

'De yeh mind?' a shrill voice blew over Maura's shoulder into her ear.

'Excuse me if yeh don't mind?' repeated the same voice in a higher tone.

Maura felt something pushing into her legs so she turned round.

'I want te get inte teh shop if yeh don't mind?' a girl about the same age as Cathy blared into Maura's face. She lowered her head to the pushchair and nodded to a small child that was eating a bar of chocolate, adding, 'I don't have much time and teh place'el be closin' soon.'

Maura moved into the shop because the girl was blocking the door with the pushchair. She had no intention of buying anything so she ignored the displays of jumpers and blouses that were gracing the new counters. She knew that if she made four right turns she would be at the door again. She should never have come in after all this time. Cleary's was always cheaper.

On the third turn Maura smelt the cosmetics before she saw the small mirrors in their silver frames sitting proudly on the glass counter. She suddenly felt she was ten years old and she was with her mammy. She was always interested in cosmetics so she slowed her flight to a walk and peered at the displays.

The woman in the picture wasn't smiling, but with skin resembling porcelain reminded Maura of Josie. She didn't read the name of the face powder the model was advertising. Cathy had already told her that Josie didn't wear makeup during the day and although the shop was illuminated with electric lights it was still daytime.

While she stared at the picture she imagined she could feel her mammy's presence, and she hated Josie. And it wasn't because of the face powder. She was thinking about shoes. The shoes she should have worn the day she had made her confirmation. The black patent leather shoes with the small strap across the instep she would have been able to wear to school for the summer if Josie had brought her into town to buy them instead of giving her mammy the money.

Like all children of working-class families, Maura was dressed in new clothes twice during her childhood – when she made her first holy communion, and when she was confirmed into the Catholic faith.

Both days were special for the children and highlighted a stage of growing up. When they had made their communion they moved from the infants to the primary school, and when they had been confirmed they moved into the high school. But the joy for most of the children was the new clothes, and the small sums of money they received from their relations and neighbours.

'Are yeh all right there?' the saleslady asked Maura.

Maura folded the tissue she had used to wipe her eye and said, 'I'm fine.' She knew the black debris in the folded tissue was her mascara. She turned her face to one of the mirrors and when she was raising her crumpled tissue to her other eye she said, 'I have a bit of dirt in my eye.'

'Help yourself,' the saleslady said retrieving a box of tissues from under the counter and placing them beside the mirror.

Maura wiped the smudges of mascara from under her lower eyelashes and sniffed. A whiff of perfume flew across her nose, and for a second she thought her mammy was standing beside her. Her mammy never wore makeup but she always wore perfume. She would have cried again if she hadn't felt anger in her heart. And she wasn't angry at the memory of the black patent shoes with the little strap across the instep. She was still angry with Josie but for the first time she saw that it wasn't her sister's fault that she had to wear the brown-laced shoes for a whole year after she had made her confirmation.

Maura had so few happy, or joyous memories from when she was growing up that she seldom recalled any events from her childhood. While she patted her face to check that she hadn't spoilt any more of her makeup when the tears had burst from her eyes, she struggled to forget about her confirmation clothes.

Pink, pink and blue, were the colours on her cheeks and eyes. They were also the colours of her confirmation clothes. She had worn a blue dress and a pink coat. Una had made her clothes and she had taken her into town when she had bought the material. She had also brought her around Arnott's and Cassidy's so they could see all the dresses that the shops were selling.

On another day Pauline had taken her into town to buy her hat, and a small handbag. They were the most enjoyable days she could remember. On both days when her sisters had bought everything they had taken her into Bewley's café on Grafton Street and they had enjoyed tea and cream cakes.

The colour pink was still in Maura's thoughts when she had left the department store and was making her way towards O'Connell Street again. The clock over a jeweller's shop told her it was nearly half past five. She was still too early to go to the cinema. She knew that the last showing was after half past seven. She also remembered that there was another picture house somewhere near Grafton Street so she decided she would walk around to Bewleys and have some tea and cream cakes. She wanted to hold on to the memory of when she had been there with her sisters.

The pavements were more crowded with people in a hurry

to get in front of Maura when she was passing the GPO again. And the busses and cars were endless when she was waiting to cross the road at Astons Quay. The sour smell from the River Liffey drowned out the remains of the perfume that had followed her out of Arnott's, but she was still fretting over the memory of her confirmation clothes.

'Pink,' Maura spat the word to the skirt of the woman walking in front of her. She recalled the day all those years ago when she had tried on about six different pairs of shoes before the black patent ones. She had dutifully walked up and down on the carpet. She remembered the shoes had felt like light little wings when she heard her mammy ask the girl, 'Do you have them in pink?'

By the time Maura had completed her walk up to the top of Grafton Street she had decided that her mammy had never cared any more about her than she had about her other sisters.

Chapter Nine

U ncle Tony's here,' Kevin called out from the back of his daddy's car.

'S-so he is,' Sean grumbled. His sons didn't hear him because they had their bodies pressed together to see the car that was in their driveway. Sean was annoyed because Tony had parked his car in the driveway. He thought it was all very well for his brother-in-law with his double garage and enough room in his driveway for four cars.

'He has two new ones,' Kevin shouted when he was scrambling out of his daddy's car.

'Three contradicted his younger brother Brian,' and ran after Kevin to look at the football stickers that were always on the windows of his uncle's car.

While his boys were arguing over the importance of the different football teams, Sean brought Jerome out on the pavement and they watched a bus from the size of a pea coming up the road until it had passed them. He enjoyed the smell of the roast pork when he pushed in the hall door and wondered if there would be enough meat for two more. He picked up a slice of the carved meat off the tray that was on the kitchen unit and put in into his mouth and followed the boys through the kitchen and out into the back garden.

'There yeh are Sean,' Tony said, his plastic chair grating noisily on the ground because he had stayed sitting on it when he pushed it back.

Sean nodded his head at his sister Joan's husband then glanced at Flo who had remained sitting on the chair opposite Tony. 'O-on yer own?' he asked looking back into the kitchen where Flo should be fussing about with the dinner. The pots were on the hob, but the taps were still straight. The vegetables should be steaming away. His joy at seeing Tony started to evaporate; he wondered where Joan was.

Tony stood. He didn't know what words to use. He flapped his hands around his chest and hips as if he was wearing a tailored jacket that needed smoothing.

For a few seconds as he waited for his brother-in-law to say why he was here Sean envied his friend's good looks. He liked Tony, he'd known him before he had married his sister. In his late twenties Tony still played football and he trained twice a week. He didn't smoke, and he never drank more than a couple of pints at any one time.

Sean thought a smile as he ran his eyes over Tony's maroon sweater, and wondered if he ever wore the same one twice. 'Stay where ye are,' he said, 'I'll get another.' He pulled his eyes away from Tony's long denim-covered legs and took his time retrieving a plastic chair from the corner of the patio. He liked bad news slowly. He thought it must Joan.

Tony left his chair shoved out from the table and waited for Sean to sit down.

'C-come on,' Sean said, 'w-what's up?'

'Maura's in teh Mater,' Flo said, leaning into the table and stubbing out her cigarette. 'It's her shoulder. She's goin' te be all right. Joan and Cathy are with her now.'

'Donal is on the way up,' Tony said.

'There's no n-need teh worry about Jerome, we can k-keep him here,' Sean said. His plastic chair creaked when he shoved it back so he could look down the garden at the boys playing about with a ball. He knew that Joan still went to work. 'What's teh score on the s-shoulder?' he asked.

The snapshot was black and white. A neighbour had taken it with a Kodak box brownie camera. Tony was one of the six children that were lined up under the window of a house. One of the children he played out with had shown it to him. After he had seen the picture Tony had asked his gran Bella why he was darker than the other children.

Bella had told him that his daddy was from a far off country where all the people had very dark skins. Tony didn't ask about it anymore. He was only seven but he had learned in school about how poor people were in African countries. His teacher had shown the class pictures of where the nuns and priests went to work. He had never seen his mother either but Bella told him she lived in England.

Until he married Joan the only family Tony had known was his gran Bella who was his mammy's mother. Donal had been his best friend since he was seven when they had both joined the Ballyglass Football Club. It was through his long, and close friendship with Donal that Tony had gotten to know the Malone family.

For days after the evening Joan had told him why she had been in England, Tony was astonished that he hadn't known anything at all about why she had been away. Until this morning at the hospital, and he saw how quickly Cathy, Donal, and Joan had acted together when they suspected what had happened to Maura. While the doctors were attending to Maura, the four of them; Donal, Cathy, Joan and himself were huddled in a corner sorting out who would be told what, when, and by whom.

While he deliberated what he should say to Sean, Tony brushed crumbs that weren't there off the table, and examined the wall that separated the gardens for faults in the brickwork, and moved his elbows from his knees to the table three times.

While Tony was trying to find the words to tell his brother-in-law what Joan suspected about Maura, Sean's mind raced away about what could be the matter with Maura's shoulder. He watched Tony move about on his chair and was sure his sister couldn't die from broken bones. It just meant being in hospital for a while and that wouldn't be for long, a week at the most. He had just braced himself for the worst from Tony when Donal walked out into the garden.

Chapter Ten

Donal's usual hello smile was weak when he nodded to Sean before he sat in the plastic chair that Flo had vacated ten minutes earlier.

'What's the story?' Sean asked. His chair grated on the gravel again as he moved it to sit in front of his brother. Donal and Tony were sitting sideways to the table with their backs to the house. Sean had his back to the garden with his hands on the knees of his short legs.

'There are a couple of things that need sortin' all right,' Donal, said showing Sean the top of his head where the hair was getting thinner by the month. He kept his elbows on his knees when he raised his face, tilted it to one side and held his older brother's frightened gaze.

'Do yez want tea or a beer?' called Flo from the kitchen door.

'How long f-fer dinner?' Sean asked.

'A good half hour,' Flo said, nodding down the garden. 'I'm goin te feed teh boys first, and put Angela down fer her nap.'

'I'll get t-teh beers,' Sean said. He felt that if he walked a few steps his breakfast would drop back down to his stomach. He couldn't remember ever seeing Donal so distressed before so he patted his brother on the back before he went into the kitchen.

Donal nodded gratefully, but not because he needed a beer. He wanted more time to get the words together to tell Sean what was up.

'G-go on,' Sean said, while he ripped the top off his bottle of beer.

Donal had never been able to flower things up like his youngest brother Liam, or Cathy who both thrived on drama. When it didn't exist they created it. They could soften bad news better than any politician. He started with the phone call from Cathy at six o'clock that morning. The Garda were in the house, and Maura was in the Mater hospital.

'The Garda?' Sean said lowering his beer from his mouth.

'Yer right in thinkin' it was her shoulder,' Donal continued. He knew his brother liked to be right. 'She had been staying the night with Nula's mother and brother in Phibsboro. In teh early hours of the mornin' teh pain got so bad that Noel's mother called an ambulance and she was taken into teh hospital.'

Sean inhaled and began doing his breathing exercises.

'It was about seven when the Garda brought Cathy down te my place and when we got to teh hospital Nula was already waitin' fer us,' Donal continued. 'Maura was sedated and she was waitin' to have X ray's.

'Why teh Garda?' Sean asked. He gulped his beer

'We're not too sure at this stage.' Donal said. He inhaled deeply. He wanted to tell his brother the truth, although he was still only imagining what had happened to his sister.

'Did she have a fall or somethin'?' Sean asked.

'We didn't see Noel or his mother because they had left when Nula arrived,' Donal said. 'It was Nula who told us that Maura kept calling out, "Stop," and "I'm sorry," when she was in teh ambulance.'

Sean turned to Tony and asked, 'Is this true?'

'It was nine by the time Joan and myself got to the hospital, and the Garda were still there. They think that Maura has been beaten.'

'Mugged?' Sean asked putting his beer back on the table.

'No, Sean she wasn't mugged,' Tony said, shaking his head from side to side in short slow movements then added, 'She was in her nightdress when she arrived at the hospital.'

Donal was still finding it difficult to believe what Joan and Cathy had decided had happened to Maura. 'Accordin' teh Cathy, Maura had teh pain teh night she came home.'

'C-canada?' Sean gasped.

'That's what we're thinkin',' Donal said, wiping his face with his hands, 'and it's teh most likely. Apparently some of teh bruises and other marks are a few weeks old.'

Sean pressed his fingers into his eyes, moved his hands around his face, then held his head in his hands. Tony and Donal watched him in silence for a few seconds, then surveyed the marks on the plastic table.

'The thing is,' Donal said picking up his beer like he needed something to hold on to, 'we are only surmisen'.' He spoke slowly and he emphasised each word and continued, 'She doesn't have te say anythin'.'

Chapter Eleven

Joan moved her head about so she could see what was behind her in the mirror of her little Ford Fiesta. She saw Cathy shifting about in the back seat: 'It's a bit tight there, isn't it?' she said.

'I'm grand, I'm grand, stop yer worryin' fer God's sake,' Cathy insisted. Her lovely face was framed between her knees for a second before she was able to get her feet on the floor behind Joan's seat, 'I should have got in teh other door,' she panted. She was still laughing when she poked her head between the front seats and said, 'Are yeh all right, Maura?' She moved around some more and tried to get comfortable behind Joan's seat.

Maura closed her eyes. She had most of the top part of her body in plaster so how could she be all right. After a few seconds she said, 'I'm fine.'

Cathy wasn't comfortable but was determined to be agreeable in the small car even though she failed to understand why they weren't using Tony's much bigger one. She accepted Joan's explanation that she was nervous with driving big cars.

Joan didn't tell her younger sister that Maura had begged her to take her out of the hospital and not let Sean or Donal come. She was also pleased not to have Tony or Donal with her because she felt that Maura would talk to her more openly than she would if they were there. After all a woman getting beaten by her husband wasn't easy to talk to other men about even if they were her brothers.

'I'm terribly sorry, Maura, about shoutin' at yeh fer te sit up straight so much,' Cathy said, pulling on the back of Maura's seat so she could lean forward. When Maura's head jerked slightly from the movement of the seat Cathy put her hand on her sister's shoulder and added quickly, 'No, Maura, don't turn round it's enough that yeh forgive me.'

Joan had been as disappointed as Cathy with their sister's behaviour and attitude since she had come home. Maura had been cold, boring and distant. She had constantly changed the conversation so that she was talking all the time. She had reminded Joan of Josie except that Josie wasn't cold. 'There's no need to be sorry for something you didn't know about, Cathy,' she said. She knew from the scowl on Maura's face when she saw Cathy walk down the ward that she hadn't been pleased to see her youngest sister.

Like Cathy, Joan wanted to be friends with Maura but she wasn't going to allow her to bully Cathy like Josie used to do. She had asked Cathy to be in the house when they got back from the hospital. Then when Cathy asked Donal to be at the house so she could see the doctor Joan thought that Cathy should be with her because it was Cathy that would looking after Maura. She didn't tell Cathy that Maura didn't want her. She also decided that Maura wasn't going to pick and choose who would look after her.

But just the same Joan's heart was full of sympathy for Maura. When she had seen the wretched state of the girl after she had come back from having her X-rays she remembered when she had been raped. Although she still had never been able to recall the physical act she never forgot the terror she had felt when the old man had slapped her across her face. The doctor had told her that her arms were bruised, and her shoulder was hurting because the man had held her down on the floor. She still didn't remember what the man had done to her, but there had been other evidence to show that she had been sexually assaulted.

From the moment she had seen Maura's tired face lying on the white pillow, all Joan could think about was how lonely she had felt when she had been in England waiting to have the baby that she hadn't wanted. She had allowed her Aunt Sue and her family to take care of her but she had never talked about what had happened. She had often blamed herself for being in the wrong place at the wrong time. She also wondered what she would have done if the old man had lived. She was adamant that whatever problems Maura had with her husband it wasn't her fault that he had beaten her.

After she had talked to the doctor at the hospital Joan had decided that Maura had probably come home for good; and if she were right then her sister would be living in Plunkett Road. And that was also still Cathy's home, and as far as they all could tell she was happy doing her own thing. If Maura was going to live in Plunkett Road then she would have to get on with Cathy. 'Are you sure you don't want to stay the night with us, Cathy?' she called out.

'I'd luv te, Joan, but I can't. I've got hundreds ev things teh do,' Cathy replied, moving forward on her seat and adding quickly, 'but at the same time if yez need me just phone and I'll come runnin' down.'

Maura made to turn round, but the plaster that encased most of the top of her body restrained. She still asked, 'What have you got to do?'

'We're gettin' teh treasure hunt ready te night,' Cathy said, pulling on Maura's seat again. 'I've been elected te write out all teh questions.'

Maura closed her eyes and sighed loudly.

Joan patted Maura on her knee and said, 'It's a game we play for to raise money for the football club.'

Maura turned her head and looked out the window.

Joan rolled up the window on her side of the car, then drove slowly towards the exit gates of the hospital.

'Doreen is comin' up this evenin' and we'll go over all teh questions that Donal has given me, and I'll have all day tomorrow teh type it up,' Cathy said.

'What about work?' Maura asked.

'I got teh certificate for teh week,' Cathy said, poking her head between the two front seats and speaking softly as though she was telling a secret when she added, 'Teh doctor saw me first thing this mornin'.'

'What for?' Maura demanded, glaring at Joan because she couldn't turn round to the back of the car and glare at Cathy.

Cathy leaned forward and whispered into Maura's ear, 'Fer teh look after yeh.'

Maura closed her eyes. She still wasn't sure if she wanted to stay with Joan or go back to Plunkett Road. She recalled how nice Tony had been to her when she was in the hospital, and he owned a bigger share in the Beggars Lodge than her brother so he would be more likely to give her a job.

Growing more concerned about how Cathy would manage Joan asked, 'What did the doctor write on the certificate?'

'Abdominal somethin',' Cathy giggled, then added quickly, 'It's not me readin' this time; even Donal couldn't read teh writin'. I don't know how teh chemists manage with prescriptions. Anyway, I feel like I'm cheatin' now.'

'Why?' Joan asked, smiling over at Maura.

'Well,' Cathy replied, 'if yer goin' te be lookin' after Maura then you should have it. I haven't sent it in yet. We could change teh name if ye like.'

While Joan and Cathy were laughing Maura managed a weak grin. She was as jealous of Cathy as she was of Joan. She envied the freedom that her youngest sister had do as she liked.

Nothing that Cathy and Joan chatted and laughed about while they completed the half-hour journey to Joan's house interested Maura. They were driving towards a building site and two tall, wide, wrought-iron gates held up by a pillar on each side were standing as though they were guarding all the rubble behind them.

'Is that the convent?' Maura asked.

Joan stole a glance over to where some of the old building was still standing and said, 'Was the convent.'

Maura continued to stare at the ruins and said, 'What happened to all the nuns?'

'They died,' Cathy said.

Maura had never been in the convent, or any convent. The only knowledge she had of nuns was what her mammy had told her about the ones that had taught her in the boarding school she had gone to. It wasn't much because every time she had asked a question her mammy would walk out of the room. 'Was there a fire or something?' she asked.

'They died off,' Cathy said, turning her head to look back at the tall gates. 'Hundreds ev convents have closed down in the last few years,' She exaggerated, 'And yeh can blame smaller families and better education.'

Maura sighed and closed her eyes.

'The convents have been getting fewer novices since the war,' Joan said.

'Women don't have te put up with their families sending them into convents to get them out of the way, or to get themselves a place in heaven,' Cathy cut in. She always felt sorry for nuns. She was ten years old the night she had cried herself to sleep after one of her teachers had told the class that she hadn't seen her sister who was a nun for twenty years. 'God tenite,' she whined, 'imagine bein' locked up in an old buildin' like that and spendin' all yer days prayin' fer teh sins ev teh world.'

'All nuns didn't do that,' Joan contradicted. She recalled the nun that had stayed with her when she was having her baby in England. 'Some of them are nurses.'

'Teh thing I can't understand,' Cathy said as she tried to move her foot again, 'is how they knew about teh sins we were all committin' if they were all locked away and they didn't read teh papers.

Not now Cathy, Joan thought. She had no idea where her young sister got her ideas from, and she was great fun to listen to. She could almost hear Maura closing her eyes. They were nearly home so she hoped that Cathy would be satisfied when she said, 'You are absolutely right about fewer girls becoming nuns these days.'

'And girls don't have te get married te have babies either,' Cathy said, leaning forward so Maura would hear her, 'most ev us are well able te manage on er own.'

Chapter Twelve

onal was rolling up the water hose when Joan turned her small car into the cul-de-sac where her new four-bedroomed house stood in the middle of seven others. He had used the time waiting for his sisters to wash his car.

'Is he cleanin' yer windas fer yeh?' Cathy called out when she saw the water flowing down the driveway.

'I doubt it,' Joan replied, steering her car into the wide driveway. 'Housework was never one of Donal's favourite hobbies.' She smiled over at Maura and pulled on the handbrake.

'Neither was gardenin',' Cathy said, tapping Maura on her shoulder; 'I'm hopin' yeh'll join me when yeh come home in persuedin' er baldy brother te start diggen teh big spread we have out the back in Plunkett Road.'

'Why don't you have a garden digging party and ask the football team?' Joan suggested opening the door of the car, 'Donal will buy the beer if he doesn't have to do any digging.'

'I'll go over fer Jerome when yer ready,' Donal said softly when he helped Maura out of the car. 'Take yer time,' he added when Maura started to walk in front him.

Maura giggled as she said, 'It's only my shoulder.' She was determined to let her brother see she would be fit enough to work in a short time. She walked into the house on her own. The pale walls reminded Maura of the hospital. She had slept most of the time, and every time she woke Joan and Cathy were there. She remembered other faces, but she could put them out of her mind now. Her most vivid memory was the pain when she was in Noel's house. She noticed there were no flowers in the sparkling glass vases before she closed her eyes again. But the light coloured painted walls still reminded her of the hospital and she imagined she could feel the pain again.

She had been with Noel before the awful pain had begun. They had been dancing when the pain started in her shoulder, then her neck, then moved to her arm. She now sat in a straight chair staring at the wall listening to Joan and Cathy giggling in the hall.

Donal had been unhappy about Maura since the evening he had watched her get into Noel Larkin's car. He hadn't told Sean or Joan and he was worried in case he should have. He couldn't remember ever having to take any responsibility, or even make small decisions about his family before. 'Is the pain any easier?' he asked. His sympathy for her moved between the pains she was suffering now, the beatings her husband had given her, and her disappointment with their mammy not being at home.

Football had never interested any of Donal's sisters and dancing had never appealed to him so they seldom had much in common to talk about. But Donal loved his sisters and he knew they had cared for him when he was a child.

Maura raised her head from her hands smiled feebly and said, 'The tablets are very good.'

'Looks too good teh smoke in, doesn't it, Maura?' Cathy called out when she walked into the room with a big ashtray and sat down on one of the four chairs that were neatly placed around the table in the middle of the room. She sniffed twice while she opened her packet of cigarettes and said, 'I love the smell of new paint.'

Maura moved her mouth in the shape of a smile and said, 'It is a lovely house.' She took a cigarette from Cathy, then cast her eyes around the room as though she was assessing the value of all the furniture.

'Well, if yer in teh business then milk it fer all yeh can get,' Cathy laughed, then poked her worried-looking brother in his arm and said, 'That right, Donal.'

How on earth does she always know what to say, Donal wondered while he waved his head at his youngest sister. Cathy was a conundrum to him. He didn't know what to make of her most of the time.

For some months now Donal knew that Cathy wasn't happy with her job anymore. He knew by how often they came into the Beggars Lodge that her group of friends had broken up. Some of them were married, some had moved away, and some went to other places for their drinks and entertainment.

'What are yeh goin' teh do with yerself now fer teh rest of teh day?' he asked. He glanced at Maura expecting her to be as amused with Cathy as everyone else always was.

Assuming Donal had looked to her for support with Cathy, Maura said, 'Do you have to stay out of work?' She turned to Donal and smiled weakly. When Cathy opened her mouth wider than her eyes, Maura put a hand on her arm and patted it like Cathy was a child and continued, 'I mean, if you wanted to go back earlier? Or you need the money? Or the company needed you?' She finished her enquiry with looking at Donal.

Donal's anxiety over Maura turned to shock. He suspected from her animated tone and the stern expression on her face that she expected him to tell Cathy that she should go back into work now that she was going to stay with Joan. He looked at his watch as if it would move him to another room.

Enough is enough Cathy thought. She looked hard at Maura and said, 'I don't give a shite about teh company.' She held her sister's cold expression and continued, 'And as fer money I have friends that will help me out if I run short.'

Maura closed her eyes.

Biting back her temper, Cathy said, 'Teh main reason I won't go back to work is because I will be at home fer yerself.'

Donal sat up straight and said, 'Yeh can go back teh work any time yeh like but yer doctor gets angry with yeh if yeh do.'

Maura gave her full attention to taking her cigarette out of the ashtray.

'It makes yer doctor look like he doesn't know what he's talking about,' Donal said. While they ate their sandwiches Joan told Maura what a treasure hunt was. He saw Maura wasn't interested until Joan said they all ended up in the Beggars Lodge when Maura raised her eyebrows.

'We're bringin' them business,' Cathy laughed, then patted her sister on her hand and added, 'and we all have a great laugh.' She exchanged glances of concern with Joan when Maura continued to avoid looking at any of them while she thought Maura would wear the spoon out from twisting it. But her good nature prompted her to say, 'Yer welcome teh come if yeh feel up to it.'

Chapter Thirteen

Would you like to lie down for a while, Maura?' Joan asked when she had come back into the room after she had waved Donal and Cathy away. Although she was hoping to use the rest of the afternoon to talk she saw that Maura looked wretched. She estimated that Tony would be home in a couple of hours so she didn't have a lot of time.

'I'm not tired,' Maura replied lifting her elbows off the table, 'the tablets are very good.' She moved her neck and arms. It was important for Joan to see that she only had some bruises and they would be all gone in a week or two. She was sure that Tony would ask Joan if she was well enough to work again. 'Tell me,' she asked in a demanding tone that matched the scowl on her face, 'does Cathy ever take anything serious?'

Determined not to lose her temper, Joan broadened her smile and asked, 'Like what for example?'

'Her job, for one thing,' Maura replied, slapping her hand on the table.

Joan spoke soft and slowly, 'Cathy works in a garment factory.' She paused for Maura to look at her and continued, 'They hire and fire numbers, not people. She is what was called in the old days, a hand.' She paused again and renewed her smile: 'At one time I thought she would be great working in a shop, she has both the personality and the manners.'

Jealousy glowed from Maura's eyes when she raised her head.

Joan continued, 'I must admit that at times I think she wouldn't have enough patience with difficult people.' She mistook the gloss of envy in Maura's eyes for feelings of pain so she softened her voice: 'Anyhow she likes her time off, and she ends up with more money, even with her time off working in the factory, than she would if she was in a shop and turning in every day.'

Maura didn't see her reflection in the spoon she was glaring at because her mind was focused on the few shops she had worked in before she had gone to Canada. She had hated the vegetable shop because it was so cold and dirty, but she wasn't going to admit that now so she said, 'At least shop work is clean.'

Joan wasn't going to tolerate Maura deriding Cathy. She stood and started to stack the small plates as she said, 'Now let's have a coffee, tea is all right with a sandwich. Coffee is better with a cigarette.'

Maura lifted her face from the spoon and said, 'Mammy worked in one of the big stores in town.'

'That's right,' Joan replied, 'in Grafton Street.' She pulled the spoon out of her sister's hand while she added, 'But she didn't work.'

Maura snorted a giggle.

'She served,' Joan replied to her sister's frown and said, 'don't you remember how she was always talking about the ladies who used to want her to serve them?'

Serving for Maura was no different to working. She served people in the restaurants. The size of her tips depended on how well she served the customers. She closed her eyes to the sounds that her sister was making with the plates, but she was really squeezing out the memory of when her mammy had been served the day she had bought her awful brown shoes for her confirmation.

'Anyway,' Joan continued, 'Mammy didn't have to give up

anything from her low wages, and she didn't have to be home on Saturdays to do housework. In fact Mammy never had to do any housework at all before she was married.'

Maura stood. She didn't want to hear about all the work her older sisters Pauline and Una used to do. She had heard enough from Cathy. She followed Joan out to the kitchen.

'Do you still like jelly?' Joan asked, opening another door on one of the cupboards that were along the wall of her large kitchen.

'I have never liked jelly,' Maura giggled. 'What do you want to know that for?'

'For after dinner,' Joan replied, opening another door.

'What makes you think that I like jelly?' Maura asked. She thought her sister's kitchen must be as big as the living room in Plunkett Road. And it boasted every piece of equipment that could be bought for the modern cook.

'Because you used to make two of them every Sunday before you went away to Canada.'

Maura moved about so that she could rest her arm that was in plaster on the table. She wasn't going to say she had made jelly because it was easy so she said, 'It was always eaten.'

Everything was always eaten in those days Joan wanted to say but she knew that this wasn't the time to annoy her sister. She sat down to wait for the coffee machine to stop squirting on the long worktop that covered two double units, a fridge, a freezer, a washing machine and a clothes dryer. She still had no idea how she was going to get her sister to tell her who had beaten her and why. She had been relieved when the Garda had said they were satisfied that Maura's injuries had not taken place in Ireland. 'How is your arm now?' she asked.

'It's fine,' Maura replied, recalling the pain, the Garda, Noel, and Nula all together. She shuddered at the memory of being helped into the ambulance. There had been two nurses and a doctor examining her, Joan and the doctor asking her questions, and there was a woman standing at the end of the bed writing. When she woke up in a hospital ward Joan was holding her hand and Cathy was sitting beside her. The last thing she remembered was Joan saying, 'We'll have a long talk tomorrow.'

Stupid as Maura was she knew that Joan was going to ask her about how she got the bruises on her arms and fractures in her shoulder. While she watched Joan's small body move between the sink and the worktop, she decided she would listen to her sister, but she wasn't going to tell her anything. It was important to humour the girl if she wanted her sister to get her husband to give her a job.

'Do you want cream?' Joan asked, smiling as she poured out the two coffees.

Maura blinked her eyes and rested her head in her hand.

Joan poured a drop of cream into the two cups.

In an effort to delay the interrogation she was expecting from Joan, Maura said, 'I was just thinking that Cathy could take up hairdressing.'

'And why do you think that?' Joan asked.

Maura pulled her coffee towards her.

Joan prayed for patience while she took an ashtray from the windowsill over the sink and sat down again.

'She would make better friends,' Maura said, 'all her friends talk about is sex and the factory where they work.'

'And what else would young girls have to talk about?' Joan asked. The idea of Cathy learning about hairdressing brought her eldest sister into her mind so she said, 'Maura, you sound just like Josie.' It was true, Josie was still a snob, and she was still afraid to upset their mammy, Joan thought as she ignored the angry glow on Maura's face. At the same time she wasn't surprised that Maura was offended. When she was growing up she had also been afraid to upset her eldest sister. A ray of hope swept over Joan. She thought that if Josie could change, then maybe Maura would. Until three hours before she was married, Joan would have been very hurt if she had been told she was like Josie. But Maura hadn't come home for her wedding so she wouldn't have seen the new Josie that the family now knew. She smiled as she whispered, 'I did say sound like.'

Maura closed her eyes, and sighed.

It's now or never, Joan thought. She opened her cigarette packet as she said, 'I think I can safely say that Josie would never have allowed any man to beat her up like you have allowed Carl to do.'

The seconds went by slowly while Maura polished a teaspoon with her thumb. She then lowered her head into her shoulders and stared into the centre of the spoon while she kept rubbing her finger up and down the handle of it and wondered if Carl would hit Josie.

Joan slapped the table with the flat of her hand, then stood, walked over to the sink, opened a drawer sharply and then shoved it in and out rapidly. The contents in the drawer made a noise like the large spoons, spatulas, and knives were screeching from pain as they bashed against each other. She pulled a large serving spoon from the drawer, banged it on the table and snapped, 'Now Maura, have a good look at yourself.'

Maura stared at the large shining spoon for about five seconds before she picked it up. She held it out as if it was a mirror and studied her reflection.

Fleeting flashes of the memory of her own pains from that dreadful Saturday afternoon when Peter Cunningham had died passed through Joan's mind. 'Does Pauline know?' she asked. As if in answer to a prayer Joan imagined she saw her eldest sister appear in the doorway from the hall with a towel over her arm and her combs and scissors in her hands. The imagined vision prompted her to say, 'We could do with Josie here now.'

Maura looked terrified when she raised her face from the spoon.

'To do your hair,' Joan said. She leaned across the table and took hold of the top of the spoon. Maura kept her eyes on the long silver stem while Joan pulled it through her fingers, and she was still gazing at it when Joan laid it down on the table. Joan then leaned back in her chair and asked softly, 'Does Mammy know?'

Maura closed her eyes. The images of when her husband had leered after Josie eight years ago blending with the memory of her confirmation shoes made her want to cry. She had never liked Josie, but Josie had never hit her. Nobody had ever hit her until Carl had slapped her across her face. She had no idea what Josie would do if anyone hit her. She closed her eyes again to block out all her memories, licked her lips, turned her face towards the cooker and said, 'I never told her.'

Joan inhaled and said, 'You know as well as I do how Mammy knows about everything even though she hasn't been told.'

'I really don't know,' Maura said to the table. She could see the four new long-sleeved, high-necked sweaters that Carl had bought her the week before her mammy had come out to Canada last year. She also remembered how good Carl had been when her mammy had stayed with them. He had even lost his job because he had taken extra holidays off so he could be with them all the time. But her mammy had never asked her why she was wearing long-sleeved jumpers all the time.

Years of ice-cold resentment, and jealousy towards her older sisters had started to thaw in Maura's heart when she had been walking up to Grafton Street on the Friday evening. At the same time she wouldn't admit she missed having at least one of them in the house in Plunkett Road. Right now she admitted in her thoughts that Joan was right, Josie would have done her hair.

'Maura, we only want to help,' Joan said, leaning over the table and taking hold of her sister's hand and giving it a pull.

Maura turned her head to the cooker. The slight pain that

ran down her arm was enough to remind her of when her husband had told her that if she told anyone anything about her business they would want to know everything. She returned her face to the table and said, 'I don't belong here anymore.' It was always someone else's fault when she didn't know what to do so she added quickly, 'I've been forgotten.' She moved her head sideways to look at the cooker again, then rubbed the side of her nose with her hand and sat up straight as though she had been given a cue from the cooker. Her eyes were clear when she said harshly, 'Nobody remembers me.'

Joan wondered if Maura was right. The family very seldom talked about her. And Maura never wrote to anyone. Recalling the last time Maura was home she said, 'It's hard to believe that it's eight years since we were all at home at the same time.' They were so short of beds that Una had stayed with Angie Dolan, herself and Cathy had stayed with another neighbour, and Donal had stayed with Tony. 'Does Pauline ever talk about us?' she asked.

Maura closed her eyes.

Joan's sharpest memory of Pauline was the evening when her sister had come home after spending the previous night with her mammy's friend Ena. Her mammy had been so furious that she had stayed in bed for two days. Joan didn't know why but ever since then any time when anyone mentioned Pauline's name her mammy would walk out of the room.

Tired of being asked about Pauline, Maura said, 'Sean told me that Josie was in Limerick for the last two weeks,' She recalled that when her mammy was out in Canada she hadn't asked to go to see Pauline. When she had mentioned it to Carl he told her it was none of her business.

Joan was also thinking about Pauline. She was ashamed now that she hadn't asked her sister why her mammy had been so angry with her all those years ago. 'There's plenty of room in Plunkett Road for you and Jerome if you want to stay,' she said, hoping that Maura would tell her one way or the other. You know yourself that mammy will appreciate another pair of hands with the housework. And I imagine Cathy will be delighted with the company.'

This wasn't the talk Maura was expecting to have. She shoved her chair back with her feet and moved her legs sideways so that she could cross them and rested her hands on her knees.

Joan prayed her older sister Una would walk into the room. Maura needed someone who wouldn't put up with all her nonsense, and Una would get answers, but Una wasn't going to walk in any more than Josie had been here a few minutes ago. She stared hard at the table and wondered what Pauline was like now but she couldn't get a picture of Pauline's face. 'Does Pauline ever talk of coming home?' she asked.

'Sometimes,' Maura lied. She hadn't seen or spoken to her sister in Canada since Christmas. As if she was following a fly that was moving slowly around the room, Maura raised her head and ran her eyes around the wall units. This wasn't the talk she was expecting to have. Joan should be telling her how brave she was for all the pain she had endured with her shoulder and her arm. She remembered she wanted her sister to get her a job so she smiled.

Thinking that her sister wanted her cup filled again when she rested her eyes on the coffee-maker, Joan stood and lifted the jug out of the machine. She put her hand gently on Maura's shoulder and said, 'There's just enough for a top-up, Tony will be in soon and we can make a fresh pot.'

'Carl doesn't beat me up,' Maura said. She waited until Joan was sitting back down and topping up her own cup before she said, 'Yes, he has hit me, I won't deny that, but it's no more than most husbands do.'

Joan's hand started to shake.

'I know you are not married all that long, Joan,' Maura paused, so she could absorb the astonishment in her sister's eyes. She grew in confidence as her younger sister continued to stare at her. She lifted her hand off the table and moved it up and down like she was chopping potatoes with a knife. Her little finger gently touched the table as she said every word when she continued, 'It just happens.'

'Jesus Christ,' Joan whispered.

The shock that was glowing on her young sister's face encouraged Maura to tell Joan about some of the real facts of married life. When she stretched her hand over to get a spoon her eyes were drawn to the swirling of the coffee in the glass bowl that Joan was still holding. She saw that Joan's hand was shaking and she felt sorry for her. She remembered the first time that Carl had hit her.

Please Una will you walk in the door, Joan prayed. She wanted to cry for Maura.

'Most of the time I deserved it,' Maura continued as she picked the spoon up off the table. She glanced at Joan then lowered her eyes to her cup. She looked up once while she stirred her coffee.

Although her fingers were sore from squeezing the handle Joan continued to hold on to the coffee jug. She wanted to put it down because the smell of the coffee was making her want to be sick but she knew if she stood up her stomach would start to hurt her again. She spoke to the dark roots on the top of her sister's head when she asked, 'What did you do?'

'It's not important,' Maura said smiling as she added, 'to tell you the truth I don't even remember.' She coughed a giggle and waved her head: 'At the time I felt more sorry for Carl than myself because he was so upset.'

Seconds passed before Joan realised that her sister meant every word she had said. She nodded her head in agreement. She decided she would learn more if she didn't argue. She removed her glasses because she didn't want to see the smirk on her sister's face.

'Most of this,' Maura said jerking her head towards her shoulder and passing her good hand down the plaster as she added, 'is because I neglected it after I fell in the snow.'

That must have been at least nine months ago Joan calculated resting her wrist on the edge of the table because her fingers were tired from holding the coffee jug.

'Anyway,' Maura continued, waving her hand as though she was brushing away a fly. She removed the spoon from her cup and slapped it on the table as she said, 'Pushing is not the same as beating.'

Glass always makes a sharp sound when it breaks. The sound of the coffee jug on the tiled floor came after the crack of the spoon slapping on the table that had made Joan let go of the handle.

'Leave it,' Joan shouted into her lap when Maura made to move. 'Tony will be in any minute.' She then covered her hot cheeks with her hands and pressed her fingers as tight as she could into her face to prevent herself from using her hands on Maura.

They both watched in silence at the patterns the brown liquid made as it travelled along the tiles on the floor. They resembled a black plant growing tentacles. Joan found it calmed her temper.

'Can you buy a jug on its own or do you have to buy the whole lot again?' Maura asked, nodding her head over at the coffee machine.

'I've no idea,' Joan replied, swallowing her anger then added, 'Anyhow it's not important.' She felt drained and useless when she sat back in her chair. She looked for and counted outlines of animals in the coffee dredges on the floor until she heard the rattle at the front door.

Chapter Fourteen

Half an hour before Joan had brought Maura out to the kitchen, Donal has stopped his car outside his family home in Ballyglass. 'There's no need fer yeh te come in with me, Donal,' Cathy said placing her hand on her brother's arm. 'It's not like it's night time and teh house'll be all dark.'

'Are yeh sure?' Donal asked raising the handbrake, then glanced at his watch. It was nearly four and he knew that Tony wanted to leave the Beggars Lodge early because he was going to cook the dinner.

'Absolutely,' Cathy replied. She wanted to be on her own. She was both annoyed with, and feeling sorry for Maura. She needed to think about what she could do to help her sister. 'It's been a great help with yeh stopping off in teh village fer me te get teh shoppin'.'

Ever since Donal had learned about Joan being assaulted he had lied to Cathy about the number of young girls that were attacked when they were on their own. 'If yer sure yeh'll be all right,' he repeated. He didn't want to go into the house with her because he didn't want to talk about Maura anymore.

Although Cathy didn't know about what had happened to Joan she pretended to believe him when he insisted on going in the house with her when he brought her home. She enjoyed the attention.

While Joan was sitting in her kitchen searching for animal shapes in the coffee grinds moving on the tiled floor, Cathy was running around the house in Plunkett Road. She moved from the kitchen to the bathroom, to the living room, and the three bedrooms with a duster in her hands. When she found something in the living room that should be upstairs she brought it up straight away. Instead of leaving her worries in the room she had left, she added another one in the room she went into.

As her thoughts dwelled on one thing a branch led off to another. Although she tried to convince herself that the main trunk of her worry was her job, the branch that kept waving and wouldn't bend was how she saw her life when she was the same age as Maura.

Unlike most of her friends Cathy had no intention of getting married because it was what girls do. She had only ever had one boyfriend and she had never really liked him. He was only interested in touching her breast. She was sorry that she hadn't tried to do better at school. When she had gone to work in the factory she had expected she would learn to be a dressmaker like her sister Una. She had planned to start her own business like her sister Josie had done in hairdressing.

But she had spent her days in the factory machining up sleeves, making collars, joining side seams, and stitching in labels. All she had learned was how to use a fast sewing machine. Before she had seen the sorry state of Maura she had a dream. She was now working on turning her dream into a plan.

It was five o'clock when Cathy was gazing out of the kitchen window while filling the kettle. She thought about Jerome when she saw a few children playing out on the road. The quiet young boy brought her thoughts to the child's mother. By the time she was plugging in the kettle she was thinking about all her sisters. Josie had bought the kettle.

When she was running some water into the pot to soak it after she had tipped her scrambled eggs onto her plate Cathy thought that she would make an effort to learn to cook. Una was right when she had said that we all can't be as good as Josie but we could try to do better. Josie had bought the pot, and Josie had bought the toaster that Cathy had made her toast in.

Although Cathy envied her eldest sister she was never jealous of her. Josie had her own business. She was also married to a lovely man and she had two children. She was also very generous to all her family. The only fault Cathy could find with Josie was that she spoilt their mammy.

When she heard another couple of children calling out on the road she raised her head to the window. She smiled at the new curtains that Una had made a couple of weeks earlier. She laughed at the memory of her red-haired sister washing all the paintwork in the kitchen before she cleaned the windows and put the new curtains up. She was spreading butter on her toast when she thought that her Uncle Fred was wrong when he had said that Una should have joined the army when she went to England.

World War Six would be startin' before the universal war five was even over if er Una was in the army, Cathy thought. Una walked like a sergeant major but that was because she was tall and heavy. And she was always rushing around. Cathy went on to see her sister more like a policewoman with the way she was always asking about everything. She was like a detective most of the time.

By the time Cathy has finished her meal she had decided that apart from Maura she didn't measure well compared to any of her sisters. Even Pauline who she didn't know much about had a lovely big house in Canada.

'I can't even compare them to each other,' Cathy mumbled while she walked across the hall so she could look at the photographs of her family that were on the wall in the living room. 'They're all different,' she murmured when she was searching for an old snap that had been taken when the family were living in Arbour Hill. She smiled at the photograph when she noticed that when Josie was fourteen she was a head taller than Pauline, and she wasn't even twenty months older than her.

There were so few photographs of when her older sisters were young that Cathy had framed all the ones she could find. She had cut away all the peeling edges and made a collage. Her daddy used to borrow a camera from his brother every summer. When Maura was born he bought two rolls of film so they had sixteen snaps every year. Una and Pauline had taken away some of them when they had left home.

Not for the first time Cathy felt separate from her older sisters. Because they had moved to Ballymore before she was born she wasn't in any of the old snaps. She rubbed the glass like she could remove the creases in the old pictures while she remembered that they were all old enough to be her mother. She then enjoyed a memory of when Una had told her that when they had moved to Ballyglass some of the neighbours believed that one of them really was her mother. She had no memories of Arbour Hill or Ballymore because she was only a year old when they had moved to Ballyglass.

Underneath the frame with the old snaps, the one with the school photographs was also a collage. The oldest picture was one of Sean when he was ten. Josie had given him the money to buy it. She had also paid for all the other school photographs as well.

'Yeh were right, Una,' Cathy whispered, resting one of her fingers on the photograph of the young girl with all the freckles on her face and the two long plaits hanging down from her neck resting on her chest like ropes with bow ribbon on the end of them. 'But it's not fer me, and good luck te yeh with goin' back.' But just the same she felt sad when she moved her finger to the tall girl with the lovely sad face and the straight hair resting on her shoulders. She was thinking that it must have been awfully embarrassing for Josie when she was standing at the back of the class of children that were two years younger than her. She ran her fingers along the picture of Josie while she said, 'Although yeh were workin' when I was goin' te school if I had known that yeh had been kept away so much te mind the other children I would have tried harder fer yeh,' She rubbed her finger on the picture of the small girl with the broad smile and the curly hair and continued, 'Like yerself Pauline, I just didn't like school. I will make yez proud of me,' she added, wiping the picture with the tissue she had used to dry her eyes.

Chapter Fifteen

Expecting the footsteps she heard in the hall to be Tony's, Joan shouted, 'Take it easy.'

Tony stood in the doorway and surveyed the mess on the floor, then raised his head to Joan and asked, 'Are you all right?' He knew by the colour of Joan's face that she wasn't all right. He noticed her glasses were on the table before he saw the cast in her eye was more noticeable than usual. It always was when she was upset.

Joan laughed lightly as she watched her husband's forehead grow ridges of flesh when he raised his eyebrows and closed his lips. It was a poor, though comic imitation of Maurice when he couldn't think of what to say to someone.

Tony continued to smile back at his wife as he moved a couple of steps into the kitchen. He then put his hand lightly on Maura's shoulder and asked, 'You ok,'

'Much better, much better, thank you,' Maura giggled.

'Good,' Tony replied. He raised his hands to his waist level, and with his palms towards the floor he flapped them up and down while he said, 'Stay where you are, the both of you.' He patted the pockets of his jacket, and walked backwards into the hall the way he had come in. A minute later he opened the back door and came in with a bucket of sand, a sweeping brush, and a small shovel.

While he cleaned the floor Joan closed her ears to her sister's rendition of how efficient she was with cleaning up spilled food in the restaurants where she had worked.

While her stupid sister droned on, Joan willed herself not to cry. She suspected from the moisture she felt in her knickers she had started her periods when the shudder went through her after the coffee jug had crashed and although she was only a month overdue she had been hopeful.

'Spotless,' Tony said. He wanted to tell Maura to shut up. He went out the back door with the bucket and tools.

'What's for dinner?' Joan asked her husband when he came come back into the house and smiling out at the plastic bags of shopping that were on the floor in the hall. Tony closed the door of the cupboard under the stairs that housed the vacuum cleaner before he answered, 'There's a choice of beef or chicken.' He worried over his wife while he walked back into the kitchen. He rested his back against the fridge then folded his arms.

'Beef or chicken what?' Joan asked.

Tony crossed his feet and looked down at the floor, 'I should think that's up to Maura after all she is the guest of honour.' He told himself again not to dislike his stupid sister-in-law just because she was like her mother.

'Absolutely,' Joan said.

'As long as we're all hungry,' Tony said recalling how Maura had played with her food when she had been to dinner the day after she had come home. He could see and feel that Joan was forcing herself to be funny. He wondered what the two sisters had talked about. Donal had shared his concerns about Maura when he had come back to the Beggars Lodge after he had left Cathy home. 'It's a pity that Cathy couldn't be here,' he said, 'she is a pleasure to cook for. She eats everything.'

Maura couldn't even force a smile while they discussed the dinner. She was thinking of Cathy and how fond Tony seemed to be of her. When they had settled for chicken kievs, egg fried rice and stir-fry vegetables, Tony ushered Joan and Maura into the sitting room so that he could get on with cooking. 'I don't need any help, or distractions,' he said.

Joan made a fuss with punching some pillows so that Maura would lie down on the couch. 'I'm sure you will feel better if you sleep for a while,' she insisted.

'I'm not tired,' Maura giggled.

'Even so,' Joan insisted. She turned on the television and drew the drapes over. 'The doctor said you were to lie down every couple of hours,' she lied.

'I haven't come to interfere,' Joan said from the hall, smiling as she watched Tony stand up straight, and move his head towards the back door away from slicing his onions before she added, 'I haven't come to help either.' She laughed as she watched him blink his eyes again and move his head back further from the chopping board.

'How is she?' Tony asked rubbing his nose with the back of his hand.

'The shoulder will mend,' Joan replied removing her glasses and rubbing her eyes.

'More important to me,' Tony said, 'how are you?'

'I'm all right. In fact I'm much better than she is, and that's without a broken shoulder, or arm, or whatever they put her in plaster for,' she said, turning on the tap and filling the kettle.

Chapter Sixteen

Joan held her finger over her lips when she opened the door to Donal. She then pointed to the first door along the hall and said, 'She's asleep?'

Donal responded to a movement at the kitchen door where Tony stood with an apron hanging from his neck and a large spoon in his hand. He held out a bottle to Tony but he couldn't muster his usual smile.

'Did yeh buy that or did yeh nick it from the firm?' Tony asked.

Joan chuckled when she saw Donal's chin recede. She didn't know why but she felt that Donal wasn't impressed with Tony's joke. She walked in front of her brother and pushed in the door into the sitting room. 'She has to have some food in her stomach before she takes her tablets,' she said as she walked over to the couch and pulled at the quilt she had placed over Maura an hour earlier.

On opening her eyes, Maura knew that her brother was in the room because she could see the lime green socks he wore. He had sat down in the chair that was at an angle to the couch because he didn't want to look at Maura all the time. When he had sat back his feet were straight out in front of her.

'I must have fallen asleep,' Maura said, trying to smooth her hair with her hands. The skin on her face felt tight like it always did before she put on her makeup. Her eyes were dry and she could feel her hair sticky and damp around her neck.

'I'll bring you in a cup of tea,' Joan said.

'Yer lookin' much better,' Donal lied, sitting forward and pulling in his legs so that Joan wouldn't trip over them when she was leaving the room. 'The couple of hours sleep has brought yer colour back,' he lied again. He had never seen her look so pale and small. He wondered if she knew how dreadful she looked and it had nothing to do with her hair, her makeup, or her clothes.

The plaster on her shoulder made it awkward for Maura to sit up. She stretched her legs out, and looked around the room as though she wasn't sure whether to call Joan or ask Donal to help her to get up.

Donal went over and held out his hands.

'I hope I sleep as well as that tonight,' Maura said. She straightened her back, and moved her neck, then walked a few steps before she let go of his arm. It was also important to show her brother she would be quite fit in a week or two.

'How's the shoulder now?' Joan asked.

'I want the bathroom,' Maura said, closing her eyes and lowering her face to her feet.

'Upstairs,' Joan said, handing the spoons she was bringing into the dining room to Donal. She then put an arm around Maura's shoulder and encouraged her over to the bottom of the stairs as she said, 'Come on, you can use my makeup for now, and I'll pin your hair up.'

Chapter Seventeen

Joan pointed to a door in the far corner of her bedroom and said, 'It's in there.'

Maura moved her eyes around the large bedroom that was covered with matching doors. 'What is?' she asked.

'The bathroom.' Joan said and walked over and opened the door into a small room that showed a shower, a hand basin, and a toilet. She held the door open while she said, 'If you like I'll help you to have a bath later. Wash you face for now; or would like me to—'

'No, that'll be fine. Thanks,' Maura whimpered, running her eyes around the room again. The long doors of her sister's wardrobes reminded her of the weeks before she was married when Carl had taken her around the apartment he was going to rent when they had come back from Ireland. They all had lovely big rooms and fitted furniture.

While Maura was in the bathroom Joan was kneeling on the floor beside a pile of small bottles, tubes, and coloured containers.

'What are they?' Maura asked when she returned.

'I don't know why I keep them,' Joan replied.

'What are they?' Maura repeated as she continued to peer into the box.

'Makeup,' Joan replied picking a small tube of rouge off the floor. Most of them are Cathy's. She gave them to me for when I used to do gigs. I think these will do you for now,' she said scooping the rest of the bottles and tubes up off the floor. She dropped them into the box and said, 'you can take any of them.'

'These are not cheap,' Maura moaned rubbing one of the little containers her fingers.

The bottles rattled when Joan shook the drawer. 'Most of them are very good; they stay on even when it's hot.' She chuckled as she added, 'a few of them are mammy's. All the eye colours and mascara's are Cathy's.' She slid the drawer back into her dressing table.

Maura scowled and continued to fondle one of the bottles.

'Will they do for now?' Joan asked pushing in the drawer with her knee.

Maura picked another bottle off the bed.

Joan was now tired of her sister not answering. 'You can to go through them yourself?' she snapped.

'No, these will be fine,' Maura replied. She managed a little smile when she added, 'I'm surprised at mammy buying make-up.'

'It was something to buy when she was going around the shops with Pam.'

'That's her friend?' Maura said recalling the tablets, and Sean talking about her mammy's friend when they were sitting in his garden on Friday. She closed her eyes. Friday seemed like years instead of days away.

'Sit down and I'll have a go at doing your face,' Joan said.

Maura nodded over towards the little bathroom and said, 'I'll manage fine in there.'

'How about your shoulder?'

'It's great,' Maura lied. 'I can move my head better than I have been able to do for weeks,' she said, holding her head up and bobbing it about by way of a demonstration. She knew that Joan could influence Tony into giving her a job in the pub.

Joan pulled out the drawer again and left it on the top of the dressing table. 'You might like to have a quick look at the rest of these then,' she said, 'come down when you're ready.'

Chapter Eighteen

Have you always been fond of cooking,' Maura asked, smiling at Tony and helping herself to more egg-fried rice.

'No,' Tony returned, 'and I don't think I ever will be.' He glanced at Donal who was sitting opposite him and added, 'But one of us has to find out what all the fuss is about.'

'Why? Maura asked, her smile fading when she moved her eyes quickly from Tony to her brother. She was still annoyed with him for sticking up for Cathy over not going back to work.

Donal wasn't going to talk about the Beggars Lodge with Maura so he said, 'Tony was trying to impress Josie,'

'I thought it was Cathy you always fancied,' Joan said to Tony.

Tony suspected what Donal was worried about, but he wasn't going to allow Maura to work in the Beggars Lodge again. He placed his elbows on the table and held his glass of wine in front of his mouth like it was a microphone and said, 'We are thinking of adding a restaurant to the Beggars Lodge.'

Maura moved her smile to Joan.

Intimidating little bitch, Tony thought as he watched Maura move her rice around her plate. He decided that Maura wasn't going to bully his wife into getting her a job.

'Are you going to do the cooking yourself?' Maura asked, smiling at Tony.

'What about yourself?' Tony asked returning Maura's smile. 'I expect with your experience that you could run a kitchen with your hands tied behind your back.'

Joan wanted to laugh at the stunned expression on her sister's face. 'I thought you promised that job to Cathy,' she lied. The uncomfortable silence was broken when she said, 'Tony has enough cookery books and woks. All future family presents should be for the garden as Tony is now going to grow his own vegetables.'

Joan and Maura stayed sitting at the table while Donal and Tony cleared away the dishes and started the washing-up.

'How's the shoulder now?' Joan asked. She waited while her sister stared out of the window for nearly a minute before she said, 'Now is a good time to take one of your pain killers; after you've eaten.'

Chapter Nineteen

While Joan and Maura were drinking their coffee, Cathy was sitting at the table in the living room in Plunkett Road with her friend Doreen.

'I never knew there were so many roads and streets in Dublin,' Doreen said, bringing her face down closer to the street map Doreen had spread out on the table.

'It's a growin' country all right,' Cathy said, moving her finger around a circle she had made with a pencil on the map, 'this is where the treasure hunt will be.' She pointed to a dozen crosses she had made with her pencil and added, 'All these places are where they will find teh answers to teh clues that we'll give them.'

'I've never been on a treasure hunt before,' Doreen said, raising her head from the map, 'what happens if someone doesn't find teh answers?'

'That's where teh fun comes in,' Cathy smiled down at her short friend. 'Yeh have te promise me now that yeh won't give teh answers te anyone before they set out on teh hunt.'

'Yeh know me, Cathy I won't remember any of them,' Doreen sniffed and she sat down.

'That'll all depend on teh fellas that sidles up te yeah and starts whisperin' in yer ear,' Cathy said, handing her friend a box of tissues. She was used to her friend sniffing and she had never known her to have a cold but she didn't want to get any dribbles on the map that Donal had loaned her.

'The fellas never sidle up te me,' Doreen said, 'and yer right I'd probably tell them anythin' if they did.' She sniffed again and added, 'I think I'm goin' te be an old maid.'

'There's no such thing as old maids anymore,' Cathy said, glancing over at the wedding photographs on the wall. She wondered if there would ever be one of her, and she was never going to tolerate being called an old maid or a spinster. She showed Doreen how she wanted her to fold the map.

'I hope I never get divorced, Doreen said, folding the map. 'It must be worse that bein' a widow.'

'Not if yer fella is sleepin' round with other women, or beatin' yeh,' Cathy returned. She had known Doreen since she was old enough to play out, and the girl had never been pretty. With her thoughts again on her sister and recalling how Maura's shoulders were curled over, Cathy decided that her sister had become deformed from her husband beating her. For an awful moment she wondered if Doreen had been beaten when she was a baby. It would explain why her nose was squashed and turned up so much, and why she was always sniffing.

'Yer right about getting beaten,' Doreen said, rubbing her nose with the back of her hand, 'but teh sleepin' around happens because teh fellas are not getting it at home.'

'Get what at home?' Cathy asked, sniffing to stop from smiling.

'Yeh know, what fellas want te do with their mickey,' Doreen whispered.

'Who told yeh that?' Cathy said, slapping her hand down on the table.

'I heard Betty Fox tellin' me ma at teh bingo last week.'

'And I dare say that Betty Fox would know all about that,' Cathy said, opening the envelope that Donal had given her and pulling out the sheet of paper with all the clues written on it, 'that little slut is on her third fella in four years. And she has three babies to prove it.' She remembered when the girl was running after Liam before her brother had joined the Air Force when she said, 'What did yer ma say about her?'

'Yeh know me ma. She never says very much,' Doreen said, sniffing again, 'but when we were walkin' home she said that teh government should never have given teh unmarried women's allowances because it only encouraged girls te sleep around and not worry about havin' babies. She said that children need a father as much as they do a mother.'

'She's right about girls sleepin' around,' Cathy said, smoothing the paper with the questions written on it. 'Children need a family,' she added, recalling she was ten when her daddy had died, and apart from the housework he used to do she had never missed him. She could still recall how she used to worry about having done something to upset her mammy when she was waiting for her daddy to come home from work.

'What do yeh want me te do,? Doreen asked, running her hands over the map.

'That area with teh pencil mark around it is where the treasure hunt is goin' te be,' Cathy said, placing her finger on the cross that showed where the church was, 'all the contestants will have te call in te teh Beggars Lodge te get teh questions and teh clues and have their time recorded.' She moved her finger a fraction, 'And that is where the pub is. Just beside the church.'

'Will they be goin' te mass first?'

'Only if they want te,' Cathy said. 'It's not compulsory and they'll have plenty ev time.' She bowed her head as if her friend had given her an idea. 'Mass'll be well over by seven so they can go into the Beggars Lodge and wash their holy communion down with a pint.' She bowed her head again, 'I'm sure that Donal and Tony will be delighted with teh business. They won't be settin' out until about eight. So if yeh know anyone that's goin' yeh can tell them that.'

'How long will it take them then?'

'That's part ev teh challenge, and that's why yeh will have te write down teh times fer when they leave and when they come back.' Cathy returned. She placed her pencil on the first question written on her sheet of paper. 'I want yeh to put a circle around teh Tolka Bridge and put a number one on it.' She watched Doreen's finger moving down the main road, 'That's where the first question ends.'

'What's the question?' Doreen sniffed.

'How many stops before I find water?' Cathy ticked the question on her paper.

'What kind ev stops?'

'There's two answers te that one but they have te be very clear with their answer. They can count teh bus stops, or they can count teh traffic lights. So when you're checkin' teh answers yeh have te make sure they have written teh words "bus stops" or "traffic lights". It won't be enough just te write teh numbers.'

'Supposin' teh road is all flooded. Yeh know yerself that teh pipes are always burstin' on Mobie Road.

'That'll be unfortunate fer teh people that are livin' down there but it won't count as an answer. Now find teh third turnin' on teh right goin' inte town and draw another circle.' She waited until Doreen had moved her finger, drew the circle and inserted a number two, then told her the question.

Doreen had drawn the last circle and inserted a neat number twelve before she said, 'They won't be able to do that one.'

'Why not?' Cathy asked. She read the question again.

'Because teh church'll be closed. By teh time they have done all teh other stops it'll be nine before they get back to teh village,' Doreen said sniffing again, 'that's why. Yeh can't expect them te see what's written on teh bottom of teh statue if they can't get inte the church.'

'Yer right,' Cathy said, bowing her head in approval and adding, 'Good thinkin', Doreen, I always said yeh were a clever girl.' She raised her eyes to the wall again before she said, 'It's only nine o'clock, so we have plenty ev time te think up another one.'

'Can't we leave it at eleven questions? Yeh know like there's eleven men on teh football team.'

'There yeh go again, with yer bright ideas,' Cathy said, scanning the three sheets of paper with the clues she had written down. 'It'll make Tony happy with reducing teh number ev questions.' She bowed her head when she said, 'We'll leave it at eleven and I'll make sure te tell Tony it was yer idea.'

'Yeh don't have te do that,' Doreen sniffed.

'Eleven is enough.'

'I mean tell Tony.'

'Yes I do, and I'll also tell him te give yeh a pint without yer payin' fer it.'

'I don't drink pints.'

'That's right yeh don't. He can give yeh two half pints instead,' Cathy returned and held her hand up to indicate that it was all settled. She didn't want to think up another question.

'I like Tony,' Doreen said, folding up the map.

'We all like Tony,' Cathy replied, raising her head to the clock. She hadn't put a match to the fire because she was going over to Angie Dolan. She didn't want to tell Doreen to go.

'I never believed what Betty Fox was always sayin' about him before he married Joan,' Doreen said. pulling a tissue out of the box and blowing her nose.

'What was teh little slut sayin'?' Cathy bellowed, shoving her chair back.

'Yeh must ev heard it.'

'Heard what?'

Doreen wanted to leave. She shoved her chair back and kept her eyes on the table as she said, 'I know it was a terrible thing te say, but yeh must ev heard it just the same.' She was standing behind her chair when she added, 'It's years ago now, and he wasn't goin' out with yer sister then either.'

'I never heard anythin', and yer not goin' anywhere until yeh tell me,' Cathy bellowed pointing to the seat of the chair that her friend was standing behind.

Doreen stayed standing and she looked over at door before she continued, 'Betty Fox said that Tony didn't go with girls because he was fond ev fellahs.'

'Yeh mean that she said he was queer?' Cathy yelled.

'I never said it teh anyone else,' Doreen moaned and leaned into the table and pulled out another tissue. She wanted to cry. 'Anyway she used te say that about every fella that didn't go out with her.'

'Did she ever say that about er Donal?' Cathy demanded.

'I never heard her say anythin',' Doreen lied. 'Jeasus Cathy she'll tear me eyes out if yeh tell her I told yeh.'

'She'll do no such thing,' Cathy said, 'because she won't be able te find yeh.'

'I'm not goin' anywhere,' Doreen cried.

'By the time I'm finished scratchin' her eyes out she won't be able te see yeh,' Cathy said draping her arm around her friend's small shoulders and moving her over to the door.

'I never believed a word ev what she said,' Doreen whimpered when she was in the hall.

'Thanks fer helpin' me with teh questions,' Cathy said, 'and don't worry about Betty Fox. She's probably sayin' teh same thing about you and me.'

'Why would she do that?' Doreen gasped.

'Because neither ev us are runnin' after any fellahs.'

'Jeasus, Cathy,' Doreen laughed, 'she couldn't do that.'

Pleased to hear her friend laugh Cathy said, 'And why not? After all it's true. Neither ev have ever run after a fellah.'

'We're girls,' Doreen gaggled and poked Cathy in her stomach. 'It's only fellahs that are queer.' She ran across the garden towards the house next door and threw her leg over the low railing.

Cathy stayed standing at the hall door and watched Doreen jump over the railings of four more gardens and go into her own house. After a few minutes she decided she would ask Angie about Donal. Angie knew everything about everyone.

Chapter Twenty

Off key musical beats coming from the pots, dishes, and cutlery were competing with Tony's singing as they came into the room from the open window, and through the wall from the kitchen. Joan rubbed her belly; the cramp and soreness were gone. She then propped her elbows on the table and rested her chin on her knuckles while she tried to think of something to talk to Maura about. She felt every bit as tired as her sister looked but Joan knew she would be fine after she had a good night's sleep.

Although she knew her sister wasn't listening, or even interested, Joan talked about new and old houses in Dublin. It was her job. She worked for an estate agent. She intended to bore her sister into wanting to go to bed.

Maura's head swayed and her eyes moved between the table, the window out to the back garden, and the door. She avoided resting her eyes on Joan every time she swooped them up to the window. After nearly ten minutes, with the exception of the tin alley opera from the kitchen, the only sound in the room came when Maura coughed.

Neither the windows nor the walls had told Maura what to think, or to do. For the first time in her life she was completely on her own.

Joan was tempted to tell her sister that if she expected to get her way by coughing like their mammy always did then she should have ten children and play their emotions off against each other. For an awful moment she wondered that maybe Maura had deserved a clout. But right now Maura looked so lonely, and lost in one of Tony's jumpers; two sizes too big for her; with her wispy hair pinned back, and her face badly made up, that she was sorry for being angry with her.

The shrill sound from the ring of the phone made Maura jump. She watched Joan gently kick the small trolley that held the telephone over towards the table, then draw a length of cable from the back. She trembled when Joan said, 'It's for you,' and held the receiver out to her. Her face lost its glow when Joan said, 'It's Sean.'

Chapter Twenty-one

Joan knew it was Tony leaving when she heard the hall door close. The small clock on her bedside locker told her it was just gone nine. There were no other sounds in the house so she thought that Maura must be still asleep. She dragged her body over to her own side of the bed and stretched her hand out for the mug of tea she vaguely remembered Tony leaving there.

She turned on the small radio and snuggled under the covers again. The cold tea was waking her up, and the news bulletins that were bursting from the radio went over her head because she was thinking about the conversations she had had with Pauline, Una, and Carl. She decided that she would do what Pauline had suggested and take it one day at a time with Maura.

It was half past nine when Joan was tuning in her radio in the kitchen. She selected a station with music because she didn't want to hear about anything that was going on in Ireland or the rest of the world. When she was walking back to the kitchen after picking up the post from the hall she smiled into the half-opened door into the front room.

Because she hoped that she would find Pauline sitting on the couch Joan couldn't resist pushing in the door. She went into the room and sat down on the same chair she had been sitting on when she had been talking to her sister all those miles away. Because she wanted it to be true she told herself that Una was right when she had said that there were too many of them for them all to be writing or phoning each other all the time. It helped her to feel less mean about not phoning either of her sisters in Canada before.

She shuffled the half-dozen letters and made a small tidy bundle by placing the small ones at the front, then flopped back in the armchair and thought about her short talk with Carl. She had to tell him twice that she was Maura's sister. When she closed her eyes to the memory of the Canadian drawl, she thought how glad she was that she had phoned Pauline first.

No matter how tightly Joan closed her eyes when she lay back in the soft armchair she couldn't get a picture in her mind of what Carl had looked like when he had come home with Maura over eight years earlier. All she could remember was that he was very tall. Still, she thought as she pulled on the arms of the chair to get up, he remembered that she existed even if he thought she was still a child.

The familiar music that heralded the news coming from the radio in the kitchen told Joan that it was ten o'clock and time for Maura to have her tablets again. She was hopeful that her sister would be ready to talk to her now that she had rested.

'I smelt the toast,' Maura said, smiling weakly when Joan came into her room with a tray that held tea and toast for two.

'It never fails, does it?' Joan said, putting the tray down on the end of the bed. She made a fuss as she helped Maura to sit up. 'I take it you slept all right?'

'I don't even remember getting into bed,' Maura said, covering her face with her hands, then moved them down her hair while she ran her eyes around the newly decorated room.

'How's the pain?'

'It's different, more sore than painful,' Maura replied, then winced as she moved her neck about.

'Eat some toast so you can take a couple of your tablets,' Joan said, straightening the curtains she had drawn back. 'It's been thirteen hours. It's great you could go so long. You probably won't need them at all in a day or two.'

'What are they?' Maura asked easing her body to a sitting position.

'I never thought of asking to nurse or the doctor,' Joan said. She had no experience of taking medication. She giggled as she added, 'They won't be the same things that Mammy has.'

'Should you not be in work?' Maura snapped. She didn't care if her mammy's tablets were laced with poison

'When I'm ready I'll phone in. I often work from home,' Joan replied, praying her sister wouldn't ask her what it was like working for an estate agent in case she would want her to get her a job.

When they had finished their toast and Maura had taken her tablets, Joan helped her sister get comfortable. After she had removed the tray, and opened another window, she brought in an ashtray and said, 'I want you to promise me you'll never tell Cathy or Mammy that we smoked in the bedroom.'

'Why not?' Maura demanded.

'It's not Cathy so much as Mammy,' Joan replied, handing her sister a cigarette. Cathy would be careful, but Mammy wouldn't care. 'I told them it was Tony's rule.'

'Why?'

'I always tell them Tony said,' Joan replied and held the lighter for her sister, then lit her own cigarette before she said, 'because Mammy would never go against Tony.'

'Why?' Maura couldn't imagine her mammy being afraid of anyone.

'Tony doesn't approve of smoking.'

Maura rested her head on the pillow and closed her eyes.

'Have you not seen the pair of them?' Joan continued, 'and the way they leave their cigarettes burning all over the place. It's a miracle they haven't had a fire down in Plunkett Road before now.'

Maura managed a smile. She hadn't seen her mammy at home for eight years. But she remembered that her mammy used to leave cigarettes burning in all the ashtrays.

'These are exceptional circumstances and you're not as silly as Cathy, or as selfish as Mammy,' Joan lied. But she needed to get Maura into a better mood before she told her about her phone call to Carl. She hoped that by praising her over Cathy she would improve her temper and her attitude.

Again like when they were in the dining room after they had finished their dinner and Tony and Donal were washing up, Joan created conversations. This time she rambled on about, gardens, jobs, housework and cooking, while they smoked their cigarette and finished their tea. Maura nodded her head but she had nothing to say.

Chapter Twenty-two

Although she turned the pages of the album, Maura wasn't really interested in the photographs of Joan's wedding. Joan couldn't think of anything else to talk to her sister about and she was about to tell her about her phone calls to Canada when the phone rang. After she had said hello into the mouthpiece she handed the phone to Maura and said, 'It's for you.'

The door banged when Joan closed it sharply after she had left the room and went upstairs. She needed to get as far away from Carl as possible even if he was only on the other end of the phone. She was also worried because she hadn't told Maura that she had phoned him. She was lying on her bed going over all the possible things she could say and, if necessary, deny when she had to go back downstairs again and face her sister, when she heard the shrill voice.

'Joan,' Maura screamed from the hall.

Joan swung her legs off the bed and ran out on to the landing. When she looked over the top of the stairs she saw that Maura was holding the body of the phone to her chest like it was a baby.

'Can you give me the boys' phone numbers?' Maura called up through the posts in the banisters.

'Which one?' Joan asked as she walked down the stairs?

'The three of them,' Maura said, smiling benignly, then lowered her eyes to the floor and started nodding into the phone.

Joan picked up a small red plastic-covered book off the small hall table in the hall and handed it to her smiling wet faced sister. 'They're all in here,' she said then started walking towards the kitchen.

'Wait.' Maura called out, 'Carl wants to say hello.' She tilted her head at an angle and coughed a giggle, as if she was saying, 'you lucky girl' and held the phone out.

'He-ll-o.' Joan placed the body of the telephone on the coffee table. She held the receiver away from her ears when Carl began thanking her and watched Maura go through the pages in the small red book. She returned Maura's broad smile with a nod. 'It's no trouble at all. We are all delighted to have her here,' she said loudly, then gave the phone back to Maura.

'Yes, I'm listening. It's me, darling,' Maura was saying into the phone when Joan was walking over to the door.

'Stupid, stupid, stupid girl,' Joan shouted at her cooker. It was the first time in her life that she wanted to break a couple of plates. She contented herself with banging a few knives as she made a sandwich for their lunch. She was tempted to use too much salt on Maura's. She rehearsed what she would say when Maura asked her about phoning Carl to tell him about her shoulder. She prayed that Una would walk into her kitchen because she was dreading Maura walking into the room screaming at her.

Thinking about Una brought her mind on to Pauline and she recalled the long conversation she had had with her sister in Canada. And that Pauline hadn't been surprised about Maura and had assured her that the family should be able to help her now that they had proof. Within minutes of talking to her, Joan was able to picture Pauline's curly hair and feel the warmth in her voice. Pauline had asked about all the family including the children. They had both laughed and cried. She decided she would talk Tony into going out to Canada for Christmas when she heard a noise in the hall.

'I've put your book back on the table,' Maura sang, walking sprightlily into the kitchen. She sat down at the table and rested her chin in one hand and patted her hair with her other and said, 'That was a great surprise.' She then used both of her hands on her hair and continued quickly, 'I must look dreadful, although I feel a lot better.'

'Is it all right with you if we eat in here?' Joan said, turning round from plugging in the kettle.

'Gawd yes,' Maura returned, slapping her hand lightly on the table and giggling as she stood. 'I'll just go to the bathroom first.'

Joan wasn't surprised when Maura said she would go back to Plunkett Road. She expected there would be many more phone calls to and from Canada and she really didn't want to know how worried and upset Carl was. She had heard enough during the last ten minutes.

Joan wanted to get any bad feeling between them about her phoning Canada out of the way so when Maura came back she said, 'I'm sorry, Maura, if you're annoyed with me for phoning Carl.'

'Gawd no, not in the least,' Maura said, her eyes wide and sparkling. 'Carl is not annoyed either.'

Joan removed her glasses. She didn't want to see the shine in her sister's eyes.

'Honestly Joan,' Maura continued, 'he's delighted I'm out of hospital.' She giggled and leaned forward, took Joan's hand and gave it squeeze. 'Carl knows there is a difference in the times between here and Canada.' She patted her sister's hand. 'He has been worried out of his mind all day.'

I'll bet he has, Joan thought retrieving her hand. She didn't want to hear any more about Carl so she said, 'Anyway it will be better for Jerome to be down in Plunkett Road.'

The ashtray was a seashell Joan had picked up off a beach. It had lost its gloss from all the cigarettes that had used it. Maura was smiling at the grotty and faded-looking shell like it was a beautiful work of art while she nodded her head in agreement. She could still hear her husband sobbing.

'There are more children for him to play with down there,' Joan continued when Maura raised her head and sniffed, 'and he knows some of them.'

'That is exactly what I was thinking,' Maura said, slapping the table. She raised her eyebrows so she could look at Joan with her head lowered while she rolled the end of her cigarette again, 'Carl said that too many homes would only make Jerome nervous.' She then sat up straight and raised her face and whinged, 'He has been so worried.'

For a second Joan imagined she saw Una standing in the doorway with her hands on her hips looking around the kitchen wall and shaking her head in disbelief. She wondered how Cathy would cope. She decided she would phone her so that she could be prepared. While Maura prattled on about how upset her husband was Joan lowered her face to the floor. She thought of Una again when she recalled her sister had said that Tony was a good cook but he was a dreadful cleaner. The pedal bin still reeked of garlic and onion.

'Are you all right?' Maura asked when Joan continued to stare at the floor.

Joan raised her head.

'Your job,' Maura said, 'did you phone in like you said you were going to?'

'Yes,' Joan lied. Her job was the last thing on her mind. 'What about yourself?' she asked. She thought that Maura might tell her something about her life in Canada now that she was happier. She took another cigarette that she didn't want, and slid the open packet to her sister and asked, 'How long of a holiday do you have?'

Maura withdrew a cigarette from the open packet, then closed her eyes against her sister's enquiring stare and held her hand out for the lighter. She lit her cigarette and blew smoke up to the ceiling as though she was saying a prayer and said, 'You should have stayed in the room and heard Carl.'

Joan felt shivers in her mouth.

'You would have heard him say that I was to have two months' vacation before I was to even think of getting another job,' Maura said. She dropped her cigarette into the ashtray and stood, inhaled deeply through her nose and smiled smugly at her sister while she performed a courtesy and said, 'I must go to the bathroom.'

Chapter Twenty-three

Road traffic never bothered Joan. She never drove fast anyway. But while she was driving over to Sean's house she said a prayer of thanks for the clear roads. She endured rather than listened to Maura rattle on about the club she had been to with Noel and Nula. And how great she had been when she was working in The Beggars Lodge. She smiled when she thought about how relieved Donal will be now that she won't be looking for a job anymore. But she continued to worry about how Cathy would be able to cope with the Maura that was sitting beside her now.

'At least it's not raining,' Joan said to the white cloud that was floating across the bright blue sky. She wasn't expecting her sister to be listening to her but she said, 'I hate driving in the rain.'

'So does Carl,' Maura giggled, 'especially since he bought his new car.'

'What about yourself?' Joan asked. She didn't want to hear anything about her sister's husband. 'Pauline told me that you get dreadful weather in the winters. She hates driving in the snow.'

'It's the ice that Carl worries about,' Maura said, shutting out the memory of when her driver's licence had come and Carl had told her she wasn't going to drive the new car. She started a smile when she thought that all that would change now. She would have to drive now that they were going to move.

Determined to get an answer Joan repeated, 'What about yourself?'

'I leave all the driving to Carl.'

'Like Maeve,' Joan said, leaning over the steering wheel so she could see the front of her car because she was passing a bus as she added, 'she doesn't have any choice though because Maurice won't let her drive.' She was turning into her brother's driveway when she said, 'I don't know, or care who told you that all men beat their wives. But it isn't true. Some do, and they also beat their children. But it is not normal.'

Chapter Twenty-four

I can see yeh've got yer a-appetite back,' Sean smiled approvingly when Maura stabbed her fork into another sausage in the dish that was in the centre of the table and moved it to her plate.

'The Irish sausages and bread are a disaster for the waistline,' Maura giggled.

'Are yeh t-tryin teh s-send me a message?' Sean laughed. They were all laughing when the phone rang.

'I'll get it, Daddy, Sean's eldest son,' Brian said.

'Yeh might as well. It'll be fer yeh at this time anyway.' Sean didn't want to leave the table. His mind was cleared of most of his worries about Maura. He had no idea that the winters in Canada were as bad as his sister had described when they were in his workshop. He wasn't surprised that the doctor in the hospital in Canada hadn't seen that her shoulder was so bad. They must be so busy with so many people slipping in the snow.

'It's Carl for you, Maura,' Brian called from the door.

Maura threw her knife and fork on the table and ran out into the hall through the kitchen door and closed it behind her. She then closed the door into the dining room before she picked up the phone.

'At l-least she's eatin' well,' Sean said nervously. When Maura had thrown her knife on the table he was reminded of when she used to stamp her feet to get her own way when she was a child. He put the memory out of his mind because he wanted to believe she had become the nice person that had been in his workshop thirty minutes earlier.

'She's not teh only one,' Flo said, nodding her head down the table to where Maura's young son was sitting.

'Ah sure Jerome eats his dinner every day,' Sean agreed.

Joan returned the little boy's smile and said, 'If Maura agrees would you keep him here for a few days? I think it would help Cathy if she didn't have to look after the two of them straight away.'

'I was thinkin' that meself,' Flo agreed.

The living room door swung open and Maura swooped in shouting, 'Carl sends you all his love.' She sat down at the table. She changed her mind about picking up her knife and fork and passed her hands down her hair while she said, 'I know it's dreadful.' She giggled, 'I'll have it done in the village in the morning.'

Chapter Twenty-five

Cathy opened the hall door and watched Maura walking up the front garden path. 'Luvly,' she said brightly, 'really luvley.' She closed the door. 'Josie could do as good but it's luvley just the same.'

'Any phone calls?' Maura asked, handing Cathy a plastic bag with some biscuits and cream cakes. She scanned the small hall table then ran her eyes up and down Cathy's bright red, tight -fitting flared trousers.

'No, not yet,' Cathy lied while she tugged at the hem of her long-sleeved, navy blue polo-neck jumper and watched Maura remove her jacket. She knew she had a good figure; a perfect size fourteen and she refused to allow herself to see Maura's examination as a criticism, or get angry with her sister when Maura held out her jacket to her for to hang it up. 'Go on in,' she said and nodded towards the living room. 'Teh fire is lightin', and I put teh kettle on when I saw yeh gettin' off teh bus.

'Any phone calls?' Maura asked, then walked into the front room expecting Cathy to follow her with an answer.

'Just a call from yer two brothers, yer sister, and Flo,' Cathy replied to the packet of biscuits she was tearing the wrapper off. She wasn't surprised when she heard Maura shout out her name but she took her time with making the coffee and arranging the kimberley biscuits on a plate.

'They're from Carl,' Maura shouted from the hall. Her eyes sparkled when she raised her head from the small white card and cried, 'he really didn't have to, you know.' Her eyes were filled with tears when she ran her hand over the cellophane wrapping on the bundle of red roses that were on the table.

Cathy wanted to drop the tray with the coffee and biscuits into her sister's lap but she forced a smile and said, 'Could yeh move them to teh side a bit so I can put teh coffee down?'

'Poor Carl,' Maura moaned, picking up the flowers. She waved her head at her sister before she slapped the flowers back on the table again after Cathy had put the tray down.

'Have yer coffee,' Cathy said. 'It'll cheer yeh up.' She pushed the flowers back towards Maura with the back of her fingers. She wanted space on her side of the table for her elbows when she sat down. She intended to try and talk to Maura again and she still wanted to be friends with her. She settled in her favourite place just inside the door with her back to the wall and at a right angle to Maura who had her back to the fireplace.

Maura dabbed at her eyes with a tissue while she flicked the small card over as if she was searching the back and front for a secret message. She picked up the small envelope and pushed two fingers into it and held it up to her eyes.

Cathy thought her sister was going to drink from the little packet that had held the card by the way she sat up and let her head fall back so she could examine the inside of it.

Satisfied the envelope was empty, Maura crushed it into a small ball and threw it into the fire. She watched the paper start to unwrap when the flames engulfed it before she said, 'He's thinking of coming over to help me go back.'

No surprise really, Cathy thought. She pulled another chair over, raised her feet onto it, and nudged the flowers back a bit more. She replaced her elbow on the table, took a biscuit then sat back in her chair and asked, 'When?'

Maura read the card again and said, 'He has been so worried.'

The bastard, Cathy thought. 'What difference does he think

that will make?' she asked moving the plate of biscuits nearer her sister and said, 'Have a one. They're gargous.'

A couple of biscuits rolled off the plate when Maura pushed it away, then moved her chair so she could cross her legs. Her small stomach was still full from all the sausages she had eaten before she came home to Plunkett Road nearly eighteen hours earlier.

Cathy picked the biscuits off the table and put them back on the plate. 'It's grand that yeh'ev had yer hair done. I told yeh that teh hairdressers would be able te fit yeh in on a Wednesday mornin'. All teh octogenarians go in then because teh place isn't busy and they get their cuts and perms fer half price.'

Maura closed her eyes.

'Still yer hair is luvly,' Cathy continued biting into another biscuit. She was chewing when she said, 'I wasn't implying that yeh were that old. Whenever he comes we'll all be delighted teh see him.' She offered Maura a cigarette. She lit her own and when she was passing over the lighter she said, 'There's plenty ev room here fer teh three ev yez.' She thought her sister was going to cry with pleasure when she watched her move her head up and down in agreement.

For a few seconds the feelings of warmth and contrition that Cathy had felt for Maura since Sunday started to chill. She remembered she had promised Donal and Joan that she would manage, so with a refreshed heart she said, 'I left a vase out on teh drainin' board fer yer flowers.'

Maura picked up the card and read it again. She smiled smugly and handed it to Cathy. 'I'll do them in a minute.'

'The most beautiful girl in the world, my wife Maura,' Cathy read. She sniffed twice: 'Very nice indeed, she said,' and handed the card back.

Maura's eyes filled up with tears again. 'He's been worried out of his mind.'

'I should think he would be,' Cathy said, dropping her feet

off the chair and asked, 'How is yer shoulder now? I think it's time fer yer tablets. I thought I'd do us a boiled egg and some toast fer er lunch.'

Two hours later Cathy hacked off the ends of the flowers and put them in the vase with water while Maura was lying down upstairs in her bed. She tried to do a dreadful job but she thought they still looked lovely. She cut two of the roses short and put them in a drinking glass and placed them on the windowsill in the kitchen, then carried the vase upstairs.

'Not up here,' Maura cried when Cathy walked into the bedroom room holding the flowers out in front of her. She raised her head off the pillow and waved her hand at the vase, 'put them down on the hall table.'

Walking back down the stairs Cathy held the vase of flowers out in front of her as if it was a dead rat. She went into the kitchen and emptied the water out of the vase. As instructed by her sister, she then placed the vase of flowers on the hall table. She placed it on a corner spot where she hoped it would get knocked off. She found the card where Maura had left it on the table in the living room end, held it under the tap until the ink started to run away, and slid it under the vase.

With her temper still hot, Cathy moved back from the small table and stood smiling at the roses for a few seconds. She wondered what she would have to do get someone to send her flowers like that. 'Yer lovely,' she whispered to the red petals, 'but yeh should have been left where yeh were.' She touched one of the flowers and added, 'Just like Angie's.' She felt like the back of her hand had been brushed with a feather when one of the petals fell off. She thought about all the rose petals on the grass in Angie's garden while she picked the petal off the table and dropped it into the vase. 'Ah sure it's not yer fault,' she said, and she went into the kitchen for a jug of water.

Chapter Twenty-six

od fergive me,' Cathy hollered and continued to laugh. She straightened the net curtains and moved away from the front window in the living room. She had been watching the grey and black smoke spurting from the rusty pipe that stuck out from the back of her brother Maurice's Austin A40. She had struggled not to laugh at Maura's mortification and her brother's red face when he helped their wounded sister into his small car. She was still laughing when Maeve came into the house and closed the hall door.

'I hope he'll be able teh get her out without breakin' her neck,' Maeve said, joining Cathy at the window. The pair of them watched the car turn the corner at the top of the road. Maeve looked at the clock and asked, 'How long de yeh think we have, Cathy?'

Cathy straightened the curtain. 'A good three hours,' she said, 'three days if yer husband isn't in the AA.'

'Cathy, yer gettin' as hard as Una,' Maeve said, pulling on her short skirt, and starting to laugh again.

Cathy walked over to the table and said, 'Give es a hand teh pull this thing out.'

'It's fine as it is, sure there's only teh three ev us,' Maeve said and followed her friend anyway.

'We need teh get it out from teh wall fer er elbowroom,' Cathy insisted, and started to drag the heavy table on her own.

'We all have te be comfortable fer teh first general meetin' ev er company.'

At five-feet-three inches Maeve looked heavier than nine and a half stone because she wore her skirts very short. Her dangling earrings swung towards her mouth when she leaned over to help Cathy pull the table out from the wall. 'Yeh make it sound all grand,' she said.

The doorbell rang.

'That'll be yer ma, now let her in while I get teh pads, teh water, and teh glasses,' Cathy said, giving one nod to her friend as the doorbell rang again, then took three placemats off the long shelf that was fixed to the wall between the chimney-breast and the boiler while she repeated, 'Go on, let yer ma in.'

'Cathy, are yeh sarious?' Maeve hollered, bobbing up and down like she wanted to go the toilet; pulling at her short skirt she asked, 'What fer?'

Cathy stood at the table with one hand on her waist and tried to deliver her brother's wife a hard glare. 'We can't have a meetin' without yer ma so go and let her in.'

'I didn't mean me ma,' Maeve hollered, pointing to the small plastic boards Cathy was wiping with the sleeve of her jumper, 'I mean them things.'

Cathy laid the placemats on the table is if she was going to serve a meal and repeated, 'Let yer ma in.'

'I saw them pullin' away,' Angie said, tilting her head back so she could see through her glasses. She frowned at the table in the middle of the floor, then glanced out the window as if she was expecting to see the A40 was still at the front of the house. The heels of her feet came out of her slippers when she stood on her toes so she could see up the road. She shoved her glasses up on her nose and patted her rolled-up ponytail, then turned round and frowned at the table again.

'Don't worry,' Cathy said, taking three exercise books out of a brown paper bag. She placed them in the middle of the table and added, 'They'll be back.'

'Jeasus, Mammy don't start us off laughin' again,' Maeve said and pulled her skirt down, 'I feel guilty enough as it is with her arm in plaster an' all.' She dragged three chairs over to the table. 'Come on, Ma, Cathy said we've got three hours and she's got everythin' ready.'

'At the very least,' Cathy called from the doorway. She walked into the room with a jug of water and three glasses. 'Her appointment is fer ten and yeh know yerself they always keep yeh waitin' for at least an hour.'

'What's teh watar fer?' Angie demanded when they were seated at the table. They also had new pencils and exercise books resting on plastic mats in front of them. The plastic mats had the Beggars Lodge scrawled diagonally across the front.

'It's symbolic fer now,' Cathy said pouring water into Angie's glass. 'Don't worry, Angie, we'll have a drop of Harvest Bristol Cream when we're finished.'

'What's symbolic about water?' Maeve asked.

'Mike said it was important,' Cathy said, looking over to Angie. 'Shall we start?'

Maeve frowned at her ma, and Angie shrugged her shoulders.

Cathy began, 'We need a chairman, a treasurer and a secretary. I suggest Angie fer treasurer, Maeve fer secretary and meself fer chairman.' She paused for a couple of seconds. She wasn't expecting hysterics but she thought Maeve would want to know about them needing a chairman when they were all women.

'That's fine by me,' Angie said, turning her face up to the ceiling.

'I think Angie would be teh best fer treasurer because she's good at addin' up. Maeve fer secretary because she's teh best we have fer teh spellin' and she does lovely writin'. Meself fer

chairman because I have teh best line teh Joan, Tony and Donal.' When her two partners nodded, Cathy continued again,
'We need te make these appointments befcre we can get started with teh meetin'.'

Angie looked from Maeve to Cathy four times and said,
'That sounds fine te me.' She pulled her chair into the table
and asked, 'Are yeh sure yeh want te trust me with teh money?'

'I do,' Cathy replied, 'what about you, Maeve?'

Maeve sat up straight, gripped the edge of the table and
asked, 'What do we all do?'

'That's exactly what we're havin' this meetin' fer,' Cathy said,
'so that we can all know and agree what er individual jobs are. It's
also important that we all know each other's as well as er own.'

'Go on about mine first,' Maeve said, letting go of the table.

'Every time we have a meetin' it'll be yer job te write down
in yer exercise book what we talked about and what we decided te do.'

'Will I start now?' Maeve picked her pencil up off the table.

'A good secretary would,' Cathy said, bowing her head to
her friend, then brought her glass of water up to her mouth.

Angie shoved her glasses up on her nose so that her hand
would cover the smile on her face and asked, 'Do yeh like water, Cathy?'

Cathy forced herself to swallow the water in her mouth.
'Not particklarly,' she replied. 'And yerself?' she asked.

'I drink a gallon a day,' Angie said, straightening her glasses
again. 'But I always have tea, milk and sugar in it.'

Cathy slapped the table and stood and said, 'I'll make some
coffee while yeh start writin' down what we've done so far.'
She gathered up the glasses and the jug of water. She stood in
front of Angie and said, 'I'd love te keep these and throw them
over Mike when he comes home again. I really would.'

In the kitchen Cathy pictured her sister Josie's husband
laughing his head off at her. She was very fond of Mike so she

convinced herself that she deserved the joke he played on her with insisting that she had a jug of water on the table when she had a meeting. After all she had pestered and bullied him into telling her how she should go about making money from her idea of an organized cleaning group.

'All done,' Maeve called out when Cathy brought in three coffees, and placed them with an ashtray in the middle of the table. 'Can I write it all out neatly when I get home?'

'Excellent, excellent,' Cathy replied, winking at Angie and adding, 'yer catchin' on quick.' When Maeve had accepted an encouraging nod from her ma Cathy asked, 'Now are yeh all right with Angie fer treasurer?' She tapped Maeve's pad with her finger and said, 'Yeh'll have teh write Angie all teh time and not yer ma.'

Maeve recalled her last couple of years at school. She hated writing stories because she could never think of what to write about. She had put all her energy into writing neatly, and she never used a word that she couldn't find out how to spell. She didn't have a favourite aunt or uncle to write about. And she couldn't stand cats. 'I'll do me best,' she said.

'Yeh haven't said yet, if yeh trust yer ma,' Cathy persisted, winking at Angie again.

'Of course I trust me ma,' Maeve hollered. Her earrings bounced off her cheeks from moving her head so quickly between Cathy and her ma, 'I mean Angie, of course I do. Now what is her job about?'

If anyone other than Cathy had asked Angie if she would be part of her cleaning group she would have said no. And she would have encouraged Maeve to say no as well.

Cleaning was the only work Angie had ever done. She was thirteen when her mother died. She was fifteen when her brother had bought her a suitcase and found her a place with a respectable family in Dublin. She knew that her husband wasn't long for the world when she had married him. When her two daughters were born she had prayed that God would allow her to live long enough to see them both with good office jobs.

Doctors, dentists, bank managers, civil servants, and accountants all married girls that had nice clean office jobs. Angie had known that before she had met her husband. There was nothing that she didn't know about grand people who lived in grand houses.

Although Angie had only worked for one family and they had always treated her well, she had been in a number of grand houses. The lady of the house where she had worked had often loaned her to her friends when extra cleaning was needed before and after a dinner party. Every house she went to had a typewriter. She used to dance on the tiled floor in the kitchen in time to the taps the lady of the house was banging out on the heavy machine when she was typing her letters.

When her legs were tired of dancing Angie would gaze out on the lovely garden in the grand houses, and dream about the day when her own daughters would sit in a lovely room, in a lovely house, and type lovely letters, to lovely people, for their lovely husbands. She knew they were her husband's letters because when the lady of the house didn't come down for breakfast the doctor always gave Angie the list of letters he wanted his wife to type for him that day.

She was eighteen when she started going to the pictures every Thursday with the young man that came to do the garden every week. After four months she found out why her brother had sent her away from her home in Kildare. Like all young girls Angie knew that she had to give a fella his court when he had taken her out. It had been raining one evening and she had been standing in the small recess of the doorway of the grocers shop with her young gardener. It was also the fourth time she had allowed him to slip his hand up her jumper when they were kissing. She hadn't been surprised, or annoyed because she enjoyed the little shivers that swarmed over her body when he cupped her small breasts in his hand. He had never squeezed her like her daddy had done. She had felt him hard against her stomach before but when he started to rock his body and she heard the rattle of the door behind her she froze.

It was three weeks before Angie could get her memory to admit that her daddy had taken her into his bed a few months after her mammy had died. She had decided that her brother must have heard the headboard on the bed rattling against the wall. Like the way the door in the grocer's shop had done when Albert had got excited.

With her thoughts swinging between her daddy squeezing her breasts, and liking the way Albert had fondled them she told the priest everything she could think of when she went to confession. She had to tell someone who wouldn't be able to see her and know who she was. The priest told her to pray every day and that God would forgive her. He also told her to marry her young man.

Less than six months after Albert had passed away, Angie missed him in her bed more than she grieved for the money he used to bring home. But unlike most of her neighbours in the tenements he always brought home some money every week. She had continued to clean for her lady, and her friends when she could after she was married so she managed to pay her rent and always have food on the table. She also continued to dance to the sounds of the typewriter.

Miriam was two years older that Maeve, and Angie was very proud when her eldest daughter qualified from the technical school with her certificate in shorthand and typing. She was satisfied when Maeve chose to leave school at fourteen and train to be hairdresser. It was a good trade and she would never have to do cleaning. By the time that Maeve had changed her mind about hairdressing and went to work in a department store Miriam had met and married her accountant.

Cleaning as a career for Maeve still didn't appeal to Angie but working with Cathy did. Also the money for the work was much better that when she had started as a young girl. Although she thought Cathy's idea of them forming a company was daft she was sure it would be fun. And none of them had anything to lose anyway.

Cathy tapped the table and said, 'Angie will handle all the money.'

'What money?' Maeve hollered. 'We don't have any.'

Patience, Cathy thought. 'We will. We will,' she said, pushing her chair back and crossing her legs, 'that'll be top of teh agenda fer teh next meetin'.'

'What's an agenda?' Maeve asked.

'It's the list of things we'll talk about, and make decisions on,' Cathy replied.

'Write down money fer teh next meetin',' Angie said, nodding her head in agreement.

'Today we have teh talk about er tools anc er workers,' Cathy said. She opened her packet of cigarettes and offered one to Maeve, 'Angie will start us off because she has the most experience.' She lit her cigarette nodded to Angie, then sat back in her chair.

With the next meeting scheduled for the following week, the three new business partners were on their second sherry when they heard the A40 stop outside the front gate.

'Her bones must be set or they would have kept her in,' Cathy said, moving back from the window. 'I expect we'll be hearin' that her man is delighted out of his mind.'

Maura had extricated herself from the low front seat of the A40 before Maurice had closed the door on his side of the car. With the top of her body still bent forward she made good speed up the garden path as though someone had set fire to her jacket and give her a smack on her arse.

She returned Maura's smile but Cathy was unable to force herself to beam as brightly as her sister. She put the lock on the catch after watching Maurice walk around his car twice. She often wondered if he counted the scrapes and dents on the grey banger every time he parked his car outside her house. 'No,' she replied to Maura's expression when her sister had finished turning over the pieces of paper that were on the hall table. 'Sure it's early yet anyway,' she said and moved in from the door to let Maurice walk in. 'And anyway,' she snapped when Maura picked the phone up and put it to her ear like she was checking that it was still working, 'he wouldn't want te talk te me.'

Maurice nodded his head at the withered roses that were hanging over the vase on the table and whined, 'I think they could go now.'

Cathy didn't say hello to her brother either. 'They're not mine,' she snapped. She moved her eyes away from Maurice's scowl and asked Maura, 'How did yeh get on at teh hospital?'

'Fantastic,' Maura said, throwing her head back and looking down her nose and repeated, 'Absolutely fantastic.' She glanced down at the small table again, then exercised all her dramatic skills with bending her body and waving her hands; she walked around the hall repeating, 'Absolutely fantastic.' When Maurice raised his arm and started rubbing the back of his neck she punched him lightly in his chest and giggled.

'Give us yer jacket,' Cathy said, winking at the embarrassed expression on her brother's face. 'Go on in,' she said, pointing to the living room door. 'Yeh can have a drop of me sherry te celebrate.' For a few seconds she didn't know which of them she was finding the most annoying, her brother or her sister.

There were times when Angie wanted to hug her son-in-law. And it wasn't because he was tall and handsome with bright blue eyes and light ginger curly hair. It was because she knew he craved attention and a little love from his mammy. 'Hello Maurice,' she said when he walked into the room.

Angie wasn't surprised when Patsy was born less than ten months after Maurice and Maeve were married. She was concerned when Emir was born two months before Patsy had her first birthday. She worried that Maurice would be like his daddy, and her own daughter would also have ten children.

Six years had passed since Emir was born. Angie had never asked her daughter why she hadn't become pregnant again. But she continued to worry because Maeve was only twenty-eight and Maurice's mother had been in her early forties when Cathy was born.

The silence continued when Maura followed her brother into the room. For some years now Maurice was used to the living room in his family home being tidy, but he wondered why the table was pulled out from the wall. He suspected the three women had been playing cards especially as Angie and Maeve were sitting at the table instead of on the easy chairs beside the fire. He sat down in the low chair under the window and watched Cathy pull a chair over to the table for Maura.

'Did ye go in te see teh doctor with her, Maurice?' Cathy asked, handing her brother a can of beer.

'No,' Maura answered, and giggled before she added quickly, 'there was no need.'

'I was outside all the time in case she needed me,' Maurice said. He wanted to let Cathy know that he was prepared to do as much for their distressed sister as herself, Joan, Sean, and Donal had done on the Sunday. 'She was seen te straight away,' he said.

'That was for the x-rays,' Maura said. 'The important thing is that my shoulder, ribs and arm are all perfectly set.' They were her injuries and she would give out the medical reports.

'I didn't know about the ribs,' Maurice said, raising his eyebrows and scowling at Cathy.

Neither did Cathy. In fact nobody in the family knew what bones or rib were broken in Maura's body. All the doctor had told Joan was that there were some fractures that he suspected weren't healed properly. And the best thing for her was to be in plaster for a few weeks.

'Well yeh know now,' Cathy said, and raised her sherry to her lips.

'They have done an excellent job,' Maura said, raising her head and inhaling deeply. Her voice filled the room and she moved her head as though she was talking to a group of people that were arguing when she said, 'I should have the plaster off in six weeks.'

'Does that mean yeh'll be here till then?' Maeve asked, wondering how Cathy would be able to put up with the little bitch for that long. She also worried if Cathy would continue with the cleaning group if Maura were still here.

Maura delivered Maeve a cold hard stare.

Cathy was furious when she had seen Maura turn her head to Maeve then lean her body towards her hands and lower her face to her feet. 'Mammy will be home by then, and she'll be delighted te see Carl here as well.' she shouted over to Maura. She was prepared to continue to appease the little bitch and endure the insults the little bitch delivered to herself, but not to Maeve. She inhaled with the intention of asking if Carl was serious about coming home when she heard a crack.

Angie had brought her hand down sharply on the table. She had seen the hurt on her daughter's face. The third time she slapped her hand on the table she was leaning towards Maura.

Jeasus ,Angie don't hit her, Cathy prayed when she saw Maura pulling her head back.

'I wouldn't worry about yer shoulders bein' bent over like an old woman, Maura,' Angie said, her head swaying with tem-per. She slapped the table again, stood and continued, 'Yeh can get physiotherapy fer that when yeh get teh plaster off.'

'Yer right, Angie,' Cathy agreed, 'they can do wonderful things these days with bashin' yer bones about.'

'And yeh can get it done in Canada,' Angie continued, her body trembling with anger. Her bottom denture moved when she inhaled before she shouted into Maura's face, 'Yer not even thirty yet.'

Maura moved back from the table.

'De yeh know that car ev yers is spittin' a lot of black smoke?' Angie shouted over to her red-faced son-in-law. She shoved her glasses up on her nose, then reached down to the floor for her handbag. She stood and nodded a broad smile to her daughter, then walked toward Maurice and snapped, 'It's not good fer teh children out there.'

Maurice looked like he was going to cry.

Angie had changed her mind about Cathy's scheme for forming a cleaning group when she had seen how enthralled Maeve was when they were talking about it. And she wasn't going to allow Maura to look down her nose at her daughter. Maeve had already endured enough smirking from her own sister. Her heart was heavy when she walked towards the door because she thought her eldest daughter Miriam was too much like Maura.

Out in the hall Cathy wrapped her arm around her friend's shoulder and said, 'Well done, Angie.'

'I hope I haven't made things uncomfortable fer yeh, Cathy,' Angie said biting on her denture as if to make sure she hadn't spit it into Maura's face. She moved her bag to her other arm. 'I'm sorry if I have,' she said, but she couldn't suppress her smile of satisfaction.

'We're all sorry, Angie,' Cathy said, hugging her friend again, 'even Maurice, he just can't handle it.' She squeezed the small bony shoulder again: 'It was a great meetin' though, wasn't it.'

Angie returned Cathy's laugh. She wanted to go back into

the room and take her girl with her but she said, 'I was right proud of Maeve.'

Delighted that Angie was going to work with her, Cathy squared her shoulders and said, 'We're goin teh make a great team.'

'We're a company now,' Angie said, tucking her handbag under her arm then trotted down the path in her tatty slippers.

Cathy closed the door with her foot when she went back into the living room. She didn't care if her sister saw her winking at Maeve. She enjoyed the silence in room while she moved her chair then sat down and said, 'Angie's right.'

'What about?' Maurice asked.

'What she said before she left,' Cathy said.

Maura removed one of her shoes and started to separate her toes with her socks still on.

Cathy was angry with her brother for being so stupid. She counted the cigarettes in her packet, pulled one out, lit it and said, 'That car ev yers is smokin' dreadful.'

The phone rang.

The shoe hit Maurice in the face, and Maura had pushed Cathy away from the door by the third ring on the phone. Cathy avoided looking at Maurice when they heard the door close with a sharp crack after Maura ran out into the hall. She pulled her chair into the table, and while she was trying to think of a reason why herself and Maeve could leave the room before her sister came back in so that they wouldn't have hear about Carl's suffering again, the door opened as sharply as it had closed.

'It's for you,' Maura said, closing her eyes at Cathy then added, 'I'm going up to lie down.'

'Finish yer sherry it'll help yeh relax,' Cathy said, 'Yer shoe is over there.' She pointed to the floor beside Maurice. She left the door open when she went out to the hall. She was expecting the call to be from Joan. She raised her eyebrows when she heard a male voice say, 'Hello Cathy.'

It was two years since Cathy had seen the man that was talking to her on the other end of the phone. But she had no trouble picturing his head of wild frizzy hair, while she wondered if she had enough milk. She was remembering that Dominick Dwyer's glasses were thick like the bottom of milk bottles.

Even now eight years after the first time she had met the only child of her mammy's friend, sometimes when she washed a milk bottle she would gaze into it. One time she had used two bottles like they were a set of binoculars. She couldn't even see the basin in the sink. She still wondered how he found his glasses when he woke up in the mornings because his eyesight must be so bad.

With her heart full of pity for the man on the other end of the phone, Cathy closed her eyes and listened. 'I will indeed,' she said about four times. 'He's got a lovely voice,' she sang to Maeve when she came back into the living room. She enjoyed the waves of curiosity that flowed around the room during the ten-second silence before she volunteered, 'That was Dominic Dwyer.' She acknowledged Maeve's frown and said, 'He's Ena's son.'

'Is mammy all right?' Maurice asked. He wanted to leave the room when his injured sister cast him a cold glance. All the years he had resented his injured sister passed over his thoughts and froze. At the same time he was willing to believe that it was Maura who had gotten her dates wrong about his mammy being away when she came home. It was easier than admitting that his mammy didn't want to see her.

Maura picked up her sherry.

Cathy saw her sister's hand shaking. 'Mammy will be home any day from Wednesday week,' she said.

'Are they enjoyin' themselves?' Maurice asked.

'I expect so, but I never asked,' Cathy returned, 'I couldn't care less if they are or not.'

'Did he say what time or anythin'?' Maurice asked.

'He said he'll ring again at teh weekend,' Cathy said, disappointed that her brother hadn't asked her why she didn't care if her mammy was enjoying herself.

'I should imagine he would have said somethin' if they weren't all right,' Maurice chuckled.

'If yeh want te know yerself yeh can ring Dominic back. He's down in Ena's house,' Cathy snapped. She closed her eyes and started to think about her own plans. She was glad that they would have another meeting before her mammy was home. She moved her legs to let Maura pass when the phone rang again.

But Maura didn't move, and neither did Cathy. Maura's hand shook when she crushed out her freshly lit cigarette.

Maurice said, 'I'll get it.' He left the door open when he went out to the hall. The silence in the living room enabled the three girls to hear Maurice say, 'Hello.' Maurice always spoke loudly when he was anxious. They heard him shout, 'How are yeh? Yes she is. How're yeh doin' yerself?'

Cathy and Maeve watched Maura getting herself ready to sprint. Maura was at the door before her brother called from the hall, 'Maura, it's Carl for you.'

Keeping her eyes on the floor, Maura waited in the hall until Maurice had moved back into the living room, then closed the door.

Maeve was still feeling snubbed by Maura and hurt that her husband hadn't tried to tell his sister off like her ma had. She didn't want to be in the room when Maura returned so she stood and said, 'I'll go round to the school now.'

'Yeh have another fifteen minutes,' Maurice whined. He could feel Cathy's temper, and he didn't want to be the room on his own with her.

'If yer worried about Maura being on the phone when we walk out te teh hall, Maurice, yeh can rest yer mind because he doesn't talk te her fer more than three minutes,' Cathy said. 'He only phones her te remind her not te tell us that he beats her.'

Apart from the door, the only exit Maurice could see from the room was the window, and he was tempted to climb out of it. He was afraid that Cathy was going to lose her temper, and he dreaded her telling him why she didn't care if their mammy was enjoying herself.

'We all heard yeh when yeh answered teh phone,' Cathy continued. 'I wouldn't worry about him not havin' much te say te yeah because he didn't want te talk te me either. And I'll bet yeh anythin' yeh like that he'll never set his old foot in Ireland again.' She turned to Maeve: 'I'll walk out to teh door with yeh. I don't want te be here when the little bitch comes back in. I think I might clout her one when she starts tellin' us how upset her git of a husband is.'

For five long seconds Maurice watched the top of his wife's head while she stood at the table and packed her cigarettes and exercise book into her handbag. The silence was broken when the handle of the door rattled and Maura moved slowly and silently into the room. She held her head down and walked like she was blind and sat down before she raised her head to Maurice and said, 'That was Carl.' She paused and sniffed as if to make sure he was listening: 'He is delighted that I am getting better, but he is still very worried.'

When Cathy and Maeve were walking down the front path Maura was telling her brother how relieved Carl was that her bones and ribs were healing. She didn't notice that Maurice wasn't listening to her. It was enough that he nodded his head when she told him how worried her husband was about her all the time.

'He won't have teh guts te come home,' Cathy said to Maeve as she was closing the gate.

Chapter Twenty-seven

Maeve was early so she walked slowly around to the school to collect her girls. She willed her mind to ignore the memory of the scowling face of her husband and concentrate on the meeting. At the same time she also believed that Maurice had every reason to be grumpy because his sister had used him. The selfish girl had only wanted a driver to take her to the hospital. She thought that Maura was worse than Josie had ever been. And it was so obvious with the way little bitch was going on that she was determined to keep Joan and Cathy from hearing what the doctors had to say about her injured shoulder and arm.

Serves him right, Maeve thought, and he'll have to miss his football on Saturday to make up his money for having the day out of work. She went on to wonder if her husband had felt as stupid as he had looked when Maura wouldn't let him say anything about when they were at the hospital.

And Carl on the phone: Maurice had looked wretched when Maura had closed the door in his face after she had gone out to the hall.

Still, the anxiety Maeve was feeling about her husband, and Maura had dented her excitement about the meeting. She desperately wanted them to have a go at three of them working together. They wouldn't make a fortune, but they would make some money. Her mind was soaking up a possible sense of achievement while she walked towards the school. She had always felt she had let her mammy down because she didn't do as well in school as her sister Miriam.

Until Cathy started going on about the three of them working together Maeve had not seen herself as doing anything other than bringing up her children and looking after Maurice. Right now she wondered if she was bringing up Maurice and looking after the children. She raised her head from the pavement and laughed. She wondered what Cathy would say if she told her what she was thinking.

She was so engrossed in her thoughts over Maurice and her new venture with Cathy and her ma that Maeve didn't recognise the A40 when it stopped to let her pass while she waited to cross the road. She ignored the first honk from the driver; she always did. She ignored the second honk. The third honk made her jump because it was loud and long. It had come from the car behind the A40. She ignored both of the cars while she crossed the road and walked on to the school.

Chapter Twenty-eight

Daddy's home,' Emir cried out when they had turned the corner at the top of road. She was short like her mammy, but she clearly inherited her bright blue eyes and her light curly hair from her daddy.

Maeve had also seen the Austin A40 parked outside their house. She allowed her youngest daughter to slip her hand from hers and run down the street.

'Did Daddy not go into work after he had taken Aunt Maura into the hospital?' Patsy asked her ma. Patsy promised to have a long body like her daddy. She was the tallest girl in her class at school. Both Maeve and Maurice were very proud of her school reports. Everyone said she looked like Maeve, but Maeve had always seen her eldest daughter looking like her own sister Miriam, and Patsy was a lot more caring about other people.

Maeve smiled down at her eldest little girl and said, 'It was too late when they came out.' She was in no hurry to face her gloomy husband so she sauntered slowly behind her children. When her daughters ran up the garden path she wanted to keep walking. She needed more time to grow some courage to be able to listen to Maurice when he started complaining about Cathy. He was standing at the hall door when she reached the front gate so she walked up the path.

'Are yeh all right?' Maurice whinged when he closed the hall door after Maeve had walked in with her head in the air.

'Why?' Maeve asked.

'Yeh seemed miles away when yeh were crossin' teh road,' Maurice moaned, hitching his jeans up on his waist. 'Did yeh not hear me hootin' at yeh?'

'Was that you?' Maeve asked, hanging her jacket on the ball at the bottom of the banisters. She stared into his red face and said sharply, 'I've never taken any notice of fellahs honkin' their horns at me since teh day I was married.'

The evening meal was called tea but the food was the same as for dinner. Maeve started getting the tea ready straight away. She continued to dwell upon her meeting. Her mind had now married her venture to Maurice and how he would help or hinder her. She talked through many imaginary scenes in her head while she peeled the potatoes, then washed and chopped the cabbage.

'Are yeh doin' the dinner now?' Maurice called from the doorway of the small kitchen.

Maeve turned her head from the sink towards the door so Maurice could hear her and said, 'We can have it early. I have a job this evenin' and I can get it done early now that yer in. I can get down from six till eight.' She carried the pot of potatoes over to the cooker, removed the pork chops from the fridge and slapped them down on the work unit.

'That'll be fine,' Maurice said, 'is it too soon to set teh table?'

Maeve wanted to say, 'I didn't ask yeh if it was all right te have the dinner early,' but she couldn't: 'Give it fifteen minutes,' she snapped.

Maurice glanced at his watch and said, 'I'll go and get a paper then.'

A very unhappy and bewildered Maurice was glad of the walk to the shop to get his evening paper. He needed a few uncomfortable thoughts to leave his head. He thought his family were being unfair to Maura. If his sister said she slipped in the snow then she must have. He snorted a sneer into the pavement at the idea that any woman would deny that her husband had beaten her at all, let alone break any of her bones. No woman or girl would be that stupid. He also thought his sister was right to do what her husband wanted. After all he knew her better than they did. And Carl was right too; he didn't phone all the way from Canada to chat about himself. He thought that Maeve was too friendly with Cathy.

But Maurice couldn't avoid his oldest worry when he passed one of his neighbours. The woman was in her seventies and was living on her own. She was a nice friendly old girl who went to the bingo with Angie every week. She was small and had grey hair like his mammy. He recalled the cold expression on Cathy's face when she had said she didn't care if their mammy was enjoying her holiday. He wasn't concerned about his mammy's holiday. He wondered how his mammy would manage in the house on her own if Cathy went away like his older sisters.

A young man's voice he knew well calling out a greeting brought his thoughts to his youngest brother Liam. 'How yeh doin'?' he called back. He felt some relief from his worry over his mammy when he smiled and waved over to one of his young brother's friends. He went on to think that Liam would probably come home to stay for good. He knew that his brother was going to leave the English Air Force next year. He decided that either Liam would come home or Donal would move back into the Plunkett Road if Cathy went away and his mammy were on her own. He didn't have enough room for her and anyway he didn't think his mammy would want to live with children in the house.

With his evening paper tucked under his arm, Maurice faced his Austin A40 parked at the kerb outside the house. He imagined that he could still hear Angie's sharp voice when she complained about the black smoke. And he knew he didn't need a new exhaust. He needed a new car. No. He needed money to buy a new car. He buoyed up a little when he smelt the pork chops as he opened the front door and walked into his house.

'I said I'll do that.' Maurice nodded his head into the door-way that led to the living room.

'It's done now. I had teh time,' Maeve said, turning the gas off under the pan of pork chops. 'Sit down, the chops are love-ly.' Her temper had cooled when she had decided that there was absolutely no need to tell Maurice anything about her new venture with Cathy and her ma until they had more of their plans ready.

Chapter Twenty-nine

Can we play out fer a while after dinner, Mammy?' Patsy asked when they were halfway through their silent meal.

'That's up to yer Daddy,' Maeve said. She had forgotten about the children going to bed. The main reason why she had taken on the late evening jobs was because she could get the girls to bed before she went out. She was cutting her pork chop when she said, 'I'm goin' out earlier than usual this evenin'.'

'Will Daddy be puttin' us te bed as well?' Emir asked, smiling brightly.

'De yez want me to?' Maurice asked.

'Yes Daddy,' the two young girls chorused. They were prepared to put themselves to bed if they were allowed to play out.

She was only two when her daddy had died so Maeve had never known him. She had never really missed him until she saw the fuss her own girls made of Maurice. She started to feel angry again at her husband for the times she had seen him looking down his nose at her ma. Prayers don't get you everything yeh want, Maeve went on to think while her mind was on her daddy. But just the same she believed it would be God's will if she had a son. At the back of her mind she wondered if there had been something on the little balloons that Una's husband Jack had given Maurice to use when they had sex after Emir was born. He hadn't used them for over a year and she still wasn't pregnant yet.

'Are ye doin' cleanin' fer teh caravan, Mammy?' Patsy asked.

Maeve lifted her head from her dinner, smiled at Emir and said, 'I am indeed.' She willed her heart not to beat any faster.

'What caravan?' Maurice asked frowning.

'Eres,' Emir said. At six years of age she didn't feel the slight tension that was in the air between her mammy and daddy. 'And we have nearly three hundred pounds,' she added, proudly.

Her jaws were exhausted but Maeve continued chewing her meat. She didn't want to swallow it. She took another potato she didn't want. She wasn't going to tell Maurice about the caravan until she had five hundred pounds, but right now she didn't care if he knew or not. After all it was him who had said it would be grand if they had a caravan for the weekends in the summer. Like her sister Miriam had.

The silence was too much for Emir so she cried out, 'That's an awful lot of money.' She pushed her head forward, then turned it up so she could stare into Maurice's eyes when she said, 'Isn't it, Daddy?'

'It certainly is,' Maurice said, 'I could buy a new car fer that.'

'No yeh couldn't,' Patsy said, shaking her head so rapidly that her flushed cheeks trembled when she cried out, 'Only Mammy can spend it. It's all in teh Post Office.'

'They're mindin' it fer us,' Emir shouted, nodding approvingly at her sister. 'That's teh best way. Then nobody can steal it, or anythin'.'

'I didn't say I would steal it,' Maurice said, embarrassed with having to defend himself.

Maeve put her knife and fork on her plate. She thought that Maurice had had enough humiliation for one day and she was sure if she had another mouthful of food it would choke her. 'Let's get back te playin' out,' she said. 'If it's all right with yer daddy, then it's all right with me.'

'Yeh were told not te say anythin' until Mammy said yeh

could,' Patsy said to her sister behind her arm after Maurice went out to the kitchen to make the tea.

'It's all right,' Maeve assured her girls, 'he had te be told sometime. Don't worry I won't let him have it te buy a car.'

'But we'll need a car fer te get out to teh caravan,' Emir said.

'No we won't,' Patsy cut in, 'Uncle Donal'll drive us out. He has a nicer car anyway.'

Maeve wanted to laugh at the way the children had handled their daddy over the money she had saved. She knew he was still embarrassed over the Post Office book and the three hundred pounds. She was also adamant that he wasn't going to spend the money on a new car. She decided earlier that if he could work on Saturday to have the day to take his stupid sister to the hospital then he could work a few more and buy a better car.

Maurice came back with two mugs of tea. 'Yez can play out fer an hour,' he said.

'Are yeh goin' teh bring yer post money book with yeh?' Emir called over to her mammy. She was sitting under the window tying the laces on her old shoes.

'No Emir, I'm not,' Maeve laughed lightly while she stooped behind the armchair to get her bag. 'I think that'll be in safe hands here.'

Chapter Thirty

Cathy struck a match and held it to the papers sticking out in the fire grate while she thought again that her sister was a lazy little bitch. 'I take it he didn't want to stay?' she said.

'Who?' Maura asked lifting her face from her magazine.

'Jerome,' Cathy snapped. She wanted to pull the magazine off her sister's lap and throw it into the flames that were creeping around the papers in the grate.

'He played out all the time he was here,' Maura replied and turned another page in her magazine.

Jesus, Cathy thought, why can't the girl answer one question? 'Yeh can set teh table while I cook the dinner,' she said while she poked the fire to loosen the papers. She knew by the way the papers were twisted that Joan had set the fire. She was grateful to Joan for doing it but she still thought that even with her arm still in plaster Maura was quite capable of getting the fire ready. She didn't ask her sister what she had done with her day, before or after Joan and Flo had and come over and Maura didn't tell her.

'The poor little mite,' Cathy mumbled when she crossed the hall to the kitchen. She had removed the chops, and the frozen peas from the fridge before she saw the pot on the cooker. She smiled at the white balls covered with water. She suspected that Flo had probably been glad to be in the kitchen peeling the potatoes just to get away from Maura babbling on about how distressed her husband was.

The kitchen was spotless and Cathy knew by the way the wiping cloth was folded that Flo had also cleaned the kitchen. She knew she would hear about how distressed her sister's husband was again when they were having their dinner. She focused her mind on how her family were doing all they could to help the silly girl, and wondered if Donal would bring her favourite chocolate gateau with him.

As Donal hadn't come yet, Cathy decided to phone Flo and Joan to thank them for setting the fire and cleaning the kitchen when the phone rang. Even before she had lifted the receiver off the cradle she heard her sister's feet thump on the floor. Maura was standing at the door when Cathy said, 'Hello.' She turned round to her sister and said, 'It's fer you.'

'Who is it?' Maura asked, taking a step back.

'Him,' Cathy said dropping the phone down on the small table and walked back into the kitchen.

'Who is it?' Maura repeated.

'Him that lives in Canada,' Cathy called out from the kitchen.

'Hello darling,' Maura said into the phone. She stretched over and closed the kitchen door.

'Not when I'm in here,' Cathy mumbled and opened the door. She left it open while she walked across the hall into the living room. She also turned up the volume on the radio. She didn't want to hear her sister on the phone. To make sure she didn't hear her sister's voice she picked up the bundle of magazines off a chair and walked to the far end of the living room and sat down.

After she had turned the pages of one of the magazines so that the front cover was on the outside and not in the middle Cathy saw that all the magazines were folded on the same page. There were six magazines all opened on the same topic page. One had a coffee stain on it. 'Fer God's sake,' she mumbled when she read the first question on the "Dear Monica" page. She wanted to cry for her sister that was talking on the phone.

For half an hour Cathy and Donal listened to the merits of the Canadian education system.

'Are yeh thinking of doin' the same thing as Una?' Cathy asked.

Maura's knife and fork made an arch when she rested her wrists on the edge of the table. She had no idea of what her sister Una was doing.

The cutlery reminded Cathy of two soldiers with swords forming a guard of honour at a wedding. 'Are yeh thinking of goin back te school?' she asked.

'Why would I want to go to college?' Maura giggled.

'Una is gettin' on great and she loves teh studyin' and eve-rythin'', Cathy said, holding her hand out to Donal for his plate.

Maura shoved her chair back and picked up her own dinner plate and stood. 'You stay exactly where you are,' she said, wav-ing her free hand over the table like she was calming a group of old people at a bingo session and shouted, 'I can make the coffee. 'You've been on your feet all day.'

'Yeh can't stand and use a sewin' machine,' Cathy said.

'Donal is standing all day,' Maura returned, smiling smugly at her brother.

Three weeks Donal had recalled, when he was leaving the shop with the chocolate gateau for the dessert. He was opening the door of his car when he decided that he knew his injured sister better now than he did before she had left home. He felt very sorry for. He didn't agree with Joan, or Cathy that Maura was stupid. She was weak. When she had pulled her chin in, killed her smile and closed her eyes at Cathy he thought of his eldest sister. Josie was the family snob, and she always pulled in her chin like Maura had just done when she didn't know what to say. He smiled at the memory of how Cathy enjoyed teasing

Josie about working in a factory. He worried that Cathy was going to start annoying Maura.

Although Josie and Cathy had become good friends since Joan was married, Donal saw that Maura was very different to his oldest sister.

'I'll bring you home again, Kathlee-en,' Maura's voice croaked from the kitchen.

'She never was much of a singer,' Donal said.

'That's not singin',' Cathy whinged. 'Teh least she could do is learn teh words.'

'I suppose yer right,' Donal replied, smiling.' He had no idea because he never sang or listened to the words of songs he heard on the radio. His thoughts went back to when he was driving up to the house and he had recalled he hadn't agreed with Joan that Maura was like his mammy. He smiled again. He had never heard his mammy sing.

Listening to, and watching his two young sisters since he had come into the house for his dinner convinced Donal that all his sisters were different and that none of them were like his mammy.

Unlike Josie, and Maura, Donal didn't choose to forget how selfish and emotionally abusive his mammy was. Unlike Una, Pauline, and Joan, he just never had any need to remember. He was a boy so he had not been expected to do cooking and housework like his sisters had. It was the Sunday afternoon after Joan and Tony's wedding when all his brothers were in Sean's and Una had told them about his mammy's spending habits that he started to understand why his sisters were always fighting so much.

'I'll give her a hand,' Cathy said, shoving her chair back. 'I don't want her te break any of Josie's lovely cups.'

'Leave her,' Donal said, 'Josie'll buy yeh new cups.' His eyes and heart were smiling at the memory of when Josie was cooking the breakfast the morning after the afternoon in Sean's house. Thinking back to that Monday morning over two years ago, now all Donal could remember was how concerned Josie had been about Cathy. It was the first time he had seen his eldest sister make a fuss over anyone other than his mammy.

'I know she will,' Cathy said, sitting down. 'But just the same I won't be able te tell "her" out there in the kitchen off because of her disablement.'

'She won't let the cups fall,' Donal said, recalling when Cathy used to call Josie 'her' all the time.

'I hope yer right,' Cathy said. 'It'll be me that'll have te clean teh floor.'

'If she breaks yer cups I'll buy yeh a whole new set,' he said. He never learned what had happened between his eldest and his youngest sisters but he hoped that something would happen between Maura and Cathy before Maura went back to Canada.

'I hope she can boil water better that she can sing,' Cathy whined.

Donal prayed Cathy would go deaf for a couple of minutes. He turned his head toward the door where the croaky sounds were getting louder because Maura was walking across the hall.

'Carl is absolutely delighted,' Maura sang when she came in with one coffee and placed it in front of her brother. She waited until she had come back into the room again with a coffee in both of her hands and placed one cup in front of her sister and said, 'The plaster is a nuisance of course, but I have got used to it now.'

Cathy picked the large knife up off the table. 'Still yeh need to be careful fer awhile yet,' she said.

Maura closed her eyes at her sister, and then smiled at her brother, waved her arms about and said, 'I am absolutely fine.'

For a second Donal felt dizzy. He worried she would ask him for a job in the Beggars Lodge.

'That's grand,' Cathy said, cutting into the chocolate gateau.

She handed a slice to Maura, and added, 'Yeh can practise with the washin' up.'

Maura babbled on about how happy Jerome was with staying with Sean and Flo. Cathy spooned her chocolate cake into her mouth. With every mouthful of her cake she swallowed the temptation to ask her sister how she would know how happy her son was when she hadn't gone out to see him once.

As if Maura could sense what Cathy was thinking, and to prevent her sister from asking any questions, she babbled on. She was so engrossed with keeping the attention on herself she talked about her friend Nula.

Donal imagined he could taste the frozen peas he had eaten with his dinner. He moved his chair back from the table as though it would prevent him from hearing anything about her friend's brother, and he still hadn't told anyone about Noel's visit to the Beggars Lodge and him taking Maura home.

When Maura paused to drag on her cigarette he said, 'How's teh job doin', Cathy?'

'We're busy all teh time Cathy said, 'and lookin' forward to er bonus.' Then just as she had expected, Maura stood. When Maura was walking down the lobby she said, 'I don't want to talk about the job in front of her. She's not interested, and she doesn't listen anyhow. If yeh want her te shut up and listen te anythin', tell her about the Beggars Lodge.'

Donal coughed.

'The fire is going down,' Maura said when she came back.

'Leave it,' Cathy said, catching her brother's arm. 'There's plenty ev burnin' left, and anyway it's a bit warm fer now.' She expected that Donal would be leaving before the hour was up. And she intended to go over to Angie later so if her sister wanted the fire she could do it herself.

Maura picked up her spoon and started to play with her dessert.

Cathy hoped that because Donal was sitting with them

Maura would give her some idea of when she was going back to Canada. 'Have yeh phoned about yer ticket yet?' she asked.

Maura put down her spoon and walked over to the mantelpiece. 'Any Sunday?' she said when she sat down again and opened her packet of cigarettes. 'I have to book it twenty-four hours before I want to travel.'

Cathy returned Donal's smile with a nod and asked, 'Will yeh have teh pay anythin' extra?'

'That's not a problem,' Maura returned with a throaty laugh, 'Carl said I was to pay whatever it cost.' She lit her cigarette.

Cathy put another slice of cake on her own plate and said, 'You can help yerself when yer ready.' She looked at the two smooth round dents in the side of Maura's slice of gateau and called out, 'Yeh should finish yer eatin' before yeh start smokin'.'

One glance at Cathy was enough to tell Donal that Joan was right when she had said his young sister would need them all to keep calling in or she might break Maura's other arm. As a way of telling his youngest sister that he was pleased to be with her, Donal said, 'All teh dinner was lovely, Cathy. Tony could get a lesson from yeh fer cookin' teh pork chops.'

Maura coughed. She hadn't seen Tony since the day she had come out of the hospital.

Silence never bothered Donal. He welcomed the quiet in his flat over the Beggars Lodge when the pub closed. Now sitting with his injured sister, he worried that she would ask him about a job in the Beggars Lodge again. And Maura still hadn't said when she would be going back to Canada, or if she was going to go back at all. 'Will yeh be gone back to Canada before Mammy gets back?' he asked.

Maura didn't know because she was waiting for her husband to send her the money to buy her ticket. She wasn't going to tell Donal or Cathy that so she said, 'I haven't made my mind up yet.'

Enough is enough, Cathy thought. She stood and walked

over to the back window. 'Any more news on Flo's kitchen yet?' she asked. She already knew but she wanted to talk about the garden she was looking out on. 'Flo'll be delighted when it's all done,' she said. 'It's always teh women that have teh most work te do when there's building goin' on.'

'How de yeh make that out?' Donal asked.

'All teh cleanin' up that has te be done every day.' In spite of all the aggravation that Cathy had suffered with her sister her mind was saturated with dreams and plans for herself. She turned round and asked, 'Did yeh get me invitation?'

Donal sat back in his chair and said, 'I'll do me share ev diggin' and I'll buy the beer.' He was prepared to do anything to help her as long as she was living at home with his mammy.

Cathy was delighted and while her brother was still smiling she said, 'I don't have any shovels, and I'll also want another load of manure.'

Maura had no idea what they were talking about, but she knew what manure was so she turned her head towards the garden and asked, 'What do you want manure for?'

'I'm goin' te grow rhubarb again,' Cathy said, pulling back the curtains. She ran her eyes over the small field of tall grass and weeds and continued, 'And before yeh ask me what I want the rhubarb for I can tell yeh that I'm goin' te make hundreds ev pies fer Donal te sell in the Beggars Lodge.'

Donal felt dizzy.

Fifty pounds here and fifty pounds there, Cathy thought while she smiled at the wild, and overgrown bit of land that was the back garden of her family home.

PART TWO

Chapter Thirty-one

The second meeting of the cleaning company took place the day after Maura returned to Canada.

'What de yeh think, girls?' Cathy asked passing round her cigarettes. Maeve had read out the minutes of the last and first meeting and the decisions that had been taken.

'Do yeh mean about yer woman not bein' here, and it bein' nice and peaceful like?' Angie asked, shoving her glasses up on her nose.

'That's got nothin' te do with the second meetin' ev er company,' Cathy said lighting her cigarette and handing the lighter to Maeve. 'Could we make a go of it?'

'What have we got te lose?' Angie patted the sides of her head, then nodded to Maeve who was writing the date in her exercise book.

'About two hundred pounds,' Cathy said.

Maeve stopped writing, looked at her ma and hollered. 'Each?'

'Between teh three of us,' Cathy said. She watched Maeve write the two zeros after the number two.

Maeve passed her hand over the page she was writing on as if to clean it of everything except her script and her writing would stand out more. 'Will yeh give up yer job at Frank's?' she asked.

'They're goin' teh give me up,' Cathy said, 'six years ev me life down the drain. 'I heard it from teh top.'

'Who do you know at teh top?' Maeve asked.

'Bella,' Cathy said, tossing her head back proudly.

'That's high enough.' Angie shoved her glasses up on her nose. 'It's always teh tea lady that knows everythin' first in places like that.'

'They'll be gone by Christmas,' Cathy said, opening her exercise book and added, 'I'll be hangin' on fer any redundancy I can get.'

'Another one'll open somewhere,' Maeve said, recalling Maurice talking about the government giving grants to companies to open up factories. She also recalled him complaining that the factories closed down when the grants had run out.

'I hope so,' Cathy said, coughing a soft laugh. 'We don't want anyone stealing er work.' She picked up her pencil as a signal for them to get on with the meeting. She raised her voice and said, 'Joan is goin' te lend us two hundred pounds fer te get started.'

Maeve added a full stop to what she had written down so far and said, 'That's a lot ev money,'

'Joan is goin' to show us how to do teh book keepin',' Cathy continued, 'I think we all need to know about that in case one of is sick or somethin'.'

Maeve looked up from her writing and said, 'I'd never be able te do it all on me own. Cleanin' has never been seen as a great job te be doin' but with the three ev us workin' together we can earn erselves a livin'. With better jobs now fer women, especially with part-time work fillin' shelves in the supermarkets. All the small places are now findin' it hard te get teh few hours cleanin' a week that they want.'

She'd sell milk to a cow, Angie thought. She un-crossed her legs, turned into the table and asked, 'What places do we have te start with?'

Cathy withdrew a sheet of paper from underneath her pad and read, 'We have Teh Beggars Lodge, teh hairdressers, teh record shop, teh chemist, teh travel agent, teh bookies, teh flower shop, and teh sweet shop.' She stretched her arm over to Maeve and put her hand on top of her friend's pencil. She could see that Maeve was almost frantic because she had only written down the Beggars Lodge. She waved the paper she was holding and said, 'I'll give yeh this list te take home with yeh.' She then passed the sheet over to Angie.

Angie counted nine shops on the list. 'How did yeh get them places to want yeh do teh cleanin'?'

'I went in and asked them after teh last time I had me hair done,' Cathy said, pulling on her cigarette. That's when I got teh idea in teh first place. The hairdresser was furious because her cleaner hadn't come in.'

'What times do they want them done?' Angie asked squinting through her old spectacles at the list of shops and places. She knew them all.

'Most of them are fer early mornin' or evening, but teh bookies and teh flower shop want some done durin' teh day,' Cathy said. She waited until Angie had finished raising her eyebrows and pursing her lips reading the list for the fourth time to ask, 'How many girls do yeh think yeh can get te work fer us?'

Angie looked up at the grey ceiling and scratched the side of her leg: 'With Maeve and meself I can count on four.' She sniffed and pointed to the sheet of paper and said, 'Two ev them are doin' some ev these places anyway.'

'None ev them are goin' te lose their jobs,' Cathy returned quickly. 'I'm hopin' they will agree te let us pay them instead.'

Angie continued to rub her leg.

Worried that Angie would not want to take anyone's job from them, Cathy said, 'Angie I don't have any trainin' te do anythin' else. I expect that Maeve is right and other factories will start up but I'm fed up with teh clockin' in and clockin' out. I suppose I could try Dunn's but I couldn't stand teh buss'in inte town every day. Donal said it's getting people he can trust te get on and do teh cleanin' when they turn in. He said that they deliberately worked slowly so that they would get more hours pay.'

'That's because none ev them want te pay very much,' Angie cut in.

'That's teh point, Angie, all teh places on the list want teh cleanin' done as quickly as possible, and they want it done properly. I'm hopin' that you will be able to estimate the time it will take and we can give a price for the whole job. After all, you have the most experience. Efficiency is what is goin' te make us successful. We will get paid fer teh job not teh hours worked.'

Angie put down her pencil and though for a few seconds. She knew Cathy was right. 'Fer the moment we can call them jobs,' she said. If we can get teh te girls workin' fer us they can take their time if they want te.'

'But we want te get workers that will turn up on time and knuckle down,' Cathy said, moving her eyes between her two partners.

Though not as experienced as her ma, Maeve nodded her head in agreement and said, 'The few times that I wasn't able te do teh flower shop I had nearly twice teh cleanin' te do teh next day. And they didn't pay fer teh day I couldn't get it. Someone just swept teh dirt under the shelves. And all teh bins were overflowing as well. And Cathy is right about the busses. When I worked in teh cake shop before I was married and until teh few months before Patsy was born sometimes I didn't get home until after seven.'

Encouraged that Maeve agreed, Cathy smiled with expectation of success and said, 'Except fer teh few houses we have te start off with, we will bring our own equipment and cleanin' stuff. All they will have te supply will be teh hot water.'

Maeve stopped writing. 'What about teh vacuum cleaners? And the floor mops?'

'That's what we'll need te buy. And a couple ev them baskets on wheels. We can keep them in the small shed behind the Beggars Lodge. We won't need everythin' fer every job,' Cathy said, 'one of teh complaints that came up all teh time when I was talkin' to teh owners ev teh shops was that their cleanin' powders were always goin' missin'.'

Angie suppressed a laugh. She waited until her daughter finished writing and said, 'Sounds te me as if yeh have it all worked out.'

'I think it's great,' Maeve said, smoothing her exercise book. 'Not many people want te do teh small cleanin' jobs, especially when teh places only want a few hours a day.'

'Efficiency and reliability is what we are offerin',' Cathy said, 'if we can get an organization goin' that will guarantee their cleanin' done we have a fair chance ev makin' enough money te give us all a fair wage. The ones I have on me list are all prepared te pay us somethin' extra every month if we can get their cleanin' done fer them every day.' She looked at Angie and asked, 'Can we do it?'

'Cathy Malone,' Angie said loudly, 'if I could do this sort ev plannin' I wouldn't have been doin' cleanin' all me life. I'd be a bank manager.' She shoved her glasses up on her nose and smiled at her daughter.

Encouraged, Cathy said, 'Let's make one list of teh shops, and another list of teh times they want teh cleanin' done.'

'We have all these places fer cleanin' every day.' Angie moved her pencil up and down the list of places. She shoved her glasses up her nose and raised her head. 'Some are fer twice a day, some mornin's, and evenin's, and some either mornin's or evenin's.'

'There's nothin' wrong with yer ma's readin',' Cathy said, smiling at Maeve. 'All we have te do is put them all in teh plan.'

Angie leaned back in her chair and folded her arms. 'We

have you, me, Kate, Beth and we have Cathy in teh evenin's te te get started with.' She looked down at Cathy's list again, then tilted her head back so she could see her two partners through her glasses that were resting on the end of her nose. 'It's teh sortin' out and teh rememberin' whose doin' what and when.'

'Can't we do a chart?' Maeve said.

'I can't. Can you?' Cathy asked, glancing at Angie.

'Can I turn teh pad sideways?' Maeve asked. She could almost see her caravan on the page of her exercise book.

'Yeh can turn it any way yeh like,' Cathy said.

Maeve flipped over a new page and turned her pad sideways. 'Do yeh have a ruler?' she asked, smoothing the paper with both hands. She then gazed at the photographs on the wall and tried to remember her last year in school.

Cathy ran her eyes around the room.

She couldn't remember the last time she had seen a ruler in the house. 'Do yeh want it fer measuring?' she asked.

'I'll need teh do some straight lines first,' Maeve said, 'anythin'll do that's long enough.' She extended her hands over the table to show the length she needed.

Cathy shoved her chair back from the table and said, 'I'll find somethin'.' She looked in the press that held the boiler, along the bookshelves, behind the television set, she pulled the cushions off the easy chairs but she couldn't find a straight piece of wood. 'Start yer list,' she said and went out to the kitchen.

'I'll make it six days,' Maeve said, smoothing her paper again. 'This is only rough fer now.' She apologised to her ma, then raised her head at the sound of Cathy in the hall.

'This is all I can find that's long enough, and straight,' Cathy called out from the door.

'Cathy, are ye serious?' Maeve roared, while Angie lowered her head and waved her face to her slippers.

'Yeh can put teh bread board underneath yer pad so teh handle won't slope up yer pencil,' Cathy advised.

Maeve's earrings bounced off her cheeks when she nodded approval. She lifted up her pad so the Cathy could put the breadboard on the table. She then replaced the pad and used the back of the carving knife to make the straight lines.

Cathy pointed to the makeshift ruler when she was sat down and said, 'Be careful now, that thing is sharp. It was me Granny Duffy's.'

Creamy blue, Maeve decided when she remembered how to make the chart. She certainly wasn't going to have one of the green caravans. Her confidence grew as she explained what she was doing and how they would be able to use it.

'That is grand, Maeve.' Cathy nodded her head to Angie who was beaming at her daughter.

Maeve tore the sheet of paper out of her exercise book and placed the chart in the centre of the table, then flipped back to the first page on her exercise book.

Angie picked up the sheet of paper with all the lines drawn across and down it. She counted eight spaces down the page before she said, 'If we can get that many te start we'll do all right.' She flapped the sheet of paper in front of Cathy and shouted, 'This is great, Maeve.'

Cathy tapped her friend's pad with her finger, beamed approvingly and said, 'Write Maeve done teh chart.' She returned Maeve's smile and added, 'Will do a good one fer photocopying.'

'That's another good idea,' Angie said. 'I'll get one filled in fer teh next meetin'.'

'When yeh do teh good one bring it round and I'll get Joan te make us a dozen on her photocopier in work.'

'We can have one fer every week and keep track of teh days and times,' Angie said joyfully, then placed her hand in the middle of the table as though demanding attention and continued, 'There's one thing we need te get agreement on before we go any further.' She rested her hands on her lap like she had seen Maura do and enjoyed a few seconds silence while her two partners waited.

'Go on, Angie,' Cathy shouted, glancing at Maeve. 'We've have had enough ev that poesin' from me sister te last us until she comes home again so put yer hands on teh table.'

'Well, it's about teh few hours I do on a Monday and Friday mornin',' Angie said, rubbing her elbows.

'What about them?' Cathy asked, pulling the sheet of paper with the names of the places they had for cleaning over to her.

'It's not there,' Angie said. 'I'll put teh money inte teh business but I have te do teh job. I've already talked te me client and that's the way he wants it. He wants me te do teh cleanin' all teh time.'

'But yeh go te mass on a Monday and Friday mornin',' Maeve said, 'yeh told me yerself that yeh do.'

Angie pulled her chin in like she had seen Maura do and enjoyed watching her friend and daughter exchange frowns. 'I told yeh I go pass teh church,' she said, 'but I never said I go te mass.'

Cathy was amused with Angie's body language. She also suspected she cleaned for her brother Donal because she had seen an envelope with Angie's name on it in her brother's flat. She also knew her brother had never cleaned a cooker so she said, 'If the money is goin' inte teh business then all we have te do is put yeh down fer them two times.' She picked up her pencil and asked, 'What's teh name of teh place.'

Angie sniffed. 'I told yeh it's a client, and I can't tell yeh teh name.'

'Are yeh carryin' on with someone, Angie?' Cathy teased.

'Cathy Malone,' Angie shouted, clenching her teeth to hold her dentures in place. She glanced at her daughter and continued to holler, 'I don't know how yeh could even think that I was carryin' on.'

'Jeasus, Angie I was only jokin'',' Cathy said and waited until her friend had stopped panting and displayed a few creases around her eyes, then tapped the chart Maeve had made and asked, 'What are we goin' te call it fer the chart so that we'll know if yer workin' or not?'

'I don't care what yeh call it,' Angie said, removing her glasses and wiping her eyes. She didn't even want to start a smile.

'What will we do if yer sick and yeh can't turn up?' Maeve asked, wondering if she should tell Maurice that her ma didn't go to mass on Monday and Friday mornings. It was the only thing he praised her for. 'Teh reason why we're organisin' teh group is so that all teh places can relay on us?'

'I'll make it up in me own time,' Angie retorted, giving her attention to cleaning her glasses. 'I'm never sick. Only a cold now and then.' She held her glasses up to the light and said, 'It's not like I'll be needin' maternity leave.' She put her glasses back on and stared at the chart that Maeve had drawn and said, 'Me days can be flexible.' She made a mental note to buy her client a couple of extra small pots.

'I'll take yer word fer that, Angie,' Cathy said, 'yeh have never lied te me yet.'

Chapter Thirty-two

Settled in the easy chair beside the fireplace Angie asked, 'Are yeh lookin' forward te yer mammy comin' home?'

'I think so,' Cathy replied, peeling the top off the bottle of sherry. She held the bottle out, laughed and shouted, 'I'll tell yeh one thing fer sure; she's a lot easier te get on with than Maura.' She filled the three glasses and said, 'Not a word te me mammy about er venture.'

Surprised that Cathy would think that her mammy would talk to her about anything, Angie held her hand out for her glass of sherry and asked, 'Who knows about us?'

'From me; there's Joan, Donal, Mike and Tony,' Cathy said, handing Maeve her glass of sherry. 'Have yeh told Maurice yet?' she asked.

'I'm not goin' te until were ready te start.'

Cathy often thought that Maeve was too good for her brother. Maurice was bright; he read the papers every day and talked about politics and Irish history. But Cathy measured people by how kind they were to other people, and she had always found him to be mean and selfish. She couldn't believe that he would hit Maeve like Carl had beaten Maura but she had never known Maeve to do anything or go anywhere without Maurice's approval.

'But I'm still doin' it whatever he says,' Maeve said, twisting her glass of sherry by the stem. She raised her head and added, 'He'll be happy enough when I buy teh caravan.'

Cathy wanted to encourage Maeve while at the same time she didn't want to interfere with her relationship with Maurice. She had been both surprised and delighted when Maeve had come on the treasure hunt on her own. She raised her glass and said, 'I think we'll make a perfect team. We'll be er own boss and we can make er own hours, and we'll make money.'

The girl is dreaming, Angie thought, raising her glass, but she admired her for trying.

'Anyway can I count on the pair ev yeh te help out at me garden diggin' party?' Cathy asked, nodding over to the back window. 'It's all arranged fer Saturday week.'

'Could yeh not do it fer a Sunday?' Maeve asked.

'I could, but some ev teh neighbours might complain. Yeh know yerself what they're like with unnecessary servile work on a Sunday,' Cathy said, walking over to the back window. 'I have already decided on Maurice te be in charge and see that all teh fellahs do teh diggin' properly.'

'Yeh'll never get Maurice te give up his football fer te dig yer garden,' Maeve said. She joined Cathy at the window, pulled back the curtain and smiled at the tall grass and all the weeds and said, 'It's desperate.'

'I'll get Maurice round here all right,' Cathy said.

'How?' Maeve laughed.

Cathy brushed a fly off the windowsill. 'I'll tell him that me mammy wants it done.'

Maeve straightened the curtains. 'I thought that yer mammy never went out to the garden.'

'She never does and she doesn't know anythin' about wantin' it dug over because I haven't told her yet.' Cathy replied, walking back and sitting down again. 'It's me price fer buyin' teh house. Liam and Donal are talkin' about buyen teh house fer me and er mammy.'

Maeve opened her cigarette packet. 'I'm havin' one more and then I'm goin'.'

Very clever of them, Angie thought. She believed they were buying Cathy to live with, and look after their mammy.

It was a lovely, calm, warm evening in the middle of October when the three directors of the new cleaning company greeted Maurice at the front gate of his house. The slightly bent grass of the lawn on the neat and tidy garden twinkled from the lights coming from the living room window, and the hall.

'Is everythin' all right?' Maeve asked, smiling although her heart skipped four beats. The sad face of her husband told her that his car was never going to drive away from the kerb. She convinced herself that she didn't care. He was still not getting her money to buy another one.

There was enough light coming from the hall for Maurice to see the curiosity on the three women's faces. He noticed that none of the expressions were friendly so he started rubbing the back of his neck, 'It's a lovely evenin', and I was talkin' te Tommy,' he said, nodded his head towards the adjacent house. He then opened the gate wide for them to come in.

'We're not stoppin',' Cathy said, 'we only came round fer teh walk.'

As promised, Maurice had come around to the house at eight o'clock on the Saturday morning of the garden-digging party. He had ten lads from the football digging and turning the earth all day. The lads had great fun competing with each other. The more beer they drank the deeper they dug. Maurice was on cloud nine when he came into the house at four o'clock in the afternoon for his mammy. He had expected her to go out to the garden and thank the boys. He nearly cried when he learned that his mammy had left the house without even sayin' goodbye to anyone.

Over to her friend again, Cathy thought when she saw tears in Maurice's eyes. She was near to crying with him when she said, 'All that money and teh pair of them in and out ev dryin' out places.' She sniffed to stop her tears from flowing and added, 'They should've had a few kids.'

Maurice knew Cathy was talking about Pam and Joe O'Mara. He recalled the afternoon when Una had told the rest of the family about Joe O'Mara wanting to buy Maura when his mammy had been pregnant with her.

'Teh garden is great, Maurice,' Cathy said. 'I'll make yeh proud of me when I get it all sorted.'

Chapter Thirty-three

After she had bolted the doors and switched off all the lights downstairs, Cathy wasn't surprised she could still hear the same music when she had turned off the radio in the kitchen. And when she had turned off the one in the bathroom she could hear the same sounds above her head. The music grew louder as she climbed the stairs. She wondered if her mammy needed the sounds in the house when she was on her own or if she was just too lazy to turn the radios off. On the other hand maybe she didn't hear them and she thought that perhaps her mammy was going deaf.

Her mammy's bedroom door was open, but Cathy gave a little tap on it before she walked in. There was a book on the floor beside the bed, and the ashtray was full of half-smoked cigarettes. Before she switched off the bedside light, she pulled back the curtains, and opened the top window to let the smell of stale cigarettes escape from the room.

When she had switched on the light in her own room Cathy thought about the morning when Joan was married and her sister had refused to let her smoke in her room. The two years rolled back when she pulled the curtains over. She willed her mind to forget about everything her sister had told her a couple of hours ago. With every tear that rolled down her face she forgave her sister for behaving in a reserved and distant way when she had come home from England. 'I didn't know,' she whispered into the tissue she pulled out of the box that was on the overcrowded bedside locker. She also decided that her sister was right about not smoking in the bedrooms. She picked up the ashtray, brought it downstairs and put it in the bin in the kitchen.

On returning to her room, Cathy was tempted to kneel at the side of the bed and say some prayers. But she had so much to pray for she thought she would be there all night. Also she was cold. The house was cold because her mammy had let the fire downstairs go out.

With the curtains drawn back again so that the morning light would waken her, the room seemed bright when Cathy lay on her back in her bed waiting for sleep. Among all the thoughts that were flitting in and out of her head the ones that were staying there the longest were about men.

Cathy had never met the man who had raped her sister but she knew he was the father of the man that Joan worked for. She dismissed the thought that her own daddy would do such a terrible thing. She couldn't think of any man she knew that would either. She was glad the old man had died from the heart attack. He didn't deserve to live.

After she had decided that she was never going to get married, Cathy started to think about her daddy again. She was only ten when he had died, and she couldn't remember much about him except that everyone said he was a lovely man, and that he had worked hard and he loved his children.

While she lay in the silent room trying to remember her daddy, Cathy concluded that he couldn't have loved her mammy all that much or he wouldn't have spoilt her the way he had. Her most vivid memories of him were the Saturdays when he came home from work at one o'clock. He never asked if her mammy was in. After he had walked into the living room he would go out to the toilet, then he would climb the stairs to see if she was in bed.

On the very few occasions when her mammy would be at

home on a Saturday her sister Sue and her husband Fred would come up to the house after tea and the four of them would play cards for the evening. Even though her daddy was always happy when her mammy was at home, Cathy hated those Saturday evenings because the television was always turned off.

But Cathy liked the Sundays. Her mammy used to stay in bed to rest her back. After their dinner her brothers used to go off to play football. Her daddy washed up the dishes, and gave Joan, and herself the money to go to the pictures. When they came home from the pictures she never minded helping Joan to get the tea because her daddy was also in bed resting his back. 'Restin' his back, me ars,' she mumbled, pulling the covers over her face.

While Cathy was lying in her bed reliving her evening with Joan and Flo, Donal was lighting the gas under a pan of bacon slices. He was hungry but he was still only going to allow himself four sausages and two small eggs. His mind wandered over his family while he opened a tin of baked beans and emptied them into a small pot. He lit the gas under the pot and put a dinner plate on top of it.

By the time he had taken the hot plate with his fry on it off the pot of beans, Donal had decided that himself and Liam were right to buy the family home in Plunkett Road for his mammy and his youngest sister. He had scraped what beans weren't stuck to the bottom of the pot onto his plate by the time he had decided that when Cathy was married she would be able to live in the house with her husband. He knew that Liam would not be coming home to Ireland to live, and all his other sisters and brothers had their own homes.

It was getting on for one o'clock when Donal was running cold water into the pot so it would be soaking for Angie to clean on Friday morning. When he was sitting down to eat his food, he wondered why his beans always stuck to the bottom of the pot. By the time he had finished his supper he decided that if Liam didn't buy the house with him he would buy it on his own. He sugared his tea twice when his mind was going over what Joan had said about his mammy living on her own if Cathy moved out. Joan said that either mammy would have to live with her because she had the extra bedroom, or him, or Liam would have to move back home. He put more milk in his cold tea and recalled Joan saying that she wouldn't have her. He gazed sadly into his cup and stirred the milk into the tea and thought about going home to Plunkett Road to live.

Donal had never tried to count sheep when he couldn't sleep. He found it much easier to try to remember how many cars he could hear going along the main Ballyglass Road. He never remembered the number of cars he had counted next morning as he usually fell asleep. Tonight he was counting his sisters because he was trying to find a home for his mammy if Cathy changed her mind about himself and Liam buying the house for the two of them.

Starting with Josie, Donal decided that his eldest sister would have his mammy to live with her but he knew his mammy wouldn't go there. He wondered about Una. She was still a bit hard but she was always fair, but his mammy wouldn't be able to get on with her at all. He felt ashamed that he didn't know Pauline. He could remember that she looked like Sean and Maurice and that she always used to have sweets in her handbag. And anyway England and Canada were too far away from his mammy's friends.

Chapter Thirty-four

Staff Nurse Monica was looking forward to the end of her shift in the maternity hospital when she walked into the centre of the waiting room a little after three on a Wednesday afternoon. In her usual efficient manner she called out, 'Mr. Malone.' She twirled on the heel of her polished black shoes, then walked backwards away from a small group of men that were hunched over a table as if they were playing cards.

The four men stood and looked at the nurse.

The nurse scrutinized the four faces for a second and said, 'I take it one of you is the husband of Cathy?'

'No,' the four Malone brothers chorused.

'We're her b-brothers,' Sean stammered.

The tall handsome brother raised his arm and said, 'She's not married.'

'Has she had the baby?' Donal, asked, swiping his hand over the hairless crown of his head and inhaled deeply.

'The baby?' Maurice asked. 'Is it all right?'

Donal pulled at the lapels of his jacket like he needed something to hold on to and asked, 'Is Cathy all right?'

The nurse held Donal's gaze, and spread her arms as if she was going to embrace the four of them at the same time. She spoke like a nun when she bowed her head and said, 'Come with me.' She slid her hands into the side pockets of her white dress and added, 'The doctor will see you in a few minutes.'

'Is she all right?' Donal asked again.

Sister Monica lifted the heels of her shoes off the ground, as was her habit when she was expecting to face awkward questions. When she grew an inch taller the four brothers dropped their eyes to her feet. They watched her take a couple of steps backwards like she was going to dance a reel. She turned on the ball of one foot like a champion Irish dancer and glided into the passage she had come from like she was on skates. She stopped at a door and opened it sharply. The bright light from the sun made her look a little more friendly when she pushed the door away from her and waved at them to go into the room.

Donal was the first to move. He walked into a small cold bright room that had six low chairs spaced evenly around the walls and a low rectangular table in the middle of the floor. When all the Malone brothers had shuffled past her sister Monica executed a nun's head nod as though to say well done for being able to walk and said, 'The doctor will be in to see you directly.' She held Donal's gaze for a few seconds, then slid one hand into the pocket of her dress and pulled the door over with the other.

Liam stood at the window and buried his face in his hands. He recalled the evening he had sat with Mike when Joan was in labour and he had had to leave to catch a train before her baby was born. He pressed his hand into his small face and prayed, 'Dear Jeasus please don't take our Cathy this time.'

Sean could hear and feel his heart thumping over the grating sounds of the chair he was dragging nearer to the table. Flo had had three babies in a hospital and he had never been asked to wait to see a doctor before. But he had seen other men that had been. He was frightened, he was embarrassed, and he was angry. He was angry with the snobbish nurse for the way she kept looking them up and down. He was sure she was laughing at them. He was embarrassed because he was in his working clothes. He was frightened because Flo had taken a mini cab to the house he was working on to tell him to get to the hospital straight away.

Religion always influenced Sean's thoughts and decisions. When he was a boy in school he accepted the teachings of the Roman Catholic Church. He learned the Ten Commandments and the Six Precepts of the Catholic Church by heart. He had found them easy to accept because he had never wanted another God. He didn't want to kill anyone. He went to mass on all holy days, and he went to confession every month.

Apart from thinking a few prayers for successful building contracts, the only time Seam prayed for wealth was when he backed his horse in the Grand National. And that wasn't for the money because he never spent more than a pound between two horses. He always felt clever when he picked the winning horse. He couldn't think of any words but his heart was bursting with a prayer for the life of his youngest sister.

Maurice had attended the same school as his eldest brother. He had been taught the same catechism, and he had accepted the Catholic doctrine. The only sin he had ever had to wrestle with was the fourth commandment. "Honour thy father and thy mother." He had never liked his mammy or his daddy, but he obeyed both of them. He was ashamed that his mammy wasn't here but to ease the sin on his soul he was ready to excuse her and blame anyone for not telling her. 'Does Mammy know?' he asked.

'I don't know,' Donal said, glaring at his brother. He wanted to thump him because he thought that Maurice should know that their mammy only went to hospitals when she was dragged there.

Sean stood and walked over to the small window. He didn't like his mammy either but he had never allowed it to worry him like Maurice. But just the same his mammy should be here. Cathy wasn't married, and none of them knew who the father of her baby was. His thoughts were so concentrated on believing that God wouldn't let her die as punishment for becoming pregnant and not marrying the father of her child that he didn't see the car pull up in front of the window. When he saw the white collar on the man in the black suit get out of the car he nearly fainted. 'H-how d-did Cathy g-get here?' he asked.

'Ambulance,' Donal replied, exchanging a worried frown with his eldest brother.

'On her own?' Sean bellowed, lowering his face to his working shoes. He examined his hands, then stuffed them in his pockets again.

'Angie was with her,' Maurice said. 'She went out to wait fer Joan.'

Donal stood. He was at the door to go out to the hall again to find Angie when the nurse walked in and a small tanned lady wearing a white coat over a lemon sari walked into the room.

The doctor was in her middle thirties and after bowing and smiling to each brother in turn she closed the door slowly and quietly before she sat down in the chair that was nearest to her. She looked at all the brothers as she clasped her hands and let them rest in her lap.

Sean prayed that the foreign woman would be able to speak English. 'We are a-ll her brothers,' he said, 'er s-sister isn't m-married.'

'Cathy is going to be all right,' the small lady said, nodding her head in turn to each of the four pairs of anxious eyes staring at her. She had lowered her eyes to her hands as if she was going to read some notes from them when they all heard a loud thud.

Fer God's sake, Donal, could yeh not wait a few minutes? Liam thought as he walked around to the back of the chair and started pulling his brother to lift him off the floor.

The doctor remained seated, smiled and nodded her head

as if she was used to seeing men faint. When Donal opened his eyes the nurse told the brothers to sit down.

'Angie,' Donal mumbled, moving his body forward to stand.

'I'll find her,' Maurice said. He spoke to the floor as he stepped over Donal's legs and added, 'You stay where yeh are.' He left the room without waiting for a reply.

'T-the b-baby?' Sean asked. He was already thanking God for Cathy. But he couldn't get the thought of Joan's first baby out of his mind, and he knew Cathy wanted her baby more then she wanted a husband.

'A little girl,' the doctor smiled and waited while the brothers exchanged glances and nods. 'She is a small baby, but she's breathing on her own, and five pounds is quite good for two weeks early.'

Liam leaned his small shoulders towards the doctor and said, 'Are yeh sayin' that the two ev them are goin' te be all right?'

The doctor moved in her chair, pulled at her sari and bowed her head. She was used to coping with anxiety when she talked to her patient's relatives but she had never had to deal with four anxious brothers at the same time before. But she had been brought up in India so she knew about large families.

The door opened slowly and Maurice eased himself into the room. 'Angie is waitin' fer Joan,' he said. He nodded his head to the nurse, then sat beside Donal. He avoided looking at his brothers.

Nurse Monica thought that the doctor looked like she was joining the brothers in prayer when the small woman leaned forward towards the table.

Experience in dealing with members of an anxious family after a premature birth had taught the doctor that the stress became mitigated when the baby was given a name.

'Cathy has called the baby Susan,' she said. She waited a few seconds for one of the men to look pleased before she added, 'Cathy said I was to be sure and tell you that.'

'Has she been christened already?' Maurice asked, looking like he was finding it difficult to see when he frowned and squinted.

The doctor looked over to the nurse.

At twenty-nine the girl from Navan had been a nurse since she had left school. During her two years of working in the maternity wards she had never known a baby to be baptised straight after it had been born. She threw her head back as if she was jolted by a memory and said, 'When we gave Cathy her baby she said, "Susan, little Susan." She said to tell them Susan.'

Body language and the worried facial expressions displayed on her young patient's relatives told the doctor that they probably wouldn't understand if she went into detail about what was the matter with Cathy. She examined her hands for a few seconds then said softly, 'Cathy has some internal bleeding and we need to take her to the theatre.' She moved to stand while she continued, 'It happens sometimes.' She paused again. 'There can be a number of reasons and it will be better for Cathy if we find out what the problem is and treat her straight away.'

'Does she know?' Liam asked, recalling when he had taken Joan down to Cornwall after she had come out of the hospital she had told him that she didn't remember anything about having the baby.

'Cathy has known all along that she was likely to have a difficult birth,' the doctor said.

Donal broke the nurse's hold on his shoulder when he sat forward in his chair. 'She never said anythin',' he said. He swept his hands up his face, over his head and down his neck. Cathy hadn't said anything to him, and he had asked her every time she had been to the hospital.

'Susan is a lovely name,' Nurse Monica said.

'W-what exactly is t-the matter w-with Cathy?' Sean asked. He was sure the nurse didn't want the doctor to tell them that his sister was going to die. He didn't care how dirty his hands were when he linked his fingers together in a strong grip. He recalled the priest getting out of the car and asked, 'How bad is she?'

The doctor rested her small hand on Sean's fist. 'The worst that is likely to happen is that she will not be able to have any more children.' She rocked the hard fist and raised her dark eyebrows and said, 'We will know more when the x-rays come back.'

'Can we see her?' Donal asked.

The doctor nodded her head to the nurse.

The nurse patted Donal on the shoulders and said, 'You stay sitting down.' She looked at her watch. 'I'll see if the midwife will allow one of you to see her.' She knew the midwife that was in charge when Cathy was having her baby. She was a small woman in her middle fifties who had fixed and hard opinions about the increasing number of young single girls that had been coming into the hospital to have babies over the past few years. She hadn't been able to remember an occasion when the midwife had allowed anyone other than a husband to see a new mother before the patient was back on the ward.

'Has the consent form been signed?' the doctor asked the nurse.

Maurice raised his head from the table and asked, 'What fer?'

Who is her first next of kin?' the nurse asked, moving away from the door to let the doctor leave the room.

'Mammy is,' Maurice said.

'I'll s-ign it.' Sean said glaring fiercely at Maurice. 'Er m-mammy is in England with another o-one ev er s-sisters.'

Maurice stood and said, 'I'll see if Joan has arrived,' and left the room.

'I wonder how many sisters Cathy has?' the nurse said to the doctor when she had closed the door.

'She could do with one of them here with her for a couple of weeks,' the doctor said. She rested her hand on the nurse's arm and added, 'I'll see about Cathy having a visitor.' She also knew the midwife.

When the nurse and doctor had left the room the brothers exchanged glances and frowns of anxieties but nobody said anything. The silence was broken when the door opened quietly and Sister Monica walked in pushing a small trolley. Sean moved the chairs nearer the table, and watched in silence while she manoeuvred and parked the trolley in the corner of the room behind Donal.

Liam hated hospitals as much as his mammy. He survived every visit he had made to the morbid places by finding something amusing. 'Have yeh come fer take some er blood?' he called out to the nurse.

Sister Monica was still trying to think of an answer for Liam when everyone's attention went to the light rattle of the door and they watched it open slowly.

'Joan is outside with Angie,' Maurice said, coming back into the room with his shoulders hunched over. He frowned at the trolley and moved away from the door.

Liam couldn't resist another wisecrack when he saw the solemn and depressing face of Maurice. 'Yer just in time teh roll yer sleeve up,' he said, nodding sharply at the nurse, 'Sister Monica here is goin' te take some blood from teh lot of us.'

Sean leapt out of his chair in time to catch his brother when Maurice's knees bent.

Liam laughed all the time he helped Sean pull Maurice into a chair and shove him around until he stayed sitting up.

'Don't worry about him,' Liam called out to the nurse, 'he passes out when his wife is sewin' a button on his shirt.'

'Is he all right?' the nurse asked Sean who was pulling on the belt of Maurice's trousers.

Sean continued to pull at the belt on his brother's trousers while he said, 'I'm s-sorry about that.' He noticed the nurse was quite pleasant when she smiled. 'L-liam is right about teh n-needles,' he added, smiling.

Sister Monica stayed hunched beside Sean until Maurice had opened his eyes. She pulled on his hand and said, 'I'm not taking any blood from anyone.' She went back to her trolley and disturbed the silence with the rattling sounds she made while she fumbled around with a small machine on the trolley she had brought in.

Sean stayed standing and put his hands back in his pockets. He glanced from Donal to Maurice and said, 'Are you two all right?' He didn't really care, but it helped to postpone the worst fears he was imagining over Cathy.

Four months of trying to find the man who had made Cathy pregnant flashed across Donal's mind. Right now he had no idea what he would do if he knew. Also there was nothing the father of the child would be able to do for Cathy now. He decided he would forget about the father of the baby and help Cathy bring up the child. He prayed that she would be all right. He was sure she would make a great mother.

Liam placed a hand on Sean's shoulder when he joined him at the window. When Sean didn't flinch or move away, Liam moved his hand towards Sean's neck, gripped a large lump of flesh and squeezed it.

'I know,' Sean said, 'I'll try,' he added, looking into Liam's soft face. He jutted out his chin and rubbed it roughly with both of his hands in an effort to stop the shivers that were running up and down inside his mouth. He folded his arms across his chest so that Liam wouldn't hear his heart thumping.

The doctor came back into the room. 'One of you can see Cathy before she goes to the theatre,' she said, handing the nurse the clipboard with the consent form.

'What de yeh think ev er sister Joan seein' her?' Maurice suggested raising his face from the floor to the nurse.

'I'll get her,' Liam said and left the room.

Sean was concerned about Joan seeing Cathy now. It would remind her of her own tragedy. He then remembered that Joan had her own babies now and Cathy would be pleased to see her sister. The main thing is that Cathy would know that her family were here.

'I-I'm t-teh eldest brother,' he said, stretching out his hand to the nurse. He signed the form, handed it back to the nurse and asked, 'How m-many cars have we got with us?'

'Why?' Maurice asked.

'B-because neither of you t-two are d-drivin' f-fer a while,' Sean said, moving his eyes over to the light tingling noise that was coming from the trolley.

'Just a few hours,' the nurse said from behind Donal, then added. 'A pint of Guinness would do you all a world of good.'

'It's a bit early,' Maurice sniggered.

'I know you are all worried and don't feel like celebrating,' the nurse said, 'but the Guinness would be a tonic for you all right now.' Her shoes made a squelching sound as she turned to move towards the door with her trolley.

Donal gazed at Sister Monica's straight back and firm shoulders. When she turned after she had pushed her trolley into the corridor he asked her, 'Can we go out to the front now?'

Sister Monica smiled at Donal and said, 'There's nothing unusual about either of you fainting from the stress you were under. I have seen doctors pass out for less.'

She had to inhale so that she could breathe but Joan endured the heavy sweet smell when she walked into the small room. She focused her mind on the second time she had suffered the stench of blood and perspiration.

'I held the baby,' Cathy said, holding out her hand.

Joan brought Cathy's hand up to her mouth. She didn't want to cry. 'I know,' she said.

Cathy picked up the edge of the sheet and started to wipe her sister's eyes and said, 'I have a little problem with teh bleedin' and I didn't bring anythin' with me.'

'I'll bring you in everything you need later,' Joan said.

'I was enjoyin a grand laugh with Angie when me waters broke,' Cathy winced, then closed her eyes.

'What were you laughing about?' Joan asked, wiping her nose with the back of her hand.

Cathy didn't reply.

'Good,' Nurse Monica said smiling, 'the pre-med has worked.' She undid Joan's hand so she could feel Cathy's pulse. 'Your sister is going to be all right,' she said, 'you can stay with her until they wheel her out.'

While Joan was waiting with Cathy her brothers and Angie were waiting out in the front hall of the hospital.

'D-e yez have enough s-staff te manage f-er when C-cathy is laid up f-fer a while?' Sean asked Angie.

Angie nudged Sean in his arm, shoved her glasses back up on her nose and said, 'Are yeh looking fer a few extra bob ye-rself, Sean?'

Sean chuckled and said, 'No I'm not.' It took him a few seconds to realise he had taken Angie seriously. 'I was j-just t-thinkin' that if yez w-were s-short that Flo w-would come over and give y-yez a hand.'

Angie placed a hand over one of Sean's, patted it gently and said, 'Thanks Sean, and I'll call if we need yeh.' She raised her head, squared her shoulders and added proudly, 'We're all organised.' She shoved her glasses up on her nose again, 'It's all been planned fer. All good businesses have contingency plans fer emergencies.' She lifted her bum off her chair and slapped it back down again: 'All professional ones, that is.'

Chapter Thirty-five

Neither Cathy nor Maurice were interested in the soap opera on the English channel that was starting on the television. Whether an eleven-month-old child was able to follow the story wasn't important to Cathy, but her daughter would be asleep before the first credit rolled up the screen.

The room was warm, and Maurice wanted to take off his shoes and settle down for the evening like he used to on a Saturday when he was living at home before he was married and he had been to a football match. It wasn't Saturday and he hadn't been to a football match. He had come in from work to see if Cathy and her daughter needed anything.

Along with his mammy Maurice was the only one in the family living in Dublin who hadn't attended the requiem mass for Pam O'Mara six months after Suzie was born. It was another two months before Cathy learned why her mammy hadn't attended the requiem mass for her friend.

Pam O'Mara had lived in Terenure on the other side of the city. To get there from Ballyglass, Cathy would have to take three busses so she had stayed the night with Joan and the two of them had made the journey over in her sister's little car. As they weren't related to Pam, or Joe O'Mara, the Malone family had sat in seats at the back of the church. Cathy saw the wild bushy hair of Ena's son Dominick before she saw her mammy's tall friend sitting in the second row from the altar. There were a number of small grey-haired women in the same row so she had assumed that one of them was her mammy.

The mass over, Cathy stood with, Joan, Sean and Donal outside the church waiting for the coffin to be brought out when a mini cab pulled up in the middle of the road. They joked at the idea of somebody being late for a funeral when her mammy stepped out of the cab and mingled with the rest of the people who were coming out of the church.

It would be another week before Cathy learned why her mammy had been late for the mass, and the only time Maurice had refused to do anything for his mammy. Maeve told her that her mammy had phoned and asked her for Maurice's work phone number. Maurice had refused to come home from work and bring her to the church.

Cathy had grown fond of Maurice since Suzie was born. He checked the pram and the pushchair every week to make sure the brakes were working. She enjoyed sitting with him waiting for Suzie to fall asleep when he called in.

Maurice's emotions towards Cathy had also changed since Suzie was born. He admired her for keeping her baby and bringing her up on her own and he loved the little girl as much as he did his own two daughters. He also admired her for getting her cleaning business working.

The theme music for the soap opera *Coronation Street* oozed from the television announcing the commercial break. To prevent himself from falling asleep with Suzie, Maurice sat up in his chair. This allowed him to see the top of the mantelpiece and he noticed a light blue envelope with small red and dark blue stripes around the edges. The writing was so neat that he shoved his head forward to look it.

'It's from Pauline,' Cathy said.

Maurice stared at the letter as if it was a sacred relic.

'Yeh can read it,' Cathy said, 'it will save me teh time with tellin' yeh.'

Telling me what, Maurice wondered, stretching out his hand to pick up the letter? It was over seven years since his sister Pauline had been home from Canada, but he had never forgotten the last time he had seen her. He looked over to the table where she had been sitting waiting for their mammy's sister Sue and her husband Fred to take her to the airport. The memory encouraged him to imagine he could see her small body counting out her Irish money and giving it to Cathy and Joan.

Cathy watched Maurice read the letter. 'I'm lookin' forward to seein' her,' she said.

Maurice read the letter again and recalled he had suggested that their mammy would probably be home before she had left. His heart felt heavy now because she had replied in her soft sad voice their mammy would not be home until long after she had gone. 'She doesn't say anythin' about Harry comin' with her,' he said, folding the letter and sliding it back into the envelope.

'She is divorced,' Cathy said, 'I thought yeh knew.'

'I fergot,' Maurice lied, his face turning red.

'I think most of us have fergotten about Pauline fer too long,' Cathy said.

Maurice recalled when he had asked his mammy if she had heard from Pauline since she had gone back to Canada she had delivered him such a cold hard stare he had felt sick.

'Just because Pauline didn't write to any ev us doesn't mean that we shouldn't have written to her., Cathy said firmly, 'even if we didn't know about her wanting to come home fer good until Joan told us.'

'I never knew about her wantin' te come home fer good,' Maurice said, moving in his chair as if he was going to get out of it.

Suzie was fast asleep now and Cathy had a company meeting in half an hour but she thought Maurice should know about their forgotten sister so she said, 'Before Pauline came home she wrote to mammy and asked if she could come fer good with her children.'

Maurice recalled there were so many of them that Una had stayed with Angie. Donal had stayed with Tony Murphy and Joan and Cathy had slept with a neighbour. 'I expect that Pauline changed her mind when she saw how little room there would be,' he said.

'No she didn't,' Cathy replied, and sharply. She thought he probably really didn't know so she said, 'Mammy didn't want her to come home because Harry was sending her money.'

'Did Mammy tell her that?' Maurice asked.

Cathy didn't want to tell her brother what her mammy had done with the letter and how her friend Ena and Sue had found out. She looked at the clock, then walked over to her daughter and un-strapped her from the lounger. 'Ena told her,' she said and went upstairs with Suzie.

Maurice was in the hall when Cathy walked down the stairs. 'I'll be off now,' he said, 'and let yez get on with yer meetin'.'

Chapter Thirty-six

Angie wiped her hand over the gold letters on the box she had taken from the bookshelf. She hadn't expected to find any dirt on the box because she knew that it was dusted twice a day. She smiled at the four large letters on the lid that were starting to peel away. M was for Maeve, A was for Angie, C was for Cathy and S was for sisters.

Four years and we are still going, Angie thought, recalling when Donal made the box and had given it to Cathy for a Christmas present the year the factory had closed. And ever since that day the company was known as MACKS. Her thoughts were going over the four months after Maura had returned to Canada when she heard a tap on the window. She went out to the hall and opened the door for her daughter.

As usual the room was warm. As Maeve waited with her ma for Cathy, she removed the bank statement, the week's working schedule, and some fresh charts from the box and asked her ma, 'Did Cathy say anythin' about teh parish hall?'

'Not a word, and I wouldn't expect her to until we have er meetin',' Angie replied, shoving her glasses up on her nose. She was now more pleased for her daughter than she was for Cathy that the three of them were able to secure a good weekly wage from their business. She was also sure they were successful because of their meetings.

As the housing estates expanded, the shops and services in the Ballyglass Village also grew. By the time Suzie was born there were two dentist surgeries, another hairdresser, a solicitors, an estate agent, an optician, and other small shops. With more women working they also had houses to do, and this was so successful that they could choose the days they would do the cleaning. They had three girls working with them. Cathy, Angie and Maeve did the cleaning when their girls were sick or away. The little business grew because they were reliable.

The agenda had taken on a set pattern: the bank balance, the coming week's schedule, and a report on the clients.

Cathy ran her pencil down her sheet of paper and said, 'We've lost two and gained one.' She then ran her pencil through two lines on her paper and added, 'From the end of the month yeh can strike out teh wool shop, and the shoe repairer.'

Angie crossed the two shops off her list.

'What's new then?' Maeve asked, raising her head from her writing pad. With so many of the small shops closing down she wasn't worried. They only wanted a few hours a week. But they were easy to do because they could be done anytime during the day.

'We have the parish hall,' Cathy said, resting her elbows on the table, 'anytime between eleven in the evenin' and four teh following day, every day except Sunday.'

'I'm not surprised,' Maeve said, pushing her chair back, crossing her legs and folding her arms as if she was expecting an argument. She nodded her head and repeated, 'I am not a bit sur-prised.' She slapped the table with the flat of her hand and added, 'They can afford it.' It was a good contract. She estimated twenty or thirty hours a week. And the hours were very flexible.

Angie sniffed to stop from laughing and handed Cathy a cigarette.

'The contract is ers if we want it,' Cathy said, then put the cigarette into her mouth, picked up her lighter and added, 'I'm workin' on teh church.' She watched Angie look down at her tatty slippers and wiggle the foot that was raised on her crossed legs, then continued. 'I know we need teh talk about it even though it's a good number.' On seeing the concerned look on Angie's face when her fried raised her head she said, 'De yeh think it's about time yeh invested in a dacent pair ev slippers, Angie.'

Theology had never interested Angie, but she was often ashamed of the way priests treated women. But she always felt comfortable with being a Catholic. 'I never thought I'd see the day,' she said. She kicked off her slipper and began massaging her foot and whined, 'I hope they pay, yeh know what they're like.' She recalled the time when she had helped a friend to clean the church after a wedding because the woman who usually helped her friend was sick. She wasn't expecting to be paid but she had been horrified when her friend had told her that none of the women that cleaned the church ever got paid.

'They want us to start the hall next week,' Cathy said, stretching her arm into the centre of the table and picking up a copy of the chart that Maeve had designed for them on their first meeting. Mike told them it was called a schedule. She waited until Angie had completed pampering both of her feet and said, 'I think we should do it.'

Maeve studied the schedule for a few seconds then said, 'We can do teh work erselves in teh beginnin'. It'll be different because the room is big. Not as much dustin' te do, but plenty ev sweepin' cn the floors.'

'I can take Suzie with me in teh mornin's,' Cathy cut in.

'Teh mornins'll suit me fine as well,' Maeve chimed.

'What do they want us te do?' Angie asked. 'They always want a lot fer their money.'

'Sweepin' teh floors, dustin' the chairs, tables and window-sills,' Cathy said, sitting up straight and folding her arms, 'like everyone else Angie the good old Catholic Church has te move with teh times. As it is they're finding it hard te get teh volunteers te run the bingo.'

Business is business, Angie thought and said, 'We'll do it.' She gave her daughter a sharp nod: 'After all, we are all professionals here.' She threw her head back and added, 'They'll know what it's like te meet a devil if they're an hour late with payin'. She showed traces of a smile when she asked, 'How much?'

'I had a look at the place and teh floor has teh old lino so it will be easy te sweep. Dependin' on the weather we will have te mop it over every couple ev weeks. Also there is a little kitchen at teh back. But the chairs, tables and teh windowsills will do once a week. Fer us I estimated three lots of four hours a week,' Cathy said. She glanced at Maeve and added, 'We can do them when we like except on Sundays.'

'How much are they goin' te pay yeh fer the twelve hours?' Angie asked.

'I told them thirty,' Cathy said, looking up from her sheet of paper.

'It more than makes up fer the two shops,' Maeve said. She also thought it was enough with the work they had. She wanted her ma to ease up on what she was doing, and she was also thinking about doing a course in hairdressing.

The meeting closed at nine-thirty.

Maeve handed Cathy her sherry, then leaned back in her easy chair and ran her eyes around the newly decorated room like a smug cat that had just spotted a pint of cream through the open window of an empty kitchen and said, 'We've done really well, haven't we?'

'Yer as sharp as a knife,' Cathy replied, stretching over for her cigarettes. 'Yeh'ed buy and sell teh lot of us in a minute. I sometimes wonder if yeh were one of us and me mammy sold yeh years ago.'

Maeve jolted up in her chair and cried, 'Cathy, are yeh serious?' She pulled her short skirt over her knees. Her eyes were wide open and her face was scarlet when she looked at Angie. Her mind flashed back to the afternoon in Sean's the day after Joan was married and said, 'Yeh don't need any more sisters.'

'That doesn't mean that I shouldn't like yeh fer me sister,' Cathy said, 'I know all about Maura and yer definitely more like a Malone than yer husband is.'

Angie was surprised at how often Maurice had allowed Maeve to have her way over the past few years. 'I never paid a penny for yeh,' she said, 'but in teh last few years I've wondered if I got teh right baby te take home from teh hoskible.'

'Well me mammy can't sue teh hospital fer given her teh wrong baby with Maurice because he was born at home,' Cathy said and raised her glass as if she was making a toast. 'Whatever has made him so different to teh rest ev us will have te remain a mystery. Fred said that we got er enterprizen from er Granddad Duffy,' Cathy said.

'Enterprizen? Maeve laughed loudly. 'What enterprizen was he talkin' about?'

'There's Josie with her hairdressin', Sean with his buildin', Donal with the Beggars Lodge, Liam with his pub in Spain, and he's opening one in Canada, and there's us with MACS.' Cathy raised her glass to Maeve, 'We also have yerself with yer caravans and rentin' them out.'

'And you with yer rhubarb,' Maeve added.

'That's a lot ev enterprisin' fer one family,' Angie chimed in and raised her glass. 'Some people go through their whole life with doin' nothin'.'

'Everyone does somethin', Angie,' Cathy said, 'even if it's only sittin' on their ars watchin' television.

Less than a month after Pam O'Mara died, Sheila Malone was still a constant visitor to the nursing home where Pam had died.

Chapter Thirty-seven

After what she had estimated to be the fifth phone call from a girl called Gladys, Cathy kept a record of all the phone calls that came for her mammy. When Gladys stopped phoning, Cathy assumed she had died. Within a week Phyllis and an over-friendly man called Terence were phoning every day. Every time a mini cab came to the house to take her mammy to the nursing home, Cathy would remember her Uncle Fred saying, 'Money buys people but it doesn't buy family or friends.' She sipped her sherry while she wondered how many people in the world would be happy with never having a family or a friend if they had money.

'When did yeh see Fred?' Maeve asked, cutting into Cathy's thoughts.

'It must be over six months now, out in Joan's,' Cathy said, 'he had us all in stitches talkin' about when he first met Sue, and Granny Duffy.'

'Did he ever know yer Granddad Duffy?' Maeve asked.

'He said he did,' Cathy replied, recalling the only time that her Uncle Fred came up to the house after her Aunt Sue had died was when Joan had been married. 'But I don't believe him. He was really tellin' us what Sue had told him. He said he remembered teh shop they had in Clanbrassil Street and that Granddad Duffy had no feelin's in him fer anythin', only makin' money.'

'What happened to teh shop?' Maeve asked.

'The miserable awl git was too mean te make a will so Granny Duffy's brother helped her to sell everythin' and he invested the money so she wouldn't have te work anymore,' Cathy said. She had never liked her Granny Duffy because the woman used to cheat when they played cards. She paused to drink her sherry, then looked at Maeve and asked, 'Anyway was teh caravan all right when yeh went down yesterday?'

Maeve laughed loudly and asked, 'Which one?'

'How many have yeh got now?' Cathy asked, glancing over at Angie and winking.

Maeve pretended to be annoyed when she roared, 'Cathy yer dreadful teh way yer likin' me te yer Granddad Duffy.'

'If teh cap fits wear it,' Cathy returned. 'Anyway there's nothin wrong with havin' feelin's fer money. It's what it can do fer yeh, and what yeh do with it that matters. Yeh won't find many people that work fer nothin'.' She turned her chair so she would be facing the back garden. She loved to look at the French doors that led out on to the new conservatory they built after the two of them and Mammy had bought the house from the corporation. She knew that Liam and Donal would pay her a wage to stay in the house with their mammy but she was determined to pay her share. She needed money as much as anyone else.

Less than two hours after Donal had taken her home from her sister's house on the evening Tony had cooked a lovely dinner for Fred, Donal, Joan and herself Cathy lay in her bed trying to imagine what her mammy's life had been like before her daddy had died. She wondered if her mammy had taken money from the till in the shop when her daddy wasn't there.

Seven maids, Sue had told her husband. And they were only the ones her aunt could remember. Sue had no memories of her mammy cooking a meal all the time they had lived over the shop. The maids had done everything.

During all the time Fred had talked about her Duffy grand-parents Cathy learned that Sue had only gotten to know her mother after the shop had been sold and the three of them had moved into a rented house in Rathmines. It was a small house but it had a garden at the front. After sorting through everything that Fred had told her, Cathy decided that her Granny Duffy had probably hated the baldy-headed little bully who had been her husband.

'Are yeh still goin' te do teh tomatoes again?' Angie asked.

Cathy smiled as she often did when she thought about money. 'I made a hundred pounds on the tomatoes last year,' she said, turning back from the window and recalling Liam making a fuss about buying the house and him saying that it would be an investment for him and Donal and that she could always buy him out later. She could only afford a third of all the payments and the extension cost nearly as much as the house.

Angie held her glass up like she was making a toast and said, 'They were lovely.'

Cathy's thoughts were more on money than on vegetables when she said, 'A hundred pounds here and a hundred pounds there, it all adds up.'

'That's great, and yeh were only playin' about with them,' Maeve cut in. 'It's a huge garden goin' te waste. I couldn't believe teh size of it when yeh were havin' the extension done.'

'Have yeh spent it all yet?' Angie asked.

'I bought teh greenhouse,' Cathy sniffed, returned to her chair and added, 'and I've got fifty fer teh van.'

'What van?' Maeve shouted turning to look at the clock, 'Sure yeh don't even drive.'

'There'll be no need fer anyone te drive it because it won't be goin' anywhere,' Cathy replied. She finished her sherry, leaned over and put the empty glass on the mantelpiece. She took her time and shifted in her chair, then snuggled down before she stretched out her legs. She winked at Maeve, then rolled her eyes towards Angie and said, 'I'm goin' te let yer ma sell teh tomatoes from outside of her house.'

Jeasus, Angie thought uncrossed then re-crossed her legs. She pulled her skirt over her knees and shouted, 'Teh pair of yeh are goin' mad.'

'I hope yer jokin', Cathy,' Maeve said, 'we have only got rid ev teh pile ev junk on teh end ev er road. The neighbours won't buy be happy te see another one. And anyway Emir was delighted with teh few bob yeh gave her fer delivering them. And yeh said yerself it was better than havin' people callin' at teh door every day.'

'I'll take some over to teh house fer me friends all right,' Angie said, shoving her glasses up on her nose, 'but I won't do no van fer yeh.'

'Be nice to yer son-in-law then,' Cathy, 'he's bringin' on all me plants fer me.' She stood and walked over to the back window.

'He's nursin' them like they were babies,' Maeve said. She followed Cathy.

Yes, Cathy thought, squinting her eyes to see down to the bottom of her garden. Maurice had been very good with help-ing her to bring on her rhubarb, and nurse her tomatoes. She was thinking he was like Josie with her hairdressing. The two of them worked hard at what they could do, and they were always delighted to help. 'I intend te have teh back all done before Pauline comes in September,' she said, opening the door and stepping out on to the concrete path to take in her wash-ing. 'It'll have te be done fer Suzie anyhow.'

Maeve followed Cathy down the narrow concrete path that ran parallel with the clothesline. 'It's bigger than ours,' she said, holding the pegs for Cathy. 'The builders must have made a mistake when they put teh walls up in the first place. The must've given all the houses on Plunkett Road half of teh garden that belonged to them,' she said, pointing down to the gardens that backed on to Cathy's.

'It looks like some ev yer rhubarb is ready fer pickin',' Angie called out from the doorway. She stood on her toes so she could see the big dark leaves that were standing proudly along the bottom of the long garden.

'It's nearly fourteen inches long,' Cathy said, smiling at her garden. 'Donal has asked me fer all that's ready.'

'Don't tell me that yeh have talked him inte making his own wine?' Angie hollered.

'He said he knows a man in Navan with a van who goes around the town sellin' fresh eggs fer a few small farmers, and he could sell teh rhubarb as well,' Cathy said, 'and anyway nobody gets er Donal te do anythin' he doesn't want te do.' She held up one of her daughter's little dresses. The dress was one of four that her sister Una had made and posted over from London. She was repeating what Una had told her when she said, 'Nobody does anythin' they don't want te do.' She went on to think about Maura going back to her husband.

'Who does Donal know in Navan?' Maeve asked.

'Again yeh know Donal, he never tells us anythin' until he has to,' Cathy said, feeling a little uncomfortable because of her own decision not to tell anyone who the father of her daughter was.

'Navan is only a few miles up the North Road. Teh men often come down to teh Beggars Lodge fer a pint,' Angie said, lowering her face to her slippers. She needed to hide her smile. She believed she knew why Donal went to Navan. And Cathy was right about her brother. She also knew he would tell her in his own good time, if there would be anything to tell her at all.

Chapter Thirty-eight

The neat and tidy piece of land in the back of Joan's house was less than half the size of the back garden in her family home in Plunkett Road. The chill in the air when she opened the bedroom window reminded Pauline she was in Ireland. But she wasn't home, and she knew she wouldn't be home until she stood in front of her mother again.

During her sixteen years living in Canada there were times when Pauline wanted to choke every person she met who had been to Ireland for a vacation. 'I don't know how you could have left such a beautiful country,' they would insist after they had talked about the fresh air and wonderful friendly people.

Every time she heard the beauty of her home country, and the people who still lived there praised Pauline was often tempted to ask them if they had met one of her four brothers, or one of her five sisters. Although her two older sisters Josie and Una were living in England she knew from Una's letters they went home to Ireland twice or three times a year. They were unlikely to meet Maura because she was still living in Toronto. She sighed watching a cat chase a bird. Both the cat and the bird reminded her of Maura. The cat encouraged her to see Maura as pretty and vain, and the bird she saw as Maura darting away every time she tried to talk to her.

But Pauline never did ask any of the people who had been to Ireland about her siblings. She smiled and said she had been sad to leave her country, but in the late 1950s there were so few jobs in Ireland that she had left with her husband to start a new life in Canada.

Then after her first, and only visit home to Ireland, Pauline would find an excuse to move away from anyone who wanted to talk about Ireland. She didn't want to think about her family, and she didn't want to be asked about her husband. She had no idea where Harry was, and she didn't want to be reminded about how he had gotten all his money. But more important she didn't want to remember how he had abused their twin daughters.

Pauline wasn't without news of her siblings. She had regular letters and phone calls from her sister Una. Una was nearly a year older than Pauline and lived in London with her husband Jack and two sons. During the last few years she also saw her youngest brother Liam a couple of times a year when he came out to Canada to see how the Irish pub he had opened with a friend in Toronto was getting on.

Liam is Pauline's favourite brother. She knew he had never approved of her decision not to contact any of her family in Ireland after the last time she had been home, but he never judged her. He had helped her to survive the last few days before she had left.

Well they were right about the fresh air, Pauline whispered, inhaled the cool air down into her lungs. then closed the window on the breeze. On turning round, Pauline cast her eyes around the small room. The door to the closet that had its body over the stairs was open. When she saw the empty clothes hangers she lowered her eyes to her case on the floor.

Lifting her suitcase onto the bed, Pauline recalled she had never had a room to herself, let alone a bed when she had been living at home. She also recalled how cramped the family had been in her family home when she had come home all those years ago for her sister Maura's twenty-first birthday. Her younger brothers and sisters had all grown so much during the four years she had been away that she had barely known them, and along with wondering if she would know them now she also wondered if they would want to know her. She had a few bridges to build to her family.

At least I remembered what the weather is like in October, Pauline thought when she opened her suitcase and saw her new jumpers. The sounds of laughing coming from the room below made her decide that she would leave her case until she had eaten. It was only gone ten o'clock and they wouldn't be going to Plunkett Road until after lunch. The voices grew louder when she was walking down the stairs.

'We never have pancakes for breakfast in Ireland,' Joan said, smiling at Jenny and Kate then added quickly, 'but I'll make you some if you would like me to. I like them myself.'

'Gawd no,' Jenny said, her blond straight hair brushing the neck of her sweater when she waved her head. 'This bread and orange jam is super.'

'I'm not worried about the marmalade but leave some bread for me,' Pauline called from the doorway. She smiled at her two daughters as she walked into the lovely big kitchen. She pressed her hands into her stomach. She had been on a diet for the last two weeks and managed to lose half a stone. The smell of the toast made her feel she was back up to ten stone again; too heavy for a woman who was only five feet two. Still, she thought, I need some comfort eating.

'You still on coffee?' Joan asked, pushing back her chair.

'She lives on it,' Kate said, wiping her hand across her blond fringe. She wasn't used to her hair cut across her forehead, but she had lost the toss when her mammy had said that one of them would have to change their hairstyle before they came to Ireland.

'Now watch your manners, you two,' Pauline admonished moving into the kitchen. 'You have to set a good example for your young cousins while you're here.' She rested her back on the long unit and added, 'Your house is beautiful, Joan.'

'Mom, you should see them getting Tony ready,' Kate called

out. Like her sister Jenny, she was more interested in her young twin cousins than she was in her Aunt Joan's house.

'Were we as cute when we were babies?' Jenny asked.

'It's far too early in the day for me to remember,' Pauline lied. She covered her face with her hands to block out the memory of when her girls were two years old. She felt some comfort with her daughter asking her because it meant that Jenny didn't remember when they were babies and their daddy was still living with them. She patted her short curly hair and asked, 'Where are they?' She glanced out the back door expecting to see Joan's two little girls in the garden.

'Tony's taken them down to get the paper,' Joan said, turning on the coffee machine and asked, 'Did you sleep all right?'

Pauline shoved her head back and raised her face to the ceiling like she was saying thank-you to the bed that was in the room above the kitchen and said, 'Like a top.'

'What's a top?' Kate asked.

'I've no idea, but it means that you have slept well,' Joan said. 'I think you will have to learn another form of the English language while you are here.'

Rattling at the hall door brought Jenny and Kate away from the table. They were both in the hall when Tony opened the front door. The two young girls smiled at their uncle, then ignored him. They were only interested in his three-year-old twin girls Rose and Lily. They took charge of one little girl each and Tony joined Pauline and Joan in the kitchen. He draped an arm around Pauline's shoulders and pulled her towards him and said, 'How is my favourite sister?'

Before he had married Joan the only family Tony had known was his grandmother Bella. His mother had brought him home to Ireland from England when he was six weeks old. She left him with her mother and returned to England on the next boat out of Holyhead. When he was eight years old Bella told him that his skin was always dark brown because his father was from the West Indies.

He called his grandmother Bella, but Tony always felt she was his mammy. When he learned that he had a real mother and father he included them in his prayers. He always said a special prayer for his mother because she had brought him home to Bella instead of leaving him in the hospital.

Although Tony hadn't shouted "favourite sister" the words sounded loud in Pauline's ears. She had never been anyone's favourite anything. And she was sure that she hadn't been a good, let alone a favourite sister to any of her family. She brought her arm around Tony's waist and gave him a thank you squeeze. She moved back when she felt something pressing on the bottom of her legs and her feet.

'Gawd Mom, isn't she cute?' Jenny said, smiling down on the dark curly hair of her young cousin Rose while the little girl pulled on her daddy's shoelaces. She stepped back into the hall so that Rose's twin sister Lily could move into the kitchen with her daddy's slippers.

'Did we do that when we were small, Mom?' Kate asked while her young cousins removed Tony's shoes.

'I don't really remember,' Pauline lied again. It was also the first of hundreds of lies she had told her daughters that had bothered her since she had decided to come home. She watched Kate and Jenny take the children's coats off, then help them put on their slippers. She turned round to Joan and said, 'Three from fourteen, that's eleven years ago.'

Joan poured coffee into the two mugs and said, 'I wouldn't be able to remember when either of mine first smiled at me.'

Pauline smiled gratefully, pulled out a chair and sat down at the table. She laughed with Joan and Tony while they listened to the children as they moved about the rooms. She buttered her toast in a dream and sifted through her memories of when her daughters were babies and tried to recall some funny stories to tell them.

Chapter Thirty-nine

While Pauline was enjoying her toast her second eldest brother Maurice was walking around from his house in the Ballyglass housing estate to his family home in Plunkett Road. It was a ten-minute journey that he made every Saturday when he wasn't working overtime. It was a fine day and the weather forecast promised the rain, if it came at all would be later in the evening.

On an ordinary Saturday Maurice would be thinking about the football match he would be going to in the afternoon but today his thoughts were troubled with all the fuss that his family were making about his sister Pauline coming home from Canada. He found it easier to think about his sister coming home than he did to worry about why she had stayed away for so long.

Although Cathy and his mammy were buying the house from the Dublin Corporation, Maurice, his sister Joan, and his brothers, Donal and Sean also had a key to front door. This was because if Cathy wasn't at home and his mammy was in bed they could get into the house. Sometimes his mammy stayed in bed all day.

'Anyone home?' Maurice called out when he opened the hall door. The absence of a pushchair in the hall told him that Cathy was out with her young daughter. The silence encouraged him to suppose that his mammy was either gone out or she was still in bed. He hoped she was out.

Sheila Malone was sitting in an easy chair by the side of the fireplace facing the door when Maurice walked into the room. She delivered a weak smile at her son, then closed her eyes.

'I take it that Cathy is out on a job,' Maurice said after he had gotten over the shock of finding his mammy on her own.

'She was already gone out when I came down,' Sheila replied.

Maurice sat down in the low chair under the window facing his mammy and said, 'I expect Pauline will be round shortly.'

As though her son had said something rude to her, Sheila leaned her head back, threw Maurice a cold hard stare, inhaled on her cigarette, and glanced at the window over her son's head.

Maurice recalled the evening he had been sitting at the table with Josie, Joan and Cathy playing cards when Pauline had come in after she had stayed the night with their mammy's friend Ena. His mammy was sitting where she was now. 'I will know her,' he said nervously, recalling his mammy had walked out of the room before Pauline had taken her coat off.

'Is it cold out?' Sheila asked.

The twelve years seemed like twelve weeks to Maurice now. He recalled Josie banging on the bathroom door after their mammy had been in it for over an hour. He had helped Josie to move all the beds around so that their mammy could have a bed to herself in the big bedroom where all the boys slept. 'I don't suppose she'll know me either,' he said, 'and she's never seen teh girls.'

Furious with her son for not answering her question about the weather, she was concerned about getting someone to take her down to her friend Ena by lunchtime. She had hoped that her son Donal would have arrived by now. He always asked her if she wanted to be taken anywhere when he called in. She stretched out her right foot, then slowly bent her body over and began rubbing the front of her leg.

'Have yeh a problem with yer shin or somethin'?' Maurice asked, pulling his feet in so he could lean over his knees to see his mammy's leg.

'It gets a bit itchy now and again, that's all,' Sheila said, turning her head sideways and smiling at her son. 'I expect they will take me down to Ena's.'

'If they start gettin' sore yeh should buy those elastic stockin's that Angie wears,' Maurice said. He didn't care if his mammy never managed to get down to Arbour Hill to her friend. He was surprised she hadn't stayed the night with Ena. She usually did when one of his sisters were coming home from England. He heard a sharp crack as though a windowpane had broken.

The sting Sheila felt in her hands after slapping them on the chair was always mild compared to the fright she gave her children.

It was some years now since she had resorted to slapping her hands on the arms of her chair. By way of further showing her impatience with her stupid son, she pulled some chairs out from under the table when she pranced around the room as if she was searching for something. She then went out through the French doors to the conservatory.

Maurice observed how smart and fit his mother was for her middle sixties. It spite of the fact that she was five feet two and weighed nearly twelve stone she turned and twirled about the room like a fat little sparrow. She still wore her grey hair short and curled. Although her face had developed some wrinkles around her small eyes, and her mouth, her cheeks and forehead were still smooth. She had no trouble hopping up and down the steps to get in and out of the conservatory.

After about five minutes listening to an assortment of rattles and scrapings from the conservatory, and then from the kitchen, Maurice leaned forward as though he was going to get out of his chair and called out, 'Are yeh lookin' fer somethin'?' When he heard the front door open, he walked out to the hall.

When she had seen that her son's car wasn't parked on the road, Sheila closed the door.

'Have yeh lost somethin'?' Maurice asked again.

'I left my bag upstairs,' Sheila said, walking over to the stairs. She rested one foot on the bottom step and bent down to rub the front of her leg again.

'Stay where yeh are. I'll get it fer yeh,' Maurice said.

'It's the navy one. It should be under the table beside the bed,' Sheila said sweetly.

After placing the heavy bag on the table in front of his mammy, Maurice glanced at the clock then he sat in the low chair under the window. He watched in silence while his mammy emptied the contents from one of the vanity bags she had taken from the navy one he had brought down from her bedroom.

Sheila raised her head from the eight small bottles lined up in front of her and said in the gentle tone she used when desperate, 'Would you mind getting me a glass of water, Maurice?'

Maurice gazed out the kitchen window while he washed and dried the glass twice to kill time so he could avoid sitting back down in the low chair watching his mammy take her vitamin tablets. 'There yeh are,' he said, placing the glistening glass of water in front of her. To avoid the monotony of watching her slowly read the labels on her bottles of pills, while she did or didn't swallow one or more from every bottle he went out to the back garden. He allowed his mammy five minutes to take her medicines before he returned. He stood for a couple of minutes looking out of the front window, then turned round to his mammy and said, 'Will yeh tell them I was round and I'll be in after teh match?' and left the house.

Chapter Forty

Cathy Malone had decided the Church Hall was a grand little earner before she heard banging on the door. 'I'll get it,' she called out to her eleven-year-old niece Emir, 'you stay where yeh are with Suzie.' She opened the door to a young boy of about ten years.

He held out three used books of bingo cards and said, 'Me ma gave me these te bring down fer teh box.'

'Yer just in time I was about te lock teh box up,' Cathy said, turning the cards over to check there was an address or a phone number on the back of each book.

The young boy picked his bicycle up off the ground and cycled away.

Cathy smiled while she inserted the used bingo books into the slot on the top of the cardboard box. It was the best idea Angie ever had to give two pounds for the one that was picked out at the start of the next bingo session. They didn't have to sweep them all up off the floors when they cleaned the hall. She slit the cellotape at the bottom of the box and pulled out the plastic bag with the bingo books, tied at the top, then inserted the new bag and sealed the bottom of the box ready for the next game.

The cupboard she placed the box in was in the small kitchen at the back of the hall and it belonged to the parish committee that ran the bingo, and paid her company to clean the hall. She locked the door, checked the sink was clean, and the mugs were lined up on the small shelf.

It won't be long now she told herself, pulling the chain of the toilet. Six months at the most. She pulled the chain harder. On the third pull the water gushed into the bowl. She sniffed the musty odour in the small room while she checked there was soap on the hand basin. Imagine needin' a car to do cleanin' work, she went on to muse in her head, recalling they had been asked to do another house in Ballymore, then another two, and then another three. She polished the new mirror she had hung up herself.

Satisfied that the mirror was gleaming, Cathy returned to the hall. She stooped and held her arms out to the little girl that was running up to her. 'All done,' she called down to Emir.'

'It didn't take yeh long,' Emir said, brushing the crumbs from the biscuit that Suzie had been eating while she had been sitting in the pushchair.

'That's because me prayers were answered,' Cathy said, lifting her daughter into the pushchair.

'Yer prayers?' Emir hollered.

Cathy smiled into the bright blue eyes of her brother Maurice's eleven-year-old daughter. 'Yeh know, the things yeh talk to te wall about when yer lyin' in bed and thinkin' about what yeh have te do when yeh get up in teh mornin'.'

'What has yer prayers got te do with yeh getting yer job done in two hours?' Emir asked. She had never talked to the walls. She shared a bedroom with her older sister Patsy.

'When it's my turn te do teh hall, and it's not on teh list fer te mop teh floors I always pray that it won't rain teh day before,' Cathy said, pulling on the straps around her little girl's shoulders. 'Now you take teh pushchair and I'll take teh trolley and we'll get over to the Beggars Lodge so I can put me stuff away then we can be home in time te have er lunch before we are invaded by er Canadian relations.'

While Emir fed Suzie a mashed banana and some toast, Cathy made two toasted sandwiches. She looked round the kitchen before picking up the tray to bring it into the living room. She hoped that Pauline would be as impressed with the new kitchen as Una had been when she saw it in the summer.

'Are yeh nervous at all?' Emir asked, stretching out her hand for the salt.

'I suppose I am a little,' Cathy said, smiling, then nodded a wink, 'but don't tell anyone.' She picked up her mug of tea, placed her elbows on the table and held the mug to her lips and said, 'Aren't we all?'

'Is it because of Suzie?' Emir asked, then felt her face grow hot. She had never asked why Cathy wasn't married. The brightness faded from her face when Cathy gently plonked her mug on the table.

Cathy moved her head slowly so her eyes shifted from her mug to Emir's scarlet red face and said, 'No, Emir, and I never will ever be nervous about Suzie.'

Emir bowed her head of cropped curly hair to hide her face.

'I know Emir,' Cathy said, patting Emir on her soft small hands, 'and it's all right.' She noticed the half-painted finger-nails on her favourite niece's fingers and said, 'Yes, yeh should have said it, and I'm glad that yeh did.' She walked over to the cabinet where she kept her cleaning company records and pulled out a small coloured bag returned to the table, sat down again and said, 'I know yer not even eleven yet, but yer smart and even if yer cheeky with it yeh can tell teh rest of teh family any time yeh like that I have no regrets at all about Suzie.'

Suspecting is not the same as knowing, and Cathy knew that her brothers had suspected a few of the boys she used to go the pub with to be the father of her baby. She never had steady boyfriends, but she had learned how to create and spread gossip when she had worked in the garment factory. She had her reasons for not telling her family so she allowed the gossip to make its full round until it died out.

'I'm not always cheeky.'

'Not as cheeky as I was at yer age,' Cathy said, unable to keep her smile from showing in her eyes, 'and I don't regret that either.'

'I'm terribly nervous,' Emir said, confusing nervousness with excitement.

Cathy opened the coloured bag. 'And so yeh should be with those hands ev yers.' She glanced at the clock, then closed the bag and said, 'Finish eaten yer sandwich and I'll give yeh a present.'

While Emir cleared away the table and washed up after they had finished their lunch, Cathy collected up the toys Suzie had pulled out and put them into the large plastic box she kept them in. She thought briefly of all her family as she handled each toy. For a second she was sorry she had lied to Emir about being nervous about Suzie. She wished it had been Una or Angie who had asked her. Una always knew what to do and Angie always knew what to say.

In response to a firm clicking sound from the back door closing, Cathy looked down the garden. She saw Emir's little bum roll from side to side as she hurried down to the bottom of the garden to put the tea leaves on the compost heap. She counted the years between the two of them and then her own and Pauline's. The years hadn't changed since the last time she had counted them. She was still fourteen years older than Emir, and sixteen years younger than Pauline.

Cathy had never felt like an aunt to any of her eight nieces, or five nephews. She had never even met two of them. Aunts were old and they always told you what to do. She had only known one aunt. That was her mammy's sister, Sue. There were times when she was growing up she felt Josie, and Una were her aunts instead of sisters because they were always telling her off, or telling her what to do. But Pauline had never bullied her.

Although she was only about seven when Pauline had left home, Cathy remembered she was small and she had never shouted at anyone like Una and Josie used to. When Emir waved to her from the garden, she pulled the curtain back and shouted out, 'Leave the kitchen sparklin' now.' She then told herself again she was very lucky to have so much support from all her family with Suzie. 'Even Maurice,' she whispered, picking up the corgi car and placing it with the other five under the television. She wondered if Maurice was still hoping for a son. She often thought that when he had bought the cars for Suzie he had really bought them for himself but he was too stupid to admit it. She sat down at the table, opened the bag she had taken from the cabinet and waited for Emir to finish in the kitchen.

'Yer kitchen is spotless, and gleamin',' Emir sang from the door.

Cathy closed the bag and held it out to Emir and said, 'There's teh bottles ev nail polish I promised yeh. And if yeh don't stop bitin' yer nails I'll take them back. Yer settin' me daughter a dreadful example.'

The small bottles rattled when Emir squeezed the bag, then opened it. 'Thanks Cathy,' she said, 'there's hundreds here.'

'Why are yeh nervous about meetin' Pauline?' Cathy asked, wondering how much the young girl knew about how her Granny Malone had treated the aunt Emir had never met.

'It's not Pauline so much as the twins,' Emir said, raising her eyes up from the bottles of nail polish. She put the bottles back into the coloured bag and as though she was confessing to a secret she joined her hands and whispered, 'They are comin' from Canada, and they're goin te have loads ev lovely clothes and be snobbish.'

'Yeh watch too many ev them American films,' Cathy replied, 'and anyway Canada is not America.' She recalled how snobbish and cold Maura had been when she had been home four years earlier. 'Teh English emigrated to Canada, and teh Irish and Italians emigrated to America.'

'What has that got te do with me cousins havin' lovely clothes?' Emir bellowed.

'I was talkin' about them bein' snobbish,' Cathy bellowed back. 'The English are snobbish and they brought all that te Canada when they emigrated.'

'I see what yeh mean,' Emir lied, thinking about how her cousins in Drogheda who always made her feel poor. Her Drogheda cousins were two and three years older than her. They were her mammy's sister's children and although she didn't see them very often they were always boasting about their holidays in Spain. 'Some Irish people are terrible snobs,' she said.

'Name one,' Cathy said, expecting Emir would say her Granny Malone, and her Aunt Josie.

'Me cousins in Drogheda,' Emir replied.

'Well yer cousins from Canada won't be like them,' Cathy assured her niece. Pauline could never be a snob.'

'Anyone would think teh Queen was comin' with all fuss that has been goin' on fer weeks,' Emir laughed and added, 'Me mam even had me dad clean out teh coal bunker.'

'The coalbunker? Why? Did he do it?'

'He did,' Emir nodded furiously, 'meself and Patsy were afraid he would throw the slack over her.'

'Nobody wears lovely clothes these days,' Cathy said, 'I expect yer cousins'll be wearin' jeans and sweaters like yerself.'

Chapter Forty-one

Built in the 1960s, the church stood on a rise of about thirty feet, that everyone called a hill, in what used to be the middle of the Ballyglass village. Pauline didn't know anything about architecture or building bricks but she always thought the new Church was a lovely building. Built from light grey fancy concrete bricks, the church was like hundreds of other new ones that had been erected in all the towns and city suburbs around Ireland since the end of the Second World War. 'Is there a mass at this time?' Pauline asked when Joan had stopped the car to allow a group of people to cross the road. She looked at her watch and added, 'It's only just gone half past two.' She swung her head to the church and saw there were other people walking up the steps. She also saw that most of the women were wearing large bright hats.

'Probably a wedding,' Joan returned.

'At this time of the day?' Pauline recalled that both she and Una had been married in the same church, but their weddings had been at eleven o'clock in the morning on a weekday. Una had been married on a Wednesday, and she had been married on a Monday. If it hadn't been for the church Pauline wouldn't have recognised the Ballyglass village. Many of the small shops like the butchers, sweet shops, and the shoe shop where she used to work were all gone. 'Today is Saturday,' she said.

Joan had driven past the church and she was turning into the housing estate when she said, 'Most weddings are on a

Saturday now.' She giggled when she added, 'The mass and the promises are the same.'

Promises: Pauline knew Joan was referring to the wedding vows. She had broken hers, and she hadn't been to mass since the day Harry had left the house.

The last thirteen years of Pauline's life faded from her memory when Joan drove through the Ballyglass village. Although the whole area had changed there were still a few places she recognised. The old convent was gone, and the cinema was now a supermarket. New and old houses seemed to be fighting for space between the new and old roads. She knew she was home the second she stepped out of the car and she saw the sun was shining on the high land in the distance at the end of Plunkett Road. 'I see nobody has moved the mountains,' she called over to Joan.

Working for an estate agent Joan was fairly up to date with the housing developments inside and outside the city. 'Not yet,' she laughed, 'but I think somebody is trying to find a way.'

While Joan watched the four girls get out of the back of her car Pauline looked around the road and smiled, nodding her head. Some of the houses had removed the railings and filled the garden with concrete. She assumed from the black stains in the centre of the wide concrete path that was across the road that it was used to park a car.

'Can Rose and Lily play out?'

Joan turned round to a young girl and said, 'Not today.' She ushered her two little girls into the front garden while she added, 'We won't be staying long.'

Chapter Forty-two

'The compost heap is goin te be moved over te that corner,' Cathy said, pointing down to the bottom of the garden.

'Why?'

Cathy turned round sharply. The voice she had heard wasn't Emir's. She glanced over the head of the stranger and saw Joan with Suzie in her arms standing at the door into the conservatory beside Emir. 'Pauline,' she said before she looked at the stranger again.

'I'm so glad you don't know me,' Pauline lied.

Cathy tried to cope with the shock of the grey hair and the strong resemblance to their brother Sean and asked, 'Why?'

'Because I wouldn't know you either, if I hadn't been expecting to see yeh,' Pauline lied again, bringing her hands up to cover her cheeks and mouth as if to stifle a scream. Thirteen years older than the last time she had seen her, Pauline would have known her young sister if she had seen her in a small crowd, perhaps a supermarket or a department store. She immediately recalled the evening they had played cards with Una and Joan. It had been the Sunday before she had gone into town with Una, her brother Liam, and Una's young son Shea. While Cathy was walking over to her, Pauline recalled when they were in Eason's and Una bought a bundle of jotters and exercise books to encourage Cathy to go to school.

'I suppose we all have er failin's,' Cathy said, putting her arms around her sister.

'Oh God I can't stand it,' Emir said, moving back to go into the house. 'You must be Jenny,' she said to a young girl who was standing in the doorway.

'No, I'm Jenny,' said another voice from another blond young girl over the shoulder of the first one.

'I'm Kate,' the girl in the doorway said.

Emir moved her head quickly from one blond-haired cousin to another. They were both taller than herself, and they wore blue jean and sweatshirts. 'I'm yer cousin Emir,' she said when she found her voice.

The three girls stood in a triangle smiling for a few seconds. Jenny turned back into the living room and pointed to the photographs on the wall and asked, 'Are they all our mom's family?'

Emir was so used to seeing all the family photographs on the wall under the clock that she rarely looked at them anymore. She moved into the room to look at the pictures. 'I don't think everyone is there,' she said.

Stunned at the size of her mammy's family, Kate gasped, 'Gawd.' She stood behind Emir while the two girls tried to follow their cousin's narrative of who was who in the photographs and when they were taken. Other than their aunts Una, Maura, and Joan the names meant nothing to them, so they soon became more interested in what was going on out in the garden.

Kate could see a tall, dark-haired woman holding her mom in a headlock. The woman had her chin on the top of her mom's head and she was crying. 'Is that Cathy?' she asked Joan who had come into the room to see what they were doing.

Joan nodded. 'And who do you think this is?' she said, holding Suzie out from her and turning so that Jenny and Kate could see her face.

'It must be Cathy's baby,' Jenny said.

Suzie moved her head sharply from Jenny to Kate, then to Emir, then out to the garden. When she saw Rose and Lily she wriggled until Joan put her down on the floor. She gave them all another bright smile, then rambled out to the conservatory to help Rose and Lily take all the toys out of the boxes.

Five minutes later Pauline sat on a stool in the conservatory and watched her three little nieces gaggle away to each other. The children gave her toys to hold, then took them back, then gave them back to her again. She knew she should go into the living room and be with her own girls but she needed some time to get used to where she was. She also wanted to allow the anger she was feeling towards her mammy drain out of her heart.

Every scene Pauline had imagined about how she would feel when she came home had no comparison to what she was experiencing now. She had expected to be nervous, she knew she would cry, but she had never imagined she would feel angry. She was angry with herself for allowing her mammy to bully her into staying away from her family. She should have been there for Joan, and for Cathy when she had her baby.

'Mom, are you all right?' Jenny asked, kneeling down and placing her hand on her mom's knee. 'Cathy has been crying. She said you are warm and cuddly.'

'She means I am fat,' Pauline said. She walked back out to the garden. She admired the lovely lawn as she made her way down the path to see what was behind the fence at the bottom. 'It's a different house,' she said to Jenny who had followed her.

'Emir has a sister that is ten months older than her but they are not twins,' Jenny said.

The light breeze rustled the falling leaves on the tree in the house that backed on the bottom of the garden. She remembered it used to be covered in lilac blossom in the early summer. She was in her family home but she knew she wouldn't be able to feel the joy of it until she had met her mother again. She draped her arm around her daughter's shoulder and said, 'Cathy was younger than you the last time I saw her.'

Chapter Forty-three

Using the rules of the game and making the right decisions were important to Maurice. He never decided which soccer team he would pull for until he had watched twenty minutes of a match. He appreciated fair play and tactics more than he did goal-scoring. He clapped when yellow cards were given out, and he cheered when the referee held up a red one.

There had been no red or yellow cards today. There had been no goals either, so with ten minutes left to play Maurice made his way through the crowd to the exit. He wanted to be in time for the first bus.

'Hello Maurice,' Bella Murphy said, reducing her height to five feet when she shrank her head into the neck of her anorak. Every time she saw her grandson's brother-in-law she wanted to give him a bar of chocolate. She would remember when Maurice was a young boy and Tony used to bring him home. Tony was always bringing boys home after his football games, but none of them were able to eat as much as Maurice Malone.

Maurice bent down to the little grey-haired lady, held his hand out to take her shopping bag and said, 'Been down to the butchers, Bella.'

'Fer me sausages,' Bella returned, letting Maurice take her bag. 'I expect there's load ev excitement with yer sister comin' home after so long?'

'There always is excitement when any ev me sisters come

home, Bella,' Maurice said, draping his arm around the little woman's shoulder and easing her in from the pavement in case the bus swung in.

'Sure yez are a grand family,' Bella said, 'yer mammy has been blessed with teh lot eve yez.'

A nod of his head and a smile was all Maurice could do. He didn't agree. He knew it was a common saying in Ireland but he had never thought that any woman was blessed with ten children. He was an avid reader of Irish history, and he often cried for the millions of people that had died during the famine, and the millions of men, women and children that had immigrated to other parts of the world.

Luckily for Maurice, the bus came along before he had time to give his opinion on how blessed his mammy was. As was usual, late on a Saturday afternoon, the lower deck on the busses coming from town were full of women returning to Ballyglass with their shopping.

Maurice gave Bella her shopping bag after she had found a seat. 'I'll go upstairs,' he said.

Disappointed that he didn't stay with her because she wanted to hear the latest new about his sister Pauline, at the same time she knew he was better able to climb the stairs than the women with their shopping so she said, 'Thanks Maurice.'

The upper deck was filling up but Maurice found a seat at the back. He was early enough to miss the crowd that would have been at the match. He wanted to be on his own so he could think about what he would say to his sister when he met her in his mammy's house.

How can yeh know about somethin' if yer not told, Maurice mumbled in his thoughts? He was trying to find excuses for his mammy, and his sister for what had happened the last time Pauline was home. At the same time he knew in his heart that his mammy had been a bitch.

The bus had careered past three stops before someone stood to get off at the next stop. Maurice was pleased, because it meant that at least one other passenger would get on. Every time the packed bus drove past a stop he would remember the times when he had had been coming home from school and he had to wait for an hour before an empty bus came along.

It was always the winter times Maurice recalled when the buses were full. Like many other children that had moved out of the city to the new housing estates, Maurice had to travel back to where he had lived before to go to school. The schools weren't built until five years after the houses.

By the time the bus had stopped outside the church, more people were getting off than were getting on. Maurice looked out of the window and waved to Bella who still lived in one of the few old cottages that had been there before the new houses were built. She used to tell him about when Ballyglass was a small village.

Watching Bella cross the road, Maurice remembered when he used to listen to Bella read. She had only just learned and she was so pleased with herself that she would read for anyone who would sit and listen to her. While they talked about the book she was reading she would tell him about the Easter Rising and how difficult life was for all the people.

Four minutes later when the bus was at the top of Plunkett Road, Maurice wondered what his family would be like now if Bella had been his mammy.

'There yeh are Maurice,' Cathy called out from her mammy's easy chair beside the fireplace when her brother walked into the living room.

Maurice saw Pauline was sitting at the table facing him, though for a second he thought the grey-haired woman was his mammy.

Pauline wanted to cry when she saw her handsome brother. With his face and body filled out, she thought her daddy had walked into the room, and for a brief moment she wanted to slap him across his handsome face.

Maurice met her halfway and returned her warm hug. His stomach was still churning when he sat down in the low easy chair under the window.

Chapter Forty-four

New house, shops, schools, factories, garages and petrol stations lined the new roads that Joan drove along when she made her way over to Sean's house.

'Gawd mom,' Kate said, pulling on the back of Pauline's seat so she could get a better view of the short grey-haired man that was standing in front of a car waving his arms at Joan like he was helping her to land an aeroplane while her aunt eased her car into his driveway. 'Sean is more like you, Mom, than Maurice is.'

The car gave a slight jerk when Joan yanked on the handbrake. She turned her body round to the back of the car and said, 'Sean gives a better cuddle.'

'Fat people usually do,' Pauline said, undoing her safety belt.

Two young teenage boys standing behind the woman with the short brown hair caught Jenny's attention. She assumed the boys were the cousins Emir had told her about. She thought the taller must be the eldest so his name would be Brian and the other one would be Kevin. They were both taller than their daddy, but they had the same curly hair and round faces.

While Flo and Pauline were hugging, crying and drying their eyes, Sean helped Joan, Kate and Jenny to get Rose and Lily out of the car and into the house where Sean's five-year-old daughter Angela waited patiently in the hall, expecting to be asked to take charge of her two little cousins.

Pauline stood at the window looking down the back garden. Her two daughters, and Sean's two sons were moving around by the wall of Sean's workshop. The three young girls were sitting cn low plastic chairs around a small table, folding pieces of coloured paper. Pauline had never seen her girls with boys before and she thought they looked awkward by the way they were moving about. She turned round when she heard the door open.

'Y-yer lookin' worried there,' Sean said, placing the two chairs he had brought in with him on the floor. 'I hope yer not thinkin' that yer girls won't be safe with Brian and Kevin.'

Safe? For a second Pauline recalled how she used to worry that Harry would come back for her children. 'Just wondering what they are talking about?' she said.

'The same as we did when we were their age, I imagine,' Sean returned.

'We never talked to boys when we were their age,' Pauline said, 'we went to separate-sex schools and girls played with girls and boys played with boys.'

Sean's only concern was that they would have enough room around the table for the eleven of them to enjoy their tea so he said, 'Children will always fine somethin' te talk about.'

Yours probably would, Pauline thought.

Flo came in from the kitchen and spread a white cloth on the table.

Pauline picked up a corner and rubbed it between her fingers

'It was yer Granny Duffy's,' Flo said, 'Sue gave it te me before she died.'

Pauline felt a wave of old memories flow through her whole body as she fondled the linen cloth. Her early and older life passed along the white cloth like the crest of a wave. 'It's damask,' she said, raising her head to her brother as if she was asking him.

'Yeh can call it what yeh like,' Sean said smiling. He thought the table looked like an altar with the polished cutlery and glasses shining. 'Flo only takes it out ev teh box fer special occasions.'

Pauline ran her eyes over the gleaming stainless steel cutlery and glasses that Flo had laid out so beautifully but she couldn't prevent her mind from recalling the times when her Granny Duffy used her highly prized tablecloth. She was five the first time they all went to her Granny Duffy for tea. It was the Sunday after Josie had made her First Holy Communion.

As if he was reading her mind Sean said, 'I know what yer thinkin' about, and I n-never enjoyed meself, at any ev t-them.' He chuckled: 'I d-dreaded not bein' able te get teh little cup back on teh s-saucer. And I was always s-starvin' when we left because teh s-sandwiches and cakes were so small.' He nudged Pauline in her arm and made a diagram in one of his hand with his finger and continued, 'She used te cut the c-crusts off the bread and then cut the sandwich inte six fer God's sake.'

Pauline had never spoken a word against her mammy's mother but she was a different person now to what she had been when had left her family home. 'I don't think any of us liked her,' she said wondering if her granny and her mammy were snobs because they knew that her grandfather was a gypsy.

It was getting on for seven when Flo served the dessert. It was a chocolate gateau she had made from a recipe Josie had given her.

Thinking about her weight, Pauline said, 'I think I will have to go for a three-mile walk after I have eaten this.'

'You could come to the disco with us,' Brian suggested.

'What disco?' Pauline asked.

'The one you are too old to go to,' Kevin said, scowling at his brother for even suggesting they could take his grey-haired aunt. 'Jenny and Kate can come,' he added quickly when he saw his aunt frown.

'Please mom,' Kate pleaded. 'We have never been on a date before.'

Everything Pauline knew about discos she had learned from television. They were very different to the dances she used to go to when she was a teenager. For one thing the dance halls and ballrooms she used to go to never sold alcoholic drinks. And nobody took drugs then. 'You are all too young,' she said.

'Not as long as they have their money,' Sean said.

Brian was looking forward to walking into the disco with a new blond, good-looking girl that none of his friends had seen before. 'The whole street is going,' he said.

'It's only round in the school hall,' Flo said, 'they're raisin' money fer somethin'.'

'Music instruments,' Brian said.

Pauline had never seen her girls dance, she recalled that she couldn't dance before she went to her first Cheili. She held her hand out to Jenny and said, 'Get my handbag. It's over on the sofa.'

An hour later while Joan and Flo were upstairs settling the three young girls down in bed, Pauline helped her brother to wash up. She raised her head from the sink and looked down the back garden recalled her girls talking and laughing with their cousins like she had seen other teenagers do. 'Your boys are very handsome,' she said.

'So everyone tells me,' Sean replied. He was more proud of how well his sons were doing at school than how handsome they were. 'They're b-both stayin' on te do teh leavin'.'

Pauline knew her brother meant the School Leaving Certificate. She had hated school. She often felt envious of Una because her sister had always wanted to go to school. It was because she had been kept home so often and she had missed what was taught while she was away. By the time she was twelve she hadn't minded when her mammy had kept her at home from school to mind her younger siblings.

Then when she was fourteen the only job she was able to get was working in shops. 'That's great,' she said and prayed her girls would be able to catch up with their peers before they finished school.

Chapter Forty-five

Pauline watched Tony and Donal wave their arms about like they were practising a ballet movement in the back garden of Joan's house. 'What are they doing?' she asked her sister.

'Wasting time, the pair of them,' Joan replied, 'they'll do anything but take a shovel in their hands. Come on, let's find out what great plans they have come up for the garden this time.'

'I'll follow you in a minute,' Pauline said. She wanted to cry because her brother had no hair on the top of his head. She was nine the day she had come home from school and was told she had another new brother. I was only a child, she reminded herself, recalling she had hated the little baby. 'We already had two babies on nappies,' she whispered to the curtains, remembering he was eighteen months before he had any hair.

As she watched her brother greet Joan with his wide smile, Pauline recalled the day she had come home from the corner shop without the pram with the baby in it. She thought about Josie again, and she wondered if her older sister was so tall and slim because she used to push the pram around the streets for hours at a time.

Donal swung his head and stretched his neck to look over his sisters' heads and around their legs. 'Are they back?' he asked, moving to the edge of the garden so he could look down the passageway that led to the front of the house.

'No, not yet,' Joan said, glancing at her watch. 'They should be though.' She had been so engrossed with telling Pauline about Donal's girl she had forgotten the children had gone out for a walk. She turned her back on a wave of smoke coming from a fire that a neighbour had started and said, 'I wonder if they're lost?'

'No,' Pauline called out over another gust of smoke. 'They may have lost their way but they are not lost.'

Another stream of smoke blew across the garden. Tony fanned his face with his hands, then gestured for them all to go back into the house. 'Where did they say they were they going? he asked.

'They didn't, they just wanted to go for a walk, to see around the houses,' Joan said closing the back door.

Pauline walked down the hall and opened the front door. 'They have probably been talking so much that they didn't watch for shops, and traffic lights so that they would know their way back,' she said to Joan who had followed her recalling they hadn't stopped talking about the disco, and the boys and girls they had met since they had woken up.

'That's the trouble with all the housing estates,' Joan said. 'There aren't any traffic lights, and very few shops. And all the houses look the same.'

Pauline raised her head and searched the sky.

'The rain is hours away yet,' Donal said impatiently, more concerned about the children being lost than getting caught in a shower of rain.

Pauline pointed over the top of garage on the far side of the road. 'That's where they will be.'

'Where?' Donal demanded. All he could see in the near distance over the roof of the garage was the steeple of the church.

'At the church,' Pauline said, praying her daughters would remember what her friend Jack had told them to do if they ever got lost.

Tony showed some confidence because he didn't want to

worry Joan. He started walking slowly towards his car while he said, 'anyway it's time they were back.' He smiled Joan and added, 'Sorry dear but the digging will have to wait for a while.'

'I'll stay here,' Pauline said, shoving Joan gently after Tony and added, 'You go as well, you'll only worry more if you are waiting here.' She recalled the games Jack played with her daughters about what to do if they got lost.

She turned to her brother and said, 'You go as well but take another road.' When he hesitated she said, 'Go on. We are expected in Plunkett Road in half an hour.'

Donal hesitated. This was the first time Pauline had ever told him what to do.

'They'll be waiting there for you,' Pauline said, shoving her hands in the pockets of her trousers; she rocked on the heels of her shoes and looked up to the top of Joan's house and added, 'You can see the steeple of the church from their bedroom window.' Her face glowed like she had just solved a major engineering problem. 'They'll know it's near and they'll make for it and wait for one of us to come for them.'

'I'll take the car and go round there,' Tony said, 'you two wander up and down the road. I'll come back straight away if they're not there.'

Less than ten minutes later, Donal smiled with relief over Pauline's shoulder and waved to Kate and Jenny when Tony turned the car into the driveway. 'They've been taught, haven't they?' he said.

Pauline beamed the greatest smile she had ever shown. 'Do you still like cocoa?' she asked.

'Not particularly,' Donal replied, frowning. 'What do yeh want te know that fer?'

In spite of her brother's baldness, Pauline was seeing him as a five-year-old when she said, 'The third time you were lost we didn't go out looking for you, we went straight to the police station.'

'I don't remember,' Donal said.

'It was where we found you the first and second time,' Pauline laughed. 'The policeman said you had walked in and asked for the cocoa. It was what they had given you the first time one of the policemen brought you into the station.' She was still laughing when she said, 'And yes they have, and by an expert,' her eyes shining with pride even though her heartbeat was only starting to slow down. She was also looking forward to telling her friend Jack.

Chapter Forty-six

Small light grey, and white clouds floated in the sky when Donal drove over to Plunkett Road.

'That's the Beggars Lodge where Tony and Donal work?' Jenny said, turning her head so she could continue to see the building they had just driven past.

'They own it,' Kate said.

Pauline smiled at her brother. She wondered if her daughters had set out on their walk to find the pub.

'Emir told us yesterday,' Jenny said, sitting forward: 'Will you be working there while we are here, Mom?'

Pauline swung her head around to the back of the car and bellowed, 'Why on earth are you asking me that?'

'Because Aunt Maura did when she was home,' Jenny said, smiling at her mom.

Pauline moved her smile between her two daughters and said, 'Well I have no intention of working in the Beggars Lodge, or anywhere else for that matter.'

Donal eased the car to a stop and pulled on the handbrake to wait for the traffic lights to turn green. He recalled that although he had recognised Maura's small body and pretty features he hadn't known the girl at all. He remembering Pauline was always quiet, and he prayed that she hadn't become like his sister Una and likely to fight with his mammy. His mammy was now a lonely old woman.

Heartsick and scared, but determined to stand up to her

husband, Pauline had returned to Canada over twelve years earlier and told Harry to leave, or she would go to the police and tell them everything she knew about his job. At the time she hadn't been concerned about his job, or how she would manage for money. She needed to get him away from her babies before he shook one or both of them to death when they cried.

Believing she had made a harder stand then than when she had decided to come home and face her mammy, Pauline was astonished when the bitch greeted her like she had only been away for a few weeks, then walked out of the room.

The last time Pauline had stood at the window looking down the back garden she had been watching Cathy's little bum. It was the Saturday morning of Maura's twenty-first birthday party, and Cathy was pulling rhubarb before the men erected the marquee. She remembered the day like it was yesterday. Una had called her over to the window and asked her if she had intended to make rhubarb pies for the party. The garden was so full of high grass and weeds that they were barely able to make out what Cathy was doing.

'You will wear your lovely new slippers out,' Pauline snapped at her mammy's feet the fourth time the small grey-haired lady had walked past her. 'I'll just check on the children,' she said to Cathy and left the room.

'Pauline's right,' Cathy said, 'but I'm more concerned about me carpet than I am about yer slippers.'

The hall wasn't any colder than the living room but Pauline felt the heat on her face disappear as though a draught of wind had swept in from the garden. She was about to climb the stairs when the bedroom door opened and her daughters came out.

'She snores, Mom,' Jenny whispered. 'Suzie is not even two years old and she snores.'

'Cathy always did,' Pauline said, hugging her two girls, then pushed in the door for them to go into the living room in front of her.

'I hear that you two have been walkin' around Dublin this mornin',' Cathy called out when the two girls had come into the room.

'Not the city,' Kate said, 'but Emir is going to ask her daddy if she can stay out of school to take us into town during the week.'

Cathy bowed her head and smiled. She knew Maurice would not allow either of his daughters to take time out of school, as sure as she knew that Emir would ask him. She smiled at Kate and thought approvingly that Maurice was as adamant about his girls having a good education as any boy.

Pauline sat down in the chair that was facing her mammy. To avoid looking at the smile her mammy was beaming at her daughters, she cast her eyes over the table that was set for the dinner and said, 'We are being spoilt dreadfully.'

'Nothin' more than yeh deserve. Yeh did enough fer us all when yeh were livin' here,' Cathy said. 'It's my turn now.'

'There were more of us to share the work then,' Pauline replied, stealing a glance at her mammy.

Sheila Malone looked over her daughter's head at the window.

'We used to have roast pork every Sunday,' Pauline continued, recalling twelve of them sitting down to Sunday dinner at the same table. Elbow to elbow, they managed to eat with spoons. They never had a knife and fork until they started work. She smiled at the cutlery on the table and noticed her Granny Duffy's silver serving spoons.

They had odd plates and cups but had a proper tablecloth on a Sunday. And it was a white one, not damask like Flo had last night but an Irish linen sheet. Una used to iron it every Saturday and the following Saturday it was on one of the beds and a fresh one was ironed. She smiled with pleasure at the lovely plates and cutlery, then stretched her hand out and picked up a glass cruet set that had also belonged to her Granny Duffy.

'That's yours if yeh want it, Cathy said. 'We all got some of her pieces, and I've been mindin' it fer yeh.' She surveyed the table again like she had been doing since she had laid it out half an hour earlier when Pauline was feeding Suzie in the kitchen.

Pauline's most acute memory of her Granny Duffy was that she had taught them all to play cards, and she used to cheat. She didn't want the cruet set, but she also didn't want to hurt Cathy so she said, 'Thank you,' turned round to Donal and asked, 'What did you get?'

'To tell yeh the truth, Pauline, I can't remember.'

'Yeh got the clock,' Cathy bellowed.

'No,' Donal said, waving his head, 'Fred gave me that when Sue died.'

'Sue was mindin' it fer yeh,' Cathy roared. 'Yeh know, Donal Malone, I think yer in a world ev yer own half ev teh time.'

Donal smiled an apology, then went back to reading his paper.

Out in the kitchen, Cathy said, 'I'll let yeh cut teh meat, Pauline,' She opened a drawer and pulled out four clean tea towels and four safety pins. When they had all pinned tea cloths around their waist she said, 'I hate doin' that.'

While the twins lifted the roast potatoes from the tin into serving dishes, and Cathy lit the gas under the frozen peas and the carrots, and made the gravy. Pauline stood at a unit where the bath used to be and carved the leg of pork as best she could.

They chatted and bantered while they worked. They laughed so loudly at Jenny and Kate practising their newly acquired Irish accents that they didn't hear the hall door open.

'I hope yer not botherin' with them tin peas,' a friendly familiar voice said from the doorway.

Pauline turned round.

'What's the matter, Mom,' asked Kate when she saw Pauline with her hands over her mouth staring at the door. When she turned round to see what was frightening her mom there was a smart-looking man with a mop of snow-white hair standing in the doorway laughing at them all.

'I was invited,' Fred said, walking over to Pauline with his arms open.

'That's er Uncle Fred,' Cathy told the young girls while they watched their mom cry in his arms.

'I have never seen mom cry so much before,' Jenny said.

Neither had Cathy. 'It's all happy cryin',' Cathy said. 'The Irish always cry when they are happy.' She prayed she had done the right thing with asking Fred to come for dinner. She knew her mammy wouldn't be happy to see him. But it was Donal's idea and she was surprised he had come.

'I never do,' Kate said.

'That's because yer not Irish enough yet,' Cathy said, 'let's get teh dinner in before it gets cold or we will all be cryin', and it won't be happy cryin'. And I want te have it in peace before Suzie wakes up.'

Sheila Malone's children were the only family Fred had known since his mother had died three years after Pauline was born. He had watched his sister-in-law use and emotionally abuse all her children since Una was able to stand on a stool at the sink and wash cups. He was married a couple of years before he suspected that his wife was still in love with her sister's husband. He had never liked Sheila. He hated her from the moment she had told him Terry was Sue's sweetheart until he had met her.

For twenty years Fred found it easier to live with Sue's affection for Terry Malone than he did with watching Sheila bully her sister.

Like all married women of her time, and where the firm would allow them to, Sue had continued to work after she was married until the first baby came along. A baby never came for Sue, so she had continued to work until the cancer wouldn't let her. Fred never minded when Sue had spent her money on the children, but he begrudged Sheila every penny Sue had given her. He knew Sheila spent more than she could afford on her afternoon teas in Jury's Hotel, Bewleys, and the pictures.

As he held Pauline's sobbing body, Fred recalled the first time he had held her in his arms forty years earlier. He had been terrified he would hurt the three-day-old infant he had been able to hold with one hand because she was so tiny. He removed his hand from the back of her head and fumbled in the pocked of his jacket for his handkerchief and said, 'Don't go dribbling down me good suit.'

'I never dribble,' Pauline sniffed, then ran her finger along the thin grey moustache before she raised her eyes to her uncle's snow-white hair. The last time she had seen him his hair and moustache were black. She stepped back so she could pull a tissue from her pocket. Her uncle was only five feet six so she didn't have to bend her head back to look into his face. 'You are still very handsome,' she said.

'And hungry,' Fred replied, ruffling Pauline's hair and trying to remember when it was fair and there were no lines on her face.

'We are all hungry,' Cathy said, 'so go inside and take yer place at teh table because we are bringin' in teh dinner now.'

Fred wasn't surprised to see Sheila sitting at the table when he walked into the living room. She was always the first to take her place at the head of the table. He often wondered if was afraid that someone else would take her place.

'Have yeh been gettin' lessons from Josie?' Fred asked, smiling over at Cathy. His appetite came back when Donal had ushered him into a chair on the long side of the table and away from his sister-in-law. He wouldn't have to look at her when he was eating his dinner.

'There's nothin' difficult with doin' a roast dinner,' Cathy replied from the end of the table with her back to the door facing her mammy. 'That right, Donal?' she added, looking past her sister down to her brother who was sitting on the long side of the table beside her mammy and facing Jenny. She knew he didn't cook anything more than a fry and she loved to tease him about it.

'All teh good cookin' is wasted if teh butcher doesn't give yeh a good joint ev meat,' Donal said.

'That's what Josie always says,' Fred said, leaning into the table for the gravy.

'Do yeh still buy yer sausages in the butchers, or have yeh changed to teh supermarket?' Cathy asked, continuing to tease her brother, and to keep the conversation going.

'I go inta town ever Saturday fer mine,' Fred lied.

'We are going to have Irish sausages when we are here,' Jenny said, smiling at Donal.

'They are the best sausages in the world,' Kate said, 'Mom told us.'

'They certainly are,' Sheila Malone said, placing her knife and fork on her plate and resting her elbows on the table, 'they are nicer than the French, and German ones.'

'We can get Italian ones as well in Canada,' Jenny said.

'We have Indian, and Italian restaurants here now,' Donal cut in, 'we have a pizza, and a curry takeaway in the village.' He didn't want his mammy to talk about her cruise.

Fred didn't want to hear anything about her cruise either so he continued to tell the twins about their mom when she was their age.

Donal was surprised that Fred remembered so much about when they had lived in Arbour Hill and he wondered if half of what his uncle was saying was true. He observed that Cathy was as enthralled as Pauline's girls. He was five when Pauline was fourteen and they had lived in the small four-roomed house. He recalled very clearly that there was nothing funny about that dreadful toilet out in the back yard.

When nobody asked Sheila Malone about her Italian or

French sausages, she returned to eating her dinner. She nodded her head and smiled while Fred told more stories about their Malone aunts and uncles while Donal, Cathy and Pauline cleared the table.

Donal left Cathy and Pauline chatting in the kitchen while they washed up and went back into the living room. He settled himself down in the easy chair and went back to reading his paper.

Fred stayed at the table and continued to talk to the twins.

Out in the kitchen Pauline picked another plate off the draining board and began to wipe it dry and said, 'Mammy doesn't look too happy listening to all Fred's stories.'

Cathy continued to wash the cups. 'I was right proud ev Donal when he wouldn't let her talk about her foreign sausages. She has been back from that bloody cruise since the week after Maura went back to Canada and this is teh first time she mentioned anythin' about it.'

Snippets Pauline thought. She recalled how her mammy used to tell them little stories of when she was young. Her mammy used to dole them out like sweets. She remembered how she used to dream of what it would be like to have a maid to do all the housework and said, 'The bitch was always like that. She used to dish out her information when she wanted something.'

'Or to prevent someone else from talkin',' Cathy said.

Pauline laughed and said, 'I think you're great the way you talk to her. You remind me of Una. I think you are the only two of us that could live on their own with her.'

'I'm not on my own,' Cathy returned quickly, 'and you wouldn't have been on yer own if yeh had told us what had been goin' on.' She emptied the water from the basin and turned round.

'I know that now,' Pauline said, tilting her head back to look into her young sister's eyes. 'I have a lot to make up for.'

'So does teh family,' Cathy said, 'we should have written and asked yeh about yer girls.'

'Hindsight has a lot to answer for,' Pauline said.

Chapter Forty-seven

When the table was reduced to its smaller square size and pushed back against the wall, Sheila sent Kate upstairs to bring down two flowery vanity bags from under the small table in her bedroom. Jenny was delighted to fetch the silver mirror from the bathroom.

Sheila Malone set up her stall to entertain her audience of two teenage girls.

The twins stood facing their granny with their elbows on the table and their bums sticking out towards the front window and watched their granny remove tubes, bottles and small jars from one of the flowery vanity bags and place them in some order of priority on the table beside the mirror.

A rat-tat-tapping sound like a message being tapped out from a prison cell came from the ceiling in the living room. 'I'm commin',' Cathy shouted from the kitchen, then climbed the stairs.

When Pauline came back into the living room she was greeted by her daughter's backsides. They were watching their granny examining bottles, tubes, and jars. She sat in the small easy chair under the window. She exchanged smiles with Donal a couple of times when he glanced over to her after hearing shouts of praise or arguments from Kate and Jenny.

'What is vanishing cream?' Jenny asked, unscrewing the top off a small white jar about the size of a small egg. 'It smells nice,' she said.

'Who makes it?' Pauline asked.

The door swung open and Suzie toddled in.

Sheila lost her audience.

Donal and Fred put down their paper and laughed when Suzie glared from Donal to Fred a couple of times, then put her two hands on her head.

'She wants yeh to give me some of yer hair,' Donal laughed.

Pauline's face beamed with astonishment and said, 'My God, she's clever.'

'What's so strange about that?' Fred said, picking Suzie up and sitting her on his knee. 'All the Malone girls clever.'

'What about us?' Jenny asked. 'Does your name have to be Malone to be clever?'

Pauline knew her daughters were not clever, but her face lit up and she laughed loudly. She was delighted with how much her girls were getting on with everyone. They were even getting cheeky. She was bursting with pride, watching them copy Cathy's pose with both of their hands on their hips waiting for Fred to reply. She had never seen them display so much confidence before.

'Go on, Fred,' Cathy shouted, 'after all you're the authority on the Malones.'

Pauline felt a pang of sadness when she saw how engrossed her mammy was with packing away her cosmetics. Her thoughts flew back to the last time she was here and she and Una were upstairs on the bed talking about the family and how they were all bound to change as they grew older. At the time she only had been away four years.

Buried, though not forgotten, Pauline's memories of how it felt to be alone in a room with four or five people encouraged her to feel sorry for her mammy. She recalled when Harry and his father and sisters used to talk about their family as though she wasn't able to hear them.

Right now her mammy reminded her of a child who was

playing on her own with her toys. 'Go on, Fred. Tell us how clever we all are,' she said.

'That depends on how many of yeh there are,' Fred smiled at the twins.

'There are nine of us with different names,' Jenny said.

'Emir told us yesterday,' Kate said, turning to her granny and asked, 'Was she right?'

Sheila zipped her cosmetic bag closed, then continued looking at it while she rubbed at a spot on the bottom of it.

'Jenny asked you a question, Mammy,' Pauline snapped.

Worried that Pauline was going to behave like Una and snap at his mammy again Donal said, 'Fifteen, but I don't know if there are more girls than boys,'

'That doesn't matter,' Cathy chimed in. 'It's a well known fact that girls are smarter than boys anyway.'

Sheila unzipped the second flowery bag.

'Who told you that?' Pauline asked.

'Una did,' Cathy said, smiling at her brother, 'and as we all know, Una knows everythin'.'

'I never knew that,' Pauline returned.

'Oh yes. Una knows everythin' all right,' Fred agreed.

Pauline laughed. 'I mean about girls being smarter than boys.'

'If Una knows everythin' then she will be able to tell us if we are a Malone when we go to London,' Kate suggested.

'Yeh can always change yer name if yeh want te. This business of always havin' teh father's name is nonsense anyway,' Cathy said. She winked at Fred, then nodded towards Suzie to indicate that she didn't want the girls to ask about Suzie having the Malone name.

Seduced by the new row of little tubes and bottles her granny had lined up in front of her, Kate went back to the table.

'Jenny,' Sheila called, quietly looking up from her display of vitamins, 'would you bring me a glass of water please?'

'I'll get it,' Pauline said. She was determined that her mammy was not going to have Kate and Jenny dancing attention on her.

After placing the glass of water beside her mammy, Pauline returned to sit in the low chair under the window. She could just about see her mammy's grey hair moving about above the twins' backsides. She sat up straighter to try to see over their heads. She estimated there were about ten small bottles.

When Cathy saw Pauline was stretching her neck to see what their mammy was doing, she held up nine fingers, then laughed and walked out of the room.

Chapter Forty-eight

Her arms folded across her chest, Pauline stood at the door of the conservatory and watched her sister taking her washing off the clothesline. 'Nine,' she said, folding a tea cloth. 'What are they for?' she asked, sitting down on a stool recalling her mammy had never been sick.

'Some of them are vitamins, and the rest are sugar,' Cathy said.

'She reminded me of Maura, and for a second I felt sorry for her,' Pauline said.

'In what way did she remind yeh of Maura?' Cathy asked stretching her hand into the kitchen to take her packet of cigarettes off the windowsill.

Pauline recalled on the few occasions when she had gone down to see her sister in her mother-in-law's house Maura would find about five or six thing to do while she was there. Maura would find a supermarket bill and go through every item she had bought. She would clean the screen on the television. When the silly girl wasn't just remembering to do something she filed and polished her nails. 'It's like she is in the room, and at the same time she's not there,' she said. 'It's as though she has changed and at the same time she's the same.'

Cathy lit her cigarette. 'I couldn't ev put it better meself. And teh reason why Mammy doesn't seem te be teh same is because teh rest ev us have learned how te handle her. I suppose yeh could say that we have changed places. She's the child and we are the parents. All that demonstration with her two bags ev bottles is fer attention.'

'Where does she get the tablets from?'

'Pam used to be given them every time she left teh nursin' home after her dryin' out sessions. She didn't want them so she gave them te mammy.'

Pauline was twelve when she first began to dislike her mammy's small pretty friend Pam. It was half past two on a Monday afternoon and Pauline had been upstairs rocking her infant brother Liam off to sleep when the car drew up outside the hall door. It wasn't the first time that Pam O'Mara and her husband had called for her mammy to take her into town to the pictures on a Monday afternoon. But it was the first time that Pauline had decided that if her mammy didn't have her friend with all her money then her mammy wouldn't go out so much.

'What does Mammy do when she is in the nursing home?' Pauline asked.

Cathy pulled on her cigarette. 'Play cards, and go to the bookies like herself and Ena used te de fer Pam before she died. Ena doesn't go in anymore. There's a fellah called Charlie who sometimes phones her on a Monday, or Friday. Then he sends a car over fer her.'

Pauline gasped. 'What is he like?'

'From teh sound of his voice on teh phone I imagine him to be big and baldy. All he ever said was, "I want to talk to Sheila," so I hand teh phone over te Mammy and walk away. That's all I know, but I hope er mammy is on teh pill.'

'Cathy,' Pauline bellowed, 'Mammy must be sixty-five.'

'I don't care if she is eighty-five,' Cathy replied, 'she is a randy old bitch.'

Laughing heartily at the idea of her mammy having another baby, Pauline returned to the living room. She glanced at the array of small bottles that were lined up on the table like little soldiers.

'Granny takes tablets for her blood pressure,' Jenny said screwing the top back on a small bottle.

'So does Jack,' Pauline returned.

'Who is Jack?' Fred asked.

'A friend,' Pauline said, smiling and winking at her uncle.

'He used to be a detective,' Kate said proudly.

'In that case he is entitled to have blood pressure,' Fred said, lowering his face to his feet where Suzie was sitting on the floor undoing his shoelaces. 'I might have some meself if I sit here much longer,' he said. It wasn't the little girl that was pumping the blood around his body. 'Do yeh have them keys to teh drinkin' establishment ev yours,' he called over to Donal who had fallen asleep.

This was the first day Fred had been in Plunkett Road when Sheila was at home since the day he had come up to collect Joan to give her to Tony on her wedding day.

Shortly after Sue had died Sheila had made it clear to him that she didn't want to see him anymore. He had promised Sue he would do what he could to help Sheila's children so he came up to the Beggars Lodge on a Sunday afternoon every month when the pub was closed. He enjoyed a couple of pints and he played cards with Donal, Sean and Tony.

'It is time we were all goin',' Cathy said.

'Do yez want me te drive yeh round?' Donal asked.

'Certainly not,' Pauline said. Maurice and Maeve weren't married the last time she was home so she had never been to her brother's house but from what Maeve had told her she estimated it was about ten or fifteen minutes' walk.

Donal had never known his mammy to walk further than the bus stop. He waited until his mammy had put two of her tablets into her mouth and swallow some water before he asked her, 'Do yeh want me te take yeh round?'

Cathy was surprised her mammy had said she would come with them but she also expected her mammy would find some excuse at the last minute not to go so she said, 'Could yeh come back fer her in a couple ev hours, Donal? I think Mammy would like te lie down for a while te get rid ev her headache.'

Sheila smiled sadly at her son, then swallowed another of her tablets.

Donal took his mammy's smile to be a yes so he said, 'I'll come back fer yeh at about five.'

Chapter Forty-nine

Maeve was both pleased and disappointed when her mother-in-law did not come with Cathy, Pauline and the children. Pleased because she wouldn't have to worry about pleasing the selfish woman and disappointed for her husband. She despaired of Maurice ever seeing his mammy as the selfish bitch she was. Watching him look over her head as if to make sure his mammy wasn't in the hall, she recalled the evening before last Christmas.

She had responded to his whinging about his mammy going over to Joan's three times in as many weeks by telling him that it was herself that his mammy didn't want to see. 'I'm too domestic fer her,' she shouted at him from the kitchen sink where she had been washing up at the time.

'Yer what?' Maurice had whinged.

'Domesticated,' Maeve had shouted over her shoulder again. 'Yeh know like me ma doing cleanin' because I haven't got a trade.'

Maurice watched his wife's head, shoulders, elbows, bum and feet move rapidly as she sidestepped along the sink unit. She had reminded him of a robot he had seen on the television in a car factory. He felt sorry for her because he always felt sorry for robots that had arms and legs. He was reminded of a movie he had seen where the robot had saved a man's life. At the time all he could think of saying was, 'If yeh don't stop bangin' them plates yeh'll break them.'

'I hope so,' Maeve had snapped back. 'Don't fret yerself,' she added, 'I got them from me ma and she only gave them te me because she didn't like them either.'

Relieved her temper had moved away from his mammy, Maurice picked up a tea towel and said, 'Then why did she buy them?'

Maeve emptied the water out of the basin, then turned to face her husband and said, 'She didn't; she won them at the bingo.' She pulled a towel off the ring and while she was drying her hands continued, 'Anyhow, I don't care if yer mammy never comes round here. And if it wasn't fer Cathy I wouldn't set one foot in 34 Plunkett Road.'

When Maurice turned his back to drop some cutlery into a drawer in a unit behind him, Maeve's courage increased so she said, 'If yeh really want yer mother te come round here then tell her not to. She only goes te Joan because she knows that Joan doesn't want her.' She lowered her eyes from his sad face and concentrated on doing the buttons on her shirtsleeves. 'When yer finished dryin' the delph yeh can put them in the press or the bin. I'm off te me meetin'.'

Now as she watched Maurice drying his hands Maeve said, 'Yer mammy will be around in time fer tea.'

'Sit down, sit down,' Maurice said to Pauline, waving his hands towards the dark pink, Draylon-covered easy chairs.

The house was a few years younger than Plunkett Road and was also built by the Dublin Corporation. It was the same size as Plunkett Road but the layout was different with smaller bedrooms, the bathroom upstairs and a larger kitchen. Like Plunkett Road, it had a back garden big enough to build another house on.

Pauline could smell furniture polish from the long, wide bookshelves when she walked over to the window to see her daughters. They were going into the village with Patsy and Emir and they were bringing Suzie in the pushchair. 'Have you done the back garden as well?' she asked her brother.

'It's what I call a real garden,' Cathy said, 'and yeh have every reason teh be delighted with it, Maurice, so standin' round lookin' shy won't get her out of seein' it. If you don't show her, then I will.'

Chapter Fifty

Y ou have a plot,' Pauline said, raising her eyebrows when she stepped out on to a small patio. She searched her memory for anything that would tell her that her brother was interested in growing vegetables when she had been living at home. A raspberry bush hid a patio the size of a small room from the rest of the garden.

'Mind yerself on teh bush,' Maurice said, blushing with pride. 'I'll be cuttin' it back in a couple ev weeks.' He continued to move down the garden. When he reached the end he turned round and saw that Pauline was making her way over to the wall that separated his garden from his next-door neighbours.

Autumn wasn't the best time to see a vegetable garden. All the coloured fruits and vegetables like raspberries tomatoes, strawberries, peppers, and corn were harvested. Every shade of green on the leaves and stalks were turning brown. But Maurice had removed all but the necessary remnants of his plants.

Pauline had never seen a large garden so neat and tidy before. When she saw a long glass shed against the other wall she cried out, 'You have a greenhouse. Do you bring on your own plants?' she asked, smiling over at her brother, wondering why a young man would give so much of his time to working a garden.

Reading from the small cards: 'cabbage, turnips, carrots, beetroot, scallions' that were still pegged into edge of the raised beds as she made her way down the path Pauline called out, 'Is there anything you don't grow?'

'Maeve likes a variety,' Maurice replied smiling, 'and it all gets eaten.'

With her thoughts on when Maurice was a young boy, Pauline wondered if he was growing his own food because he was hungry. She had no interest in gardening but she grew some tomatoes in the summer. The smell of the earth, and the remaining plants reminded her of the early morning hours she had been in her garden watering her tomatoes the first year Harry had left and recalled how lonely she had felt. 'What do you think of Cathy with her tomatoes and rhubarb?' she asked.

'I think it's great,' Maurice replied, 'but teh worry will be a nasty neighbour reportin' her. However that won't stop her, yeh know Cathy.'

Tempted to say no, Maurice, I don't know Cathy, or you either, Pauline ran her eyes up and down the remains of some runner-bean stalks hanging over poles and promised herself she would know them both before she went back to Canada. 'You are very good to her,' she said.

Embarrassed because he wasn't used to being praised, Maurice said, 'She is a grand little mother.'

'And daughter,' Pauline said and thought she probably didn't know her brothers and sisters but she knew her mammy. Even if the woman didn't look the same as the last time she had seen her she could still remember how she was always afraid of her. 'I wouldn't live with Mammy,' she said, 'would you?'

Maurice waited a few seconds before he lied, 'I don't have teh room.'

Pauline noticed her brother's hands were shaking, 'She doesn't need much room, Maurice,' she said, 'all she needs is a chair and a bed because all she has ever done is lie on her back, or sit on her arse.'

During the silence Pauline recalled meeting Joan and Tony

at the airport in Canada three years earlier and her sister was as much a stranger to her as Tony was. She shivered when a light breeze hit her face and wondered if she would know Josie and Una. When she felt Maurice turning his head towards her she said quickly, 'You know, it's awfully stupid but when you're away you think everything stays the same where you were before.'

Maurice smiled at Pauline's grey hair, and the lines around her warm and friendly eyes and nodded agreement.

Pauline moved towards the house then turned back and said, 'I missed all my family. And I feel bad that I wasn't here to help Cathy when she was having her baby. However, I'm here now and I know that I have been a poor mother with preventing my girls from knowing their cousins.' She tipped him on the shoulder: 'Come on, they'll think we're talking about them.'

Chapter Fifty-one

The first thing Pauline noticed when she walked into the living room from the kitchen was the large television set standing in the far corner by the front window.

Noticing the look of dismay on Pauline's face, Maeve said, 'Football?'

'It's me other vice,' Maurice said, walking over towards the front window and moving the television further back into the corner and against the wall. 'It does take up half of the room though,' he added, rubbing his hands together and calling out, 'Bewleys for everyone?'

'I'll do it,' Pauline said, moving back into the kitchen, 'I haven't done anything since I have come home. I'm beginning to wonder if I'm in the right place.'

'Come up on Wednesday and yeh can do some diggin',' Maurice said, smiling.

'He's jokin' about teh diggin',' Maeve said, 'but come around anytime yeh want te.'

As Maurice placed the try with the cups of coffee on the table the doorbell rang.

'I'll get it,' Cathy said, 'it'll be the children.' Her smile faded when she opened the door and saw Donal and her mammy. She moved away from the door and said, 'Will you close it after you, Donal?' then went back into the living room. 'It wasn't the children,' she said, 'it's Mammy and Donal.'

Maeve looked at her husband and said, 'I'll put a match to teh fire.'

'No,' Maurice said, 'it's too early and it's not cold.'

'Yeh can give yer mammy my coffee,' Maeve said, 'I'll have mine in teh kitchen while I'm getting teh tea ready.'

Sheila sat in one of the easy chairs beside the unlit fire, Cathy joined Maeve in the kitchen and Pauline stood at the gate waving Donal off and waited for the children. When she saw them at the bottom of the road she went back into the house. She was closing the hall door when Maurice came down the stairs with two stools. She followed him into the living room and when he set the stools down on the floor she said, 'Are they the same ones we used to have in the kitchen?'

'The very same,' Maurice replied, glowing with pride watching Pauline smile at the stools.

'I'm thinkin' of havin' them back,' Cathy called from the kitchen.

'Yer not gettin' them,' Maurice said, placing the stools near the wall at both ends of the opened-out gate-leg table. 'Yeh got teh silver.'

'They're solid mahogany,' Sheila said, 'they were your Granny Malone's.'

'I know they were Granny Malone's,' Pauline snapped. 'I remember them in the kitchen. They must be worth something then, if they are mahogany,' she added, smoothing her hand over the shiny seat.

'They're not fer sale,' Maurice called out when he came back in with a long plank of wood that was lightly padded and covered with green Draylon fabric on one side. He placed it on the two stools so it could be used as a bench for the four girls to sit on while they were having their tea.

Remembering they used to use a plank of wood on the two stools to make a seat for four or five of them when they were all living at home Pauline said, 'What a smashing idea to cover the plank.'

'What about me stealin' them back?' Cathy called from the doorway.

Maurice turned on Cathy and said, 'I'd go to teh police.'

'I wouldn't do that,' Sheila said, and waited until they were all looking at her before she added, 'Your Granny Malone stole them in the first place.'

Maurice felt tiny shivers in his mouth, and for a second he thought he was hungry. 'From where?' he asked. The most poignant memory of his daddy's mammy was when she came to see them in Arbour Hill. She had biscuits in her big coloured bag that she shared out before she left.

Like a spoilt little girl who had the attention of her parents, Sheila Malone stretched her feet out and gazed at her shoes as she said, 'From a bishop's kitchen.' She raised her mean face to Pauline and added, 'Your granny told me herself when she gave them to us the year after you were born.'

Pauline's smile grew bright and broad as she gazed over at the wall where the stools were waiting to take the weight of the four pretty bums. She didn't believe her mammy. She remembered her daddy's sister telling her about the long hours her granny had worked cleaning a bishop's house. She wanted the story to be true because it would be some kind of payment for all the running around the church had made her do in Canada and they still wouldn't accept the twins in the school. 'What bishop was it?' she asked.

Sheila leaned back in her chair and raised one of her shoulders so she could move her arm and put her hand into the pocket of her apron. 'I don't remember,' she said, holding Pauline's stare for about ten seconds, then raised her eyebrows and smiled at her son and asked, 'Do I smell cucumbers?'

Livid at hearing her mammy deride her daddy's mother, Pauline said, 'Granny never stole anything in her life. The bishop never owned the stools in the first place. Everything in a priest's house belongs to the parish. I expect Granny removed them to dust when the bishop had his feet up on the mahogany table reading his paper. And the people in the parish bought the table and the paper for him as well.'

The frown on Maurice's face made deep lines across his forehead and his mouth was set like a dog that was going to growl. He didn't know whether to ask about the bishop or tell his mammy that they were having the last of his cucumbers.

Cucumbers had nothing to do with what her mammy had said about her Granny Malone and Pauline knew that her mammy had deliberately changed the conversation. She saw her old mammy playing the same games, and she was sure her mammy was trying to manipulate Maurice. She didn't know or care why. It was up to Maurice to make his own stand but as usual she felt some pity for him so she said, 'We were a poor family but none of us ever stole from anyone.'

Maeve walked in from the kitchen with a white bundle in her arms. 'What's the matter?' she asked the sad face of her husband, then added quickly, 'Don't tell me teh swingin' leg on that table is gone again.'

Cathy had heard the conversation from the kitchen and like Pauline she suspected her mammy was annoying Maurice so to pull the attention away from her mammy she called out, 'Maurice won't give me back me stools.'

Maeve plonked the roll of fabric on one end of the table and said, 'Catch this, Pauline.' She held one end of the fabric and rolled the rest down the table and called out to Cathy, 'Neither will I. And good luck to yer granny if she stole them.'

Chapter Fifty-two

Progress, Cathy thought when Maurice asked the four girls if they were comfortable, and never asked their mammy. 'We are all grand, Maurice, so stop yer worryin',' she said.

Pauline stretched her arm into the table and picked up a small triangular sandwich from the plate. 'They must have taken hours to do, Maeve,' she said.

'Eat up,' Maurice said, 'if they're not all gone I'll have te take them fer me lunch.' He stretched out his big hand and took a couple off the large plate nearest to him and put them on his own plate and continued, 'Can yeh see me takin' out these fancy triangles, circles and squares with cocktail sticks in them among a crowd of fellahs.'

'I guess they would be better than pancakes,' Jenny cut in.

'Pancakes?' Cathy hollered.

'Mom makes pancakes for lunches.'

Kate shook her head at her sister and said, 'Mom makes pancakes for money.'

Shocked, Cathy said, 'Do yeh mean, like makin' them and sellin' them.'

Cheeky, cheeky, Pauline thought but she didn't mind. She was delighted because she guessed that Jenny was trying to be smart like her cousin Emir. Her daughters looked as sharp, cheeky and as full of fun as Emir and Patsy. She knew her girls were copying their cousins but she still thought; all these years, what have I done? Because I didn't want to talk about the bad things I never talked about anything. I have been like Josie, avoiding, avoiding, avoiding. I talked and said nothing.

'Sounds like a good little earner teh me, if yeh can get people te buy them,' Cathy called out.

Pauline didn't know how much, or anything her daughters remembered about when she had made the pancakes, but right now she wanted to support them so she said, 'I make pancakes.' She beamed at Jenny when she lied, 'And I make them for money.' She told herself that she owed her daughters an honest lie. After all she had already lied enough with her silence about her family, and all her siblings are her daughter's family. Apart from Jack they are the only family her girls know. They very rarely see or hear from the Harpers.

'Do yeh have a shop?' Cathy bellowed.

'If you mean a store, then no she doesn't,' Kate said, 'she sells them on the highway.'

'De'yah mean out on teh road?' Cathy bellowed again.

'Sorry,' Pauline patted her chest and continued to cough and laugh. She stood: 'My tea is too hot. I'll just get a glass of water.'

Waiting for the water to run cold, Pauline continued to cough a few more laughs. She could still see the horrified face of her sister, and assumed that Cathy thought she walked along the roads selling pancakes. She thought about her two girls. They were so lively compared to the quiet and shy children she had brought home with her. She helped Anita make pancakes because she had been pleased with something to do when Kate and Jenny were in school.

God, she thought, I had to. I couldn't let them sleep over in anyone's house. Although the doctor could find nothing wrong with their bladder they were still wetting the bed until they were ten. They were too quiet and shy to go to holiday camps. And she didn't know what they had remembered about their daddy.

'Are you all right, Mom? 'Kate asked when Pauline came back and sat down again with her face flushed and her eyes still watery from coughing.

'I'm fine,' Pauline said, picking up her cup of tea. She drank some and said, 'No Cathy, I don't sell them directly myself.' She stretched into the table and took another sandwich.

'Jacko sells them,' Jenny said.

'Yeh'll cut yer finger if yeh try te cut that sandwich any smaller,' Cathy told her mammy, then turned her head to Pauline and asked, 'Do yeh make money?'

'Gawd yes,' Kate answered quickly. She tossed her head like she had seen Emir do and said, 'We have been making them since after Dad left.'

Emir seized her chance to know more about her Uncle Harry. 'How long ago is that?' she asked.

Uncomfortable with the way his mammy was playing with her sandwich, Maurice said quickly. 'I think we should have er tea and then talk about pancakes.'

'It's nearly seven years now since our dad went away,' Kate told her uncle.

'Is that right?' Maurice said, wishing his mammy hadn't come. His face was very red when he looked sadly at Pauline.

Pauline was tempted to say, no Jenny, we don't make pancakes, just to hear what her daughters would say to her. But she knew that it was the wrong time to involve her girls in an argument just to learn about what they were thinking. Instead she stood, then stretched down the table for a sandwich from the plate at the other end of the table. She nodded to the girls and she said, 'Maurice is right, we can talk about it better when we have had our tea.' When she sat down again she added, 'If I'm talking too much I'll forget to leave room for the cream cakes that Maeve thinks she's hiding in the fridge.'

To prevent his own daughters asking any more questions about their Uncle Harry, Maurice talked about his vegetables.

After he had droned on for about five minutes Pauline decided that he was just like Josie. Especially the way he gave three or four reasons for doing things even though he wasn't asked. She thought if he was writing down what he was saying he would omit all full stops and commas.

Other than giving them snippets of information so she could hold their attention, Sheila Malone wasn't used to talking to her children. Although she was bored with her second eldest son rambling on about his greenhouse she brought tears to her eyes while she smiled with interest and approval at him.

Annoyed with her husband and furious with his mother, Maeve shoved her chair back and stood. She needed to get away from the pair of them. She stretched down the table and picked up the plate that was in front of him and said, 'While yer teachin' yer mammy how to grow cucumbers I'll take teh cakes out ev teh fridge.'

'I'll give yeh a hand,' Cathy said, 'there's no point in yeh takin them out ev teh fridge if yeh don't bring them in.'

'Do you have a cow in your garden that you didn't show me, Maurice?' Pauline asked, gazing at the plate of fresh cream pastries Maeve had placed on the table.

Maurice coughed a laugh and said, 'I don't have a cow, but I'm thinkin' ev getting a few chickens.' He very seldom made a joke, but he enjoyed this one because his mammy was smiling at him.

Patsy's round face glowed with embarrassment.

'I think that's a great idea,' Cathy said.

'In the back garden?' Emir asked, already composing what she would tell her friends in school. She cupped her hands like she was holding something and said, 'Little yellow ones?'

'Mammy?' Patsy roared. She had never helped her daddy with his vegetable plot, but she pruned and deadheaded the roses in the front garden. 'Daddy's goin' te have chickens in the front garden.'

'He's certainly not puttin' them in me kitchen,' Maeve said. She had never known her husband to be funny in front of his mammy before. She held a plate of cakes out to her eldest daughter and said, 'If his mother wouldn't let him have chickens in her kitchen then he's not havin' them in mine. They can stay out in the back garden and eat his cabbages and peas.'

'Come on, Maeve,' Pauline cut in, 'the kitchen in Plunkett Road was too small for chickens when Maurice was living at home.' She wanted to cry with delight at the stunned expression on her two daughters' faces.

Cathy picked a chocolate éclair off the plate that Maeve was holding out. She cut it into small pieces for her daughter, then said, 'I don't fancy boiled eggs smellin' like cabbages, roses or peas.'

'It wasn't all that long ago when all Irish families kept pigs in the back garden and chickens in the kitchen,' Maurice said, smiling down at the table at his mammy.

'I wouldn't mind yer havin' a couple ev pigs,' Maeve said, 'as long as they don't come inte me kitchen and yeh slaughter them when I am at me meetin'. I wouldn't want te hear them screamin'.'

'You will need a barrow or something to collect the slops,' Pauline said, smiling at her mammy.

'I can almost taste the roast pork already,' Cathy said.

Delighted with his sisters for taking on his joke, Maurice said, 'Patsy can use the old pram I have in the attic to collect teh slops. I'm only intendin' te get a couple ev pigs so that should be enough fer two pigs.'

'What are slops?' Patsy asked.

'Vegetable peelings, and food remains,' Pauline said, 'the neighbours will keep them for you if you ask them.'

'Mammy,' Patsy shouted.

'Your Great Granddad Malone used to collect slops before he married your great grandmother,' Cathy said.

'The slops have to be cooked before they are fed to pigs,' Sheila said, smiling at Maeve.

'Is that right, Daddy?' Emir asked.

'You really wouldn't get a pig. Would you, Daddy?' Patsy asked.

'Would you like me to?' Maurice asked.

'Is it true about teh slops, Daddy?' Emir asked.

'I didn't know they had te be cooked,' Maurice said.

'I mean about yer granddad collecting them before he was married?' Emir said.

'I hope,' Sheila Malone called out raising her head to her son, 'that you will grow more courgettes next year. This year's were better than any I have ever had in any restaurant.'

'It's the way I cook them,' Cathy said, 'I always use butter.'

As usual Sheila made a statement when someone was asked a question that she didn't want to hear the answer to. However, Pauline had never heard her mammy praise her or any of her siblings. She suspected her mammy didn't want her grandchildren to know about her own father. She looked at Patsy and said, 'Yes, our Granddad Duffy collected slops before he married our grandmother. He worked for our grandmother's father, and he did many other jobs too. He may have been a mean man but he worked hard all his life for his family. He also sent his daughters to secondary schools.'

'Yer not really goin' te get pigs are yeh, Daddy?' Patsy said.

'Not at teh moment,' Maurice said, smiling triumphantly, pleased at the entertainment he had given his sisters and the children. 'I will have te think about how I will cook teh slops.'

'While yer thinkin' about yer pigs, chickens and slops,' Maeve said, 'Patsy and Emir can think about who will wash and who will dry the delph before they go over to their friends to watch their television.'

'Is your television broken?' Pauline asked, swinging her head round to the window.

'I hope not,' Maurice said.

'Daddy doesn't turn on teh television when we have visitors,' Patsy said.

Chapter Fifty-three

When Maurice came back into the living room after bringing the stools upstairs, he glanced longingly over his mammy's head at the big television set in the corner recess by the window.

'Would you like me to move?' Sheila asked, smiling at her son. She expected he would know that she would want the television turned on.

'Not at all,' Maurice said, stretching his arm over to the mantelpiece for a box of matches. He lit the papers in the fire grate.

'Teh fire will be goin' grand by teh time Joan and Angie come round,' Cathy said. She was sitting in the chair facing her mammy and getting Suzie ready for bed.

Sheila closed her eyes and sniffed.

'Excuse me, Daddy,' Emir called out from the kitchen doorway.

Maurice moved to give his daughter some space. 'Take yer time,' he said when he saw the china plates in her hands.

Emir and Kate emerged from the kitchen with their heads bowed over their outstretched hands carrying more plates.

Emir put her plates on the table. 'I'll get teh boxes,' she said, 'I know where they are.' She then squeezed past her daddy's long legs and ran upstairs.

'Imagine,' Kate said, tilting her head back so she could look up at her uncle, 'these are over eighty years old.' She ran her fingers over the top of one of the plates, then held the plate out to her granny.

'Yer cousin wasn't tellin' you,' Cathy said pulling Suzie's hand back from the plate at the same time as her mammy took the delicate piece of china from Kate.

No matter how angry her mammy was, Cathy had never seen her throw anything, or deliberately break a mug. She had often wondered how exaggerated the stories that her sister Una had told her about her mammy's temper. She knew her mammy was angry now because Maurice hadn't turned on the television. While she watched her mammy read the small blurred writing on the back of the plate, she recalled Una telling her that when Josie was four she had her shoulder in plaster for weeks. Her mammy had thrown a small brass brush handle at their daddy and it had hit Josie when their daddy had ducked.

The plate her mammy was studying was as thin as a sheet of paper and as light as a feather so Cathy wasn't concerned about who would get hit with it if her mammy threw it across the room. But she could sense her mammy's temper was hot enough to throw it anyway.

Loneliness is different for everyone Una had told her youngest sister. Una had also said that their mammy had been lonely all her life. Within two weeks of talking to Una and after her mammy's friend had been dead for a month, Cathy agreed. Her mammy continued to go down to the nursing home to visit other lonely patients as if she was still visiting Pam.

Sheila didn't throw the plate, but Cathy shot out her foot in time to kick the plate that her mammy had dropped into the hearth out onto the carpet.

'Don't worry.' Cathy smiled at the horrified face of Kate, 'yer granny's hands are not as strong as they used to be.' She picked the plate off the floor and handed it to her niece.

'I said take yer time.' Maurice spoke louder this time when he moved so that Emir could squeeze past him again with three old and tattered boxes in her hands.

'If yeh break them plates yeh won't be goin' te yer friend's house,' Maeve said from the doorway. She plonked Suzie's bottle of milk on the floor beside Cathy and took the boxes from Emir. 'I really must get better ones,' she said, 'these are fallin' te pieces. The tissue paper is teh same as when me ma gave them te me.'

'I can do it, Mammy,' Emir said, smoothing out the tissue paper.

Maeve raised her eyes to Suzie who was struggling on Cathy's lap trying to get down on the floor.

'Teh only place she's goin' te is upstairs,' Cathy said, picking the bottle of milk off the floor.

'It's in er room,' Maurice said, moving away from the door.

'Yer very good, Maurice,' Cathy said, smiling up at her brother.

Chapter Fifty-four

Cathy lay down on the bed and listened to the drone of voices from the room below while Suzie drank her bottle of milk. She woke with a start after twenty minutes when she heard the doorbell, then Joan's voice in the hall. She laid her sleeping little girl in the cot that Maurice had borrowed from a neighbour. She went into the girl's room, picked up a large box, then went down the stairs to get rid of her mammy.

The voices grew louder when Cathy opened the door. She placed a finger on her mouth and said, 'Keep yer voice down fer a while.' She placed the box on the table.

Maurice knew the box. 'What are yeh goin' te do with that?' he asked.

'Play snakes and ladders,' Cathy said, then added quickly, 'Emir said we could borrow it.'

Ten minutes later as if to make sure her mammy wouldn't change her mind, Cathy walked down to the front gate and watched her get into Maurice's. 'Leave teh catch on the door fer Angie,' she said to Maeve when she walked back into the hall.

'Me ma's not comin' round,' Maeve said.

'Yeh can't be sure, and I don't want te bell te waken Suzie.'

'Yeh know yerself, Cathy, that me ma would never come round when she knows that your mammy is here,' Maeve called over her shoulder walking into the kitchen.

'But me mammy isn't here,' Cathy smiled.

'Me ma doesn't know that,' Maeve said, collecting the wet tea cloths.

'She does, and she's on her way round while we are arguing.'

Maeve threw the wet teacloths into a plastic box under the sink and yelled, 'Are yeh tellin' me that yeh planned all this?' The memory of her mother-in-law's face encouraged her to smile so she lowered her voice and said, 'Yeh could have told me.'

Cathy didn't want to tell her friend about her mammy dropping the plate. 'Anyhow,' she said, 'Maurice will be happier watchin' television with his mammy than playin' snakes and ladders.'

Maeve turned on the tap and held her hands under the water. 'I'm sorry fer shoutin' at yeh.' She knew that Cathy needed all the help she could get with her mammy. 'I'm delighted me ma is comin'. I'll get the small chair from upstairs.'

Climbing the stairs to get the small low chair for her ma, Maeve thought back to the Sunday evening she was formally introduced to her husband's mammy. She had come over to the house after tea to play cards with Maurice, Joan and their young brother Liam. They weren't expecting their mammy in until after eleven.

'Her own bloody chair,' Maeve hissed, opening the door to her bedroom and recalled she had been sitting in the easy chair with her back to the front window when the awful woman had walked in. 'I wouldn't do it now,' she said, closing the door.

Joan walked over to the window and looked out at the gate as if she was making sure her brother's car hadn't come back. 'For a minute there I was afraid that he wouldn't want to go,' she said.

Cathy lifted Suzie's holdall bag on to her lap. 'I'm surprised she came in teh first place,' she said, rummaging down the bag.

She pulled out toys, and nappies and dropped them on her lap. She then pulled out a small bottle of vodka, nodded sharply to Pauline and said, 'Sit down; a drop of this'll revive yer spirits.'

'There's nothing wrong with my spirits,' Pauline said, 'but I am exhausted.'

'I don't see how. All yeh'ev done is a bit ev washin' up,' Cathy said, returning the things she had taken out of the hold-all bag, 'yeh said yerself that we have yeh spoilt since yeh came home.'

'It's my brain that's tired,' Pauline said.

The door from the hall opened slowly and the bottom of a small low armless chair covered in light pink cotton moved into the room followed by the side of Maeve's face. She spoke softly over her shoulder towards the hall door when she said, 'Yeh can close it now, and take teh catch off.'

Angie Dolan curled her small shoulders and patted the grey ponytail on the back of her head with one hand as she walked into the room after her daughter. 'I see ye'hev started without me,' she said giggling and moving about the room hugging her large handbag as though it was her partner and she was dancing. She then withdrew a bottle of Harvest Bristol Cream, put it on the coffee table and sat down on the pink chair.

Cathy frowned but didn't try to hide her smile and shouted, 'Did yeh not bring any mixers?'

Angie glanced at Pauline before she lifted her bum a couple of inches off her chair, pulled her skirt down to her knees, then dropped her bum on to her chair again. She pointed to the row of bottles in the hearth at Joan's feet and shouted back at Cathy, 'Yeh have plenty.' She then shoved her glasses up on her nose and glanced at Pauline again.

During the years she had lived in Plunkett Road, Angie had been a friend to all the Malone children except Josie, Maura and Pauline. Josie had never made any effort to be friendly with any of the neighbours. Una talked to anyone who would stand and listen to her. It was the younger children that Angie had gotten to know because they played out on the road. Pauline was quiet and she had the family chores to do on her own after her two older sisters had moved to England so she little time to give to the neighbours. Maura was always mean and spiteful.

Maeve's face was bright and proud when she said, 'This is me ma, Pauline.'

Pauline closed her eyes as though she could shut away the embarrassment she was sure everyone was able to see on her face. She stood, then leaned over to Angie and kissed her on the side of the face and said, 'I hope you will forgive me but I don't remember you at all.'

'Sixteen years is a long time te remember anyone,' Angie said. She wouldn't have known Pauline either if she hadn't been looking out of her front window when Joan had brought her up to her family home yesterday.

Chapter Fifty-five

I take it that everyone is comfortable?' Cathy said when they were sitting around the fire.

'Not really,' Angie said, flapping her elbows. I don't have anythin' te rest me arms on.'

'I wasn't askin' you,' Cathy returned, 'I was askin' Pauline, she's goin te tell us all about her pancake business.'

Astonished to hear Cathy talk to a woman as old as her mammy as if Angie was a child, Pauline said, 'Take mine. My chair has arms and I like low chairs.'

'No Pauline stay where you are,' Joan said, 'mine will be better.'

Maeve put her hand on Joan's arm and said, 'I'm the one that should be movin'.' She looked down at her giggling mammy and added, 'Me ma'll see better from this one.' She leaned into the table and moved the glasses while she said, 'Now watch that yeh don't spill anythin'.'

Pauline recovered from the shock of the way Cathy had spoken to Maeve's ma when she watched Angie's shoulders vibrating. Angie's glasses fell into her lap because she was laughing so much that her head was bent over towards her knees and her chin was in her chest.

'Well, yer not gettin' mine,' Cathy shouted again while Angie was putting her glasses back on. 'Yer getting as bad as me mammy with wantin' special attention.'

Angie flapped her arms into the sides of the chair; then

brushed her hands along the floor and shouted, 'Honestly Cathy, look at me.' She then tried to swing her arms like a soldier and roared, 'I could paddle up the Liffey in this chair.' She raised her head in response to Joan's loud laugh; 'I look like yer brother Maurice when he's sittin' under teh winda in Plunkett Road.'

'Waiting for his mammy te say thanks for coming round to see me, Maurice,' Joan cut in, then laughed louder.

With her glass in her lap again, Angie had to move her head around the four laughing faces to find Cathy because she couldn't see with her eyes crossed and tears running out of them. She shouted, 'I'm sorry, girls, but I couldn't wait anywhere fer yer mammy te say anythin' te me.'

Flutters of guilt and shame crept into Pauline's thoughts while she laughed. Although she had no love in her heart for her mammy she had never laughed at her before. She was sure they were all laughing at Angie being offered three chairs, and at the same time she believed her sisters and Maeve were laughing at her mammy and Maurice. She also worried about telling them about making pancakes.

'Yez are spoilin' me,' Angie cried when she could get her breath from laughing.

'Angie is right,' Pauline said after she had taken a tissue and passed the box back to Maeve. 'Maurice looked very uncomfortable yesterday afternoon when he was sitting on the low chair under the window in Plunkett Road. And I felt I was sitting on the floor myself. Chairs like that are all right for a short time, but you do need something to rest your arms on if you want to be comfortable.'

'Then you're not sittin' on it,' Cathy yelled.

'I'll tell yeh what we'll do,' Maeve said, 'we'll put me ma's chair between Pauline's and mine and we can share teh arms.'

Taking care not to knock over the glasses on the coffee table, Joan and Maeve moved the chairs and they all sat down again.

'Yez look like three stupid nuns waitin' fer te go te heaven and yer not sure yeh'll get in,' Cathy yelled, running her eyes along Maeve, Angie and Pauline sitting in a straight row they had made with the three chairs.

'Cathy, this won't do at all,' Angie cried, continuing to giggle. 'I'll be grand if yeh want me te wave te yeh all evening.' Her chair was so low, when she had elbows on the arms of the chairs on each side of her, her own arms were coming straight out from her shoulders.

'Yeh look like yer hangin' from a cross,' Cathy yelled.

Joan saw that Angie's hand was three inches above her head. 'More like she's holding her hands up so that we can all take her money,' she said.

'I'll never make it te me mouth with me sherry,' Angie complained.

Pauline laughed so much at Angie imitating the queen's wave to the exasperated expression on Cathy's face that she was close to wetting herself. Apart from needing to pee, she hoped that when she was away from Cathy she would be able to dream up something to say about making pancakes for money. In the small room upstairs she recalled her daughters delight when they had told Cathy about the pancakes. She had never known them to make up a story before.

Guessing her daughters had said she made pancakes and sold them on the highway because they wanted to say something dramatic, Pauline was proud of them. After all it was only half a lie — she had made pancakes and they were sold on the highway.

Walking down the stairs, Pauline remembered Una telling her that lies always get you into more trouble than what you started out with. By the time she had opened the living room door, she had decided that Una was right. And so were her daughters, but she still couldn't think of any fun or laughs she had had when she had been helping her friend to make the pancakes.

'I've topped up yer drink,' Cathy said when Pauline came back into the room, 'and as yeh can see everyone is comfortable.'

Much as she wanted to have a dramatic story to tell Pauline she wasn't able to make one up. 'I think that Kate and Jenny have become infected with the Irish way of exaggerating things,' she said. 'All I did was help my next-door neighbour Alisha make pancakes and they were eaten on the highway.'

'Did yeh make money?' Cathy asked.

'No Cathy, I didn't,' Pauline said. 'Alisha made the pancakes for her brother and his friends who worked on the highways.' She felt sorry for disappointing Cathy with not having more to tell her. 'I helped for a while when she had the flu one winter.' She picked her drink up off the table and said, 'Sorry, Cathy but I couldn't let the twins down when we were having our tea.'

'Well we're not sorry that yeh came. Not the least bit,' Cathy said. 'We've all got er houses cleaned up fer a start. Maurice hosed out the coalbunker, and Angie broke out and bought a new pair ev slippers.'

God almighty, how does she always think of something funny at the right time, Pauline thought, laughing when they all watched Angie pull her feet out from under the coffee table and tuck them under her chair.

Angie patted Pauline on her knee as she said, 'I'm glad yer home, and I hope yeh can put some manners on yer youngest sister while yer here.'

Listening to her young sister relating stories and experiences about their cleaning group, and Cathy growing tomatoes and rhubarb, Pauline wondered what her daughters had told Emir about their life in Canada. She expected that her young niece had told Kate and Jenny as many stories as she was hearing from Cathy, Angie, and Maeve. She prayed she hadn't let her daughters down by not having much to say about making pancakes.

'That's the lot till Friday,' Cathy said, dividing the last of the vodka between the four glasses on the coffee table.

'What's so special about Friday?' Pauline asked.

'We're havin' a ladies night at the airport,' Cathy said. 'Tony and Donal will bring us out and come out again after we have had a few drinks at the airport when we meet Josie.'

Chapter Fifty-six

Envy more than jealousy encouraged Pauline to stand up straight and pull in her tummy when she saw her eldest sister walk through the arrivals at Dublin airport. She had never been close Josie, but unlike Una she had never fought with her. Until she had told her husband to leave their house or she would go to the police, Pauline had never fought with anyone. Watching her tall beautiful sister walk like a countess among the crowd of other passengers, Pauline prayed she wouldn't have to fight with her now. But she would if she had to.

Hearing about something is a great deal different from living through it, and Pauline knew this as much as any of her family. She also knew that the Josie she remembered was not the same girl that her sisters had been talking about all week.

Recalling some of the praise that Cathy had been showering all week on their eldest sister, Pauline watched Josie toss her straight golden-brown hair away from her face. She smiled, almost laughed, when she noticed the young girl walking behind Josie and thought she must be Eileen. For a second she wondered about the tall, skinny, blond, long-haired boy Eileen was looking up at and talking to. She realised it had to be Josie's son Rory because he had the same small eyes, and nose as Josie.

Efficient, that's what Josie is, Pauline thought when Josie turned back to check that her children were still with her. She could find no reason not to believe Joan and Cathy when they had told her that Josie didn't boss them around anymore, but she also knew that she would only believe them when she found out for herself. There were times when she had been living at home that she had been as much afraid of Josie as she had been of her mammy.

Rory and Eileen gazed out into the large group of people that were crowded around the opening in the barrier while their mammy pulled at the bags they were carrying.

Pauline laughed lightly, watching Josie walk after her children when they ran over to Cathy. She still had her hands on the barrier because she was nervous and she needed something to hold on to.

Tears of shame glistened in Josie's eyes when she realised the grey-haired woman standing beside Joan was Pauline. She had expected to see some changes after twelve years. Some of Una's hair was grey, and Sean's hair was grey. Josie always noticed people's hair.

'I hope yer not thinkin' ev takin' out yer tints and dyes until we get home?' Cathy said, hugging her eldest sister.

'Una never told me,' Josie whispered into Cathy's ear.

'Well Una doesn't know everythin',' Cathy said, taking the bag from Josie's hand. 'Go over and give her a hug. I think she's more nervous than you are.'

She couldn't be more nervous Josie thought, allowing Cathy to take her bag while she said, 'Pauline has nothing to be nervous about.' She prayed that Pauline would forgive her for what their mammy had done.

Josie was fourteen when she started to serve her time as an apprentice hairdresser. It was the last time she had worn her hair cut short just below her ears, and a with straight fringe across her forehead. It was the only style her daddy knew how to do. When she was sixteen she was cutting all her siblings' hair.

Even without her high heels to give her height, Josie was

the tallest sitting at the table. She looked like a mother hen checking out the chicken run before she let her children out to play while she moved her head and ran her eyes over the lounge.

Cathy put her arm around Eileen's shoulder, gave it a squeeze and said, 'Yeh know yer Auntie Una isn't comin'.'

'What makes yeh say that?' Flo asked.

'We could do with her teh mend teh trousers,' Cathy replied, running her hand down one leg of Eileen's jeans.'

'After all the trouble Mike went to, to cut them up,' Josie snapped. 'I have to confess to doing her hair though.'

'Yeh mean not doin' it,' Flo said.

Eileen removed her crochet cap, then ran her fingers up the back of her neck and waved her head to show her long partly curled and partly matted dark-brown hair. 'Mammy permed it,' she said proudly, her brown eyes shining with laughter at her aunties nodding in unison like they were a group of chorus girls.

Just gone thirteen, Eileen Cullen was a supporter of every anti-establishment group, and organisation that had been born since the middle eighties. While she was telling Flo and Maeve about how Mike had put the cuts in her jeans, Cathy joined Pauline in observing their elegant older sister. Josie's eyes flittered all over the airport lounge. Cathy was glad she wasn't one of the people walking about as she watched Josie's eyes drop from their head to their shoes.

They were sitting in a corner booth, and Josie's seat gave her a good view around the lounge. Most of the people walking around wore coats or jackets, and there were cases and bags tucked under nearly all the tables and chairs.

'Are yeh thirsty, Josie?' Cathy asked.

Josie jerked her head away from watching Joan at the bar and replied quickly, 'Not in the least.' She then started to unbutton her jacket for something to do. She looked like she would have been more comfortable sitting in the lounge of the Brighton Grand Hotel during a Tory Party Conference. Although her royal blue suit had narrower lapels than those favoured by Margaret Thatcher, Josie looked every bit as smart and as well-groomed as the British Prime Minister.

'Yer looking well, Josie,' Flo said, suspecting Josie was searching for her mammy. During the fifteen years she had been married to Sean she had never known her mother-in-law to go out to the airport or the harbour to meet her children when they were coming home. And more often than not the selfish woman was out when her children arrived at the house.

'We're all lookin' well,' Cathy said, picking her beer off the table, 'but as usual Josie is the most glamorous.' She thought Josie looked worried.

Chapter Fifty-seven

O h my God,' Josie gasped, running the water to clean the sink. She hadn't been sick since she was pregnant with Rory. She would have laughed if she hadn't felt a cramp in her stomach. As the cramp was fading she decided to have a bath after she had her breakfast. All Josie's pains and worries went away when she had a bath.

Although she was only forty-two she hadn't been unduly concerned when her periods had been two weeks late. Or when she had gone two months. Nearly half of her customers were middle-aged so she knew everything about the menopause.

'Where's Granny?' Rory called from the hall, then walked into the kitchen.

Josie stared at her tall skinny, long-haired, fair-haired son for a couple of seconds then said, 'She's down in Ena's.' She smiled approvingly at her favourite child, then looked around the room for a clock. 'What is the time?' she asked. When Rory went into the living room to see what time it was she decided she'd buy a kitchen clock when she was in town during the week.

'It's just gone ten,' Rory called from the bottom of the stairs.

Every time Josie saw her son's skinny torso, she wanted to cook him a meal so she opened the fridge. A nice batch loaf was smiling at her and there was a full tray of eggs. Hearing a rattle at the front gate, she closed the fridge and walked over to the sink and looked out the window. She saw Cathy waving to a neighbour. To assure herself that she was seeing all right, Josie swiped back the net curtain. She then saw Eileen turning a pushchair into the garden. She dropped the curtain just as Cathy was waving to her wide-open mouth.

'Mornin', Josie,' shouted Cathy when she opened the porch door.

Josie accepted Cathy's greeting by way of bowing her head, then helped Eileen to lift the pushchair into the hall. 'Where have you two been so early in the morning?' she demanded.

'Three of us,' Cathy corrected, bowing her head to the pushchair.

It was eleven when they had arrived home from the airport, so Josie had been only able to get a glimpse of Cathy's little girl as the child lay sleeping in her cot. She wagged her head rapidly sideways in disbelief as she gazed down at a miniature Cathy. 'Ouch,' she cried when she bent down to hold Suzie while Eileen was undoing the straps so that the child could get out of her pushchair. Holding her stomach with both of her hands, Josie sucked air in through her teeth stood up again and panted as the sharp pain that had caught her around her waist, back and stomach faded.

'Are you all right, Mammy?' Eileen asked, looking at Cathy for confirmation about the pain she had just seen in her mammy's face.

Josie gasped as she let the air out of her puffed-up cheeks giggle and said, 'That was a nasty one.'

'A nasty what?' Eileen asked, leaving Cathy to take care of Suzie and watching her mammy continue to rub her stomach.

'It's only my periods.' Josie smiled at the concerned face of her daughter.

'Yer gettin' old now, Josie,' Cathy said, kissing Suzie, 'yer old enough te be this one's granny.' She then held her daughter out to her older sister for inspection, and added, 'This is yer famous Auntie Josie.'

Josie watched Suzie look down at her pushchair, then put her arms out to Eileen. She smiled at Cathy and said, 'You never looked like that when you were her age.'

'That's because yeh never looked at me properly,' replied Cathy watching Josie stand up straight and rub her back.

Probably, Josie thought. She could remember so many babies being born that they were all the same to her. She saw her son at the top of the stairs and remembered she was going to cook. Rory looked so thin that he reminded her of a giraffe's neck. She thought of food again and asked Cathy, 'Is it all right to use the eggs in the fridge?'

'That's what they're fer,' Cathy replied, 'but are yeh feelin' all right? How is the pain in yer belly now?'

'It will go away when I eat something,' Josie said and walked into the kitchen.

An hour later Josie rested her arms on the kitchen table and ran her eyes over the empty plates and cups. She hated wasted food as much as Una did. She was delighted she had heard Eileen tell her Green Party friends that if everyone cooked like her mother there would be very little hunger in the world. The pleasant memory barely dented her confused and sad emotions. When she raised her head to stare down the kitchen and out to the back garden, she didn't see Cathy, Eileen, or Rory as they walked back and forth waving their arms and shouting to each other because her mind was elsewhere. She had been relieved she was wearing her housecoat when Rory insisted that Cathy gave them a tour of what she called her farming venture. She didn't want to know.

The church bells tolling the Angelus told Josie it was twelve, and that she should be getting herself dressed, but she couldn't think of one reason why she should hurry. Her mind glossed over their conversation when they were eating their breakfast. She hardly recognised her family from all Cathy had told her.

When Cathy, Maeve, and Angie had started the cleaning

group, Josie had thought they were mad. But as Mike had told her, they had nothing to lose. He wasn't the least bit worried about not getting the hundred pounds he had lent them to buy the small amount of equipment they needed.

It was nearly four years since her husband had showed Josie the cheque that Angie had sent him six months after he had had loaned the money to them. Josie had been so proud of her young sister she had cried. The three women weren't making a fortune, but they worked hard and earned a living. Josie still prayed that their success would continue while Cathy had to be at home with Suzie. And now Cathy was growing tomatoes, cucumbers and rhubarb, and selling them. Cathy said she enjoyed the garden and with only herself and Mammy at home they wouldn't be able to eat them all. All she had to do was fill the boxes with the fresh vegetables. Donal had a friend that went around Kells selling eggs so he sold her vegetables as well.

Her young sister was welcome to all that work if it made her happy, Josie thought as her thoughts drifted to Maeve who had invested her money in buying caravans, and renting them out during the summer months. And now she was doing a course in hairdressing.

Casting her eyes over the table, Josie noticed Suzie's little plate. The child had eaten all her toast. She wondered if her family knew who his father was and they were keeping it from her because they were afraid she would tell their mammy. Thinking about her mammy didn't add any cheer to Josie's mood, and Cathy had hardly mentioned her at all. The slight pain in the bottom of her stomach became aggravated while she recalled Liam had helped Cathy to buy the house from the Corporation. Raising her head to the window, she saw her children walking back up the garden so she started clearing away the table. Her stomach started hurting again as she walked back and forth from the table to the sink. She gripped the back of a chair, and when she looked up to the voices coming in the door she scowled fiercely at Cathy because the pain in her stomach was so bad.

'Jeasus, Josie,' Cathy cried, 'yeh look as white as a sheet.' She bumped into a chair as she made her way over to Josie and said, 'Are yeh sure it's yer periods?' She removed Josie's hands from the back of the chair and then used her foot to turn the chair round and held her sister's arms while she sat down.'

'Not anymore,' Josie panted, closing her eyes with the pain. 'I don't usually get the cramps as bad as this.' She sat up straight, rubbed her stomach and moaned, 'I don't get them so regular now.' She inhaled before she continued, 'The pain has never been as bad as this.' She inhaled deeply again and said, 'It's going away now.'

Cathy ran her hand over Josie's hair and said, 'Go back te bed fer a while, Mammy won't be here before two. Yeh'ev already done teh breakfast so it's not yer turn te wash up.' She felt a little shiver in her stomach because she had never seen Josie slumped in a chair, or slope her shoulders. As if it would dispel her concern, Cathy started to finish with clearing the table. 'It might have been from mixin' teh drinks last night,' she said, 'I've had a couple ev nasty mornin's meslf before now.'

The slight dampness, and the smell of steam from the hot water running in the sink blew across Josie's face. She inhaled deeply and said, 'I think I'll have a bath.'

'Go on then,' Cathy said, 'but don't lock teh door just in case yeh get another cramp.' She turned off the water. 'Yeh can use Mammy's buzzer if yeh do.'

'Mammy's buzzer?'

'It's only a hall door bell that Maurice fixed in teh bathroom fer mammy after Angie had a fall in hers over Christmas last year.'

Josie always thought about Angie when she enjoyed a sherry. 'It's a very good idea,' she said.

Chapter Fifty-eight

Maurice stayed longer today than he usually did on his short visits to see his mammy on his way to his football match. His mammy wasn't in so he sat in the conservatory with Josie's children. He frowned at Rory's long hair, but he was flattered when his nephew praised Cathy's garden. He was also impressed with Eileen's enthusiasm for organic and home-cooked foods. Although she pushed him on the subject he avoided giving his opinion about men cooking in the home.

'Are yez all set fer tenight?' asked Cathy.

Maurice hesitated; he didn't want to go but he knew that Maeve did and he was hoping to talk her into going on her own seeing that she would be with his family.

Cathy jumped at the long shrill sound of the buzzer that came from the corner behind her chair. 'Stay where yez are,' she said, getting to her feet quickly. She dropped her cigarette into the ashtray and shoved her chair back. She glanced over at Eileen when she was at the door and called back, 'It'll probably be yer mam lookin' fer a fancy towel.'

Eileen shrugged her shoulders and giggled.

The bathroom was down a short passage at the top of the stairs and Cathy was relieved to find the door was half open. When she pushed the door in fully she found Josie holding on to the hand basin. She smelled the blood before she saw it dribbling into Josie's slippers, but she was terrified at the colour of her sister's face when Josie half turned her head at the sound of the door opening. She grabbed a towel and shoved it up Josie's dressing gown between her legs.

Josie tried to straighten her back, when she turned her face sideways and cried, 'It's the pain again.' She then put her head down over the hand basin and vomited again.

Cathy leaned over her sister's back and opened the water taps, then held Josie around the waist until she was ready to be guided on to the toilet and helped her to sit on the seat. She pulled another towel off the rail and kicked it at the door to make sure it stayed open in case Josie fell over. She pulled her head back at the strong familiar smell that came from the blood on Josie's slippers when she removed them and put another towel under her sister's feet.

'This isn't teh drink, Josie,' Cathy said quietly, willing herself to be calm although she was terrified. She kissed her sister on the top of her head and asked, 'Have yeh still got teh pain? Is it the same as when yeh were in the kitchen?'

Bent over, and holding the toilet rail with one hand, and Cathy's arm with the other, Josie inhaled deeply and whined, 'It gets dreadful every few minutes.' She then squeezed Cathy's arm and she cried out, 'Oh God here it comes again.'

When Josie's pain had eased Cathy freed her arm from her sister's tight grip then went to the top of the stairs and shouted, 'Maurice.' She waited until he was at the bottom of the stairs and shouted, 'Phone an ambulance.' When Maurice didn't move she roared, 'Now!'

On the second attempt Cathy made to get her sister to stand Josie cried, 'I don't want to move.'

'Then stay where yeh are,' Cathy said, giving Josie her hand to squeeze again and sat down on the edge of the bath. 'I think yer better not standin' anyhow,' she said, leaning over and passing her hand over the top of her sister's head as if she could take some of the pain herself. She had never seen Josie in pain before.

When Maurice saw the blood on the slipper he started to feel dizzy. 'They want te know what I want teh ambulance fer?' he said.

Josie bent her head down and gripped Cathy's arm again and she cried, 'Oh my Go-o-d.'

'Fer internal bleedin',' Cathy roared, standing to hold Josie who then put her arms around her young sister's waist and screamed, 'Oh my God.' Cathy turned her head and called after Maurice, 'Keep Eileen and Rory down there. Send Eileen over fer Angie.'

For five minutes Josie shook with pain, crying and panic while Cathy's tears dropped on to the top of her head. They both prayed for the terror to go away. Cathy released her hold on Josie's head when she felt a gentle pair of hands pulling on her arms. She gladly accepted help although she didn't know who it was, except that it was a woman. She couldn't see through her tears.

'Josie,' the gentle voice said. 'I'm a nurse, I'm also a friend of Donal's.'

The girl who the Malone boys knew as Sister Monica knelt in front of Josie, smiled at Cathy, then looked up and nodded to the window for Cathy to open it. She sniffed the strange smell that Cathy had got used to, then looked over Josie's slippers and briefly examined the towel at Josie's feet.

Josie raised her head and said, 'They're worse than labour pains.'

'They always are,' Monica said, then gently tugged at Josie's hands and asked, 'Do you know what's happened, Josie?'

'They're still coming,' replied Josie, 'but not as bad.' She glanced at Cathy who was standing behind Monica, then bent her head again. 'Oh God, but they're still there.' She shot her hand out and cried, 'Cathy, oh Cathy.'

Chapter Fifty-nine

They were sitting on hard seats in a corridor in the Mater Hospital. Monica put an arm around Eileen's shoulders and said, 'And what do you think of little Suzie? Your mammy is going to be all right, I promise.'

Eileen replied with only a sad smile and started to cry again.

'I'll go up to the ward and find out how she is,' Monica said.

Cathy watched Monica until she had turned into another corridor, then put her arm around her niece and said, 'Jeasus, Eileen but she's nearly as bossy as yer mother.' She squeezed the young shoulders again and added, 'And she really hadn't a clue.'

'I wonder what she would have called her,' Eileen whinged.

'It wasn't meant te be,' Cathy said, 'now I want yeh to promise me that yeh won't ever tell yer mother I said it but she is probably too old te have a baby. She told me herself today that her periods haven't been regular fer years.'

The youngest in the family Cathy had no memories of when any of her siblings were born. She recalled Una telling her that after Donal was born she been upset when her mammy was pregnant again. She calculated that Una must have been only eleven at the time: a year younger than Eileen was now. Una had two more sisters and a brother. 'Are yeh tellin' me yeh would've liked a sister?' she asked.

Eileen nodded her head against Cathy's shoulder.

'So would I,' Cathy said, 'younger than me.' She waited until

Eileen had stopped sobbing. 'We couldn't go on with teh big families. All teh Irish have done fer years is breed workers for teh Americans and teh English.'

Eileen blew her nose into her wet tissue, then walked over to a bin and emptied the pockets of her long cardigan of other wet tissues. She walked back and stood in front of her aunt and said, 'I'll be your younger sister if you like.'

Squeezing her eyes to hold back her tears, Cathy's head touched the wall when she tilted it back and said, 'Are yeh sure?'

Eileen nodded her head

'I might start bossin' yeh about.'

Eileen nodded her head again and sat down.

'Only on condition that you become an older sister fer Suzie, but yer never te boss her about.'

'I don't want a sister to boss about.'

'Everythin' will be all right,' Cathy whispered and kissed the top of Eileen's head.

Resting her head on the wall again, Cathy gazed up at the tall cream ceiling. She swallowed to stop from feeling sick at the memory of the smell in the bathroom and wondered how Josie would have managed if she had been on her own. 'Yer right, Eileen,' she said, 'and I won't boss yeh about.'

'Unless I deserve it,' Eileen returned.

'Sisters are fer helpin' each other,' Cathy said.

'And brothers,' Eileen sniffed, 'you were great with helping my mammy.'

'She would ev done the same fer me,' Cathy said and recalled how good her brothers Liam and Donal had been with helping her to buy the house. She never thought about that day very often but when she did she called it her taxi day.

Liam had insisted on getting mini cabs everywhere. The first was from the house into town, then to the Corporation, and then to the solicitors. Then to Bewleys for a coffee, back to the solicitors, and the Corporation again, then to Jury's to celebrate. Then Liam put their mammy into a taxi to take her to her friend Ena in Arbour Hill.

Home now and happy that Josie was not in pain anymore, Cathy moved around the kitchen opening and closing cupboards. 'We'll have te have temerraw's breakfast,' she said to Eileen.

Eileen opened the fridge, bent down, moved some of the packages about and said, 'We have plenty of sausages. Will I take them out and cut them up?'

Cathy stood with her hands on her hips glaring at the light bulb as if it would tell her what to do. She loved her sister's husband, but right now she could have strangled him for getting Josie pregnant. He would have known that they were all planning to have an evening at the Beggars Lodge with Pauline home. Even if they all went anyway they wouldn't be able to enjoy themselves with Josie in hospital.

'Will I set the table then?' Eileen shouted.

'No, Donal can do that,' Cathy said, walking over to the cooker. She pulled out the grill, wondering if she could cook something more exciting for Donal's girlfriend. If only Josie were here, she thought, then felt tears she coming and said, 'Donal likes a fry, you like a fry, I love a fry and I'm starvin'.'

'So am I,' Eileen said. She took the bacon, sausages and eggs out of the fridge and brought them over to the worktop beside the cooker. 'Are you all right, Cathy?' she asked when she saw her aunt frown at the pan she had taken out of the oven.

'I'm scheming,' Cathy replied, pointing to a drawer in a unit by the sink and said, 'Get the little pointed scissors out of there. They're grand fer cuttin' the sausages. I'll do them first because they take teh longest and they'll keep warm in teh oven. The rashers get all dried up when they're kept warm.'

'What are you scheming?' Eileen asked over the noise of the cutlery in the drawer as she searched for the scissors.

'It's nothin' important,' Cathy returned, then added quickly, 'You separate the sausages and spread them out and I'll snip them.'

'Is it about Josie?' Eileen asked, snipping at the sausages.

Cathy stole a quick glance at her niece. 'What makes yeh think that? And it's yer mammy te you. Yer too young te be callin' yer mammy Josie.'

Eileen idled along towards the sink, spreading the sausages along the worktop. 'You looked worried when you were staring at the ceiling,' she said. 'Do you think that Monica was telling us the truth about my mammy.' She looked at Cathy with tears in her eyes and said, 'Mammy was so pale when we saw her.'

Pale as death, Cathy thought and said, 'That's te be expected when you have been in teh amount of pain yer mammy was in. And yes Monica was telling us the truth. Yer mammy will be home in few days.' She moved the sausages about the pan and continued, 'It just doesn't feel right that we should be singin' and dancin' with yer mammy in teh hospital.'

'You're still going,' Eileen said, watching Cathy make three little cuts down the length of the rest of the sausages. 'It wouldn't stop Josie,' she lied, then said quickly, 'I mean my mammy.' She was looking forward to Maurice bringing Patsy, Emir Kate, Jenny and herself down to the Beggars Lodge early while the band was setting up so they could mind a table for her aunts.

'There's somethin' else,' Cathy said, lighting the grill before she continued, 'there's mammy. I didn't think she would be home until late this evenin' or in teh mornin'. I have arranged with Angie te come over te be here with Suzie.'

Cathy checked the grill tray was not too near the flames while Eileen washed the small pair of scissors.

'Rory will be here,' Eileen said, 'and he'll have her in bed before you have finished your first drink.' She held the scissors up and said, 'These are lovely, where did they come from?'

Cathy placed one of her hands on the cooker and another on her waist and asked, 'And how will Rory get her te bed?' She pointed tc a drawer, and said, 'Put teh scissors back in there. They're Una's, she uses them fer her cuttin' her buttonholes.'

Eileen ran her finger over the faded gold rings on the top of the small pair of scissors. She wondered what Una would say if she knew what Cathy was using her lovely scissors for as she dropped them into the drawer and said, 'Rory will play cards with Granny and show up her cheating.'

Alongside, wondering what Josie would say if she heard what her daughter had said about her granny, Cathy felt some sadness for her mammy. 'Call Donal and tell him to set teh table,' she said.

Relieved that Cathy wasn't worried about her mammy, Eileen said, 'Of course I will.' She slapped the worktop with her hand and added, 'Now hurry up and get the fry done, I'm starving.'

'Wait a minute there,' Cathy said, 'I'm teh one to do teh bossin'.'

'I need the practice,' Eileen returned, 'now you do your job and I'll do mine.'

Cathy laughed. 'Yer goin' te make a grand sister fer Suzie,' she said, 'promise me yeh'll never spoil her.'

Her sad feelings for her mammy didn't encourage her to want to ask her mammy to come to the Beggars Lodge with them. She knew that none of them would know what to talk to her about. She sighed and told herself that her mammy had brought her loneliness on herself.

Although Cathy had left the window wide open when she had finished cooking, the smell of grilled sausages still permeated the kitchen when she walked in an hour later in front of her baldy brother with the empty plates in her hands. 'Yeh are a real dark horse, Donal.'

'I know,' Donal said, turning round from the sink where was

running hot water into the basin and added, 'Thanks Cathy, that was a lovely fry.'

'We spoilt yer day, and I'm sorry about that, Donal,' Cathy said, 'but yeh should have told me.' She walked over to the cooker. 'I could have got the place cleaned up.' She stopped wiping over the cooker and stood with her hands resting on the metal sides gazing at the black spots around the edges of the rings and added, 'Donal I don't know how I'd have managed without Monica, I really don't. I had no idea what was happenin', and I don't think that Josie did either.'

'I didn't know I was bringin' her home meself,' Donal said, walking over to the fridge to get a clean cloth from the top of it. 'We met Mammy in Bewleys and she asked me te take her home. I had intended te introduce her te yez tenight in teh Beggars Lodge.'

The cloth Cathy was unravelling was like a rope because she had squeezed it so tight while she thought of the fun they would have had if they had known that Donal was bringing a girl to tea, and with Pauline here as well. She smiled at her shy brother and said, 'She's a very nice girl, and I'll do me best teh behave meself.' She continued to wipe the cooker and asked, 'Was mammy on her own in Bewleys?'

'Just be yerself, Cathy, or yeh'll make me out te be a liar,' he replied, and said, 'Yes, Mammy was on her own.'

Chapter Sixty

Breakfast was hectic in Joan's house on the following Tuesday morning. It was an ordinary working day for Tony and Joan and they went about their usual routine of getting the children ready for nursery school.

The novelty of entertaining Rose and Lily had worn off Kate and Jenny. Today they were engrossed with getting ready for their day going round Dublin.

'There's no doubt,' Pauline said to Tony while she was cutting bread, 'but the second bathroom is great, isn't it? Especially when you have another family taking over your house.'

Tony tipped Pauline on the shoulder and said, 'You're right about the bathroom, but nobody will ever take over, and it's great to have you here.' He glanced down the hall and added, 'Thanks for taking Bella with you today. It means a lot to her to be involved with all the excitement.'

Pauline stopped cutting the bread: 'Me taking her?' she cried. 'She's taking us. Were you listening to anything we talked about last night? She's a godsend, and I am sure she'll be every bit as good as Liam.' She sighed and started cutting the bread again: 'I really am ashamed, you know, when I think of all the time and tears with learning, or trying to learn Irish, and the Catechism and then end up ignorant of things that I could use and enjoy.'

After turning on the coffee machine, Tony put half the cut-loaf bread into a plastic bag. He didn't have the heart to tell her there was only the two of them for toast. 'Bella didn't even learn her catechism or her Irish language,' he said, raising his highbrows as high as Pauline's when she gazed at him in disbelief. 'Hard to believe isn't it?' he continued. 'Bella went to school all right.' He paused: 'Well some of the time anyhow, but like over half of the other fifty children in the class she just couldn't learn.'

Pauline thought back to her last few years at the school she hated so much that she never went back the day after she was fourteen. But she was able to read and do her sums. She sat down at the small table and said, 'She was reading last night.' She stood to get the booklets they had used when they were deciding where they would go as if Tony would need proof.

Tony laughed lightly. 'I know, I know, she can read now, I taught her.' He took the toast out of the toaster and put two more slices of bread in, then folded his arms and stood facing Pauline with his back leaning against the unit. 'I can't say I approve of what she reads though, but she enjoys them.'

After a few seconds Pauline asked, 'What's wrong with what she reads?' She could remember reading fairy stories in books her Aunt Sue had bought them for Christmas. She couldn't remember the name of any book she had read, but she hadn't read many. She recalled Una telling her about one she had been reading. Una had told her the story every morning for two weeks like a serial when they were going into work on the bus. She even remembered making the beds for Una so she could read enough to tell her the next day.

'Barbara Cartland,' Tony said, smiling as he put the small rack of toast on the table and sat down facing her with his back to the hall.

Pauline picked up the coffee jug: 'I've never heard of it,' she said nervously. She felt ashamed because couldn't remember the name of one book.

'It's not a book,' Tony said, struggling to stop from smiling, 'Barbara Cartland is a writer of silly stupid romances. I wouldn't have thought it would be your type of reading.'

Pauline buttered the same piece of toast twice.

Although he was used to her now, Tony was still amused by her actions and her expressions when she was surprised. 'I'm not saying she should read Shakespeare all the time, and the romances are fine, even good for teenagers, but after all she was four when Michael Collins was shot.' He shoved his toast into his mouth to stop himself from laughing.

Pauline shoved Michael Collins into her already cramped mental notebook and sliced through her toast. When she saw the brightness in Tony's eyes as she brought her cup up to her mouth she knew he was teasing her again. 'I totally agree with you about the romances,' she said and continued to stare at him while she bit on her toast. 'However,' she continued while she chewed, 'I'm not too sure about the Shakespeare.' She took a sip of her coffee and continued, 'Do you read Shakespeare yourself?'

Surprised and amused that Pauline was teasing him, Tony said, 'No, I don't.' He wanted to keep the charade going so he added quickly, 'I like thrillers myself.'

'I've never even opened one of his books,' Pauline confessed. She sat up straight, held her head up so high she was nearly looking down her nose when she winked at him when she said, 'but I read comics.'

They were still laughing heartily when Joan came into the kitchen.

'Save a few smiles,' Joan said, boasting a wide grin and looking down the hall where they could hear Kate and Jenny laughing coming down the stairs with Rose and Lily.

When the children walked down the hall Pauline brought her hands up and covered her mouth as if she was trying to stifle a scream.

When Tony saw Pauline's eyes shining and smiling, he

glanced at his giggling wife, then turned his chair to see what was so astounding in the hall.

Pauline rocked her body as if she had a stomach pain while her daughters slowly walked into the kitchen. Rose and Lily tottered over to their aunt and started to join in her dancing. Tony opened his mouth as though he had been hit in the chest.

Kate and Jenny completed a full turn to show off their new clothes.

Pointing to Kate's legs, Pauline demanded, 'How did you get the slits in your jeans?'

'Tony made them,' Kate said triumphantly, walking further into the kitchen and looking down at her legs. 'Gawd, Mom aren't they super?' she said pulling her jeans up to her knees revealing what looked to Pauline like red woollen hats around her ankles. 'Leg warmers,' she said, turning to show Tony.

Tony shot up out of his chair and bent down to get a closer look. 'They're the sleeves of my best jumper,' he said.

Jenny hoisted up the legs of her jeans to show her blue leg warmers and said, 'Thanks, Uncle Tony.'

'Old jumpers,' Joan corrected.

After two weeks of seeing Tony wearing a different jumper every day, Pauline had wondered how many of them he had. She had also noted that none of the jumpers he had worn had been old. 'Did you do all this?' she asked her sister as she examined Kate's long red sleeveless cardigan. She squinted her eyes and looked closely at the stitching around the armholes and said, 'It's just the old blanket stitch.' She looked at Tony and added with approval, 'It's done with wool.'

Struggling to stop laughing at the idea that he would know about any kind of stitching, Tony replied, 'I wouldn't know.' He sat back down in his chair and crossed his arms and said, 'I never was one for doing any stitching, or knitting.'

Neither was Pauline, but when she had been living at home Una used to mend the sheets and blankets. By the time Una was thirteen she was able to use the old treadle sewing machine her Granny Malone had given her. Una used to cut up old sheets and use them to patch others. When the blankets became thin in the middle Una would cut them down the centre, then stitch the two sides together. It was seeing her sister do the blanket-stitching down the sides of the blankets that helped Pauline recognise it on her daughter's sleeveless cardigans.

With emotions of delight for her daughters and nostalgia from remembering her younger days, Pauline wanted to cry. The sleeves of the jumpers on Kate's ankles reminded her of when she used to shove her feet into an old jumper before she got into bed so she could warm them. Right now she was so delighted with the happiness of her two girls she said, 'Tony, I will be delighted to buy you two new jumpers.'

Still trying to look annoyed Tony held up his hand and said, 'No need, Pauline, I think I know who to send the bill to.'

'Bella,' Joan and Pauline said together.

'Bella's sewing will give Una a run for her money,' Pauline said, continuing to smile at her daughter's clothes, and added, 'You look terrific, the pair of you.'

Chapter Sixty-one

Kate, and Jenny helped Tony to strap the children into the car so he could take them to their nursery for a few hours. Jenny and Kate went with them and Tony collected Eileen and Bella and brought them back. While thay were gone Pauline made a telephone call.

Delighted that Pauline agreed with the itinerary she had worked out for the first part of their day, Bella closed her little book and whispered to Pauline, 'Did yeh make yer phone call?'

'Between four and five,' Pauline whispered.

As the bus ride into town was to be part of their excursion, Bella and Pauline declined Tony's offer to take them into town. It was half past ten when they set off and Pauline was so determined her daughters were going to have a good day that she didn't notice the sun was shining.

Half an hour after they had boarded the double-decker bus they stepped down on the pavement at the top of Parnell Square. Bella's route was to walk into O'Connell Street, then up to Stephens Green. This would also bring them to the top of Grafton Street in time for cream cakes in Bewleys.

Knowing her daughters couldn't read very well, Pauline felt sad and amused as she watched them poke their heads over Bella's shoulders when she was reading her sketch map with Eileen.

They all stood round Bella at the top of Parnell Square while she told them that the square was the second oldest in

Dublin. She didn't know about the bleak-looking, soot-covered church they were standing beside and smiled with relief when the young girls gave it a scornful stare.

They crossed the road together, and started walking towards O'Connell Street. Eileen and Bella sauntered on in front.

Afraid they would step out into the road without thinking of the traffic while they tried to get a better view of what they were looking at, Pauline stayed close to Jenny and Kate.

'Mom,' said Jenny, 'what does Georgian mean?'

'It's the name of the English king that was on the throne when the houses were built,' Pauline said, then pointed down the road to Bella and Eileen and prayed they wouldn't ask her what number George it was at the time.

They caught up with Bella and Eileen at the Rotunda building at the bottom of the square. They chatted for a few minutes about what they had seen and what they thought of Parnell Square. The history of the Rotunda Maternity Hospital was of little interest to the young girls even if it was one of the oldest in Europe. Bella insisted that they see the GPO from the opposite side of the street.

'As long as we still cross over,' said Pauline, 'because I want the foreigners to put their fingers into the bullet holes in the GPO and sing God save Ireland.'

'I don't know it,' Jenny whinged.

Eileen burst out laughing when she saw Pauline wink at Bella.

Everything was much brighter when they crossed the road into O'Connell Street. Walking five abreast on the wide pavement, Bella told them about Daniel O'Connell, and Charles Stewart Parnell. They smiled up at the Gresham Hotel and the Savoy cinema before they had to get into pairs because the pedestrian traffic increased as they got nearer to the more popular shopping area around Henry Street.

With Bella in the middle, they were able to line up again at the kerb facing the General Post Office. Bella told them they should notice the six fluted portico columns. Pauline changed places with Eileen and stood between the twins and explained what fluted columns were. Bella then told them that it wasn't finished until 1818, and that the British shelled it from a gunboat in the River Liffey in 1916.

'It's a monster,' Kate whinged.

Pauline stared at the grey imposing building and said, 'You're right, Kate, it does look like a monster.' She glanced down the line of faces, winked at Eileen and said, 'Come on, you girls have to do your singing.'

'Gawd Mom, it's cold,' Jenny moaned when they were standing in the middle of the floor in the General Post Office building looking around at the counters.

'It is high, isn't it?' Pauline said to Eileen who had her head bent back. 'You know,' she continued, joining Eileen in gazing up at the ceiling, 'I must have passed this building hundreds of times but this is the first time I have ever looked at it.'

Having completed a full circle of the ceiling and the rest of the room, Eileen said, 'I always look at them and I think most of them are a waste of money. Just think of all the homes that could be built for the cost of this one.'

Pauline couldn't think of anything equally intelligent to say so she returned Bella's wave over at the information counter where she was chatting to Kate then said, 'It must have cost a fortune to rebuild it after the fire in 1916.'

'You could build mountains with cheap labour,' Eileen said.

'You probably could,' Pauline returned. 'I was never even able to build a sandcastle.'

Outside in the warm sun while the girls were poking at the bullet holes three white-haired American women asked Eileen if she was making a wish.

They stood on the steps of Eason's Bookstore for a few minutes so that Kate and Jenny could look around and become familiar with where they were. Pauline stood in front of them and spoke firmly, 'The monster building is next door and Cleary's is right across the road.' She pulled at their hands and studied their faces until she was satisfied that they knew where they were. 'If we lose you, just wait here until one of us comes.'

Eileen smiled brightly and said, 'We can go where we like then, we don't have to stay together all the time.'

'Could Kate and Jenny come with me?' Bella asked Pauline, 'I want to show them something.' She shrunk her head into the collar of her jacket and giggled, 'I'll be all right. Kate and Jenny will look after me if I get lost.'

Pauline nearly reached across and hugged Bella. Now that she was outside the best bookshop in the world she wanted to look for something that would tell her about Ireland's history. She also felt that Eileen should have some time on her own without the twins. 'We only have thirty minutes,' she said.

Compared to her mammy, Eileen Cullen enjoyed a privileged childhood. She had never been expected to do any housework, or cooking. She had never had to share her bed with younger siblings. She had never been cold or hungry. She had never had to sharpen her pencils. She had cried when her daddy had told her that her mammy along with her aunts, Pauline and Una, had left school at fourteen – two years behind for their age because they had been kept home so often to mind the younger children.

It was nearly two years since Eileen had complained about her mammy searching through her schoolbag to make sure her pencils were sharpened. She was thinking about her mammy when she glanced over the top of the bookstand and smiled at her grey-haired aunt. Pauline looked like she was ready to cry. She picked a book off one of the shelves, walked around to Pauline and asked, 'Can I help you?'

Overwhelmed with the assortment of books, Pauline decided to swallow her pride and consult her smart young niece so she said, 'I'm looking for something easy about Irish history.'

'There's nothing easy about Irish history,' Eileen said, 'but I think the famine would be the best to start with because most of the emigration started then.' She picked up a book, read the back cover then said, 'My daddy and Jack told me most of the history of Ireland that I know.'

'Well I can't bring them back to Canada with me,' Pauline said.

'What about going back to school?' Eileen said. She wiped her nose with the back of her hand to stop from laughing when she saw the horrified expression on her aunt's face. 'I mean adult classes. They use the schools in England for evening classes for adults.'

Pauline raised her eyebrows.

Eileen wiped her nose again and said, 'You could make enquiries when you get back.'

Pauline smiled and nodded her head.

Chapter Sixty-two

Crossing O'Connell Bridge, they agreed to disagree as to the truth of the British shelling of the GPO from a gunboat in the Liffey. Bella didn't know what other buildings were there at the time, or whether they were knocked down as well. Pauline gave her a hug for all the work she had done.

Moving up Westmoreland Street towards College Green Bella said they would get the best look of the Bank of Ireland from a short distance so they crossed the road to Trinity College.

Tears came to Pauline when she gazed at the huge grey stone structure. She coughed a giggle and said, 'All Jack Byrne's money is in there.'

Eileen laughed and said, 'I didn't know Jack had money.'

'They are minding it for him,' Pauline said and sniffed but a tear rolled down her check. 'Liam told me the last time I was home,' she said. Her youngest brother was her best friend. She was twelve when he was born, and she had been kept home from school to mind him so often she had grown to love him as if he had been her own child.

Staring at the massive building, Pauline forgot she was admiring it because her thoughts were on Liam. Except for a couple of months in the summer when he came out to Canada, Liam lived in Spain. When he had left the British Air Force he opened a pub in Spain. And a few years ago he went into partnership with a friend and opened another one in Toronto.

Smiling sadly, Pauline wondered what bank was minding her brother's money. Although he didn't stay with her when he came out to Toronto she saw him three or four times a week. Her smile was sad because she knew he was sick. He was always small and skinny, but during the last year he had become like a skeleton he was so thin. He told her that he was anaemic, and he showed her the vitamin tablets he was taking, and said that he would be taking them for a long time.

Like all the children in the family Eileen loved Liam like he was her own brother. 'I didn't know that Una's husband had any money but if Liam said so then it must be true.'

Bella read from her notes, 'It was finished in 1730. It was originally Old Parliament House.'

The wide road worried Pauline again. She checked the twins were not too close to the kerb. The tall buses swayed when they came down from College Street into College Green. She was terrified that Kate or Jenny would try and make a dash across the road when there was a short pause in the volume of the traffic. She remembered she used to charge across the road anywhere when she was much younger. She moved beside Eileen, and nudged her lightly in the arm and said, 'You must admit it looks imposing.'

'It is lovely and clean compared to so many of the old buildings in London. And there seems to be a lot more space with the traffic not so heavy,' Eileen said.

Consulting her notes again, Bella nodded her head to the railings behind them and said, 'This is Trinity College.'

As if Bella had told her she had won a prize Eileen said, 'Really?' She pointed to the metal bars and added, 'In there?' She then moved out towards the kerb and looked along the railings in both directions for a way to get in.

This time Bella didn't need to consult her notes: 'We can go into the grounds,' she said pointing up towards Grafton Street, 'the entrance is a bit further up the way we are going.'

Pauline called to Kate and Jenny to follow then. She watched Eileen's long cotton skirt blow around her legs while she asked Bella, 'Have you any notes on it?'

'A few,' Bella said, shrinking her head into the collar of her jacket and added, 'I hope it'll be enough.' She followed the three young girls through the very grand Palladian arch gates and read from her notes, 'The university was founded by Queen Elizabeth the First in 1592 but that's all I know.'

Tossing her mop of frizzy hair back, Eileen wrapped her arm around Bella's small shoulder and gave her a soft hug. 'Daddy wanted to come here,' she said to Pauline who was now walking beside her.

'Why didn't he then?' Pauline asked, feeling she was in a foreign land. The greyness of all the tall buildings outshone the bright green of the lawns. She couldn't even imagine what it would be like to live here for three or four years, let alone go to the classrooms every day.

'It is intimidating, isn't it?' Eileen said. 'I don't know why, for sure, because Daddy never told me. I think it was his sister Theresa that prevented him from even taking the exams to try and get in. He has a friend who went here and he is now a doctor.'

Pauline lowered her face to the ground. It had never even been considered that any of her own family might go to a university. Secondary school would have been a luxury. 'It's another world,' she said.

'And thank God it's another time,' Eileen said.

Frowning Pauline asked, 'Why do you say that?'

'Daddy's friend is a Protestant,' Eileen replied, running her eyes over the main entrance again, 'the main reason why Theresa didn't want Daddy to come here is because it is a Protestant university.'

'Well, well,' Pauline said, feeling very small and ignorant, 'I never knew that.' She waved over to Bella and the twins, and they walked across to join Eileen and herself. They all agreed that it was a grand place and that they would come back again to see it better when they had more time. Bella told them about the Book of Kells and the great library. She was relieved when the young girls said they were hungry because she wouldn't be able to tell them any more about the place.

The next grand building they admired was a short walking distance to Kildare Street. The three young girls were amazed when Bella told them the huge grey stone building was Leinster House; the Irish Parliament, and it was built as a family residence.

'It would have suited our large family just fine,' Pauline said, smiling while she thought with so many rooms she wouldn't have had to see her mammy let alone leave Ireland to get away from her.

'Think of all the house work you would have had to do,' Eileen said.

They walked back down Kildare Street and turned left into Nassau Street. Pauline knew by the way the twins were walking close to the wall and looking at their feet they had enough until they had something to eat. 'Third turn on the left,' she called up to Eileen. 'I'm starving,' she added when Jenny turned round.

When they reached Dawson Street Bella said, 'If we go up this way we'll pass the Mansion House.'

What Bella didn't know for sure she made up when she told the girls about the English gentry that used to live in the houses in Dawson Street. She had their little minds on fire explaining the uses of the different floor levels like the maids in small attics or the basements. It was twenty minutes before they arrived at the Mansion House building because the houses got grander as they moved slowly up the street, and the girls took more time looking at them.

Eileen gasped when Pauline told her that her mammy used to go to dances in the grand Mansion.

Chapter Sixty-three

When they arrived at Bewleys in Grafton Street Pauline insisted they went upstairs. It was nearly two o'clock and most of the customers were getting back to their jobs in offices and shops so they were able to find an empty table.

They were all hungry after their walking so instead of the usual cream cakes they had chips, eggs and sausages.

Using all the muscles in her face, Pauline held back her tears. The last time she had sat in the room Una and Liam had been with her. Liam had told them he was joining the English Air Force. He was only sixteen at the time, but he had talked like he was twenty-six. She recalled the last time she had seen him two months ago. He was now getting on for thirty but he looked forty. His fair curly hair had thinned and it was grey.

'Why was it so important to come in here?' Eileen asked when she had finished her egg and chips, and trying to make up her mind if she would have one of the lovely cream cakes.

'The history,' Pauline said, and blinked her eyes. She couldn't remember anything about what her youngest brother had told herself and Una about the Irish writers and actors who used to come here.

'What is it?' Eileen asked.

Barely managing to hold her tears in her throat because she was still thinking about Liam, Pauline put her knife and fork on the table, then sat up straight and said, 'I don't know.' She looked around the room as if her young brother was somewhere close by and added sadly, 'But Liam does.'

Sensing Pauline's sadness, Bella said, 'Nobody knows all of it.' She tapped Eileen lightly on her arm and added, 'that's why the Irish are always fightin' so much.' She looked up at Pauline and winked.

'Liam knows a lot,' Pauline volunteered recalling the day she had spent with him, Una and Shea in town and how impressed she had been. She looked around the room as if she was expecting him to walk in or be sitting at another table. 'I don't think there is anything that your Uncle Liam doesn't know,' she said.

Eileen removed her knitted bag from the shelf under her chair and withdrew the Eason's paper bag and rested it on the table. 'I bought this for Daddy,' she said, removing a book from the bag.

'*Heroes of the Revolutions,*' Bella read, 'that is very hard readin',' she said.

Eileen picked up the book, rolled the pages and said, 'the print is small as well. I think it will do because it has something about all the people who fought for Ireland.'

'Does it have Michael Collins?' Pauline asked.

Eileen scanned the index: 'Yes it does,' she said, smiling at her aunt and continued, 'Daddy has other books, but they never seem to be enough.' She closed the book and continued talking while she was putting it back into the paper bag. 'Every time he gets into an argument about Ireland and England down in Limerick he buys a book and it never has all he wants in it.'

'Do you think you're Irish? I mean do you feel Irish?' Pauline asked.

Eileen thought a moment then smiled, 'I think we all do,' she said. 'I mean Rory, Shea and Liam as well as myself, and I suppose it's because we come home so much and we go to Catholic schools.'

'How long is it since you have seen your Uncle Liam?' Pauline asked.

'It must be a year,' Eileen said. 'He used to come to see mammy every six months and have his hair permed, but he hasn't been for a while.'

Bella had known all the Malone boys since Donal and Tony were ten and they started to play football together. She had known that Donal had six sisters before she had met Joan. She had also known Cathy before she had met Joan because she used to be a tea lady in the canteen of the clothing factory where Cathy had been a machinist before she began her cleaning business.

There were many times when Bella envied Sheila Malone her large family. She knew why Pauline had stayed away from her family for so long and she didn't blame her. But she often wondered why her own only daughter hadn't come home since the summer she had brought her son and returned to England without him.

Refreshed, but a little footsore Bella guided her tired group up to Stephens Green. On their way, a few narrow streets on both sides of Grafton Street invited them to explore old buildings. They turned into South King Street and when they were admiring the Gaiety Theatre Pauline said, 'If you still want to go to Arbour Hill then we should start to make our way towards the Four Courts.'

'I'd love to see the Four Courts,' Eileen said.

'In that case,' said Bella, 'we can do Stephens Green, then take the small roads down to the Liffey, and see as much as we can.'

The windows on the Shelburne Hotel glinted in the sunshine like a queen dressed in jewels, and the twins were delighted with the grandeur of it. They had a short stroll in the park before then made their way down to the smaller and narrower streets and saw Dublin Castle.

'Gawd Mcm,' Kate and Jenny kept repeating as they moved through the old narrow streets. They looked up at all the windows searching for curtains. They wanted to know if people were still living in the small dark dwellings. Bella didn't know.

Walking beside Bella, Pauline inhaled deeply when they had emerged from Parliament Street onto Wellington Quay. For a few seconds she felt like she had never left her country. 'There's your Four Courts,' she called over to Eileen, pointing across the river up to her left. She wanted to bring the twins across the Halfpenny Bridge, but it was too far down so she had to settle for Church Street if they were to get to Arbour Hill before five.

The power of the Four Courts building received little attention from the twins. They were more impressed with the tall houses that lined both sides of the River Liffey. If the Phoenix cinema had been still there Pauline would have taken them inside just to see the hard seats they used to sit on when she was their age. They turned up towards Arbour Hill at Blackhall Place.

Time rolled back for Pauline when they crossed Brunswick Street into Stonybatter. All the shops and pubs seemed much smaller than she remembered, and walking up towards Prussia Street, Manor Street appeared to be half as wide as she remembered it.

It was better than a tenement, Pauline thought when she led her leg-weary group through the small streets. She stopped outside a house, smiled at Eileen and said, 'This where we used to live.'

Standing outside the house where her mammy used to live, Eileen tried to recall if the hall door was the same as the one in the photograph her Aunt Una had shown her. 'The rooms must be dark with such small windows,' she said.

Not nearly as dark as the small cottages in Kildare, Bella thought as she said, 'One good thing about small windows with small openings is that they were not easy to break into.'

The girls laughed when Pauline told them Una and she used to tap on the windows and run away. She couldn't remember any of the homes being broken into, but she recalled the children getting in through the top window for the neighbours when they had gone out and forgotten to bring their key.

Recalling her years of playing out on the streets, Pauline whispered, 'Poor Josie.' She then pointed to one of the houses and said, 'That one.'

'What about it?' Eileen asked, scrutinizing the metal oblong window that was five feet long and three feet wide, with an eighteen-inch opening at the top.

The memory of the day was as sharp as if it had happened last week. Pauline imagined she could smell the cattle dung that used to be on the streets when she inhaled. 'One cattle-market day a bull came charging down the street, and when Josie saw it coming she tried to get into that house through the window.'

Jenny looked like she was going to cry when she whined, 'Gawd Mom.'

As if she was watching a film of some of her childhood Pauline continued, 'She didn't get all the way in because she hadn't done it before so she didn't know how to bring her knee up under her chin.' She wanted to cry at the memory of her sister's legs sticking out of the top of the window. She laughed with tears in her eyes and said, 'Her legs were waving about for nearly half an hour after the bull had gone.'

'Why?' Eileen asked.

'Because she was stuck and there was nobody in the house to help her in, and she was holding on to something and she wouldn't let it go, so we couldn't pull her back out.'

'Where did the bull come from?' Eileen asked.

'The cattle market,' Pauline said, pointing over to the church steeple in the short distance. 'It used to be just over there in

Prussia Street. Wednesday was cattle market day, and we often used to get sheep and cows along here. I think that the bulls used to run away.' She felt tearful as more memories came flooding back to her. 'Una and I could get in and out of all the windows without any trouble. That's how we got Josie out in the end. Una got over the wall of the house next door and got in through the back window and opened the hall door. Then a man went in and helped to get Josie down.'

Encouraged by the attention from Eileen and her daughters, Pauline told the girls about the swing they used to make on the lamp post with a rope, and how they all had to queue up the get their turn. She told them how they used to chalk lines on the ground and kick a tin around when they played beds.

When the young girls were rubbing the ground with their feet in the hope of finding an ancient chalk mark, Pauline told them they always got the best chalk from broken statutes of the Virgin Mary.

With her memories shooting into her head like arrows, Pauline brought them to another house off another side street and pointed to a step on the first house and said, 'Your Auntie Una cost your granny sixpence one day when she sat on that step.' She waited a few seconds while the girls examined the step and continued, 'Una sat there and polished shoes until she had used up all the brown polish in the tin so that we would have an empty tin to fill with dirt to play beds with.' When Bella hollered a laugh, Pauline added, 'Well, Una couldn't stand wasting anything.'

More memories started to fog Pauline's mind as she looked around the silent little cottages. She thought they looked for-gotten about. All the hall doors and windows were closed and there were no people about. She looked down at the step and said, 'Una had children queuing up with their shoes.'

Eileen walked over and stood on the step. 'What did Gran-ny say?' she asked.

'She didn't know.' Pauline wanted to tell her niece that her mammy never polished their shoes. Instead she said, 'It was on one of the days when Mammy was in town.' She looked at her watch and asked, 'Would you like to go into one of these houses and have some tea?'

'Really?' Eileen beamed.

'And truly,' Pauline said, 'I have a friend who lives about five minutes walk from here and she is expecting us for tea at five.'

Chapter Sixty-four

The door to number twelve rattled like it was being torn from its hinges twenty seconds after Pauline had tapped on one of the windows. She heard Kate say, 'Gawd mom,' and Eileen say, 'Jesus,' when the door flung open and the high pitched voice of a tall woman shouted, 'Pauline.'

Ena Dwyer always pulled her hall door open with a flourish. And she always shouted the name of the person that was standing on her doorstep. Most of the time she knew who was at the door because she would look through the window first. If she didn't know who was there she would shout, 'Well.' She used to frighten the life out of Una and Pauline when they were children and their mammy had sent them down to her on a message. Una used to stand out in the middle of the street until Ena had finished her roar.

Ena let go of her hall door and moved her tall body with such a swift swing towards the small group the three girls and the old lady stepped backwards as though they expected Ena to fall on top of them.

'Bella,' Ena cried loudly, swinging her arms out as though she was going to pick the frightened old lady up by her elbows. 'I remember you from the wedding,' she said in a softer sweet tone taking Bella's small hands and pulling her into the small three-foot square hall. She threw her long grey hair back over her shoulder, then tossed her head towards another open door that was just beside her right elbow.

Bella bowed obediently and walked into the little house while the bracelets on Ena's arm jangled like they were playing a tune.

'Now,' Ena shouted scanning the terrified faces of the three young girls who couldn't take their eyes off the rows of beads that hung from Ena's neck over her long, loose, flowing, flowered dress. 'Eileen,' she shouted, 'where did you get that lovely hair?'

Eileen gasped, but didn't answer.

Ena continued, 'I'm sure you had some help from your mother; after all she is wizard at her craft.' Her bracelets jangled again when she waved at Eileen and said, 'You must come in, please do.'

Eileen went into the house.

Ena's held both of her hands in front of her like she was Jesus Christ showing the wounds in his hands. 'Genevieve and Kathrina,' she sang. Her eyes glowed with approval when she glanced at Pauline and said, 'What beautiful names, for two lovely girls.' She clapped her hands like she was going to ask one of them to sing and said. 'I will have to take a gamble. Kate on my right and Jen on my left.'

Terrified to disagree, Kate and Jenny nodded.

'In you come now, in you come,' roared Ena, jangling her bracelets again.

As the two terrified young girls stepped into the house, Ena opened her arms to her best friend's daughter and said, 'Welcome home, Pauline.'

Because it blocked the light from the only window in the room when it was open, the living room was brighter when Ena closed the second door when she was in the room. This second door was commonly known as the 'cross door', and nearly all the small cottages had one. It had to open into the living room because the small square hall was only big enough for the hall door. The small hall was needed to allow some privacy to the living room from the street and to prevent the heat from escaping when the door was opened in the winter.

The slight squeaky sound from her shoes and the smell of mansion polish from the inlaid lino on the floor triggered Pauline's memory back to the last time she was here. She had been glad of the darkness of the room then. It had also been raining and that made the light even dimmer but the room was warm and Ena had made bread in the oven of the range. She had sat by the fire with her back to the window and told her mammy's best friend all the things about her life in Canada. The dark room had encouraged her to talk and cry.

When some light had swept into the room after Ena had closed over the cross door, Pauline remembered the sun had been shining the next day. She had slept until ten o'clock. When she had been sitting on the bus on her way back to Plunkett Road at seven o'clock that same evening she didn't think about the film that she had seen with Ena in the Savoy. She had forced her mind to go over all the things she knew she had to do when she went back to Canada.

'Well,' Ena panted, smiling at the three young girls standing in a row facing the range, 'I expect I will always be jealous of your Granny Malone. She has six beautiful daughters, and now I see she has at least three even more beautiful granddaughters.' She wanted to cry when Eileen raised her arms and straightened her hair band.

Pauline wanted to cry with pride when Jenny said, 'Granny Malone has two more granddaughters. They are Irish and their names are Emir and Patsy.'

Kate and Eileen nodded agreement and smiled at Jenny.

Ena clapped her hands and shouted, 'Coats and jackets.' When she saw Bella gazing at the gleaming black range she said, 'I have a gas cooker, and I use it most of the time.'

'What is it?' asked Jenny.

'It's a cooker,' answered Bella quickly.

'Coats and Jackets first,' roared Ena. 'The bathroom is in through that door,' she added, pointing behind her to a room that was at the back of the house.

When Pauline saw Bella sway on her feet while taking off her jacket, she became concerned that she was over-tired. 'Can I phone Joan and ask her to come down for us?' she asked Ena.

'Certainly not! I wouldn't hear of it.' Ena said, taking Bella's jacked. 'Phone her for anything you like. Please do, but Dominick is going to take you home.' She stretched out her arm for Jenny's jacket and added, 'The phone is right behind you.' She then disappeared through a beaded doorway that led to the second room that was at the front of the house with the jackets.

An image of a tall, skinny, and awkward-looking boy came into Pauline's mind. Dominic Dwyer was Ena's only child. She also remembered an old woman, but she couldn't recall a man living in Ena's house.

Fascinated with her Granny Malone's friend, Eileen was staring at the curtain of hanging beads swaying when Ena came back out again a second later. She wondered if the tall loud woman had thrown the jackets out the window because she had returned so quickly.

Built without gas or electricity, the small house had three rooms – a living room and two small bedrooms. The hall door was in the centre of the house, with a window on both sides at the front and one window, for the second bedroom, at the back. There was a door off the back of the living room to a small back yard and a toilet. The bedrooms were large enough for a double bed and a small wardrobe, or chest of drawers, or two single beds with a chest of drawers. Ena's living room was three feet wider than the bedrooms, and as it was the length of the house it was twice the size of the bedrooms with a small section partitioned near the back door for a kitchenette.

For a second, Pauline thought it was twelve days instead of

twelve years since she had seen the old polished cabinet against the wall facing the stove fireplace.

A triangular shelf with a curtain fringe tacked on to the edge over a small television set in a corner held Pauline's attention. There was an old photograph of a young boy with his hands joined and a rosette on the front of his jacket. It was a photograph of Ena's only child Dominic. He was a year older than Josie. They made their confirmation on the same day. She was sure that Dominic had a crush on her eldest sister, she also thought that Josie had liked him too. He used to help her to carry the milk from the dairy when it was her turn to go and get it. He never played out on the street with any of the other boys, and he used to squint when he wasn't wearing his thick glasses. He used to go away somewhere for all the school holidays. He always had a pen and some pencils in the top pocket of his school blazer.

'Well,' Ena asked, after she had handed Pauline a glass of sherry, 'how did you all enjoy your day?'

Assuming that her Canadian cousins were either too shy, or frightened of Ena, Eileen smiled into the tall woman's deep blue eyes and said, 'It was great.'

Ena struggled to hold back tears when she bowed her head in approval.

Eileen continued, 'I can now believe all the stories Una told me about when the family had lived in Arbour Hill are true.' She smiled over at Pauline as though she was saying thank you.

Beautiful like her mammy, Ena thought. She drank some of her sherry and said, 'Your Aunt Una was always smart.' As if to compete with what Sheila Malone's second daughter had told her lovely niece, Ena told them about what it was like living in Arbour Hill during the civil war.

Chapter Sixty-five

Ena cut her bread very thinly like her mother had taught and thought about her son. The smell of the fresh bread brought her mind back to when she had talked with Pauline the morning after she had stayed the night. She had been up early because she hadn't slept, and she was tired when Dominic came into see her on the Friday evening because she hadn't slept the next night either.

It was to be another night before she slept after she had lain on the outside of her bed for an hour drinking half a bottle of whisky. Still, she thought when she was cutting the bread into small triangles it had been the best talk she had ever had with her son.

'Mother, they are the only family I have ever known,' Dominic had snapped at her when she had asked him why he was so interested in the Malone family after he had asked her to tell him about the party. He had stared into the fire for a few seconds before he had added, 'And I never really got to know any of them.'

Ena regretted she had continued to live in her mother's house after the hard, cold woman had died. It was over twenty years ago now, but at the time all she had wanted was to enjoy the freedom of not having to listen to the bitter old woman complaining. She recalled the shock that had shot through her when her son had told her he had hated his summers with his father's family in Galway. He had also told her he hated his father's family and he would never feel grateful to them for paying for his school and university fees. And he would never forgive them for looking down on her.

It was getting on for six when Ena and her five guests were seated around a round table in the back room. Ena refused to call it a dining room because it was so small. 'It used to be Dominic's bedroom,' she told the girls.

'Is Dominic your husband?' Jenny asked.

'My husband was killed during the war,' Ena lied. She thought about all the photographs on the wall in Plunkett Road and prayed the girls wouldn't ask to see a picture of Dominic's father. 'Dominic is my son,' she said.

Eileen had grown fond of her granny's friend. She could see the tea Ena was pouring through the cup. She picked up the small almost paper-thin plate beside her silver fork. She was looking at the delicate painted flowers on the plate when she heard Ena say, 'It's fine bone china.'

'Can we get some of these plates and cups, Mom?' asked Jenny when Ena had finished pouring the tea.

'Sorry girls,' Pauline said, 'not these. I was thinking of getting a couple of the tiered ones for cakes and sandwiches, but not a full set.' She met Ena's smile and added, 'I don't know how I'll manage them when we get back to Canada; they have had so much royal treatment.'

'Was it your mom's?' Jenny asked, remembering the plates Maeve had used nearly two weeks earlier.

'Are they over eighty years old?' asked Kate.

Ena laughed loudly and said, 'More. It was my mom's mom's.'

Eileen held the side of the plate between her thumb and fingers and said, 'They are beautiful.'

And so are you, Ena thought. 'Very, very beautiful.' She moved her hand into the table and lifted a spoon of sugar out of the sugar bowl. 'I am almost sure that it is over two hundred years old. And I never saw my mom use it once.'

While they ate the tiny sandwiches and small cakes Ena brought her visitors into another world talking about her childhood. She told them stories about her mother and her grandmother. She brought them to India, Africa and China in her great grandfather's merchant ship. As Ena talked the young girls, they were almost able to feel what it was like to be a humble maid and marry a rich sea captain. Then a sea captain's daughter who becomes a scullery maid. When they were starting on the cream cakes Eileen asked, 'Did your great grandfather bring the bone china all the way from China in his own ship?'

'I don't really know, dear,' Ena said, picking up her small plate and running her fingers along the rim and added, 'I like to think he did.' She raised her head and smiling mischievously: 'He was a pirate and a smuggler.'

'Are you ever afraid you will break any of them?' asked Kate.

'Not as much as I used to,' replied Ena. 'I have mixed feelings about them. I feel that they shouldn't be stored away in the bottom of the wardrobe all the time. And I also believe that so much work went into making them that they should be looked after.' She rubbed her hand over the plate again and said, 'A lot of slavery was used in making these. I think of the poor people that had to dig the clay and work the fires more than I do the artists that painted them.'

While the twins were looking sadly at the plates Pauline turned round to see why Eileen was looking over her head. She knew straightaway that the tall, broad, dark-haired man that filled the doorway was Dominic. She would have known the thick glasses anywhere.

'Dominic,' Ena said when she heard him cough.

'Mother,' Dominic replied and smiled warmly at all the faces that had turned to look at him. He held out his hand to Pauline and said, 'It's been a long time, Pauline.' He flapped his hands to tell Ena to stay sitting and said, 'I'll get my own in a minute.' He smiled at the girls, then he stretched his hand across the table and said. 'You must be Bella.' He shook hands with Eileen then stroked his short beard and gazed at the twins. 'It's fifty, fifty' he said, 'so I'll go for—' He moved his finger from one to the other about six times then said, 'Kate,' and pointed to Jenny.

When Dominic came back into the room with a small stool and a mug of coffee, he smiled at Eileen when he saw her look from his mug to the neat and decorated cups they were having their tea from and said, 'I get enough of them at court,' he said, 'and the tea is always cold.'

'Are you a policeman?' Jenny asked,

'I'm a barrister,' Dominic returned, taking the last two small sandwiches off the plate in the middle of the table, 'I'm the one who gets you sent to prison.'

'Like an attorney,' Pauline told her daughters, feeling her face grow warm. It was the first time she had heard him say her name, and she couldn't see his eyes because his glasses were so thick.

'In the Four Courts?' Eileen asked. 'We saw it today.'

'I thought you would,' Dominic said, moving his warm smile to his mother a couple of times, 'the next time you come if you like I'll arrange to take you around some of it.'

'Yes please,' Eileen replied.

While wondering how Dominic knew about them going around town, Pauline wasn't surprised he was a barrister. She knew he went to university after O'Connell's because her mammy had told her.

'And you Pauline,' Dominic smiled, 'do you find Dublin has changed since you were here last?'

If Dominic's face wasn't turned towards her, Pauline wouldn't have known he was looking at her. She remembered he always squinted when he talked. She used to think he raised his cheeks so that he could keep his glasses on his nose. She also used to think he was always smiling because when he raised his cheeks he showed his top teeth. 'I don't really know, Dominic,' she said, 'because today is the first time I have ever really looked at the city.'

Dominick nodded his head as though he approved of her answer and said, 'I haven't met anyone who said otherwise. I always believed it is the reason why most emigrants come back. You have to lose or leave something to miss it.' He stretched over and put his mug on the table. 'If you have a spare evening I would love to take you out and see something of the place myself.'

'Like on a date?' Jenny said.

From the day Harry had left Pauline she had never wanted, or expected go out with another man on her own. All she could think of while the three young girls were smiling at her was that she was stealing her sister's boyfriend.

'Yes,' Dominic replied bravely, hoping that Pauline wouldn't refuse him in front of her daughters. He smiled at the expectant faces of the three girls and said, 'You Malones will never die out.' He then picked up his mug again and held it out his mother like he was offering her a toast, but he spoke to the twins when he said, 'Mother here will vouch for my good behaviour. I am sure she will promise you that I will bring your mom back safely.'

When Pauline felt the bright smiles of her daughters boring into her she said, 'I would love that.' She then felt her stomach turn over like it was telling her she wasn't playing a game. Her mind raced through her suitcase.

'How about Wednesday evening?' Dominic said, returning his empty mug to the table. 'I believe you are going over to Una on Sunday.' He smiled at the eager young faces again, 'Or whatever evening you like. I should imagine the family will want you to themselves for the last few days.'

How on earth does he know about Una? Pauline wondered

glancing at Ena, then returned Dominic's warm smile and said, 'Wednesday would be great.'

'Where will you go?' Kate asked as though she was going with them.

Pauline was so embarrassed that she looked over to Ena. She saw that Eileen was holding onto the Ena's arm and they both had their head bowed over laughing.

Dominic looked over at Kate and said, 'You are the experts. What did you see today that impressed you the most?'

Ena slapped the table and bellowed, 'Just don't say Bewleys.'

'What about the Shelburne?' Eileen suggested.

Chapter Sixty-six

For the second time in ten seconds Sheila Malone asked, 'Is that the last piece of toast?'

Josie continued to spread marmalade on her slice trying to remember how many drinks she had had at the airport the evening she had come home. Three and two; she often had that many when she went out for the evening in Kent, they all did. Except Mike, he always drove. Sometimes during the week she had a couple of vodkas and there were times when she had a sherry while she was cooking.

Raising her head from her squashed piece of toast, Josie looked past her mammy's head into the back garden, recalling the doctor asking her about how much alcohol she drank every day. She was sure the doctor was wrong and that the drink had nothing to do with her losing the baby. That happened because she was too old. She didn't need drink; she liked it, and had done since Joan's wedding. She was sure it had helped her to sleep on the nights they were down in Limerick during the time when Mike's sister was dying.

'Are you all right now, Mammy?'

Turning round quickly, Josie found Eileen had come in through the door from the hall. She smiled at the 'Feed the World' transfer that covered the front of the long T-shirt her daughter was wearing for a nightdress. 'I'm fine,' she said, 'what about you?'

Eileen swept her hair back off her face and tucked it behind her neck and walked lazily over to the table and sat down. She hung her head to one side and drawled, 'Gawd, Mom but I slept well.' While her mammy was laughing at the imitation of her Canadian cousin's accent she added, 'Oh mom, but it was worth it.' She then shot her hand out and put it on her mother's arm and said, 'Stay where you are. I'm well able to get my own cornflakes.'

'Do you know what time it is?' Josie asked, watching Eileen move her way around Cathy's kitchen like it was her own. She then swung her head round to her mammy and demanded, 'Is there any special reason why there's no clock in this room?'

'Yes Josie, there is,' Cathy shouted from the conservatory and walked into the kitchen, 'and I'm delighted te hear yer in fightin' spirits again.' She wanted to cry when she saw how pale her sister was but she continued, 'I'm waitin' fer yerself te buy me one. But under the circumstances I won't press yeh this time.' She walked slowly towards the sink, washed her hands and then stood behind Josie's chair. She then held Josie's head so that she could only look in front of her and said, 'De yeh see that picture in the corner by the window yeh?'

'If you mean that awful green one of the Chinese woman, then I won't look at it for very long,' Josie said, 'and quite frankly I wouldn't hang it in the garden shed.'

Cathy let go of her sister's head: 'I thought as much,' she said, 'and I knew yeh would insist on buyin' somethin' new fer teh new kitchen. Yeh'ev already bought teh fridge and teh freezer. I though of askin' yeh fer a cooker but I couldn't wait fer yeh te come home.' She saw Eileen's shoulders shaking as she bent her body over her bowl of cornflakes. She kept her eyes on the green picture and said, 'That dreadful thing comes down when yeh replace it with a lovely clock.' She looked down at her sister's face and continued, 'Yer not goin' te talk me out of it. A clock is what it's goin' te be. That way we can all think of yeh when we look at it.'

Josie looked at Eileen as though she was expecting her support and said, 'I have no intention of talking you out of it. Why haven't you asked me before now?'

Used to listening to Cathy bantering with her mammy, and knowing that her mammy enjoyed it, at the same time Eileen could see her mammy was sad. In an effort to get her mammy to laugh, Eileen said, 'You were supposed to put that picture in the bin the first time that you saw it. Then Cathy was to ask you to buy a clock to fill up the space.' She then lifted her bowl to her mouth and drank the milk that was left.

Delighted that Eileen was helping her to tease Josie, Cathy said, 'Not ask.' She nodded firmly when Josie started a smile and said, 'And don't go buyin' us one of them white dinner plate things that has four black lines around the sides and no glass over it.'

'If I'm buying it, I'll buy what I like,' retorted Josie smugly.

Cathy also smiled smugly and said, 'That's what I'm hopin' fer.' She winked at Eileen, 'If there's one thing er Josie has it's taste. I'm sure we'll be delighted with what yeh settle fer.' She nodded over to her mammy.

Sheila Malone smiled at her two daughters, then raised her hands and patted her hair.

Worried about Josie and fed up with her mammy demonstrating that she wanted her hair done, Cathy called out, 'I take it we'll now all have a fresh cup of tea, and when we've lit er cigarettes Eileen'll tell us about her day yesterday.'

Josie smiled at her daughter's bright face and asked, 'Other than Bewley's and O'Connell Bridge what else did you see that was so wonderful and worth wearing yourself out for?'

Every minute of Eileen's day had been wonderful. Her most vivid memory was standing on the pavement and looking at her mother's early home. 'We went to Arbour Hill,' she said, moving her smile to her granny, 'we had tea in Ena's, and Dominic drove us back to Joan's.'

Fury shone in Sheila's eyes. She pushed her chair back and said, 'While you are all chatting I'm going to have a bath.'

As her mammy walked out the door, Josie smiled at the glow in her daughter's eyes and said, 'Arbour Hill is different to Ballyglass.' The only time Josie had gone back to her old home was when she had driven her mammy down to her friend Ena the day after Joan was married.

Climbing the stairs with the intention of going back to bed for the day, Sheila Malone recalled the time she had slept over with her best friend the evening Pauline went back to Canada twelve years ago. The anger that inflamed her face darted through her body so quickly she had to grip the banisters tightly to stop from falling. Ena had removed the bed from her second bedroom and bought a table, so Sheila had to sleep on the couch in the living room.

While her mammy was walking into her bedroom, Cathy closed the door the angry woman had left open. She was born the year after the family had moved to a new house with three bedrooms, a bathroom, and a garden at the back and front. She was two when the family moved to Ballyglass so she had no memories of Ballymore either. But she had been down to Arbour Hill so she knew how different the place was. The door clicked closed as she called over to Eileen, 'Will it change yer mind about teh social order of things?'

Eileen sat back in her chair, picked up a spoon, stirred her tea and replied, 'I'm not against the social order of things as you put it. I'm against all the waste that's going on everywhere. For example it seems unfair that all the houses up here have such big gardens and all the houses in Arbour Hill have none at all.'

'We managed,' Josie said, smiling proudly at her daughter and added, 'I hate gardening.' She recalled she was her daughter's age when her third brother, and sixth sibling Donal was a year old. And it wasn't a garden she would have wanted to have. It was another bedroom and a bathroom.

Pleased to see her mammy smiling Eileen said, 'Pauline has a date.'

'Yer not serious?' Cathy bellowed. She joined Josie in staring at Eileen like she had told them that Pauline was getting married again. 'Go on,' she demanded. When her niece continued to laugh, Cathy slapped her sister on her arm and shouted, 'Josie, if yeh don't get yer daughter te tell us who he is I'll put that green picture on teh wall over there beside yer bed. I promise yeh I really will.'

For a second Josie had a vision of her daughter and sister getting picked up by a man in a pub. 'How do you know?' she asked.

Between bouts of giggling Eileen told her mammy and Cathy about their tea in Ena's and her son Dominic asking Pauline if he could show her more of Dublin if she had the time. And how Kate and Jenny encouraged their mammy to go to the Shelburne.

Satisfied that Eileen had told her everything, Cathy said, 'He's very nice, isn't he?' Remembering the thick glasses he wore, she smiled at her sister and asked, 'Do you remember him, Josie?'

Of course Josie remembered Dominic Dwyer. Every girl remembers her first boyfriend. She also recalled the cold stares Ena used to give her when she used to see them together. Staring at the wall over Cathy's head, Josie recalled the last time she had seen the tall lanky boy who used to carry the bag of potatoes for her when she was her daughter's age. 'Yes, I remember him,' she said.

The light orchestral music coming from the radio brought Josie's thoughts to the dance when she had last seen Dominic. It had been a couple of years after her family had moved from Arbour Hill. It was the first time she had seen him wearing a suit. When ladies' choice was called she couldn't find him. She had supposed another girl had asked him. She never saw him again.

Eileen put her hand on her mammy's arm and said, 'He remembers you. He asked Pauline how you were.' She rested her arms on the table and leaned towards Cathy and added, 'He knows every one of the family. He asked how your farming was coming on.'

Chapter Sixty-seven

Pauline came into the kitchen through the conservatory sat down at the table and looked at the drawing of the garden Cathy had made. She could hear the twins in the living room talking with their granny. She knew what they were shouting about because Cathy told her a parcel had come from Una. She wished it were Una that had come so she could make her something to wear for tomorrow night. Anyway she thought, Joan was probably right, her dark blue trouser suit would be fine. She had phoned Ena and checked. Still it would be nice to have something new. She looked out at the garden when she heard Cathy shouting at Rory. She couldn't believe it was the same place she used to try and make her way down so she could hang the clothes on the line when she had been living at home. She walked over to the door when she heard Josie shout from the conservatory, 'Make him earn his keep,'

Still unable to believe that it was the same garden she had known, Pauline joined Josie and said, 'Isn't it brilliant?' She smiled at her lovely sister and prayed that Josie wouldn't think she was stealing an old boyfriend by going out with Dominic.

Josie looked her sister over as though she was thinking of buying her, or she was seeing her for the first time. She smiled warmly and said, 'It is a credit to Cathy, and Maurice.'

With the thought she was stealing a boyfriend from her

sister still on her mind, Pauline said, 'I'm looking forward to meeting Mike when I go over to England.'

'Not as much as he is looking forward to meeting you,' Josie said, 'he has been doing the gardens every evening for the last two weeks.'

All the stories Cathy had told Pauline didn't help her to picture what Mike would look like. She knew from the photographs that he was the same height as Josie. She nodded her head towards Rory and said, 'How on earth did he get so tall?'

'They all are,' Josie replied, 'they are all better fed than we were.' She didn't want to think about, let alone talk about, their diet when they were children so she turned around from the garden and gave her attention to Pauline's hair. 'Would you like me to give you some highlights?' she asked.

The last thing Pauline expected her sister to care about was her hair. She recalled the hours Josie used to spend cutting and perming all the family's hair. 'Josie,' she said, 'you're only out of hospital.' When she saw her sister looked disappointed, she said quickly, 'I intend to ask you to help me choose something so I could do it myself when I get back to Canada. Maybe when we go down to see you when we go over to Una's and you are better.'

Troubled by the memory of the last time Pauline had been home and she hadn't helped her, Josie smiled warmly and said, 'That will be too late for your big date tomorrow night.' She nodded down the garden: 'Eileen told us.'

One half of Pauline's mind was telling her to accept Josie's offer to do her hair. It wasn't hard physical work. She could wash it and hold the dryer herself. She was blushing from her selfish thoughts as she turned to her sister when she felt Josie lift her hair at the back of her neck.

'I don't often get my hands on hair so thick and in such good condition,' Josie said, patting her sister's hair back into place, 'a few highlights would show off that lovely grey.' The bright blue shine in Pauline's eyes brought memories of when Una used to put shoe polish on her eyebrows to darken them so she said, 'Have you thought about dying your eyelashes and eyebrows?' She waved her arm into the living room. 'I brought some things with me to do Mammy's, and I'd be delighted to do yours as well.'

Pauline wanted to run upstairs and get Josie's lotions and curlers before her sister changed her mind or fainted. Her eyes pleaded a yes please when she asked, 'Are you well enough, Josie?'

'Of course I am,' Josie embraced her sister, 'from what Eileen has told me the twins would never forgive me if I didn't do your hair before you walked into the Shelburne.'

'Gawd Mom,' Kate called from the door into the living room, 'come and see the clothes Una has made for Granny. Three trouser suits, and they fit her perfect.' She returned Josie's smile and said, 'Are you better now, Josie?'

Josie wasn't used to children asking her how she was. She didn't know what to say so she smiled and nodded her head in approval at being asked.

'Gawd Mom, isn't Josie beautiful?' Kate said.

Laughing because she was recalling Eileen imitating the Canadian accent a little over an hour ago, Josie followed her sister and niece into the living room and she was still smiling when her eyes fell on her mammy. She nodded at her mother's pink glowing face. She assumed it was from the pleasure at the clothes that had come in the parcel from Una. She expected she would have to buy her a bag and shoes to match the suits, but that didn't matter. She would buy them when she bought the clock. She hoped Cathy would come with her and choose the one she would like for the kitchen. She decided Cathy was right when she said that cookers and fridges wear out, but good clocks last forever. Everyone would think of her when they looked at the clock in the kitchen. She was sure all the family remembered their daddy when they looked at his clock.

Chapter Sixty-eight

Cathy wrapped an old curtain around Pauline's shoulders and said, 'Yer havin' yer operation out here.'

That was fine with Pauline. She could see Rory kicking a ball around with Suzie in the garden. Her daughters and Eileen were sitting on the small stools her daddy had made for Josie, Una and herself when Josie had started school. They were all smiling as if they were waiting for a concert to start.

The concert started when Cathy said, 'There's no need te be nervous, Pauline,' and started to comb Pauline's hair.

'I'm not the least bit nervous,' Pauline returned. 'Josie has been cutting my hair since before you were born.'

'That I don't doubt fer a minute,' Cathy said, continuing to comb the grey curls on her sister's head and added, 'I'm goin' te cut it fer yeh this time.' She handed the comb to Josie who had finished taking the tubes of tints she was going to use to do the highlights.

As if they were also going to have a go at cutting Pauline's hair, the twins stood beside their mammy and listened, and watched attentively while Josie demonstrated how to part and cut her sister's hair.

'Are you thinking of learning hairdressing, Cathy?' Pauline asked.

Josie watched Cathy comb, part and clip Pauline's hair for a few seconds, then said, 'She will make a good hairdresser.'

'Maeve has already started doin' a course in teh technical

college,' Cathy said, 'and I intend to start next year when Suzie is old enough te go to nursery in teh mornin's. We intend te open er own business in a couple ev years.'

By eight o'clock that evening Pauline felt her new hairstyle was resting on a new head and the new head was resting on a new body. She glanced behind Josie out to the garden and placed four glasses on the small table in the conservatory and said, 'The children are playing cards.'

'Why have you brought four glasses?' Josie asked.

'Joan is on the way over,' Pauline returned, glancing out of the window again. 'I suppose it's as well the rain is on the way. If we sit outside the neighbours will hear what we are talking about.'

The sky was dark with clouds that were ready to empty every drop of water they had. Pauline turned on the light so that they would be able to see the table. When she sat down in front of Josie and she saw her reflection in the window she barely recognised herself with the blond highlights in her hair, and her eyebrows were dark and neat. 'Thanks again Josie for the make-over,' she said, 'I hope I didn't tire you out too much.'

'Cathy was a great help,' Josie said, feeling a little sad about that because she had wanted to do something to make up to Pauline for not helping her the last time her sister was home; she was also worried about the letter she had found on the hall table after her mammy had left in the taxi.

It was nine when Joan came. Cathy put a brown envelope with the backside of it facing up on the table, sat down and poured the four of them a sherry. She raised her glass and said, 'Here's to teh weddin'.'

Joan picked the envelope off the table. 'Is this what you found?' she asked, turning it over. Half of the front was torn away. 'Was the envelope torn away like that when you found it?' she asked Josie.

'I won't be going to any wedding,' Josie replied.

'I want to be a bridesmaid,' Pauline said.

Joan pulled three sheets of paper out of the envelope; her mammy's birth, her marriage, and her daddy's death certificates.

Like Cathy had decided when she had seen the certificates, Joan concluded there was only one reason why her mammy would have all the three certificates in one envelope. She shoved the three sheets of paper back into the torn envelope and said, 'there won't be any wedding.'

'What about a marriage?' Cathy asked. 'She is old enough, and she doesn't need anyone's consent.'

Josie couldn't think of anything more disastrous for Cathy than her mammy getting married again. She couldn't imagine herself being married to anyone other than Mike. At the same time she had enough memories of the way her mammy had treated her daddy to suspect that her mammy had never been fond of him. She dragged her thoughts back to Charlie and said, 'Eileen said he was very rude on the phone.'

'Sorry about that, Josie,' Cathy said.

'Why on earth should you be sorry?' Josie retorted.

So that was the phone call, Pauline thought, recalling Eileen answering the phone when Cathy was putting the paste on her hair.

'I should have been expectin' him te phone,' Cathy said, 'especially as he hasn't phoned fer a few weeks.' She rested her head on the back of her chair and thought for a few seconds. 'Teh only time he phones durin' teh day is when he hasn't phoned fer a few weeks.'

Recalling how her mammy had gotten dressed so quickly after the phone call Pauline said, 'he is probably dangling her, or playing hard to get.' As if she needed to be sure of what she had seen, she picked up the envelope and looked at the certificates again. She put them back into the envelope and said, 'Why would she want to get married again?'

Joan giggled, 'Maybe she's in love.'

More likely for money, Pauline thought. 'Why would Charlie want to marry Mammy?' she said. 'He must know she has ten children.'

Four of Sheila Malone's six daughters listened to a light roll of thunder in silence and thought about Pauline's question. Why would any man want to marry their mammy?

The rain that fell on the glass roof of the conservatory that had accompanied the thunder sounded like a dozen people clapping. Josie said, 'Older men usually get married because they want a housekeeper.'

The applause from the rain grew louder.

'Well he is goin' te get a big disappointment with er muther,' Cathy hollered.

Why do you want to sell the property was a standard question Joan had to ask all the people who came into the office and wanted to sell their house. And more often than not she was given one of two common answers. They were either buying a bigger house, or the house had belonged to their parents and they were now dead.

But Joan had also sold houses for couples that had to sell because their relationship had broken up. She recalled an unfortunate young man who had inherited his parents' house before he married. After three years his wife walked away from the marriage with half the value of her husband's property. 'It is also possible that Charlie is after Mammy's money,' she said wondering if the unfortunate young man had married again.

'What money?' Pauline asked.

'The house,' Josie said.

It wasn't the fear of her mammy selling the house that had made Cathy nearly faint. The rain falling on the roof above her head encouraged her stomach to reject her dinner. She looked up at the dark clouds and said, 'Mammy can't sell the house but she could do somethin' worse.'

'What could be worse than selling the house?' Joan asked.

'She could bring the arrogant little shit to live in it,' Cathy returned. She looked at Pauline and asked, 'What time is it in Canada now?'

Pauline frowned.

'Liam has teh deeds fer teh house,' Cathy said.

There was something worse than Charlie moving into the house, and Josie wasn't thinking about Cathy having another man to look after. If her mammy had gotten to know Charlie from going into the nursing home when her friend Pam was there, then he was probably an alcoholic also. She thought a prayer for Mike's father, and his sister Theresa. 'You are right, Cathy,' she said. 'We probably can't do anything about Mammy getting married, but we will have to stop her from bringing another man into the house.'

Pauline was surprised Josie was more concerned about Cathy and the house than she was about their mammy. She had also known Josie to agree with Una when Una had complained about how unreasonable their mammy was, and then change her mind when she heard their mammy bang a door. At the same time Pauline knew Josie was right. 'It's about two o'clock in the afternoon in Toronto,' she said.

'I don't believe Mammy has any intention of getting married,' Josie continued, 'she is just looking for attention because Pauline is home. She left that envelope in the hall on purpose to frighten us.' She snatched the envelope off the table and said, 'I will put this up on her bedside table.'

Chapter Sixty-nine

Cathy took her time walking up the garden path in response to the phone. She didn't want to talk to anyone. She had heard everything that could be said, and she needed more time to believe it. The only way she could stop the phone from ringing when she had closed the hall door after placing her bag on the floor was to answer it.

'Hello Charlie,' she said, trying to smile. Her chat with Charlie was shorter than usual. When she walked into the kitchen she was surprised to see the breakfast dishes had been washed and the units had been wiped over.

She had been working three mornings a week for one of the hairdressers in the village since she had completed her hairdressing course. So, with getting Suzie out to school, she didn't have the time to clean up the kitchen before she left.

It was late August, so she didn't have much to do in the garden. All the cucumbers, and peppers were all finished. There were a few tomatoes still on their withered stalks, and they would all be gone in a couple of weeks. Josie's clock told her it was half past two. She had a couple of hours before Suzie was home from school so she made a cup of tea and carried it out to the conservatory.

Sleep was what Cathy needed before she would be able to sort out the bedrooms for her sister Maura coming home. She decided if she lay awake another night she would have to go to the doctor and get some sleeping tablets. 'Just a little somethin' to knock me out fer a week,' she whispered to her feet that were propped up on the stool. She raised her face to the feathery clouds blowing across the sky and added, 'And then I can wake up and find the last three days hadn't happened at all.'

It was a couple of months short of eight years since she Josie, Pauline, Joan and Cathy had sat around the same small table and worried about her mammy getting married again. It was also three years since her favourite brother Liam had been home. She recalled some of the phone calls, and the laughs they had enjoyed, when the phone rang again. It was Jack Byrne to tell her that Una was on the plane and that his sister Freda was picking her up at the airport.

Una recognised the tallest of the three boys before she saw Freda standing behind them. She tried to smile for her sister -in-law when they embraced, but her tears came through just the same.

'I'm so sorry, Una,' Freda whispered into Una's ear while she hugged her.

Una allowed her tears to roll down her face. 'It was very good of you to come all the way out for me,' she said. She smiled down at Freda's three sons who were standing around the trolley that held her case and bag. 'They all have the Byrne hair, haven't they?' she said while she thought, dear God, let this all be a dream.

The late August sun was glaring after the shower it followed at four o'clock on the Tuesday afternoon. The brightness of the sun did nothing to cheer the two sad women who followed three blond young boys towards the car park at Dublin Airport. Neither woman made any effort to stop the boys fighting over who should push the trolley.

The eldest of Freda's sons was six, and the youngest was four. Apart from the blond, straight hair the three boys had the same round, pleasant face as their daddy. Freda still wore her blond hair straight and folded behind her ears.

Sixteen years younger than her brother, Freda was four when Jack started taking Una Malone to the pictures. It was another twelve years before Freda stopped hating Una because Una had taken the only person she had loved away from her when she had married her brother, and left her alone with her ma and da. Jack was her only sibling.

For her part Una found her sister-in-law very easy to like when she learned that Freda had been jealous of her large family. Today, while she walked behind the three young boys, and without a shred of bitterness in her heart, if she hadn't been grieving Una would have been jealous of Freda.

Before she was married Freda was a size ten. Eight years and three children later and Freda was still a size ten. Una had been a size sixteen since her eldest son Shea was born.

'I don't even know where I'm staying,' Una said, putting her case and bag in the boot of Freda's car. 'I just booked a plane and phoned Sean. There was no one there so I left a message on his answering machine.'

'If it's all right with you, Flo, would like you to stay the night with her until Sean gets back,' Freda said.

That was fine with Una. She had no objection to staying with Freda, but she wanted to be with her family. She knew where Sean would be and she didn't want to cry alone. She turned round to the back of the car to talk to the three young boys. Her heart nearly broke at the sight of the three young obedient young faces that looked back at her. They reminded her of her brothers Maurice, Donal, and Liam when they were children.

Brian opened the door to Una. Freda left her children in the car and went into the house with Una to see if there was anything else the family wanted her so. They found Flo weeding in the back garden. Una picked up a small garden fork and started to help her while Freda and Brian sat on the new plastic chairs and watched them for a few minutes.

Now twenty-two, Brian was a taller and leaner version of his daddy. He was a trainee manager for one of the supermarkets where he had worked weekends from when he was sixteen. He liked the work so he stayed on after he had sat for his leaving certificate. He was relieved his Aunt Una had come because he didn't know what to say to his mammy about his uncle, even though he knew she was mostly worried about how his daddy would manage in Spain than she was about the death of his uncle.

When Una and his mammy were sitting on the grass talking he said, 'You go on, Freda. Kevin and Angela will be in soon. There's nothing anyone can do. I'll cook fer us all, and we'll just have to take it from there.'

Ten minutes later Kevin stood at the gate, watching the cars driving too fast along the road. He had never witnessed a road accident or seen anyone killed. But he had lost one friend from drugs and another friend of his had a brother that had been killed in a car accident. He now had three young people to pray for.

Chapter Seventy

Dominick Dwyer wondered if it would ease the pain for one of the five Malone sisters if he told them now, how he had always envied them as a family. And they all had children; even Cathy who wasn't married had a beautiful nine-year-old daughter. Pauline was the very proud grandmother of a three-month-old little boy. He still thought they should all be told everything before their brothers arrived.

When a group of five people carrying cases walked past their table, Tony said, 'I'll check again.' The women admired his suit when he patted all his pockets before he nodded his head as if he was assuring himself that he knew what he was doing before he moved away.

'It'll be grand fer Pauline if they're all on the same plane,' Cathy said. She was tired of the silence and she couldn't think of anything they could talk about while they waited for the plane to bring her brothers home from Spain, and for Pauline's to come in from Canada.

'It would be grand if none of them had to be on the plane at all,' Una said, then covered her face with her hands.

Expecting that Una would give them all a history lesson on their youngest brother, Josie stood and said. 'I'll just go to the loo before the plane gets in.' While she fumbled around on the floor for her bag Flo said she would go with her.

'I'm sorry, Cathy,' Una said glancing sadly at Joan, Maeve and Monica. 'I was thinking out loud.'

Cathy squeezed Una's hand and said, 'And yer right, but it's happened. We have te try er best fer teh boys when they come in.'

Boys? Dominick wanted to laugh. They were all married men with children. Sean was only three or four years short of fifty.

Chapter Seventy-one

The room in the undertakers was cold when the Malone family stood in silence around the small white box on a metal stand in the middle of the room. Their eyes were stuck to the shiny metal bars on the sides of the white coffin that didn't seem like it was big enough to hold a baby.

Dominic stood between Pauline and Cathy facing Una and Josie. As a barrister he had often had to talk to, and sometimes try to reason with many angry and grieving people. Today, and at this moment it was the first time he had come anyway near feeling what it was like to be devastated. He was reminded of cartoon drawings and he was astounded at how accurate artists were able to get their facial expressions.

Maeve's round sparkling eyes were tilting at the sides down towards the collar on her blouse. Una's jowls were the clearest and the most obvious. Joan's mouth had the biggest downward curve, but then she was sobbing the loudest. He couldn't think of any reason to stop Pauline moving towards the coffin. He saw her stretch her hand over to Una. When Una clasped her sister's hand he heard her cry out, 'He was always only a baby.'

Dominic cried with the family over the loss of their brother Liam. He stopped worrying about the girls not being told why Liam had been cremated before he was brought home. He found that there was beauty and consolation in their crying together. He also thought it was fitting that they were on their own without their mammy. Although it was very sad to watch he thought it was quite appropriate for them all to move their hands over the coffin and polish the name plate with their fingers.

Chapter Seventy-two

Angie Dolan was one of the neighbours that stood at their front window and watched the Malone girls go into 34 Plunkett Road. They all knew where the girls had been and they were sad for them. Liam had always been popular with them all, and he always called in to see them for a few minutes when he came home.

Angie knew he was sick, but he never told her what he was suffering from. He left some letters with her for Una and Pauline. He told her they were to do with Cathy and the house and that she wasn't to give them until after he was buried. If they went before him she was to burn them.

Angie stayed at the window until Patsy and Emir walked up the garden path with Suzie and the three of them went into the house. She patted her net curtains, moved back from the window and started shuffling towards her kitchen. 'Sacred Heart of Jeasus,' she said to the empty room, lowering her eyes from the holy picture on the wall over the door that led into her kitchen. She then picked up a small bottle off the table and tried again to open it.

When the white plastic top on the small bottle refused to budge she looked over to the mantelpiece and smiled at the two white pills. She put the bottle down on the table again so that she wouldn't forget to ask Cathy to open it for her when she came over later. She glared at her holy picture and shouted, 'Yeh have some big bullets under that long brown dress of yers.' She held her stomach and shuffled towards the kitchen: 'Are yeh sure yer firin' them at teh right people?' She shuffled into her small kitchen for a glass of water to take her painkillers.

After half an hour the pain in Angie's heart over Liam was stronger than the pain in her stomach. On hearing voices out on the road, she wandered over to the front window again. She watched Dominic lock his car while he talked to her son-in-law. She took a couple of steps back when she saw Maurice raise his head and look at her window as though he knew she would be standing behind the curtain. She knew what he was going to ask her, but she hadn't made up her mind what she was going to tell him.

Maurice used his own key to Angie's house. 'Are yeh all right, Angie? Did teh girls give yeh a hand?' He asked patting the pockets of his jacket to make sure he had put the keys back there. He sat down on one of the two hard chairs at the small table, moving his eyes from her lined face to her legs he asked, 'Are they any better today?'

Varicose veins in both of her legs had plagued Angie since she had been pregnant with her first child. She glanced down at her bandaged legs, while she thought Maurice really did need everything spelled out fer him. She held one of her feet out and said, 'The legs are grand as long as teh bandages is done properly.' She decided not to remind him about the pains she was getting in her stomach.

In response to some young girls screaming in the road, Maurice got up and went over to the window. For a couple of minutes his mind became clear as his eyes followed the roof of a bus between the gaps in the houses as it travelled away from him. When the bus passed another one going the other way, he recalled he used to stand in this very same place looking for the bus when he was courting Maeve. When the bus came towards him he would call her and then they would go into town on the same bus. It had been a few weeks after Liam had joined the air force.

Angie watched her son-in law's shoulders shaking while he cried. She had seen him cry many times. He had cried when his girls were born and he always cried when the Irish team walked out on a football field. This was the first time she had seen him heartbroken. She dried her eyes and blew her nose then shuffled out to the kitchen and closed the door and made a pot of strong tea. She always thought it was better than whisky. She only had sherry, and anyhow that was for celebrations. When she put the tray on the table she said, 'Put two good spoons of sugar in it.'

Stirring the sugar into the dark mahogany liquid in his cup, Maurice turned over words in his mind. He had often felt jealous of the fondness his mother-in-law had always shown for his younger brother. When Angie had taken the spoon out of his hand, he raised his head and tried to find her eyes through the thick lenses of her glasses. He was still searching her face when he felt her squeeze his hand and say, 'Maurice, what can I tell yeh?'

'Angie, did yeh know?' he asked.

With her heart ready to burst with love for the lonely, heartbroken, handsome man Angie shoved her glasses back up on her nose leaned towards him and said, 'I knew he was homosexual.' She then wiped a dribble of tea on the table with her finger. 'Drink some of yer tea, never mind the spillin'.' She picked up her own cup: 'I also knew he was sick, but I didn't know what teh matter was. I thought he had TB.'

While they drank their tea in silence, Angie examined her feelings for her son-in-law. She had always thought that he was lucky to have married Maeve even if they had both been too young to know what they were doing at the time. She had known at the time that the wedding had given them the licence they both wanted to have sex. Over the years they learned to take the measure of each other and they are still fighting it out. She watched him stir his nearly empty cup and saw that he was still very handsome. She was sure that there were dozens of girls that would put their arms around him. She doubted he would ever get a cuddle from the only one he wanted it from.

She poured the rest of the tea between the two cups and said, 'I know he didn't kill himself.' She then scooped the sugar into the two cups of lukewarm thin tar.

Maurice changed his mind about drinking his tea when he looked into his cup and said, 'The police said it was teh sun in his eyes that had made him go off teh road. It gets real bad out there and even though his sight was poor he was wearin' his glasses.' He rolled the end of his cigarette in the ashtray for a few seconds: 'He died because he wasn't strong enough to survive the operation. It was the illness he had.'

'What was the illness, Maurice?' Angie asked, removing her glasses so she could take the punch when it came. She thought she already knew.

'It was Aids, Angie.'

She didn't want to see his face and she knew he would prefer if she didn't see him either so she placed her glasses on the table.

Maurice looked up at the ceiling as though he was talking to God and said, 'Angie, can I tell yeh what's botherin' me the worst.' He sniffed but he couldn't stop the tears rolling down his face. He flashed her a glance, then looked up at the ceiling again and cried out, 'He was on his own all the time.'

'Sacred heart of Jeasus,' Angie said, getting to her feet. She pulled Maurice's head over to her and he put his hands around her waist. She held his head to her chest and cried her own tears on to his lovely curly hair until Maurice had stopped wailing.

Chapter Seventy-three

The little white coffin was already on the altar when the family arrived at the church for ten o'clock mass on the Saturday morning. The family occupied four rows on both sides of the full church. Una was standing between Josie and Pauline when Father Brian Farley came out to the altar followed by Sean's Kevin, and Donal's son, six-year-old Shamus. The priest bowed to Joan who was seated at the side of the altar with Rose, Lily, Suzie and Patsy holding a guitar each.

The priest flapped his hands lightly for everyone to sit down. He then bowed to Joan again, and while she started strumming her guitar, he moved to the other side of the altar. The small family musical group played and sang a short poem, 'I'll love you always', to the tune of, 'I love you truly'.

Una nudged Pauline and whispered, 'That's the lad that joined the air force with Liam.'

Pauline looked behind her and saw Cathy kneeling down with her elbows on the rail and her face in her hands. 'Jesus,' she thought; before she turned back quickly and watched the tears roll down Joan's face. She lowered her head and prayed for Cathy. When they were near the end of the mass she wondered if she was the only one who had noticed that Cathy didn't receive Communion. She had seen Cathy move to the altar with everyone else in the row. She then walked out the other side without kneeling in front of the priest.

Young people have big funerals and Liam was no exception.

He probably did better than most people because they knew four days in advance instead of the usual one or two. Forty-two full cars followed the little white coffin across the city to Deans Grange Cemetery to see Liam's little coffin lowered into the grave beside his daddy; they had all come from Ballyglass.

The funeral reception was held in the Beggars Lodge. The sandwiches were on the tables when the family, their friends, and neighbours arrived. Donal and Maurice served the usual drinks for a funeral from a side bar.

Maurice stood behind his brother when Donal pulled down the grill at six o'clock.

'Are yeh off home now, Donal?' Maurice asked. He felt like he was floating in the sea and he didn't know whether he wanted stay there and drown, or swim to the shore. He couldn't stop his mind from thinking about his youngest brother and how he hadn't seen much of Liam since he had left home.

A peel of laughing from the table in the corner of the lounge reminded Maurice how he used to feel jealous of Liam when they were children. Maurice was five years older than his brother, but from when he was three Liam was always smarter. It was Liam that had made people laugh. Maurice was feeling ashamed that he had never thought about his smart brother very often before Sean had picked him up at work and told him about the car accident and that Liam was dead.

Despite all the efforts Donal had made to stop his thoughts from dwelling on a name for the new baby Monica was carrying, the problem just wouldn't go away. He hadn't been concerned about what the baby was going to be called until Monica had reminded him that because they had called Shamus after her dad it was only fair that he should choose a name for the new baby.

 At first he had worried because her family were expecting him to name the baby after his mammy, or his daddy, and he didn't want to. He didn't want to call any of his children after his brothers or sisters. But right now if wondered if he would get his youngest brother back if he called the baby Liam.

'Are yeh off home now?' Maurice asked again. He wanted to get away from everyone that was reminding him of Liam, and he didn't want to be the first in the family to leave. Also he didn't want to go out to the lounge because he was afraid that his sister Maura would start talking to him again.

Donal continued to stare into lounge. He had to duck his head and move it sideways to see through the rectangles of the grill. 'I'll wait a while yet,' he said, continuing to look at the same table where Maura was standing beside their mammy. She was waving her arms about as if she was singing a pop song while six other people were smiling up at her. His mammy had her head bowed staring at the ashtray in the middle of the table as though it fascinated her. When Maura sat down, Donal was able to see Maura's mother-in-law sitting beside his mammy.

Staring through another rectangle in the grill, Maurice watched another group of people sitting at another table. There must have been eight heads straining their necks as they leaned over the noise trying to hear what Una was saying. Mike had an arm around her shoulder. Flo and Josie smiled at each other every time Una stopped talking to drag on her cigarette. The conversation was interrupted when Maura bent over the table with a plate of sandwiches. Maurice pulled his head back from the grill and asked, 'Why did Maura's mother-in-law come with her?'

'I don't know, Maurice,' Donal returned, watching his stupid sister move to another table holding out a plate of sandwiches. He remembered her evenings working at the Beggars Lodge over ten years ago. He hoped she wouldn't ask him if he needed any staff this time because he did. 'I don't know,' he repeated, bending his head to look at the table where Janet Grant was talking to his mammy.

'She's very American-looking,' Maurice whined. He also thought the big woman with the grey, short hair looked as hard as nails. He disliked her the instant she threw her head back to look at him at the airport a little less than twenty-four hours earlier. He was used to Angie looking down her nose so she could see through her glasses when they had slipped. But she always shoved them back up again. He had time to look Janet Grant over when she had ignored him and Maeve in favour of Donal and Joan while they were standing around the two trolleys of cases.

Looking at her now through the grill, Maurice decided her cold squinty eyes were good company for her thin lips and sharp protruding chin. He wondered if she shaved the hair on the back of her head to show how thick her neck was. And the curls on the top of her head made her look like an old, fat teddy boy from the fifties. 'I don't like her,' he said to his brother and selected another rectangle to look through.

Neither did Donal. 'She looks a bit of a bully all right,' he replied, looking through another rectangle in the grid. 'I hope all teh family comin' home hasn't been too much fer Cathy,' he said.

Recalling the face of Cathy when he was bringing the three large suitcases up the stairs in Plunkett Road, Maurice smiled. Maeve was still laughing when they had left Plunkett Road half an hour later. 'Maura and Janet might stay with Joan when Josie and Mike are gone,' he said, leaning forward towards the grill when he saw Cathy get up from the table and introduce Father Brian Farley to Pauline and Dominic. When Brian sat down, Cathy picked up her handbag and walked away.

A couple of older people sitting at a small table in the corner caught Donal's attention. 'Is that Angie sitting beside Charlie?' he asked, smiling.

Maurice had seen them earlier and if he hadn't known Charlie was married he would have worried because the old dreamer had his arm around Angie's shoulder. He looked around for Charlie's wife, Myra. He found her sitting at another table talking to Fred. A loud peel of laughing from another table caught his attention. The tall body of Ena towered over Patsy, Emir, Eileen and Una's sons, Shea and Liam. Behind them Mike and Jack looked like they were standing guard in case the teenagers got stroppy with Ena.

The loud voice Cathy had been used to hearing on the phone described the opposite of the big bulky man she had imagined Charlie Whelan to look like. The first time she saw him she thought he was a jockey because he was so small and skinny. His face was light brown, weatherbeaten like he had spent all his time out in the open air. She was to learn from the man himself that the only animal he had ever ridden was a woman.

The third time Cathy had driven her mammy over to Charlie's house in Rathmines, Charlie had asked her to come in for a coffee. She had stayed for two hours. When she was driving home she was relieved that Charlie wasn't looking for a wife. He had enough with the one he had.

Myra Whelan was also about sixty years old. She was a head and shoulders taller than Charlie, and she never stopped complaining.

From all the stories Charlie had told her about himself Cathy estimated he must be ninety years old but she grew very fond of him.

Chapter Seventy-four

Jack, Mike, Eileen, Rory, Una's Liam and Shea went back to England the day after the funeral.

On the Monday morning Cathy went back to bed after Suzie had gone to school. She was tired but she was unable to get back to sleep so she lay in bed listening to the radio until she heard the third set of footsteps going down the stairs. As there were only four sleeping in the house one of them would be her mammy. She expected her mammy would go over to Myra Whelan and she didn't want to be on her own with Maura and Janet so she decided she would leave early for her work experience with a hairdresser in town.

Janet Grant pressed her thick arm on the table and turned round to the door. She scrunched her face while she lifted her glasses up on her nose, but she didn't say anything.

Cathy sat down on the low chair under the window. Not for the first time she saw the bulges of fat oozing around Janet arms and back between the straps of her bra. She thought the awful woman looked like a wrestler.

Sheila Malone smiled and nodded her head to her youngest daughter, then went back to watching the television and rolling the hem of her apron.

Fed up with whom she believed to be the lady of house not talking to her, Janet slapped the table and called out, 'Sheila, can we get a cab into town from out here at eight o'clock in the morning?'

'You can get a cab to anywhere at any time from out here,' Sheila replied coldly.

Prior to Maura coming home this time, it was fourteen years since Sheila Malone had seen her spoilt, stupid daughter, or Janet Grant. Although she had invited herself to stay with Maura, she had expected she would stay with Pauline. During her three-week visit, she never saw Pauline or Pauline's twin little girls.

It had never been Sheila's way to tell her children what she wanted them to do for her. If Maura had understood the hints her mammy was constantly delivering about her wish to be taken over to Pauline's house, Maura would not have taken her.

For one thing Maura couldn't drive, and Carl didn't want to go out to Pauline's house. So when Sheila said anything that hinted about the difficulties with living in an apartment, Carl brought his mother-in-law over to his mother's house.

Before she had taken her seat on the plane for her journey home from Canada, Sheila Malone vowed she would never walk around another shopping arcade without buying anything, or listen to Janet Grant ramble on about how wonderful her son was.

Janet glanced at Maura, then went back to studying her holiday brochures.

'Yer best te order it fer teh time in teh morning if yeh want te be sure of it comin',' Cathy said.

'It's not for tomorrow,' Maura said, picking up the brochure that Janet had placed in front of her and starting to read it.

'Why not if yer goin' at all?' enquired Cathy, moving her head so she could see Maura over Janet's fat shoulder and snapped, 'Yeh'ev already wasted three days doin' nothin'.'

Maura turned sideways from the table, joined her hands in her lap, smiled brightly and leaned over towards her sister and said, 'Because tomorrow is when the will is being read.'

Sheila slapped her hand down on the arms of her chair, stood, glared at Janet Grant, then walked out of the room.

Cathy threw the end of her cigarette into the empty fire grate, then rose slowly from her chair and said, 'I'll be off.'

They deserve each other, Cathy told herself when she glanced back at the house before she opened the door of her car. When she was fastening her seat belt she thought that no matter how selfish, mean or spiteful her mammy or Maura were, they didn't deserve to have to spend time with Janet Grant.

Chapter Seventy-five

The following morning in the bed she shared with Janet in the small room, Maura lay awake worrying about what her brother might have left her in his will. She wasn't worried about the money she would get because she knew her husband would tell her what to spend it on. She was dreading having him at home more often until the money was all gone.

Home for Maura was Janet Grant's house in Toronto. Carl had moved them into his mother's house a few months after Maura had gone back to Canada when she had been home twelve years earlier. He had failed to pay the rent on the small apartment where they had lived with their four-year-old son Jason. At the time Maura had been delighted with the move. She found it difficult and expensive to get minders for her son so she could go to work. She had to work because Carl was very mean with the money he gave her. He was also away for weeks at a time. She had also agreed with him that as they wouldn't have any rent to pay they would be able to save and buy a house of their own like her sister Pauline.

The bulk of Janet's body shifted in the bed so quickly that for a second Maura thought her mother-in-law was going hit her. Carl used to hit her when they were in bed. As if she could get away from thinking about her husband, she got up and went downstairs. While she was waiting for the kettle to boil, she went out to the back garden. She wasn't interested in tomatoes, or green peppers, and she hated rhubarb. She barely looked at the plants. She thought her youngest sister was stupid to be growing them for the few pounds she was getting from selling them to the neighbours and the man that sold them from a van. She also couldn't understand why Cathy was doing cleaning jobs when she could work in the Beggars Lodge for her brother Donal. She was so jealous of her youngest sister that she wouldn't allow her mind to think about Cathy completing her course in hairdressing. She sniggered at the idea of Cathy and Maeve opening their own salon.

Then Maura had never tried to understand any of her sisters. She was the last of Sheila Malone's daughters to leave her home. And, like her three older sisters, she had left to get away from her mammy, but Maura also wanted to get away from cooking and cleaning for her brothers and sisters that were still living at home. She was only seventeen when she had joined Pauline in Canada. Joan was only eleven, and Cathy was only eight.

Glancing back at the door she had come out from as if she was making sure she was in the house she had left twenty-one years earlier, Maura didn't recognise her family home anymore than she did the garden. The only time she had ventured down to the bottom of what used to be a small overgrown field was when she had watched her brothers erect the marquee they had hired for her twenty-first birthday party. Carl had been with her, and she had only been married a month.

With the exception of a few birds darting around and chirping to each other, the garden and the house were silent. She made a cup of coffee and went into the living room to look at the holiday leaflets again. She didn't want to go anywhere but she knew she would have to if Janet decided they would.

Crossing the hall, Maura heard a car engine. She wondered if it might be Cathy coming home early to make breakfast for their mammy so she turned back and looked out of the front window. There was no mistaking the girl getting out of the car was Maeve's older sister.

Fairness of any sort had never been part of Maura's thinking or vocabulary, but when she saw the new car, and Maeve's sister locking the door she wanted to cry. She reflected on Cathy, Joan and Maeve as well as the snotty-nosed little bitch walking up Angie's garden, and she thought life had been unfair to her. She was still brooding when she heard Janet Grant coming down the stairs.

'Have you a cold, Maura?' Janet asked when she saw her daughter-in-law wiping her eyes.

'No,' Maura replied, walking out of the living room. She went upstairs and sat on the toilet seat for twenty minutes and cried. 'I can't even drive,' she whispered into the toilet when she pulled the chain.

Chapter Seventy-six

Before the family had agreed there was no need for them all to be in the solicitor's office to hear the contents of her young brother's will, Josie had decided she wouldn't go. She started to wash up after breakfast when Joan had left the house to drive Suzie to school. The only reason she had stayed after the funeral was because she felt if she were with her family she would feel Liam was still with them. She didn't want any of her brother's money. She wanted her brother to walk in the door more than she had ever wanted anything in her life.

She knew she would never see his bright blue eyes, perm his fine fair hair, or listen to his funny stories again, but it didn't stop her from praying that she would. Now as she looked out the window at the children in Joan's back garden, Josie thought she would choke on the memory of how often she had dreamed of coming home from work and finding all the children were in bed asleep when the family were living in Arbour Hill. She was only fourteen and Liam was the baby then.

Josie never forgot what it was like to be hungry, so while she cleared the table she broke up the slices of cold toast and brought them out to the back garden for the birds. Although she had never dreamed that any of her siblings had never been born Josie felt as if she had. She watched the tiny birds swoop down to the grass, pick up a piece of toast and shoot up to the sky again like they had been fired from a gun, and as if they were stealing the food and were afraid they would be caught.

Small birds always reminded Josie of babies. And babies needed feeding, and minding. And small babies needed more attention than big ones. As she watched the tiny birds flitter between small trees and the rooftops of the houses she recalled Maura and Liam as small babies. 'God,' she cried up to the low clouds drifting slowly across the sky, 'I never wished any of the family dead.'

Josie had hated washing floors, making beds, washing up, and ironing. But she knew every crack in every pavement, in every street and lane between Arbour Hill and the North Circular Road. On the days when she was kept home from school to mind the children because her mammy was going into town to meet her friend's Pam and Ena, she used to put the babies into the pram and walk around the streets for hours.

When Donal was born, Sheila's mother bought her a twin Silver Cross pushchair. It was light blue with silver trimmings, and the most beautiful vehicle that Josie had ever seen. She used to wash and shine every inch of it every week.

Leaving the birds to fight over the bread, Josie went back into the house to prepare food for her family coming for lunch, and at the same time her heart was heavy because Liam wouldn't be with them.

Next to hairdressing, cooking was Josie's favourite occupation. Concentrating on her cooking prevented her from thinking, and worrying. And her worries always had something to do with her family, and her family were always hungry.

It was nearly five when Maurice walked into the large kitchen with a pile of glass dishes in his hands. 'You go inside Josie,' he said, 'I'll give Una a hand to wash up. That was a lovely meal.' He was prepared to wash every cup, saucer and pot in Joan's kitchen rather than sit in the front room listening to Janet Grant panting.

Una cleared a space on the worktop for Maurice to put the glass dishes. 'He's right, Josie,' she said, 'you can tell me what they were all talking about later. I want to talk to Maurice in peace for a minute anyway.'

Maurice was nearly four when Liam was born; too young to have noticed his mammy's swollen belly before he came home from school on the day he learned he had another brother.

'Do you think Maura really thought that we could rewrite Liam's will?' Una asked Maurice, handing him a Pyrex dish to wipe dry.

Maurice looked down the garden. Maura was standing on her own in the far corner watching the children running around. He sat down at the small table and glanced down the hall in response to the laughing coming from the front room. They were all women's voices and his first thought was to go in and drag them out and make them talk to Maura. He was ashamed of her when she complained about the contents of Liam's will. 'Yes Una,' he said, 'I really think she did.'

Chapter Seventy-seven

Cathy cut the few ripe tomatoes in bunches and placed them carefully in the cardboard boxes Suzie had made up. She had the handset of the phone with her as she made her way along the row of plants. Monica said she would phone her about ten. She looked up towards the kitchen when she heard the loud Canadian voices. At least they're out of the bathroom she thought. She didn't think she could face another morning like the last three. She and Suzie managed, but her mammy had come downstairs to use the toilet three times in an hour. Cathy wouldn't have minded if her mammy had had to come downstairs for a toilet a couple of years ago. But over the last few months her mammy had become much slower on her feet.

Well, Cathy thought, they could get on with it any way they liked. She would be gone for the day as soon as Monica phoned her.

'Where's the phone, Cathy?' Maura called down the garden from the door where she stood in the sunshine with her hands in the pockets of a white very light silky trouser suit. It had blue stripes running down the sleeves and legs. When she moved away from the house a light breeze filled out the body, arms and legs of her suit so much that her head looked very small.

Cathy watched her silly sister cast her eyes around the garden and made her way down the concrete path. 'I have it with me,' she shouted.

'I'll take it,' Maura said, holding out her hand as if she was talking to a child.

'I'll bring it inte yeh when me call comes,' Cathy said, 'Yeh can do some weedin' on yer way back if yeh like.'

Maura inhaled deeply through her nose, then turned and made her way back into the house.

Anger filled Cathy's thoughts when she returned to collecting her tomatoes. Maura's manners annoyed everyone but they were all getting a few good laughs behind her back. She wondered again who Maura, or the dragon that had come from Canada with her had been phoning so often all the time. Suzie had asked her three times where the phone was yesterday.

'Can I have that phone, young lady?' Janet Grant demanded from the doorway.

For a second Cathy thought she was going to wet herself because of the tone the fat woman had used. Then the sight of the thighs and stomach bursting through the light green knitted trousers made her want to laugh. She thought, the hard bitch makes Una look skinny. 'What fer?' she shouted.

'None of your gawd-dam business,' Janet spat out, then raised her hand and drawled, 'Just gimmie that goddamn phone.'

There was no way Cathy was going to give the phone to anyone until Monica had phoned her. The outstretched hand reminded her of a grip she saw on one of the digging machines the builders had used when they were doing the extension. She saw Maura standing at the door behind Janet with her arms folded as though she was gripping her chest from pain. 'I'll bring it in when me call comes,' she answered with more confidence than she felt, then leaned down to her plants again.

'Just gimmie that gawd-dam phone, young lady,' Janet roared, stepping on to the patio, and then slipped on some of leaves that Cathy had left on the path.

The phone rang.

Cathy walked to the end of the garden while she picked the

phone out of the tomato box. She listened for half a minute, then said, 'Jeasus Monica thanks. I'll take her out of school and we'll be there fer two on teh dot.' She turned back in time to see Maura helping Janet into the kitchen. It took her five minutes to fold over the tops of the boxes and bring them into the house and leave then on the floor in the hall. 'Teh phone is back,' she called into the kitchen, then climbed the stairs to the bathroom.

The phone was still in its right place when Cathy came back down the stairs. She pulled down the sleeves of her sweat-shirt, then shoved the kitchen door open. She stared at Maura and said, 'I'm going over to Angie's.'

Janet looked sharply at Maura as she stretched her fat arm out to take another biscuit from the torn packet in the middle of the table.

Maura dropped her head quickly to her lap where she was pressing and twisting her fingers like she was tightening a screw to a bolt. She kept her head down and looked at her sister through her eyebrows and said, 'When are you going to do breakfast?' She raised her shoulders and darted her eyes towards Janet in a gesture to remind Cathy she had a guest.

When she raised her furious eyes to Josie's clock, Cathy was reminded of Patsy and Emir. The two of them had come round every morning and helped her with the breakfasts and lunches when the family had started coming home. She recalled the laughs they had enjoyed about Janet and Maura. Her fury had waned enough for her tone to be civil when she said, 'I'm not.'

Janet sat back in her chair, banged her fat hands on the table, swiped them across it and brushed crumbs on to the floor.

Maura jumped when she heard the second slap, looked at Cathy and asked, 'What about Mammy?'

Cathy's temper rose again when Maura's mouth formed a smile that said; now I've got you. Janet patted the table lightly with her fingers like she was keeping pace with a tune on the radio. Cathy inhaled deeply, then said, 'Do her a couple of nice boiled eggs.' She held her sister's stunned expression for a few seconds and added, 'I suppose yeh can do that all right.'

'What time will you be back at then?' Maura demanded.

Cathy picked up her bag, and slung it over her shoulder. She wanted to tell her sister that it was none of her business but she didn't want to fight with her in front of Janet so she said, 'When yeh do mammy's eggs make sure yeh boil them fer ten minutes, then let it rest fer another ten in cold water, but be careful not to crack the shell. She also likes hot milk on her cornflakes.'

Chapter Seventy-eight

As usual when she inserted the key into her friend's hall door, Cathy called, 'Angie.' She picked up the post and shouted, 'It's me.' When Angie didn't answer Cathy wondered briefly if she was in. She decided she would stay until she went to the school to pick up Suzie. She walked through the silent living room to the kitchen to put the kettle on. Anger swept over her again as she thought about being so uncomfortable in her own kitchen that she wouldn't even have a coffee before she came out. 'Angie,' she called loudly as she plugged in the kettle.

She picked up the teapot to move it out of the way and found it was still warm. It was also was heavy. She removed the lid, pulled her head back at the smell of the strong tea. She then shivered with fright. Angie would never make a pot of tea and then go out. 'Angie,' she called as loudly as she could. 'Jeasus,' she moaned when she saw Angie's handbag on a chair.

Light at the top of the stairs told Cathy Angie's bedroom door was open. Her heart raced when she saw Angie's bed wasn't made. The covers were thrown back like she had only just got out of it. 'Angie,' she screamed, opening the door of the second bedroom.

Finding the second bedroom was as neat and tidy as it always was, Cathy rushed back into Angie's room and saw her clothes on the chair. 'Angie,' she screamed, running down the stairs again. 'Jeasus,' she cried when she noticed Angie's packet of cigarettes on the table.

Opening the door into a small lobby off the kitchen Cathy called, 'Angie, Angie will yeh answer me fer gods sake.' Before she had even tried the handle to open the bathroom door she stretched her hand up and unhooked the poker that Maurice had left there.

'Just in case,' Maurice had said to her the day he had altered the door. When the door didn't open on the first try, Cathy inserted the poker into the ring and yanked it. Just as Maurice had promised the door opened outwards. Angie was lying on her stomach on the floor with a towel under her head and it was clear to Cathy she had been sick. 'Stay where yeh are, Angie, yer goin' te be all right,' Cathy shouted, then added, 'Remind me te give Maurice a hug fer teh way he changed teh door so that it would open out.'

'It's not me legs, Cathy,' Angie said, raising her head so her friend could replace the wet towel with a clean dry one. She then cringed and brought her knees up closer to her stomach.

'I'm callin' an ambulance, Angie,' Cathy said.

While she was waiting for the ambulance, Cathy phoned Donal, then Maeve, then Suzie's school. Two hours later she was in the car park of the hospital when she saw Donal making way his towards her with Suzie running to keep up with him. It was five minutes past two. 'Thanks Donal,' she said. I've been worried in case they wouldn't let yeh have her.' She tried to smile.

'What am I here fer, Mammy?' asked Suzie.

Donal put his hand on Suzie's shoulder and steered her to walk with them the direction of the blood testing department of the hospital and asked, 'What's the story on Angie?'

'We're both here fer a blood test,' Cathy said, determined to be firm with her daughter. 'It's nothin'. But it has te be done fer the insurance policy.'

'Fer what?' Suzie asked frowning at her uncle.

'I didn't know meself until this morning,' Cathy said, smiling her thanks to her brother.

'What insurance?' Suzie moaned.

'Fer yer university,' Donal said and thought it would be a good idea for Cathy to take out an insurance policy for her too smart daughter. 'It has te be done. They want ye checked fer everythin' these days.'

'What if I don't want te go te university?' Suzie demanded.

'Then it'll be up te yer mammy if she gives yeh teh money te start yer own business,' Donal replied, glancing at his watch then asked Cathy, 'How's Angie?'

'They're keeping her in.' Cathy replied, 'Maurice and Maeve were there before I left her.'

Chapter Seventy-nine

The soggy cornflakes, and the green egg yolks glared at Cathy in the bin when she was scraping most of her sister's dinner from her plate into the bin. She wondered if Maura put anything into her stomach other than coffee and cigarettes. The familiar sound of the low screams and laughing of the children playing on the road was like music to her ears and drowned out the voices of Maura and Janet coming from the living room. She was delighted when she saw Maurice going into Angie's house.

Turning round from the sink to look at Josie's clock, she saw Suzie rolling up the hose in the back garden. 'Jeasus,' she whispered, 'don't ask me to choose between Angie and Suzie.' Returning to the sink, she picked up a small pot off the cooker. She smiled, suspecting her mammy had come downstairs and made herself some poached eggs and toast when Maura and Janet had gone into the village after the ambulance had taken Angie into the hospital. The small pot had some white froth around the rim. She was running cold water over her lower arms to cool them after she had finished the washing up when she noticed a bruise on her arm.

While trying to remember when she had banged her arm, Cathy recalled the last time Maura was home. Her sister had left her husband in Canada because he had been beating her. She wondered if Carl's mother was hitting her now, because she seemed to be afraid of the awful woman. By the time she was drying her hands, she heard the hall door open. She knew it was Maurice because she heard him talking to Maura. She smiled at the thought of being glad to see him. She had rolled her sleeve down when he came into the kitchen. She went into his outstretched arms and hugged him.

'Is Suzie comin' with us?' Maurice asked.

'Jeasus, Maurice, didn't yeh have yer head screwed on when yeh done that door,' Cathy said, hugging him again. 'It came away with one jerk.' She ignored Maura standing behind him with her hands on her hips. She picked up a small bag from the floor beside the fridge and said, 'We can leave Suzie down with Joan on er way.'

'You're not going out again?' Maura demanded, thrusting her head forward. 'Janet and myself are going into town in half an hour.'

For a second Maurice wondered if Maura was growing smaller. With her head and shoulders folded over he thought she was shorter than his mammy.

'We're goin te see Angie,' Maurice said, then walked down the kitchen. He turned back at the door into the conservatory and said to Cathy, 'I'll get Suzie.'

'What about Mammy?' Maura demanded, resting one fist on the table and the other on her hip. Her small shoulders rose slightly when she inhaled deeply and ran her eyes down Cathy's loose light trousers.

'What about her?' Cathy asked.

Maura wasn't concerned about her mammy. She just didn't want to be left alone with her mammy and Janet. She moved her head towards her sister said, 'Are you telling me that you are going to see an old lady that lives across the road while your own mother has been lying in bed all day?'

Shorter than Cathy by five or six inches, and her body slouched from leaning on the table, Maura had to look up at her sister. She watched Cathy rummage in her bag for a few seconds before she shouted, 'Are you listening to me?'

'I can hear yeh very clearly,' replied Cathy, slapping the sides of her bag like she was puffing up a pillow, then shoved her arm through the straps and hoisted it on to her shoulder.

'Well,' Maura snapped, shoving her head forward and up so that it came closer to Cathy's left arm. She pointed her finger out the kitchen window over towards Angie's house, and jerked her head with every word when she shouted, 'For god's sake, she's only the mother of someone who's married to one of us.' She didn't see Cathy's hand, but she heard the sound and felt the sharp pain when Cathy's hand swiped her across the face.

Chapter Eighty

I've never heard ev a jugenial ulcer,' Cathy said, 'are yeh sure yeh were listenin' right?' She was so relieved to learn that Angie didn't have cancer that she didn't care what kind of an ulcer she had. She thought her friend looked very tiny as she lay in the hospital bed. 'Are they feedin' yeh anythin' at all?' she asked.

'I'd love a dacent cup ev tea,' Angie said, raising her eyes to the ceiling in prayer.

She was bursting to tell Angie everything that had happened at home since yesterday morning when she had gone over to her to get away from Maura and Janet, but Cathy didn't want to get her friend excited, so she squeezed Angie's small hand and said, 'Yer lookin' great fer an eighty-three-year-old just the same.'

'And nineteen days,' Angie added.

'I thought it would get the ambulance all the quicker if I added a few years on to teh twenty-six we both know yeh really are.' Cathy said, smoothing Angie's hair. She smiled brightly into her friend's face and added, 'I'll have loads the tell yeh when yer feelin' better.' She wanted to cry because Angie looked so pale.

Angie knew all about Cathy slapping her bitch of a sister across her face. She moved her bum in the bed and asked, 'Are yeh holdin' together all right, Cathy?' she asked. Her heart was warm because she was thinking about her son-in-law when she said, 'Did it hurt yer hand when yeh slapped yer woman?'

'How did yeh know?' Cathy asked, recalling Angie had been asleep when she had come into the hospital with Maurice the previous evening. 'I don't remember if I hurt me hand Angie, but I'll never do it again.' She imagined she could see the frightened look in her sister's face when she continued, 'Teh poor girl just walked away, as if she was used to gettin' walloped.'

Smiling at the memory of her son-in-law walking down the ward to see her at seven o'clock that morning, Angie said, 'Maurice told me when he came in with me clean nightdress this mornin'.'

Cathy was telling her friend about the hardboiled eggs she told Maura to cook for her mammy when Angie pulled her hand away and used it to raise herself up on the bed.

'Sacred Heart of Jeasus,' Angie cried, looking over Cathy's head to the end of the ward.

Cathy turned round to see what was disturbing Angie. She was more shocked than her friend when she saw the good-looking man walking down the ward.

'Hello Angie,' Brian Farley said, smiling broadly when he stopped at the end of the bed. He held up his right hand when Angie sank back on her pillow and said, 'No, Angie, I haven't come te give yeh teh last sacraments. I hear you're going te manage on yer own fer a while yet. And I am very glad te hear it too.' His bright blue eyes moved nervously between Cathy and Angie.

Angie knew Brian, and his sisters. Only three of his mother's children had lived. Brian was the eldest and the only boy, and he had to take the worst of his father's temper after the big bully of the man had finished with his mother. The poor soul had lost three babies from his father's beatings. Brian had the same round handsome face, wide mouth and bright blue eyes as his father.

Cathy noticed that his golden tan was more obvious with

his blue open-necked shirt than it was when he wore his black suit on the Saturday when he had said Liam's funeral mass. He had joined the English Air Force with her brother. 'I'll leave yeh te talk with Angie fer a while,' she said, scraping the polished floor with her chair as she pushed it back.

Fed up with Cathy walking away from him since he had seen her at Liam's funeral Brian said, 'Please stay, Cathy. I'm not doing rounds. I'm not here as a priest.' He moved to the other side of the bed and pulled a chair over. He stayed standing until Angie sat up off on her pillows. 'I was hoping I would catch yeh here. Donal told me I might find yeh with Angie.' He removed his joined hands with their fingers linked from the bed when he saw Angie and Cathy staring at them. He then sat down as if to assure them that he wasn't waiting for another funeral and said, 'I'm goin back te Spain next week.'

Nothing about Brian Farley's clothes, or manner would tell anyone who didn't already know that he was that a priest. But he was, and both Cathy and Angie knew it. He sat with his legs crossed, his fingers entwined, and his back straight against the round backrest of the chair.

'Yer lookin' well, Brian,' Angie said.

'I can't say the same fer yerself,' Brian replied with a smile around his blue eyes. He rubbed his chin to stop from laughing and continued, 'I think yeh will have te cut down on teh fags, teh tea and teh bingo.'

Angie raised her head off the pillow and leant towards the priest and demanded, 'What has teh bingo got te do with me ulcer?' She flopped back on her pillow and glared at Cathy as if she was also responsible.

Cathy moved sideways in her chair. She didn't want to look at Angie or the priest.

'Teh excitement waitin' fer the last number on yer card,' Brian said.

'I love teh excitement,' Angie said.

Chapter Eighty-one

I have te pick up Suzie,' Cathy said over her shoulder as she hurried along the corridor of the hospital.

'No, you don't,' Brian said from four paces behind her, 'she's with Joan.' He continued to follow Cathy as she walked past the stairs that would take her out of the hospital. He let her walk a few paces before he called after her. 'Cathy if you don't talk to me I will have a blood test done that will prove that Suzie is my daughter and then I will take you to court to get my rightful access.'

Cathy hooshed her bag up on her shoulder and spun round. Her face was crimson-red from worry and fear when she started walking back towards him.

'Just who the hell do you think you are?' Brian spat the words at her then turned his back on her and started walking away. When he heard her footsteps behind him he turned his head and said, 'Yeh could have saved yer money on the blood test for Suzie. All yeh had te do was te ask me.' He walked backwards away from her and he pointed his finger at her face and said loudly. 'No, all you had te do was te tell me yeh were pregnant in teh first place.' He stopped walking. 'Cathy, I'm a priest, not a saint. However teh important thing at teh moment is that I am not and have never been gay.'

Cathy closed her eyes.

Brian looked down at his feet. Liam was the best person he had ever known. He had counselled hundreds of gay men and women in the confession box and he knew the agony some of them suffered. He looked into Cathy's eyes and said, 'That's all you want to know.' He then turned away from her and started walking quickly towards the stairs.

'Wait,' Cathy called after him.

He raised his hand and waved to her without turning round and then quickened his step.

She ran after him and caught him by the sleeve of his denim jacket: 'I'm sorry, Brian,' she said, then walked one step behind him as they made their way down the stairs. 'There's a café out on the street,' she said, 'would you buy me a coffee?'

Brian turned round with the intention of telling Cathy to buy her own coffee, but when he saw the sadness in her eyes he took her elbow and steered her out of the hospital grounds like he was a teacher taking a pupil to see the headmaster.

Cathy allowed Brian to steer her across the road, into the small café, sit her at a table for two. He bought two coffees at the counter, brought them back to the table, sat down in front of Cathy and asked, 'Why didn't you tell me?'

Cathy thought back to the week's camping she had enjoyed with seven of her girlfriends from work the summer the factory had closed. Brian had been there with a group of four blokes. They all had two sleeper tents. The competition for the fellas was two to one so she had to get one of them. She had always liked her brother's friend Brian, and he was the best -looking of the four. From the stories her friends had told her she wasn't expecting to get pregnant the first time she was with a fella.

'Why didn't yeh tell me when yeh got pregnant?' Brian asked again, pulling on her hand to make her look at him.

Tears ran down Cathy's cheeks when she raised her face. 'I wanted te keep teh baby fer meself,' she said, opening her handbag and taking out her cigarettes. 'How did you find out?' she asked.

Brian looked around the small café. He was embarrassed with Cathy's tears. He ran his hands through his dark hair and said, 'I worked it out after Donal told me yeh had a daughter and how old she is.'

Cathy nodded her head at her cup of tea, then looked at Brian and said, 'I was also afraid yer family would want te take her from me.'

Brian lowered his head to his hands. 'Yeh mean me da,' he said, raising his head.

Cathy nodded her head.

Brian sat up straight and said, 'He has been dead fer two years.'

'I know,' Cathy replied, 'I took Suzie to his funeral mass.'

'I am very proud of yeh, Cathy,' Brian said. He stood and held his hand out to her. They walked out of the café laughing.

Chapter Eighty-two

Three hours after Cathy had left Brian outside his mother's house in Ballyglass she tuned the small radio into her favourite station and placed it on the toilet seat, then stepped into the bath. The bubbles had all gone flat, and the water was cold by the time she finished recalling the last holiday she had enjoyed.

Just as she had pulled the plug to let the water out of the bath, the church bells started to chime the evening angelus. She had often made the sign of the cross when she heard the angelus, but she had never prayed. Right now she prayed in her heart that she had done the right thing by her daughter with not telling Brian when she had found she was pregnant. He had told her he was going to be a priest before they had even left the camping site in Galway.

Gazing at the pink tiles and trying to see something nice about them, Cathy thought, 'I am a thirty-five year-old woman with a nine-year-old daughter. I have no husband or boyfriend, and I don't want one either. I have my family and friends.'

'Sorry Cathy,' Maura called from the landing after she had tried to turn the handle on the door. 'I forgot, no problem, I'll go downstairs.'

With her legs out straight, Cathy sat in the bath and listened to the water running down the drain. By the time the bath was empty she was cold. She rubbed herself vigorously with the towel. She thought it would shake her brain cells up and get her thinking. She had managed her mammy with Liam alongside her. In a way she had let herself be managed, but the truth was she had accepted everything for her own ends. She wondered if she was really any better off than Maura. When she heard Janet plonking down the stairs she decided she was. She definitely was. Her mammy was a pussycat compared to the bull that was plonking down the stairs.

While Cathy was selecting, then rejecting dresses and skirts to wear for her evening with Brian, Maura was sitting at the table with her back to the garden shuffling through a collection of pamphlets. Cathy settled for her navy trouser suit and red t-shirt.

Sitting opposite Maura, Janet Grant was also sifting through pamphlets. But unlike her daughter-in-law she was reading them. When she heard footsteps on the stairs she raised her head and scowled at Maura. She hadn't forgiven the stupid girl for allowing Cathy to bully her over the telephone and the scowl was meant to tell Maura she had as many rights in her family home as any of her siblings.

As much afraid of her youngest sister as she was of her mammy, and mother-in-law Maura raised her face from the pamphlets when Cathy walked into the room. Her eyes were full of envy when she said, 'You look very nice.'

'Thank you, Maura,' Cathy replied. It was the first time Maura had said anything nice to her.

Janet turned round, looked Cathy over and sniffed.

Suzie was already in the car when Cathy left the house. She was looking forward to staying the night with Joan. 'Are you goin on a date, Mammy?' she asked when Cathy opened the door.

'Kind of,' Cathy replied.'

'With a fella?' Suzie asked.

Cathy turned on the engine and indicated that she was pulling away, then said, 'Yes.'

'Anyone I know?' Suzie asked.

'Not yet,' Cathy replied smiling, 'but you will.'

Later when she lay in bed Cathy decided she would wait until Maura and Janet had gone back to Canada to tell Suzie about her father.

PART THREE

Chapter Eighty-three

Charlie Whelan sat in the back seat of a mini cab and smiled smugly at the Irish Sea while Billy drove along the coast to Malahide. He paid Billy a generous tip, then walked beside him into the hotel.

Billy placed the cardboard box on a chair near the reception desk, shook hands with Charlie and said, 'I'll be back at ten.'

Smart in his new tailored suit, Charlie admired his small frame in the reflection of the glass door when Billy walked out of the hotel.

Within seconds a man dressed in a black suit and boasting a bow tie appeared from a swing door that led to the restaurant. 'Mr Whelan,' he said holding out his hand to Charlie and looked anxiously over the small man's head at the clock above the door.

Skilled at reading people's expressions Charlie said, 'I am a bit early, Mr James.' He patted the pockets of his jacket as if to make sure he still had his wallet. 'I wanted to be here before my guests, and I am sure you know what the traffic can be like crossing the city.'

'This way, Mr Whelan,' Mr James said and led the small man into a dining room where a round table was set for twelve people. There was a small table in the corner. 'I have reserved tables in the lounge so you can enjoy a drink until everyone has come.'

Twenty minutes later, Janet Grant ignored Una's greeting

and moved her head so that she could see behind Una's back. Una assumed Janet was looking for Maura and was about to move away from the table so that Maura could sit on the stool that was touching her legs and facing Janet when she felt a hand on her shoulder, which then pushed her down onto the chair.

Cathy moved stools, then told Pauline and Maura where to sit.

'Cathy, we'll only be here to have a drink,' Josie said, looking over to Charlie expecting him tell Cathy to sit down. After all it was Charlie that was treating them all to dinner.

Charlie smiled at Josie and picked his drink up off the table.

'She knows what she is doing,' Dominic whispered into Josie's ear, 'the plan is to keep Maura away from Janet.'

'Josie,' Cathy said, 'if Charlie is treating us all te er dinner in a place like this then the least we can do is te be comfortable. How do yeh think he would feel if we told him later that we got a creek in er neck because we had teh strain erselves when talkin' while we were havin' er drinks?'

Josie smiled at Janet.

The grey, short hair, thick neck and hard, cold face of Janet Grant reminded Sean of a policeman he had gone to see some years earlier and his thoughts shot back to that awful time with his sons.

It was fifteen years since Sean had started his small building business. He had built porches and conservatories all over his housing estate. He was now doing loft conversions. He was proud of his home and his family and he never hankered after anything he couldn't afford. Except for one very unhappy year with his sons, he was very proud of them.

His year of misery and heartache began four years earlier on an afternoon in June. He was searching through old tins for some metal paint when he found an old rusty can. He picked it up with the intention of throwing it out. It felt heavier than he expected so he opened it. When he unrolled the brown paper he found two envelopes and a plastic bag. One of the envelopes had some pills, the other had some white powder and the plastic bag had some dark brown, coarse tobacco.

Reeling from the shock of what he thought was in the old paint tin, Sean had sat down on one of his old kitchen chairs and gazed at the balls of dust rolling back and forth under the shelves near the door of his workshop. He didn't close the door when a shower of rain pelted down. For hour his thoughts stammered while he thought about what to do.

Brian had one week of school examinations to do and he was expected to get six or seven honours. Kevin was a year behind his brother and Sean's heart was almost bursting with pride at how well his three children were doing in school, football, and swimming. He believed that one of Flo's dreams would come true and one of their children would go to university.

The water dribbling down the front of the workshop from the rain gushing over the gutter, reminded Sean of the tear-streaked face of a customer he had built a ramp for. 'P-poor S-sadie,' he whispered to the dirty strip of carpet that was soaking up the water at the door. He had held his arms across his chest as if it would have burst with the memory of the tears that had run down Sadie's face when she had wheeled her son down the new ramp he had made for her. The boy was only seventeen and he would never walk or think again.

When he had been making the ramp for the young boy Sadie had told Sean every hour it wasn't the car that had knocked her son down, and made him into a vegetable. It was the drug he had taken that had caused Rufus to run out into the main road. The rain continued to pelt down and pour over the gutters and Sean imagined he could see the lovely Jewish lady with tears running down her face feeding her only son. He didn't know what he was going to do but he was determined that Flo was never going to be heartbroken like Sadie. He wrapped the rusty tin in a rag, locked up his workshop went into his house and made a phone call. 'Are the boys in?' he called out, after he returned the receiver to the cradle.

'Yes Sean they're all in,' Flo shouted over from the kitchen door,

'De yeh want somethin' done, Dad?' Brian asked, drying his hands.

'C-can yeh g-get all yer f-friends here fer eight this e-evenin?' Sean said. 'I've a d-double loft te do and I w-want te plan it o-out with yez all.'

Brian beamed. 'Great,' he said, hanging the towel on a hook at the sink, 'I'll call Mick and he can tell the rest of them.'

Kevin and Brian had worked for their daddy during the school holidays and Sean was also able to employ some of their friends. He used to take one of his boys with their friend on alternate weeks. While he had played with his favourite apple tart he tried to put faces to names as his mind went over the seven or eight boys that had worked for him over the last two years. One of the boys had always tidied up the workshop. Brian or Kevin had been always there so as to be sure it was locked properly.

'Are yeh all right, Sean?' Flo had asked. 'Yeh'ev hardly said anythin' since yeh sat down.'

Sean raised his head and said, 'Just doin' some addin' up in me head.'

It was about ten past eight when Brian came down to the workshop. He rattled the closed door and called out, 'Daddy, they're all here and there's a man te see yeh.'

Sean heard the loud voices of the young men in his living room while he was talking to the Garda at the hall door. He introduced the stranger to his sons and their friends, then the policeman opened a plastic bag and put the rusty tin on the table. Sean left the room and went down to his workshop. He had filled four black plastic bags with sticks for lighting the fire when he felt a shadow behind him and heard the Garda coughing.

Apart from his skilled men, Brian and Kevin were the only helpers Sean had during the following summer. The boys worked hard, they were respectful but they hardly spoke to their daddy. The poisoned atmosphere dissolved almost a year to the day after the evening the Garda had lectured the eight boys on the contents of the tin box. It was also the same time in the evening that Sean, Flo and the boys had come home together from the church.

It was the first time Brian had seen his daddy hand his car keys to his mammy when they were leaving the church. Although she was coping better than his daddy, Brian thought that his mammy was also too upset to be driving the car, but he didn't say anything because it was only a five-minute journey home.

For ten minutes the only sound that could be heard in the living room was the light ringing of plates and cutlery from the kitchen. Sean sat at the table staring at his hands. Brian and Kevin were slouched in the armchairs staring at their outstretched feet.

When the table creaked from the weight of Sean's elbows pressing down so he could hold his head while he sobbed, Flo shouted out, 'Leave him.' She stood in the doorway from the kitchen and waved her hand over to Brian and said, 'He's cryin' because he's thankful.'

Brian stayed standing holding his hands out like he was going to catch a ball and cried out, 'Thankful fer what?'

Flo pointed out the window in the direction towards the church and shouted, 'That it's not one of you two that's lyin' in teh coffin around there.' She shoved a towel under Sean's arm and said, 'Don't forget te wipe teh table.'

Kevin shot up from the couch and stood beside his brother: 'Is that all you're worried about? he shouted. 'An old table?'

Sean blew his nose in the towel, then nodded out the window towards the church and asked, 'Was he o-one of teh boys that was here l-last year?'

'No,' Kevin replied, walking to the other end of the table and sitting down. He waited until Brian had pulled out a chair and said, 'He was a pusher though.' He waited until his daddy had looked at him and continued, 'All teh other boys thought that we had given yeh teh tin.'

'Why didn't yeh ask us about them first?' Brian had asked. 'Was it because yeh didn't trust us or somethin'?' He looked at his mammy and said, 'We've all been afraid te even stand at teh bus stop with each other ever since that evenin'.'

As this nightmare of a time in Sean's life passed through his thoughts like a dark cloud, he glanced at Janet again. He thought he was looking at a very angry tiger with her head tilted back so that her nose was pointing towards the far wall. Her thin lips had disappeared because she had sucked them in under her front teeth, and her eyes were like slits from squeezing them so tight.

'How is Angie?' Josie called over to Cathy. She thought that Angie should be with them instead of Janet. After all she knew Charlie before his mammy did.

'Fightin' with everyone te make her a strong cup ev tea,' Cathy called back. 'Emir and Suzie are sleepin' over with her te make sure she doesn't get out ev bed and follow us all over here.'

Charlie recalled Angie as a young girl of fourteen. She used to clean the tables in a pub in the small village in Kildare where he had worked as a barman. 'It's the half-cigarettes she smokes,' he said, recalling she used to light her cigarette take a few pulls, then stub it out and put it into the pocket of her apron. He didn't know how many times she used to light the same cigarette: 'She needs to stop smoking more that she does giving up her tea.'

'Don't we all,' Cathy returned, 'I told her yer goin' te take teh two ev us inte Jury's fer afternoon tea next week.'

Janet Grant leaned into the table, stubbed out her cigarette in the ashtray in front of Charlie, then lit another one.

Disgusted with Janet, and to prevent Charlie from responding to the rude woman, Cathy said, 'Have yeh never smocked at all yerself, Charlie?'

'I still do,' Charlie said, picking up his glass of orange juice.

'I never saw yeh with a cigarette,' Cathy said, opening her handbag and pulling out her packet. 'Here, have one of mine.'

'Not now,' Charlie said, returning his glass of orange juice to the table. 'I only smoke during the night.'

'Do yeh mean durin' teh night when yer in bed?' Cathy asked, smiling at the stern face of Janet. To encourage Charlie to tell one of his stories she said, 'That's the most dangerous thing yeh can do. What about Myra? Have yeh though about her with breathin' in yer smoke while she is sleepin'?'

'I don't smoke in bed,' Charlie said.

When Charlie Whelan was seven years old he used to dream about sitting down to his dinner at a small table in a small room. Along with himself there would be a woman, a man, and a little girl. Just like the pictures he saw in books the nuns had given him to read in the orphanage. They would say grace together before they ate the chicken, and the cakes that would also be on the table.

Then when Charlie was twelve he dreamed he was sharing a bedroom with just four boys. He continued to read and he was an avid listener to all the stories he heard about the Easter Rising in Ireland, and the two world wars. He retold everything he had heard and read as if he had been the hero. Among many of his dreams he had been a British spy. He had made a fortune, and he had lost a fortune.

None of Charlie's adventures could be proved or disproved. The orphanage he had been brought up in had been demolished while he had been in England working on the motorways. He had never talked about the farm-labouring jobs he had hated from the time he was fourteen until he left for England.

On returning from England twenty years ago, Charlie went to work for Myra Drew's father in a small pub in Clanbrassil Street on the north side of the city. Paddy Drew owned the pub. Charlie didn't drink so Paddy was more than pleased when Charlie wanted to marry his only child Myra. Myra was forty-two and Charlie was fifty.

Myra had always hated the pub, especially living in the rooms above it so when her father died two years after she was married she sold it and bought a house in Rathmines. Charlie missed the pub. It was the pub he had married. He had lost his listeners. He had loved telling anyone who would listen to him about his adventures. He had told them so often that he believed them to be true. But it was Myra's money so they moved.

Having worked on farms in Ireland, and the roads, and building sites in England, there was no job that Charlie wasn't able to do; plastering, plumbing, woodwork, painting, tiling, hanging paper, laying lino and carpets. He even devised some new dreams about when he was working on the best stately homes when he had been in England. Charlie could dream about anything.

Myra listened and sighed.

Living in a house with a garden at the front and back was everything Myra had expected. Within a year Charlie had decorated every room, and while he was cutting the grass and pruning the roses in the front garden she would stand at the gate waiting for her neighbours to walk by and have a chat.

But Rathmines wasn't like the Clanbrassil Street Myra had grown up in. The neighbours didn't stand around chatting. Also Myra didn't have any children so she had nothing to talk about to the few young mothers that walked by with their children in pushchairs.

Deprived of the local gossip, Myra spent her days standing at the front window upstairs watching her neighbours going out and coming in. The only time she wasn't at the window was when she went out for the shopping. Charlie cooked all the meals, and cleaned the house.

Within a year all the decorating was finished. One day Charlie was clearing out the small front bedroom when he found the empty bottles. He was used to Myra drinking half a bottle of wine in the evenings but he had never seen her drinking vodka. He found five empty bottles and it was the day he started to love her.

Charlie was a dreamer, not an idiot. Even before he had found the empty bottles, he wondered if Myra moaned and complained so much because she had had an empty and miserable life. He also believed that people drink in secret in their own home because they need the drink. Not because they liked it.

Six months later when Charlie visited Myra in the nursing home where she was drying out, he met Sheila Malone and her two friends Ena Dwyer and Pam O'Mara.

Pam O'Mara was a patient in the nursing home before Myra had been admitted. Sheila and Ena were Pam's regular visitors. Myra had known Sheila as Sheila Duffy when she used to live in Clanbrassil Street. Myra's mother used to buy her groceries in Sheila's father's shop.

One of the few moments of pleasure Myra Drew had shared with her own mother was when they had been told that Mr Duffy who owned the grocer's shop had died. Myra was fourteen at the time and she was sure that at long last Sheila would have to work in the shop.

Like most of the gypsy son's customers, Myra attended the funeral when Mr Duffy's remains were received into the church the evening before the funeral mass. Myra wasn't interested in praying for Sheila's father. All she had wanted was to see the stuck-up little bitch crying.

The church was full and as Myra was a tall lanky girl she was able to see over the heads of all the people that were standing around the coffin while the priest was saying the prayers. The only person she saw crying was Sheila's sister Susan.

A stranger to the Clanbrassil Street area would have believed that Myra's mother, with her hard face and intense expression was praying for the bereaved Duffy family. Also a tall lady, Myra's mother was looking around for some women she expected to see. Her lips moved as though in prayer as she searched for the woman who had come up from Cork and worked as a maid for the Duffy family. It was from one of the maids that Myra had learned that Mr Duffy had been the son of a gypsy.

Chapter Eighty-four

When the waiter had served coffee, Charlie brought the cardboard box over to the table and like he was serving slices of gateaux gave all his guests a small parcel wrapped in brown paper.

'I've never been in Cork,' Cathy said after she had torn the brown paper from the small parcel. She gazed at the picture of a small cottage in the South West of Ireland and ran her hands over the plastic gloss on the cover of the book.

'I have,' Josie said, smiling down at Charlie. 'It reminded me of Hong Kong the first time I saw it.'

'I didn't know ye'hev been out to Hong Kong, Josie,' Cathy called down the table, flicking through the pages looking for a photograph.

'I haven't,' returned Josie. 'I have seen pictures, and read about it in a magazine.'

'Yeh can't believe everythin' yeh see and read in magazines,' Donal said, holding his copy of Charlie's book in both of his hands like he was afraid to open it. He never for one minute believed that the old codger would really write a book. He worried about what he had told Charlie when they had been chatting in the Beggars Lodge after they had closed the pub on the evenings Charlie had helped them when they were very busy.

It was Cathy that had suggested to Charlie that he write a book of the stories he had told her about his own life. At the time she never thought he would, and he had told her that he could write a better book about her own family. Now she thought the only reason he was giving the family a copy of his book was because he had written about them. 'I hope yeh have spelt er names right, Charlie,' she said, frantically turning pages looking for her name.

'I didn't use your names, Cathy,' Charlie said.

'How are we going te know erselves if yeh haven't used er name?' she hollered, closing her book and holding it between her first finger and thumb so she could measure the size of it. She estimated it would take her a year to read a one-inch thick book. 'Will yeh tell us teh different names yeh have given us?' she asked.

Orphans, ten orphans, Josie read on the back cover of the book. She smiled at Una, then turned it to look at the front again.

'Read the back of the cover, Cathy,' Una said, laughing.

Charlie stretched his hand down the table, patted Cathy's book and said, 'It was all your idea and I'm giving you all the money you will need to open your hairdressing shop.'

'Salon Charlie,' Josie corrected.

'If Charlie is given me teh money, Josie,' Cathy said, 'he can call it what he wants.' She recalled the first time she had met Charlie. She had passed her driving test and if she was at home when Charlie phoned, she drove her mammy over to Rathmines. Her mammy insisted that Cathy left her at the end of the road. Though bursting with curiosity to see what Charlie looked like, she was content to do what her mammy wanted. As she had lived on the north side of the city all her life, she didn't know her way around Rathmines and it was easy enough to turn the car and drive back the way she had come.

On Cathy's third trip over to Rathmines, the rain fell so heavily it seemed as if the clouds had burst The windscreen wipers couldn't keep up with the stream of water running down the front window, so when she had stopped the car she leaned across her mammy to open the door on her side so she could measure how far out she was from the kerb.

Believing her daughter was opening the door for her so she could walk the rest of the way like she usually did, Sheila caught Cathy's arm and said, 'Drive on up to the top of the road.'

'How far?' Cathy asked, more concerned about finding her way back than about her mammy getting wet from the rain.

'I will tell you when to stop,' Sheila had said.

Neither Charlie nor Myra drove but their house had a garage and driveway. Myra insisted on leaving the wide gates open all the time so that her neighbours would think they had a car. Sheila instructed Cathy to drive into the driveway when they were at the house.

Myra had been waiting and watching from the window upstairs and when she had seen the car she called to Charlie who came out with an umbrella. From that rainy day on, when Cathy drove her mammy to Rathmines she turned the car into Charlie's driveway.

While Cathy was recalling the first time she had met the author of the book she was holding in her hand, Charlie's memory was whizzing through the same times and how much he had looked forward to seeing her. He had never been pleased to see Sheila and it had always been for Myra that Charlie had phoned.

Although it was fifty years since Myra had seen Sheila Malone, she knew the snobbish little bitch the first time she had seen the small woman walk into the nursing home the day she had been sitting in the sunroom of the large house talking to Pam O' Mara.

Depending on their politics, and social attitudes, people saw St Celia's as a nursing home, a respite home, or a place for wealthy people to leave their elderly parents while they went on holiday. Una said it was a place for spoilt rich people. Whatever it was called, the two nurses that owned and ran St Celia's were never short of people to fill the seven rooms they had.

From the day he found the empty bottles, Charlie was as much concerned about the hours Myra spent looking out the window at the neighbours as he was about her drinking. To get her away from the window, he had suggested she might like to stay in St Celia's for a couple of weeks. 'It will be like going on holiday,' he had said from behind her at the window, watching one of the neighbours putting suitcases into the back of a mini cab.

Myra had never been on a holiday. She turned round to Charlie and said, 'I will have to buy a suitcase if I go for a week, and we will have to get a mini cab if we have a case to carry.'

'Sunday would be the best day,' Charlie had lied, 'there isn't as much traffic on a Saturday.' He also knew that some of their neighbours would be working on their front gardens on a Sunday and would see Myra getting onto a taxi with a suitcase.

On the Sunday morning while Myra sat in the sunroom with Pam O' Mara, wondering how many of her neighbours had seen her husband put a brand new suitcase into the back of a mini cab then watch the two of them be driven away, Sheila Duffy walked into the room.

During her two weeks' stay in St Celia's, Myra forgot about her neighbours when she became friendly with Pam O' Mara. Charlie was attentive when Vera updated him on her new friend. Myra had told him that Pam knew she was dying and she was angry. She was angry with her husband because he had another woman who had two children by him.

Myra continued to visit Pam in St Celia's for another month after she had left. Charlie was pleased that Myra was sorry for Pam but he also deduced her main reason for the visits was to see Sheila Malone. When Pam was moved to a hospice, Myra continued to visit her every day for another month. Ena came every second day but Sheila never came at all.

On her second week visiting Pam in the hospice, Myra was disappointed that her old snobbish neighbour hadn't visited her best friend, and, unable to curb her curiosity any longer, she asked Pam if Sheila was coming in to see her.

'I don't think I will ever see Sheila again,' Pam had replied sadly. She had stared at the holy picture of the Virgin Mary on the wall behind Myra's head and added, 'Sheila doesn't go to hospitals.'

Myra lifted Pam's head off the pillows and moved them so that it would be raised. The nurse said it would do Myra good to talk to her, even if she rambled on about different things. But Myra didn't want to upset, or argue with her new friend so she said softly, 'Sheila must have been in hospital when she was having her babies.'

'Just the first one,' Myra had replied, 'after Sheila had Josie she had all her other babies at home.' The Virgin Mary didn't move a muscle on her face while Pam went on tell Myra when all Sheila's babies were born. She sounded bitter, and she was, but she was angrier with the Virgin Mary than she was with Sheila. For years the Virgin Mother had all her prayers, but she had never had never given her a baby.

Myra had never yearned for a baby. She had too many memories of children waiting outside the pub for their parents to come home and feed them before they went to bed.

Pam closed her eyes at the Virgin Mother and sighed. There would be no more prayers. No more pregnancy false alarms, and no more dreadful physical examinations. She moved her legs. Although it was eight years now since Joe had found another woman, she would never forget the sex he used to force on her. First thing in the morning, during the day, and when they had gone to bed at night and sometimes he would wake her during the night to have sex. She wondered how different her life would have been if she had had just one baby of her own but she had said to Myra, 'If Sheila had been given a choice she would have preferred money instead of babies.'

What woman wouldn't, Myra had thought? 'It can't have been easy bringing up ten children,' she had said to Charlie when she had told him about her talk with Pam. She went on tell him that Pam had told her Sheila loved sex so much that she would have had a baby every year, and that Pam had told her if there was anything she wanted to know about enjoying sex to ask Sheila.

Charlie was the first man Myra had sex with. He had enjoyed sex with enough women before he had married her to know that she had not derived a lot of pleasure from it. 'Are you going to ask Sheila?' he enquired.

'I don't know Sheila well enough to ask her anything about that,' Myra replied, tossing her shoulder-length hair back in an effort to give him the impression that she wasn't interested in talking about sex with anyone.

'Then get to know her,' Charlie had said. 'From what you have told me about her all you have to do is to invite her to have afternoon tea with you in Jury's.'

Chapter Eighty-five

Charlie Whelan had never seen any flaws in any of the stories he told about the adventurous life he had enjoyed before he had started to work for Myra's father. When Myra had told him what Sheila had told her about her family he saw many contradictions.

At the same time Charlie was so pleased that Myra had stopped drinking, and she had ceased to stare out of the front windows all day, he encouraged her friendship with Sheila. He had also been pleased when she bought some new clothes, and had her hair restyled.

For six months Myra had tea in Jury's with Sheila every Monday and Thursday. Charlie wasn't surprised or alarmed when he saw that Myra had withdrawn money from the bank on Fridays and Wednesdays. Her father had left her a considerable sum, and with the sale of the pub, and the money he had saved they were able to buy the house and live comfortably on their investments. Myra had earned every penny she was spending, and she had stopped drinking.

The third bank statement showed Myra was taking even more money from the bank. Charlie remembered that Myra had bought new clothes and she was having her hair set every week. When he read the next two bank statements he started to go over what Myra had told him about her friend. He also decided it was time he met the poor woman who was living on a council estate with her youngest daughter.

Charlie wasn't worried about the money Myra was spending. While Myra was out he was enjoying himself reading. He had bought every book he could find on Ireland's history. He had new dreams about his ancestors fighting to free his country. He was so convinced that he became an orphan because all his family were killed during the Easter Rising he was planning to write a book about them. He folded the bank statement so that Myra wouldn't see it and put it into the drawer he used to keep all their financial paperwork. He scolded himself for not listening more attentively when she was telling him about Sheila's children. He couldn't even remember one name.

There were times when Charlie wondered if he had left a girl in England with a bastard. But nobody had come after him so he had assumed he hadn't or the girl had married someone else. He had always used a sheath to protect himself from a disease as much as he did to prevent the girl from becoming pregnant. While he was closing the drawer, he remembered that Sheila's daughter had a young child and she wasn't married. It helped him to see something good in Sheila that the girl had a home for her bastard child.

Summer blended into autumn. Winter brought colds and the flu. It was the middle of November when Myra stayed in bed for the weekend because she had a bad cold. She was so dizzy she could barely stand on the Monday morning when she was getting ready for her usual afternoon tea in Jury's. The only way Charlie was able to persuade her to go back to bed was to get Sheila to come over to the house for her afternoon tea.

Luckily for Charlie's temper, there were not many Malones in the phone book that lived on the Ballyglass estate. He was still angry when a young female voice answered the fourth number he had called, 'I want to talk to Sheila,' he had asked gruffly.

'Which one?' asked a female voice.

Cheeky little bitch, Charlie thought before he asked, 'How many have you got?'

Thinking it was a crank call, Cathy replied, 'Just the one.' It was ten o'clock in the morning and she was in great form. Suzie had taken her first few steps on her own.

'I want to talk to her,' Charlie snapped.

'Who will I say is calling?' Cathy asked. Her mammy was still in bed.

'Charlie,' came the curt reply, hopeful he had the right house when he heard a baby talking in the background so he added, 'Charlie Whelan.'

'Do you play the drums?' Cathy had asked.

'What difference does that make?' Charlie gasped.

'It makes a big difference to a band if they don't have one,' Cathy said, smiling. I knew a drummer once and his name was Charlie Whelan. He borrowed a fiver off me and he never gave it back.' She then held the phone out to her mammy who was walking down the stairs and said, 'Somebody by the name of Charlie Whelan wants yeh on teh phone.'

Chapter Eighty-six

A year after Cathy had taken her mammy out to Myra Whelan's house, Donal met Charlie. It was during the Christmas after his son Kevin was born. The regular barman was down with the flu, and, with the baby, Donal wanted to be at home more often, so when Cathy suggested he ask his mammy's friend Charlie to help, he paid Charlie's mini cab fare for a few evenings over the Christmas and the New Year.

Charlie enjoyed working again, but he enjoyed meeting Sheila Malone's children even more. And he also had more people to tell his stories to. His most eager listener was Maurice.

The pages of Charlie's book blew a light breeze onto Maurice's face because he was turning them over so quickly. He was afraid to read any of it. Like Donal, he was surprised the old dreamer had written the book. Although Charlie talked a lot, Maurice didn't think the old man was capable of writing an article let alone a book. He recalled he had suggested to Charlie that he should write a book. He had meant for Charlie to write about his own life. After he had read the page that said what the book was about for the third time he said loudly, 'This is not about us at all.'

'Does that mean I can sue him?' Cathy called down to Dominic.

Dominic smiled and replied, 'Cathy, you lot don't need to

spend your money with suing anyone.' He smiled at Janet and added, 'You are well able to fight your enemies when you stick together.'

Dominic's glasses were so thick Janet didn't know if he was smiling at her or the waiter who was pouring her coffee. She glared back at him anyway. She was still seething with anger over Liam's will. She was also livid because the house was empty when she had come down for her breakfast in Plunkett Road ten hours earlier. She glanced down the table to find her daughter-in-law. She wanted to scowl at the stupid little bitch for allowing Una to keep her out all day. All she saw was a smile on the wretched girl's face because she was reading Charlie's book. She watched Maura nudge Una, then run her finger down a page in the book. She couldn't hear what the sisters were saying to each other but there was no mistaking the smile and the giggle the two girls exchanged.

It was now over a week since Janet Grant had plonked her fat arse in the easy chair beside the fireplace in Plunkett Road. During all those days she had hardly noticed that none of Maura's family liked her. But she had never been used to people liking her. She picked up the book she wasn't interested in but it was something to do while she tried to figure out why Maura was suddenly so friendly with Una.

Rolling over the pages of the book, and with her thoughts on Maura laughing with her red-haired sister, Janet recalled Maura hadn't shown any desire to spend time with her sisters, or brothers. She recalled when they were in the Beggars Lodge after her brother's funeral that Maura had been on her own all the time. Now for the first time since she had been in Ireland Janet was sensing some competition from Una for Maura's attention. She raised her head to the stupid little bitch before she said, 'What page are you reading, Maura?'

'Chapter seven,' Una called back.

Charlie loosened his tie and sat back in his chair as if he was waiting for a storm to pass. He was feeling guilty about enjoying his great moment so soon after Liam's funeral. It had been Liam's idea that he should write a book about ten children that had been brought up in the same orphanage. He blinked to stop the tears because he imagined he could see all the Malone children standing around the grave while their youngest brother's little coffin was being lowered into the ground.

There were a few times when Charlie wondered if he had ever cried. He supposed he must have when he was a child but he couldn't remember. When he had been disappointed over something he would bury his sadness in a dream. When he had been bullied he would dream of getting his own back. He had only been to two funerals. The first one was Myra's father and although the people that had attended were sombre, nobody had cried. Myra hadn't cried.

For every story Charlie had told Liam, the young man had told him two. Liam had loved to talk about his family, and it was from Liam's stories that Charlie had mainly written his book. He had given up on religion the day he had left the orphanage, and he never prayed for anything. His heart was bursting with an unspoken prayer for Liam when he said, 'You will all be able to find yourselves in the book if you read it. The big difference is that all of you are not related.'

'Did yeh get a lot of money fer doin' it?' asked Cathy, polishing the shiny sleeve of her book with her table napkin. She pulled her eyes away from Charlie's smiling and teasing face, stretched her hand across the table and tapped her friend Maeve on her hand and said, 'Yeh could have a go yerself.'

'Would someone please tell me what's going on?' Josie shouted. She couldn't imagine why anyone would want to read a book about her family. They were just ordinary. None of them were famous, and now Charlie had said they were all orphans.

While Josie's brothers and sisters were bombarding Charlie

with questions, Monica was reading the book. Before anyone had answered Josie's question she asked, 'Do we find out who murdered the night-watchman?'

'What night-watchman?' Maeve asked.

'The one Sean found on the building site,' Monica said, folding over the corner of the page she was reading so she would know where she had read up to, and placed her book on the table. She believed the man in the book must be Sean because he had a stammer.

'Was he dead?' Josie gasped.

'They usually are when they are murdered,' Maura giggled.

'How do yeh know he was murdered?' Cathy asked, standing and leaning over the table to see what page Monica had been reading.

'Because he had his throat cut,' Donal said, recalling telling Charlie about the body that was found on the building site where Sean had been working but Sean hadn't found the watchman.

Used to speed-reading, Dominic skipped through the book. He remembered a court case when he had been a junior barrister at the time of Charlie's 'murder'. The young girl accused of the crime had been acquitted. 'The old fart,' he whispered to Pauline, 'has used an old murder case I told him about and written one of his dreams.'

Chapter Eighty-seven

Una was awake before she heard the heavy footsteps on the stairs. She raised her head from the pillow and turned her head to see if Cathy was still asleep. A glance at the clock told her it was nearly nine. There was no way she would be able to go back to sleep with the curtains drawn back. She was complaining in her thoughts because her sister always pulled the curtains back before she got into bed. She threw the covers back and got out of bed.

Wearing one of her mammy's housecoats, Una found Janet Grant sitting in one of the easy chairs beside the fireplace. 'Would you like a cup of tea, Janet?' she asked the bull-faced woman who looked like Winston Churchill with her head jutting forward like it was growing from her shoulders.

Janet inhaled deeply. She expected everyone would know by now that she always drank coffee. She shot her right arm out towards Una, used her left hand to push up the sleeve of her jumper on her right arm like she was getting ready to do some physical work, then inserted her left hand into the bag of biscuits on her lap and she said, 'Maura is on her way down to cook breakfast.' She pulled a biscuit out of the bag and put it into her mouth.

The belt of her mammy's housecoat hurt Una's waist when she pulled it tightly because she imagined she had the belt around Janet's throat. 'I didn't know the stupid little bitch could cook,' she said and held the fat woman's cold stare for a few seconds while she prayed Maura didn't hear her. When she was crossing the hall to go into the kitchen she promised herself she would go on a serious diet when she was back in London. She would hate to fill out a chair like Janet. She made two mugs of tea and brought them upstairs.

'Wake up, Cathy,' Una called, pulling the duvet off her sister's shoulders while she added, 'you have guests to look after.'

'Like who?' Cathy asked, stretching down the bed to pull the duvet back up again.

'Well there's me for a start.'

'Yer right,' Cathy returned, drinking a sip of her tea, 'I need te be kind te yeh.' She picked her watch off the bedside table read the time and said, 'Are yeh sure yeh can stay until I get back?'

'I'm sure,' Una replied, 'just remind me to phone Freda to let her know I will be late.' She put her mug back on her bedside cabinet, flopped back on the pillows and said, 'Do you think Maura will go back with Janet?'

'I told her she didn't have to,' Cathy replied, 'we were able to keep Janet away from her while we were in the hotel but we don't know how the bully treated the stupid girl when they had gone to bed.'

'Are you all right with having her living here?' Una asked.

'I'll manage,' Cathy replied, 'but she will have to change her ways a bit.' She sat up in the bed and looked around the room. 'Suzie can move in with me and Maura can have the small room.'

Chapter Eighty-eight

Time you were up, Una,' Freda said, pulling the curtains back. 'Pauline phoned. She will be here in an hour to pick you up.'

Two hours later Una wanted to cry because the last time she had been in the airport she had waited with her sisters for her brothers to bring Liam's ashes back from Spain. The two weeks felt like a day, and a year at the same time. The sadness she felt at the death of her young brother tempered the anger bursting in her chest because Maura had decided to go back to Canada with her mother-in-law.

'They are over in the queue,' Cathy said, pointing down to the rows of people forming lines to get their boarding passes. She walked in front of Una and Pauline as they made their way over to join the two Canadian passengers and Dominic.

'She still has time to change her mind,' Una said.

'If she does I'll never talk to her again,' Cathy replied.

Una closed her eyes. She couldn't blame Cathy for wanting Maura out of the house, but at the same time she was upset to see that Cathy was happy with Maura going back to Canada to live with Janet Grant.

They had reached the check-in counter when Pauline said, 'I don't think she will.' She watched Dominic read the labels on the suitcase, then lift one of them off the trolley, and put it on the weighing scales. He stood behind Janet while she took her passport out of her bag. Maura was standing to one side. She had her hand over the opening of her shoulder bag.

Janet held her hand out to Maura.

Cathy held her breath as she watched Maura say something to Janet and wave her head.

'She's forgotten her passport,' Una mumbled.

'No, she hasn't,' Cathy said and prayed that Maura wouldn't change her mind.

Janet looked at the trolley, then glared at Dominic.

Convinced Maura had forgotten her passport, Una walked around the line of people to get closer to her stupid sister. She wasn't going to argue with Cathy, and Maura was her sister, and she wanted to hug her. With the state Maura was in and the bullying she had to put up with it was no surprise that she had forgotten something.

By the time Una had reached the other side of the queue Dominic was easing the trolley with Maura's case still on it back from the check-in desk. He put his arm around the sad girl's shoulder and eased her away from the crowd of people waiting to check in.

Chapter Eighty-nine

Two years after Janet had gone back to Canada on her own, Cathy watched Maura get into a car outside her hairdressing salon. She waved to Maura's friend Noel and watched him drive away. She turned the key in the door and slipped the closed sign into its slot.

She didn't know or care if it was the money her sister was after when she had renewed her friendship with her friend Nula's brother, Noel. She also thought the money Noel had been awarded for the car accident was poor compensation for the loss of his leg and the ugly scar down the side of his face. He wasn't fifty yet.

It was Thursday lunchtime and although there wasn't much left to do, Cathy set about helping Angie to get the salon ready for the next two days. Friday and Saturday were always their busiest days. They had only been open a couple of months when they had a full diary for Friday and Saturday.

'Maura's lookin' better,' Angie said. She had never warmed to the selfish, sad girl but she felt very sorry for her. She also believed that Maura came in on a Thursday to avoid Maeve. She was surprised Maura came all the way to Ballyglass from Phibsboro to have her hair set after she had moved into Noel's house. She tried to make herself believe she came out to see Cathy. But she suspected the little bitch was letting Cathy know she could afford to have her hair done every week.

'Her hair has got very thin,' Cathy said, 'over teh years she has used too many chemicals to hide the grey hairs.'

'Yeh could be right there,' Angie said, sniffing to bring her glasses back up on her nose and continued, 'the girl still has te kick away teh rest ev her rotten bricks.'

'What rotten bricks?' Cathy bellowed.

'Teh foundation bricks in her life,' Angie said, throwing her head back and looking up at her friend.

'Have you been readin' more books?' Cathy yelled.

'Just a few,' Angie replied, folding the dry towel, 'yeh said yerself there's never much worth watchin' on teh television in teh summer.'

'Tell me about teh bricks,' Cathy said, sitting down.

'Well,' Angie began as though she was talking to a group of people. 'Teh bricks are the things yeh believe te be true. Yeh start te believe them when yeh are very young. And it is from these early bricks that yeh believe everythin' else.'

'Like religion?' Cathy suggested.

'A good example,' Angie replied, shoving her glasses back up on her nose, 'but they will be the second layer of bricks because yeh are forced to have them there by yer parents.'

'Go on,' Cathy encouraged, wiping her mouth. She didn't want to smile in case her friend would think she was laughing at her. 'Tell me about teh first layer ev bricks,' she said, focusing her mind on when the builders were working on the extension in Plunkett Road.

With her head bent forward so her chin was touching her collarbone, Angie closed her eyes tight and tried to remember the words she had seen in the book. She raised her head, smiled and said, 'The first ones are the foundation ones.'

Cathy recalled the first few days when the builders were starting the extension, and all the earth they had removed. The garden was in a right mess with all the sand and cement that was being mixed. She asked, 'Is it teh same if teh foundations are all made from concrete?'

Angie knew that concrete was hard and strong from the time Maurice had fitted a new gate for her. 'The foundation bricks, or whatever is used to hold up a buildin' are the most important ones, because if they break up the whole buildin' falls down. Teh first things we learn about erselves are teh foundation bricks, and we go on believin' no matter what. Fer example if we learn we are stupid then we believe we are, and teh same fer if we are clever, even if we aren't.'

Pretending she didn't know what Aggie was talking about, Cathy said, 'Does that mean that Maura will have te go back te bein' a baby te kick out her foundation bricks?'

'It means that yer sister learned at a very young age that she was special among te lot ev yeh,' Angie said, holding her hand up to stop Cathy from saying anything and continued, 'I know she has had her troubles. What with her husband hittin' her, and that awful mother-in-law bullyin' her.' She paused to draw breath and shove her glasses back up on her nose. 'Maura was so afraid ev the awful woman she couldn't tell her she wasn't goin' back with her until she was at teh airport and Dominic was beside her.'

'We were all afraid ev Janet,' Cathy said, recalling the morning Maura had asked her if she could stay. 'I agreed with her when she said it was teh only way she could get Janet te go back on her own.'

For a full minute the two women listened to the cars whiz by on the road. Cathy re-lived the year Maura had lived with her. Angie recalled how quickly the little bitch reverted to her old snobbish ways.

By the end of her first month at home Maura had got a job as a waitress in a coffee bar in town. It was the first job she had applied for, and she was hired straight away. She worked different hours, but she left the house early every morning, and she was never home before nine in the evenings. Angie was convinced the little bitch stayed away from the family because she didn't want to tell them anything about her job. She was working with young girls that had only taken the job part-time while they were trying to get something better.

The first few weeks after Una had gone back to London, and Pauline had returned to Canada had been the most difficult time for Cathy. Even now, nearly a year after Maura had moved in with Noel, Cathy expected to hear Maura running down the stairs when the phone rang. It was just like when the poor girl had been home the last time and Carl was phoning her every second day. Cathy had felt so sorry for her that she had got Joan to phone a few times so that she would get a phone call. 'Yer right about teh bricks, Angie,' she said, laughing and walking over to the small desk to take the money from the till. 'Sixty pounds,' she said, 'ten up on last week.'

'Ah sure yez are doin' great,' Angie returned, picking up a small blue box and shaking it. 'Yeh have some silver from teh old dears. And yer woman has left yeh her usual fiver.'

Chapter Ninety

Driving home, Cathy was deep in thought about what Angie had said about Maura's foundation bricks. Starting with Josie, she tried to recall if any of her other siblings had changed from the time she could remember them. She glanced at Angie after she had turned the car into Plunkett Road and said, 'Did yer book tell yeh that people never change?'

Regretting she had ever learned to read, let alone open the book she had found in the bin of the doctor's house she had cleaned for over two years ago, Angie shoved her glasses up on her nose and said, 'I still have teh book, and I'll give it te yeh teh read fer yerself. It has some very interestin' words.'

'Name one,' Cathy said, stopping the car outside her own house. She pulled on the hand brake and smiled at her friend.

'I don't remember,' Angie laughed. 'It took me two hours te read four pages. And I didn't learn anythin' I didn't already know. And yes people do change but not everyone. Accordin' to teh book we all do what suits us. Nobody makes us do anythin' we don't want te do. But like I said yeh can read it fer yerself.'

'We also change as we learn things,' Cathy said.

'That's called growin' up,' Angie said, undoing her seat belt.

A white van pulled up behind Cathy's car. Two men got out and walked across the road looking at the house numbers. One of the men walked up Angie's garden while the other walked back to the van and started pulling ladders off the roof.

'Yeh have visitors, Angie,' Cathy said, getting out of the car. When she saw the man who had knocked on Angie's door walk down to the gate and look up at the gutters she said, 'Have yeh somethin' wrong with yer roof?'

'There's nothin' wrong with me roof,' Angie returned, waving over to the man that had knocked on her door. 'It's me Sky television,' she said, smiling triumphantly.

'Yeh never said anythin' te me about getting Sky television,' Cathy said, running her eyes along the front of the houses. She counted five satellite dishes on Angie's side of the road.

'I didn't know meself til last night,' Angie said, beaming. 'Maurice is rentin' it fer me.'

Leaving Angie to supervise the men while they bolted the satellite dish to the front of her house, Cathy went into her own house to get the dinner for her mammy, Suzie and herself. As usual, the first thing she looked for when she came in was the post. She knew her mammy was up when she saw four letters on the hall table. 'I'm home,' she shouted, pushing in the door to the living room.

The long net curtain hanging from the door waved a greeting at Cathy. It was three in the afternoon, and the sun was shining but it was the end of September. By eight o'clock it would be chilly enough to light the fire that was all ready with paper, sticks and coal. She was further surprised when she walked out to the conservatory and found her mammy sitting in a chair with one of Suzie's white socks on her left hand.

Suzie wouldn't wear a sock with a darn in it but Cathy didn't say anything as she watched her mammy pass white embroidery thread through the eyes of her sewing needle and continue to work the thread under and over the lines she had already made. 'I think we are goin' te have some rain,' she said and walked out to the garden. She sat on the swing and surveyed her mini farm. All the tomatoes, cucumbers, and peppers were all harvested. Suzie had taken over growing them when Cathy opened the salon with Maeve. She glanced into the conservatory and tried to feel sorry for her mammy. She doubted if the selfish woman would have made any effort to do anything for Suzie if her daughter had not met Vera Farley. Cathy liked Brian's mother as much as Suzie adored her.

The only regret Cathy had about allowing Brian to take their daughter to meet his mother was she had not taken Suzie herself when the child was a baby. She was pleased that Suzie had continued growing the vegetables and rhubarb. It taught her the value of money and it was helping with her mathematics in school.

When he learned that Suzie's father was a priest, Maurice allowed himself to admit he didn't like his mammy. The biggest shock for Maurice was when Brian wanted Suzie to know he was her father. He had reasoned that if a Catholic priest can forgive himself for having sex and a child then he could forgive himself for not liking his mother. It had been a heavy weight lifted off his conscience. It had also become an even bigger pleasure for him to bring on the plants for Suzie to take over the vegetables from Cathy so she could save the money to take Vera to Spain to spend some time with Brian. He had wanted to cry when Suzie had told him, because he couldn't imagined how he would feel if he had never known Emir or Patsy.

Children's voices coming from the garden at the bottom of the vegetable plot told Cathy it was getting on for four. It was time to make the beds before she started the dinner. When she was in the hall ready to make her way up the stairs she saw the letters on the table. She expected they would be bills so she shuffled them quickly. Her heart skipped a beat when she saw a blue envelope with a darker blue border. She knew it would be an airmail letter.

Expecting the letter to be for Suzie from Brian, Cathy was about to prop it beside the telephone when she read the name.

She gasped when she saw it was for Maura, and it was from Canada. Turning the envelope over, she read it was from C Grant. 'Jesus,' she whispered, turning the envelope a few times and read her sister's name, then Carl's name as if she needed to assure herself that she was really seeing what was written on the envelope.

On hearing the front gate rattle, Cathy expected it was Suzie was home from school. She shoved the letter up her jumper before she opened the door.

'Angie's getting satellite television,' Suzie said.

'Nothin' more than she deserves,' Cathy returned, then added quickly, 'There's no letter from yer dad today.' She thought it best to tell Suzie before she asked her mammy if any other post came other than what was on the hall table.

'I'm not expectin' any until next week,' Suzie said, mounting the stairs.

'I haven't made yer bed yet,' Cathy confessed, following her daughter. She noticed the heel on one of Suzie's socks was threadbare so she added, 'Yer granny is darning yer socks.'

'It gives her somethin' te do,' Suzie said, pushing in the door of her bedroom. 'Vera likes te crochet.'

'What does she crochet?'

'Blankets,' Suzie replied. 'She is goin' te make me one fer a bedspread.'

Cathy had never darned socks or crocheted. She also knew Vera was managing on a pension so she said, 'I'll buy her teh wool.' All thoughts of Vera flew out of her mind when she closed the door on her bedroom. She removed the letter from under her jumper and studied it again. Like all airmail letters it was very light. Holding it up to the window she estimated it had one page, and the writing was in a dark pen, and it was large.

Cathy always thought large dark writing screamed at the reader. Like headlines in the newspapers, and posters in shops.

As if it would burn her fingers she placed the letter on her bed and sat down. Her first thought was to open it. Her second thought was to tear it up and burn it. She lay down on her bed. The white ceiling made a perfect screen for her to recall the countless times Maura had read every envelope that had come through the letterbox three or four times as if she was making sure they weren't for her. She put the letter under her pillow and went back down the stairs and got on with the dinner.

It was eight in the evening when Cathy crossed the road to Angie's house. She had her own key but she knocked and called out before she opened the door. The memory of the day she had found her friend on the bathroom floor flashed through her mind so when she opened the door she called out, 'Angie.'

'Me sight was never good,' Angie called back, 'but there'd nothin' wrong with me hearin'.'

'It's yer advice I want,' Cathy said placing the letter on the table. 'This came in teh post today.'

'It's fer yer sister,' Angie said after she had read the name.

'I can read that much meself,' Cathy said, 'but what do I do with it?'

Angie nodded her head, then looked around the walls of her living room. 'What do yeh want te do with it?' she asked.

'I'd love te know what teh git has written,' Cathy said.

So did Angie so she said, 'Look at it then.'

'I'd have te open it,' Cathy whined, turning the letter over and examining all the edges for a tear. She rested her head on the back of the chair and closed her eyes.

'Are yeh prayin'?' Angie asked.

'Just thinking,' Cathy replied, 'though I have had a few prayers answered before now.'

'Yeh could answer yer man's letter yerself,' Angie suggested.

'Have yeh got an envelope and a bit ev paper?' Cathy asked.

Angie opened a small drawer in a small cabinet. She fumbled for a few seconds, then handed Cathy an old writing pad and a packet of matching envelopes.

'Jesus, Angie,' Cathy yelled, 'how long have yeh had these?' She turned the top yellow sheet of paper over and revealed a blue one.

'It'll do the job,' Angie said, holding out her hand. 'Give me the yellah one,' she said.

'Give me yer biro,' Cathy said. She wrote 'not known at this address' on the yellow sheet of paper. The letter from Canada was so thin she was able to fold it so it would fit into the small envelope with the note she had written. 'Did yeh take yer wee-wee sample fer yer doctor this morning?' she asked Angie, handing her the letter with the gummed flap open.

'I see what yeh mean,' Angie said, bringing the brown gum up to her nose. She made to get out of her chair.

Cathy held Angie's arm to stop her and said, 'Tell me where it is. This is one task I want te do meself.'

Angie nodded her head in agreement and said, 'In teh mustard jar on teh windasill in teh bathroom.'

Cathy pulled a small stick from the pile in Angie's fire-grate. She spread a newspaper on the hearth, placed the envelope on the newspaper and used the stick for a brush to wet the gum on the envelope with Angie's wee-wee. 'I'll have te let it dry and use some sellotape te hold it down,' she said.

'Well yer not leavin' it there in me grate!' Angie hollered.

Cathy wrapped the envelope in a sheet of newspaper and stood. 'I don't suppose I could use yer iron te dry it,' she said, smiling, 'after all it's yer own wee-wee.'

'As long as yeh use plenty ev papers,' Angie replied, 'and yeh give me a lift inta town.'

'I'm not goin' inta town right now,' Cathy said, sliding her arm into the sleeve of her jacket and frowning. 'What do yeh want te go inta town fer?' she asked, moving towards the door.

Angie stood and turned her head towards the clock so Cathy wouldn't see her face and said, 'I want te do some shoppin'.'

'Are yeh breakin' out and treatin' yerself te new slippers?' Cathy asked.

'If yeh must know…' Angie replied, patting the pony tail on the back of her neck. She sniffed and shoved her glasses up on her nose so her hand would cover her mouth and continued, 'I want te buy meself s bikini.'

Cathy knew what her friend was really telling her but she thought Angie was teasing. She opened to door to the small hall turned back as she said, 'Yeh will need a passport.'

Angie retrieved an envelope from the mantelpiece, removed a small slender green book held it out to Cathy and said, 'Will this do?'

Expecting the passport to belong to Maeve, Cathy looked sadly at the green booklet, picked it up, opened it, looked at the photograph, then at her friend and said, 'Yeh don't have teh figure fer a bikini.' She smiled, closed the passport, handed it to Angie and asked, 'When are yeh goin'?'

Angie knew Cathy was pleased she had decided to go to Spain with Brian Farley's mother. She sniffed, shoved her glasses up on her nose and said, 'I have arranged with Mary Byrne te do teh towels fer teh fer salon fer next week, and teh one after.'

'I should hope so,' Cathy retorted, bowing her head as though having the towels taken care of was more important than Angie's holiday. She walked over to her friend, draped her arm around the small shoulders and kissed the top of Angie's head. 'Brian'll be as much delighted te see yeh as he will his mam,' she said.

'I'm still nervous about goin' in the flyin' car,' Angie said, raisin her eyes to the ceiling.

Cathy squeezed the small frail shoulders as she said, 'Millions more people are killed in road accidents every year than they are in aeroplane crashes.'

Angie put her arms around Cathy's waist and buried her face in her friend's breast. She expected Cathy was also thinking of her brother Liam. 'Yer absolutely right,' she hollered. 'I think I might walk out to the airport just te be on teh safe side.'

'Look at it this way,' Cathy said, 'it'll add another brick to yer life.'

They both laughed.

www.ingramcontent.com/pod-product-compliance
Lightning Source LLC
Chambersburg PA
CBHW060815120726
47909CB00006B/1934